MAKING LOVE IN THE ***WILD***

A Romantic Handbook for Adventurous Couples

Chuck Butkus

Making Love in the Wild

Published by Chuck Butkus
PO Box 4931
12304

ISBN 0-9709154-0-3

10 9 8 7 6 5 4 3 2 1

First Edition

Printed in the United States of America

Dedication

For Melanie:
I love you, beautiful lady.

I gave you your fantasy world
as long as I could.

Making Love in the Wild

INTRODUCTION

This book depicts lovemaking in the wilderness, as seen by a hopeless romantic. It is respectfully written for adult couples who want to spice up their relationship. It suggests different settings and unusual circumstances that can intensify your passion. The book contains no explicit sexual material. Instead, it blends romance, excitement and passion together by exploring adventurous lovemaking in the exciting beds of Mother Nature.

The deadlines,
appointments,
job stress,
family responsibilities,
finances,
traffic jams,
canceled flights,
bureaucracy, and
politics
of your day-to-day world put a big strain on the lovemaking core of a relationship. Using this book, you can mortar the loving foundation that the outside world may have cracked.

Making love in the backdrop of the wilderness is a unique and unforgettable experience. You feel more free and uninhibited here; there are no worldly pressures. It's easy to be childlike, and have *fun* as you loveplay. You focus on immediate, basic decisions regarding only each other-- Shall we make love, then nap, or vice-versa?

Stress melts away. When you are naturally doing physical things like hiking, swimming, or biking, you feel more alive and your libido is higher. You sleep better and love better. You are away from anything that interferes with your relationship.

You become more impulsive and stop planning details. You make simple love in the purity of nature. If your relationship is in a rut and the spontaneity is gone, the wilderness can help you get it back.

I suggest that you find a quiet spot where you won't be interrupted, put on some soft music, then read this book slowly, one full chapter at a time. If you don't like a particular chapter, go on to the next. Please don't flip back and forth; each chapter has a mood and an environment — you will lose that if you flip.

I have provided a prelude to each chapter which paints a picture of what might happen in that setting. If that environment doesn't appeal to you at the time, skip it and find one that you like. You become creative in your favorite ones, and invent more love scenes than I can depict. After living the chapters that turned you on, go back and read pages that you originally skipped.

Most of the scenarios depicted here I recommend for daytime, but they can also be enacted in the evening. The vision of my lover's body against the sunlit beauty of nature always arouses me. I bet it does the same for you.

The *Outdoor Sports* Chapter is a special insert. It gives erotic ideas you can use while enjoying a favorite recreation. You will add new dimensions of excitement and thrills to the outdoor activities that are a meaningful part of your life.

Certain scenes are written as the woman experiences it, while others are written as the man views his lady. In either case, *you* are placed in each love scene.

Some of the activities are more foreplay than culmination because they are difficult to sustain for a long time. If that's the case, then tease away!

Certain settings may seem more relaxing than love-intensifying. If you find this to be true, then relax, kiss, touch and let the stresses ebb from your body. Get rid of the rest of the world. Later, you can make love in another setting without worrying about something that could ruin an otherwise magical moment. You lower your speed, do things less urgently, and find yourself making love more passionately.

Even if you are not the outdoorsy type, you can find appealing, comfortable scenarios in this book. Each page presents one or more unique adventures. If one single love portrait appeals to you, it's worth your time to get away and do it. You have nothing to lose and a stronger, more satisfying relationship to gain. And with every visit to the woods, you will naturally progress to greater outdoor pleasures.

Don't work too hard to find these places. Just spend more time in the outdoors, and the romantic areas will jump out at you. Be spontaneous and crazy.

If you want to elevate your love life, come and do it in the wilderness. Throw away your watch, forget time, and learn afternoon delight. *Live* this book.

Chuck Butkus

For an ideal start on your romantic adventures, get a copy for each of you, and read the books at the same time over soft music, gentle light and your favorite wine or tea. This way you can dwell longer on settings that appeal more to you than your partner, and vice-versa. You may both become aroused. Later you can combine your favorite scenes and plan how to make them real.

P.S.— Leave it on the coffee table as a conversation piece. Other couples will look at you in awe!

SAFETY NOTES:

This book is written for responsible adults. The outdoors has risks different from those in suburban and city life. Use common sense, and take standard precautions in the woods. While, except for some bugs, the outdoors is very pure and normally presents few problems, you should take care to select a private setting in nature's bed.

These scenarios have been experienced by myself and other people, who have been very comfortable in the settings and environment. They may not be for you, either physically or mentally. You'll have to choose what you are comfortable and safe with.

All the water settings assume that you can swim, or are not putting yourself in a position where you have to swim.

Don't exercise beyond your body's limits. If in doubt, see a physician before living this book.

Drink plenty of water while hiking or climbing. During exertion, the body loses fluids quickly.

There are Safety Considerations and Equipment Suggestions at the end of each chapter. Please read them before beginning your adventure.

This book can't warn you of every possible circumstance or danger that you may encounter. So be alert, take precautions and use your good sense in the wilderness.

Chuck Butkus

P.S.- Make your own notes in the white space at the end of each setting regarding safety, problems and what was GREAT!

Making Love in the Wild

Thanks To:

Melanie, my inspiration and editor, for her originality, and lovingly making sure that I write as romantically as I act.

Bob Adelson, another hopeless romantic with insight into what needed work.

Lee Bardin, for his encouragement, suggestions, and criticism.

Michele Butkus-King, for her detailed editing and suggestions.

Don Hebert, for his gentle criticism of poor prose.

Rick Hickerson, for his encouragement and enthusiasm, great ideas and detailed corrections.

Patrick Hussey, ** Special thanks. I showed him the book before anyone. A romantic and crazy person like myself, he loved it instantly, added to it, and gave helpful criticism.

Tamara Manny, for her encouragement, suggestions, criticism, and support of Melanie's thoughts.

Janet Neary, for her candid comments.

Tom Pratt, for his insight as to what was initially wrongly presented.

Chuck Butkus

LisaDawn Rounds, for her reminder to stay romantic all throughout the book, and her literary criticism.

Michelle Upson, who felt that it was more of a documentary than a romantic handbook.

Bill Hubert, for helping me get it into print.

Kathy Bradley, for her editing and support.

Making Love in the Wild

CONTENTS

Chapter One:	THE GROUND:	13
Chapter Two:	THE MOUNTAIN:	23
Chapter Three:	THE WOODS:	32
Chapter Four:	BAD WEATHER:	46
Chapter Five:	THE LAKE OR POND:	53
Chapter Six:	THE STREAM:	67
Chapter Seven:	WATER CRAFT:	77
Chapter Eight:	AT CAMP:	87
Chapter Nine:	OUTDOOR SPORTS:	109
Easing into Outdoor Love		119
Footnote: How do you find all of these places?		120
Notes		122
Order form		127

Chapter One: THE GROUND

INTRODUCTION

Lying Down, Looking Up

You both are walking down a path, when you spot a small clearing. It is ringed by tiny poplar trees, which in turn, are surrounded by huge pines. It seems like a perfect spot to lie down and relax. Looking up, you share a portrait of a blue sky framed by the circle of poplar and pine. Its quiet beauty projects a peace and serenity that calms the spirit. It seems so natural just to kiss and hold each other in that environment. So you let the emotions escalate naturally.

When I was a kid and troubled by problems that seemed unsolvable, I sought spots like this, and let the serenity overtake me into sleep. As an adult, I have also found this environment to be a natural, relaxed one for making love slowly and easily.

I think you will find it the same.

In the Moss

The two of you come upon a cool green shaded area. The ground is covered with soft, spongy moss. You take off your hiking boots and socks, and walk in the moss that nuzzles your feet as you wiggle your toes. Soon four feet are dancing in the soft greenery.

Since that felt so good, you both take off all your clothes and go rolling around in the moss together. You lie on your stomach in the moss and your mossmate lies face down upon your back. You play footsies and slowly slither around, not touching each other with your hands.

Only your bodies move in the moss. The moss is fondling the entire front of your body. You change places and let the moss massage your partner while you slowly caress, skin against skin. Velvet lips touch, then brush your body as you move together.

As you kiss, touch and play, you fantasize about lovemaking in the massaging moss.... then, you make it a reality.

On a Grassy Hill

You are hiking, searching for the ideal hill to picnic upon. Through the trees, you see a sunny green hill on the south side of the valley. You cross the canyon and climb up into the sunlight.

You both are resting quietly on top of that grassy hill. No words need be said. The view across the valley is stunning, with huge oak trees, intermingled with pine. A slight breeze gently kisses your face as you pour Sauvignon Blanc for the perfect picnic. You smell the facing pine as you gaze into each other's eyes and toast.

A pair of hawks are gliding together, enjoying the currents as they sail back and forth. They are the only other couple around. You toast the hawks and this perfect place. You relax, kiss, sip wine and talk.

As you lie there holding and kissing, yearning eyes beg for love. You play Jack and Jill, both uphill and down.

The slant of a hill can be a big asset:

You are lying together with your heads uphill, immersed in lovemaking. You roll over time and again, with each being dominant for a short period of time.

Depending on the degree of steepness, there is never a worry about sliding uphill, similar to the way you would slide up in a bed. You will either stay in one place, or slide slowly downhill. Because of the uphill slant, your bodies are closer together, and touching more than in a bed. Other sensations are also different.

Or you can make love at a small angle to the hill, and slowly go a little downhill with each roll.

Then your lover lies on his back with his head downhill and you join . You will both slide downhill as you excite each other. Because of the uneven downhill slant, the angles of connections are very different and erotic.

A different kind of adventure can be had on a sandy, rather than grassy hill. This setting adds the sensation of abrasion on your back as you love your way down the hill. It takes longer than walking, but it's lots more fun.

You might need a tarp or heavy old coat for protecting the back as you slide down the hill. And a blanket to cover yourselves with— but it will probably fall off.

In the Mud

You are walking a quiet path alongside a stream. You sit and rest near a tranquil muddy bend in the brook. The frozen fruit juice you brought has thawed and is heavenly. The kiwi are juicy and sweet, like fruit from heaven.

You start eating a grape, then feed one to your mate. A grape, then a kiss. As you bite one and feel its juices on your lips, you sense other juices beginning to flow. Soon more kisses than fruit. The forgotten bunch drop into the mud.

As your lips part and your eyes open, you note the muddy grapes. Feeling a little mischievous, you pick them up and throw them along with the mud at your partner. Your partner puts the soggy bunch down your neck.

You take off your clothes and get a good clean mud fight going. You chase each other around, fall together, rub mud over each other, and wrestle in the wet earth.

If it progresses to arousal, make muddy love. Otherwise, have fun playing.

If you can find a secluded, sunny place with mud, this is really fun and can be unusually erotic. But avoid mud next to stagnant water.

If it rains while you are engrossed, it will clean you off. Otherwise, be near a source of moving water to wash up afterwards!

Don't forget to keep your eyes and mouth closed while your mudmate is throwing the muck.

In the Leaves

It's autumn, the most beautiful time of year in the wilderness. The foliage is still brilliant with shades of reds, yellows, and oranges. The leaves covering the ground rustle as you walk down the path. Remembering when you were a kid, you both work to create a huge leaf pile. A leaf fight interrupts the job for a little while.

After you run and jump into the leaves one at a time, you soon jump in together and roll around in the leaf hill. The smell of fallen leaves is like a drug that increases awareness. You chase each other and fall together in a mound of leaves.

Rolling around together in the pile, you kiss each time you are dominent. Your leafmate puts a blanket on the pile, then covers it with more leaves. You two crawl under the blanket and embrace.

If this develops into lovemaking, you can do it invisible to the rest of the world. Make love under a little blanket tent that is totally covered by leaves.

If it doesn't, you had fun, some foreplay, and were a kid for a little while. Isn't it great to be young again?

In the Warm Sand at Night

This one requires a little research and planning. You need to find a private sandy area that faces south and is heated all day by the sun.

I really like islands for this.

Select a sunny day followed by a cool evening for your lovefest.

Wait until two hours after dark to minimize the mosquito distraction, go to the spot and lie down together. The warm sand against your backs contrasting with the cool of the night is unusually erotic.

You watch thousands of stars performing only for lovers, track satellites, and kiss upon sharing the view of a shooting star. Every constellation is a reason to kiss and embrace, as is every bright star. A million excuses to kiss. Shimmering eyes embrace as you slowly and passionately make love under the Milky Way.... till the stars fade.

A warm blanket might be nice to put over the top of you.

If you're using a boat to get to the warm sand, take the necessary precautions for running a boat at night.

On a Big, Flat Rock

It's a hot day. You both have been walking for an hour and are heated. A huge flat rock rests just off the path, shaded by some pine trees. It looks so cool and inviting. You climb onto the refreshing rock and lie down. After drinking water in the screened coolness, you feel as refreshed as if you walked into the mist of a waterfall on a torrid day.

A gentle breeze fans the perspiration on your back, giving a little chill — you hug, then bond your lips. As you kiss more and more fervently, you warm up to each other. You stroke silken skin as a probing tongue finds yours. Soon fires are burning and there's only one way to douse them...

You might find the ideal rock as the ledge overlooking a stream or river. Or it might jut outward onto a lake. Maybe it's on an island, or in the middle of the woods. The rock should be bigger than a king-size bed.

Alternately, if you pick a rock that has been sunning all day, you will be making love as the heat caresses your skin. This is especially nice in the spring or autumn, or on any cool day.

For some people, a small amount of pain can increase lovemaking pleasure. You have to decide whether you want a perfectly smooth rock, or a somewhat ripply surface for a little pain intermingled with the pleasure.

Confine your wiggling to the top of the rock!

In the Middle of an Open Field

You find a large open field bordered by a country road and a grove of trees. There are no houses, tractors, cows or horses. Because the field is not fenced, you know that farm animals don't abide here.

A dozen butterflies are lighting near the center of the field, then flying up, circling, and lighting again.

You walk toward the little wings and spread the blanket nearby for a picnic. The grass is over two feet high, and it shields you from the road.

Bees are busily caressing the clover and wildflowers, oblivious to you and the butterfly demonstration.

The butterflies are landing on the moist rocks and licking the water off them. They seem to like you, and fly near your head, landing on a rock inches from the blanket. The beauty of those delicate creatures with their tongues caressing the rocks can only be seen, not described. It's a fantasy world, with you at the center.

You kiss and marvel at your good fortune— the two of you in a special little world few ever experience.

Taking a cue from the butterflies, you begin gently licking your mate on the lips. Then elsewhere. A responding satin tongue roams your body.

....You forget about the picnic and roll off the blanket together.

Take turns being on the bottom. The view looking through the grass at your lover, into a sky floating with butterflies, as bees nuzzle the clover is a unique experience.

Safety Considerations

Watch for poison ivy, oak and sumac. They will give you sensations you don't want to have .

Keep away from ant hills, bee nests, and animal holes, for exactly the same reason.

If you are spending time in direct sunlight, protect yourself from sunburn. It's tough to make love if you get one.

Possible equipment:

You will need a daypack to carry any food, wine and equipment.

Kneepads protect your knees from abrasion. A blanket, shirt or towel cushions the back.

It's smart to bring bug spray so the bugs don't join your festival.

In the event of rain, a tarp can prevent cooling down a love session. And making love in the rain under a tarp adds to the experience.

You should bring a blanket to cover yourselves up, in case of visitors. If the day is breezy or cool, the blanket makes the loving cozy and warm.

I consider water a necessity for any jaunt, however short. Hiking is an exertion, so you perspire and lose body fluids. Drink water frequently as you are walking.

Last, but certainly not least, a bottle of wine and two plastic wine glasses round out the equipment list. For my love and I, sharing wine in the woods is a reverent and romantic moment we both cherish. It seems like the natural thing to do in that beautiful wooded setting created by nature.

Chapter Two: THE MOUNTAIN

INTRODUCTION

The Beauty of Climbing

You are climbing a small mountain with lots of open, rocky areas that present magnificent views of the wooded mountainous countryside. Each of you is wearing a loose T-shirt, paper-thin shorts, climbing boots and socks. As you climb upwards, the continual stimulation of the cloth on your chest subtly arouses you. Then the perspiration makes it visually apparent.

You keep watching that silhouetted body against the mountainous view. You admire the beauty and strength of your partner's legs and behind as they stretch and navigate the inclined rock at a particularly breathtaking panorama. You take turns leading, so each can watch and touch the other's shorts on the backside.

Resting at a senic spot, you reach around front and gently massage the chest area of the T-shirt. An arm reaches back to find your shorts. The touching through clothing, without actually seeing the object of your fervor, is very erotic. Maybe even more so than when you can see it.

More touching. You each arouse the other. As you continue to touch your stimulated partner in a flimsy shirt and shorts, you envision that beautiful body and fantasize what it can do.

You approach a secluded spot, lie down and let nature take its course. If the time isn't right, you kiss a little and continue upward, letting this scene, and perhaps others, serve as appetizers for the main course.

The portrait of your lover's body against the majestic backdrop on a mountain is a combination of beauty that will steal your breath. You have to experience it.

I have spent hours looking at my climbing mate's legs and behind, letting the desire rise with the elevation. We take turns leading, giving each of us a chance to look at the other. Sometimes we make it back to camp. More often, there's no waiting.

On a BIG Scenic Ledge

You find a mountain that has several scenic views that are away from the main trail. A further search discovers a secluded scenic view perfect as a lovemaking backdrop.

When you find one, you are in for a scene few people will ever experience in their lifetime. The thrill of making love — against a mountain panorama too magnificent to be captured on film or canvas— is a rare high. You sense the height of your love cradle, as it intensifies every movement of your beauteous mountain mate. Your blood is pumping, your heart is racing, and you are so *alive* — aware of every aspect of the nature surrounding you. A cool wind brushes your bodies as you culminate.

Words can't do it justice. I suggest you try it.

Or you might use this spot for arousal, and enjoy the anticipation as you walk, or maybe run back to camp. There you can move any way and anywhere you want.

On the Top

Everything that is described in the previous page *On a BIG Scenic Ledge* applies to this scene. In this case, you have been climbing for a long time and are physically drained. You are winded, hot, and your muscles are sore. You can't wait to enjoy what you worked so hard for— the summit view.

You have reached the very top of the mountain, with a view in every direction. It is such a high to be totally enveloped in that beauty — every way you turn is a spectacular painting that no artist can capture, it can only be lived. A slight breeze cools your bodies as you relax and hold each other.

An eagle is screaming her greeting as she floats up a thermal. A parade of hawks encircle the sky above the mountain. Only you and the raptors share this summit picture.

You begin to massage your partner's neck and shoulders... then the aching calves and thighs. As the muscle tension drains, the caressing replaces it with sexual energy. You are totally relaxed with a heightened sense of touch. Your senses are ultra-wired with each kiss and stroke. Lips begin to quiver, as your bodies soar. Soon you make love on the summit. It's the *ultimate* culmination, with only the sky and birds above you, and the whole rest of the world below.

It's not easy to find a mountaintop that is isolated enough to make love upon. You can select an unpopular mountain, and go there during the late fall, or winter, or on a weekday, when no one is thinking about climbing.

But it's worth it!

In a Cave

This is as primal as you can get. Transport yourself back to the caveman days.

During your climb down from the summit last week, you came upon a small, secluded cave that looked down over the valley and river. What a neat place to picnic and make love! But you were both drained from your summit activities. You decide to return at another time as cavemen.

That time is now. You hike up to the shallow cave, lay down your furs and provisions, and take up homesteading for the afternoon. Candles light the back of the cave, while incense adds to the sensory experience. The meat cooks on a stick over a little fire. You eat without utensils and drink blood-red wine from a leather sack.

You don leather playwear and lie on the fur. First you tease each other's bodies with feathers. Then you take a small piece of the fur and slowly stroke each other's bodies. As you kiss and stroke, the caveman comes out in both of you. Eyes become eager, then wanton. Only the sparrows on the nearby tree notice the wild lovemaking that moves the fur around.

You are cave dwellers for a day. Making prehistoric love.

For this adventure you need some furs, natural or synthetic, as your loverug. An erotic touch is underwear made of soft leather— sexy, soft, and primitive. Fur underwear is even better.

Pick a shallow indentation you can stand up in. The back wall should be visible and less than twenty feet from the opening. Explore the cave so that you know you are alone.

If you see any sign of animal habitation in or near the cave, don't walk away —RUN. A *menage a trois* with a bear is a real turn off. Those cavemen had to be careful. Loving for them was both exciting and risky.

So will your prehistoric festivities.

Safety Considerations

Pick a safe lovemaking spot where you can't fall as two volcanos erupt together in the heat of rapture.

—And keep your energy level up for the loving after the climb. Eat your oatmeal in the morning, and bring your energy bars or raisins. You want to be in peak shape to have fun on top!

To minimize accidental visitors, pick the furthest view from the main trail. Here, even the voices of those climbing the main trail are muffled. Then you can be as noisy as your passion dictates.

If using a ledge, try to find an area where the inner part of the ledge is slightly lower than the outside portion. Pick a large, level ledge, where falling isn't a problem. You don't want to fly united!

Don't climb above your ability.

Rest frequently and spend that time kissing, touching, talking.

Drink lots of water on your breaks.

Protect yourself from sunburn. Hopefully, you'll lose track of time.

Bring energy bars, gorp or raisins to keep your endurance level up for the climb back down.

Possible equipment:

Hiking boots or, even better, approach shoes are a must for climbing. You need the traction and support of a good boot.

A climbing rope to help in tricky spots is a good idea. You can also tie yourselves in while lovemaking so you don't move the wrong way.

You need a daypack to haul food, energy bars, wine and equipment.

Kneepads are worth bringing. They take up little room in your daypack, and protect your knees from the rocks on the mountain while you are loving.

You may not need it, but it's a good precaution to bring bug spray for a climb. The bugs can't ruin your celebration on top.

A small tarp is a good addition. It's fun making love in the rain under a tarp.

A blanket keeps you cuddly and warm if the weather turns. You can cover yourselves up, if there are visitors.

Climbing is hard work, so you naturally perspire a lot. Bring plenty of water.

Chapter Three: THE WOODS

INTRODUCTION

Walking

You are watching from a few steps behind on the trail. Those beautiful legs are swaying that behind from side to side. The leaves and pine boughs are dancing in a friendly breeze and the birds are arguing with the squirrels. The air is pure and fragrant with the scent of balsam, the sun is bright; it's a perfect day.

You're breathing a little heavy from making the last hill, your blood is pumping, you sense every detail of your surroundings. It seems much warmer than when you started walking.

You are in a remote area— your love gives you a playful wink, then removes that loose-fitting tank. Your shirt quickly follows. Only shorts and boots are left. The walk turns into playful chasing and touching.

God, you feel so alive and aroused! That body, those legs, in shorts and hiking boots against the greenery. Should you wait until you get back to the cabin? ....

Why wait?

Dress for that sexy image—shorts and hiking boots, and see if this doesn't happen to you.

On a Log

As you stroll through the woods, you notice fallen trees and logs scattered near the path. Big ones, small ones, those right on the ground, those slightly elevated. Some have rough bark, others are smooth. Some are long, with branches everywhere, some barren.

The lush green of the forest contrasts with the starkness of a fallen soldier across the trail. You climb onto the log and walk its length. Soon you are both playing like kids, jumping over the logs, walking on them as long as you can without falling off, and chasing each other to pull down the other's shorts. You hug and kiss, standing on top of a log.

As you play in the woods, the yearning builds, and you start looking for a log that suits your mood well off the trail.

You might select a snug, branch-canopied one. Or, rather, the log out in that tiny clearing. Maybe the one framed against the cliff is appealing, or perhaps the one on the hill with the view? How about that one down in the ravine, nestled against the hill? What an assortment!

As to bark selection, a certain amount of friction is desirable for some people while making love. A small amount of pain can enhance the pleasure. Select the bark as rough or smooth, depending on your pleasure-pain connection.

You can take turns lying down on the log; while the other enjoys topping things off. Or you might find other types of satisfaction. Enjoy!

Against a Tree

You decide to get out of the hot afternoon sun by cutting through a patch of cool, inviting woods that leads to the camp. The trees in this tract are really diverse, with pine, balsam, birch, oak, maple and spruce all intermingled.

A noise from behind startles you. It sounds like a herd of elephants. You turn to see two chipmunks chasing each other in a game of tag that winds among the trees. Their leaf rustling fun seems loud against the quiet forest.

Taking a cue from the chipmunks, you start your own version of hide-go-seek, each hiding from the other behind a tree. When you find your game mate, you kiss, then it's your playmate's turn to catch you. Each capture happens against a different kind or shape of tree, each kiss original. Sometimes you chase your partner round and round a big tree, but no matter how hard you try, the tree stays between the two of you.

As the game becomes more intense with touching and kissing, you look to a tree for more than hiding behind. All you need is the right tree, and you have an endless variety of backdrops to pick from. You run to a tempting tree with branches spaced far enough apart for the two of you to lean against while standing up. You hide till you are found, then embrace against the tree.

Slowly, wanting lips envelop yours....

You undress each other, and after a long, penetrating kiss, your treemate picks you up. As you wrap yourself around him, he braces your back against the tree.

Your legs gradually drop and find the lower branches of the tree. You brace your feet on them, and, slowly swaying, twist and turn....

You can sit with your back against the tree, stand braced against the tree, whatever your pleasure. Make love any and every way you can, without climbing the tree.

You might consider that a small amount of discomfort can enhance the pleasure of lovemaking. If so, pick a tree with rougher bark.

Or you might want to bring a shirt, or jacket — something to protect the back as it rubs against the tree.

Don't pick a dead tree that could fall down and bring you to a rotten ending.

In the Low Fork or Branch of a Tree

You are following a path through the evergreens which opens up to an oak and maple forest. It's late summer, and some of the trees are starting to turn. Three squirrels run around, their cheeks swollen with gathered nuts.

You both sit on a low branch to take in the activity and the setting. More squirrels and some chipmunks appear as you quietly watch. They appear to accept you, as you kiss and hold each other.

Eyes become tender, then eager. You slowly peel off each other's clothes.

You note that the tree you're on has powerful outward spreading branches. Some are above your knees; others as high as your chest. stroking velvet skin, you think about the gentle bark on this tree.

You could pick a rougher surface, if a little friction elevates the pleasure of making love.

You begin to fantasize the love scene at that inviting, versatile tree:

You hang from an upper branch, put your legs on a lower branch, and offer your body to your lover's lips.

After a while, your lover then playfully picks you up as you wrap yourself around him. He then places your backside onto the branches of a low fork of the tree, as you brace your legs on lower branches.

He then spins around, and you pin your lover's back against the tree, straddling him while bracing your feet on the low branches and slowly twisting the branches...

Pausing to rest a bit, but very aroused, you lean forward over the low branch, with your lover holding you from behind. Eventually, he sits on the low branch while you sit on his lap first backward, then forward....

There are endless possibilities for making love. You are limited only by your imagination and endurance. Depending on the tree and your creativity, you will run out of energy before you exhaust the possibilities.

If this scene seems too much like a marathon, pick just one of the tree's uses. Or taste all of them as foreplay, go back to camp and finish what you started.

Just say no to dead branches.

Among the Giant Roots of a Big Tree

You are walking through a damp, dark section of woods where the ancient majestic trees seem to reach toward you. Although the day is sunny, you see shadows everywhere.

You come upon one of those mammoth trees with roots that extend like monstrous serpents curling around and above its base. It provides an eerie, horror-movie like background in which to fantasize:

You are in that horror movie as the hero and heroine, and have just escaped from the demented killer. You are spending the night in the woods, hiding among the giant roots.

You lie together, shielded by the roots as you hold each other. The embracing becomes more intense as the setting sun provides the right environment....

Your eyes scan the surrounding woods for activity, then lock onto your rootmate's. A hurried, darting tongue seeks fulfillment.

You begin to make love among the roots, and, bracing your legs with the roots, find new ways to move and enjoy each other.

Having made love before among tree branches in the previous setting, you find as many ways to enjoy those raised roots. In this instance, chills down your back may suit the lovemaking. Find the rougher bark for your lovebed to complete the weird setting.

Other Thoughts:

You will be making love with chills up and down your spine. It's a theater encircled by a serpent. Let your imagination fly! You are engulfed by this monstrous rooted creature in the sinister, eerie dusk of another world. Unable to escape, you make love, maybe for the last time before the creature attacks. If the loving happens, it will be an experience in fantasy. If not, run away and enjoy the fleeting sun.

Under a Pine Tree

You're walking through a pine forest. The lush bed of pine needles on the ground cushions your footsteps and muffles their sound. Everything is still. It's almost like being in a sacred place, so rather than talking out loud, you use hushed voices.

You want to extend the tranquil moment. So you duck under an inviting pine tree for a quiet embrace in a needled, scented nest. The closeness and mood are reverent and loving.

If it feels right for you, make slow, quiet love. But if the mood is too reverent, holding each other and quietly kissing is both beautiful and romantic.

You can gather fallen pine needles and make a soft, tickley bed. As you make love, the needles tantalize your bodies while the pine scent delights your nose.

As you are loving in the pine needles, the pine cones will be very scratchy. Either avoid them, or use them to your benefit.

In a Pile of Birchbark

Find a stand of birch where there are a lot of downed trees. Peel the bark off the fallen birch trees, and gather a big pile of bark for a bed.

Get enough bark for a cushiony area the size of a single bed. You have to pile it at least eight inches high in order to soften your festivities.

You open the Chardonnay, and between sips and kisses, slowly take each other's tops off— tickle each other with the bark, then with nibbling lips and flirting tongue. You can be rough or gentle with the bark, whatever increases the pleasure. As both skin and bark become heated from your passion, you discard the rest of the clothes and take turns getting your back scratched on the birch bed.

Take extra care that you don't put bark with bugs into your pile, unless you want your back tickled as you make love.

In a Surreal Setting

Contributed by Patrick Hussey

This scenario is one of complete spontaneity, and is a wild experience contrasting the rushed modern world with the serenity of nature.

You hike in the woods adjoining a super highway and are walking parallel to the highway fence. The woods grow right up to the fence. You come to a section of the fence where you have a wide-angle view of the road.

It seems so weird, looking through the mesh. Cars are speeding by in both directions, and you're placidly watching from the woods. You can see them, but they can't see you.

You open up the Cabernet Sauvignon, toast the woods and each other, and wonder where all those people are going in such a hurry. You lie together, sip wine, kiss, and watch the rest of the world go by. After your second glass of wine, your lover gets up, disrobes, and hangs his clothes on the fence. He begins dancing naked, using the dressed fence as a backdrop. You undress and join in. The dancing graduates to uncontrollable kissing, then lovemaking, with the fence as your bed.

You climb up the fence and turn around. Then, holding on to the top of the fence, place your legs over your lover's shoulders, seeking his lips.

Then your lover moves your legs downward and picks you off the fence. You wrap yourself around him, and he braces your back against the jacket hanging on the fence.

As your lover tires, you step down, bend forward and hold onto the fence, while he holds you from behind....

You are making love in the woods with a fence that divides two worlds. While you are arousing each other in one world, cars and people are whizzing back and forth in the other.

The contrast is surreal — two totally diverse worlds separated by a fence. One loving, the other spinning their wheels.

Pick a well-supported fence!

Safety Considerations

Always have a trail map and a compass. Know exactly where you're going at all times.

Don't be in the woods during the big game hunting season.

Wear hiking boots to protect your ankles and turn on your partner. Bring bug spray and use it on your legs, maybe elsewhere.

Drink plenty of water as you are hiking.

Watch for poison ivy, oak and sumac. Stay away from ant hills, bee hives/nests, and animal holes. You'll have enough excitement without them.

Don't drink so much wine that you will be tipsy walking back to camp. It's too easy to fall or turn your ankle.

Pine, willow and poplar branches snap easily! Never make love on or using the branches of a pine, willow or poplar tree.

Branches 35 feet off the ground are not a good idea. We're not talking tree-climbing; you are tree-loving. This doesn't make you a candidate for the mile-high club.

Only make love on a log where you are able to touch the ground. If the bark on the log is loose, it could break and separate from the log during your celebration, and you'll go flying united.

The one on top might want some cushioning to save scraping his or her knees.

Possible Equipment:

Drink water frequently as you are walking. A two quart canteen is the minimum to carry.

You may want a blanket to save some embarrassment if guests arrive. If it's cool, the blanket keeps you cozy.

In the event of rain, a tarp can rescue a love session from being rained out. In fact, it can add to the adventure.

Cold cream works great for removing pine tar from your body. In a pinch, butter, margarine, many lotions, or any oil also does the trick.

It's easier to carry food, wine and equipment with a daypack.

Bring bug spray into the woods. It can prevent a bad experience from ever starting.

Kneepads weigh nothing and take up little space in your daypack. They can save wear and tear for the one on top when the surface is rough or hard.

Chapter Four: BAD WEATHER

INTRODUCTION

Walking in the Rain

You are sipping Sherry in a secluded campsite. Warm, soft rain begins to fall. A crazy idea pops up as the wine warms your body. You slip out of your clothes except for a T-shirt and start dancing around in the friendly rain. Your partner joins in the play. You walk through puddles splashing, roll in the grass and mud together. You feel free, childlike, and exuberant.

You look at a playmate in a transparent, wet, muddy T-shirt. As you watch that body dancing in the rain, you feel other sensations. You embrace and fall to the wet ground.

The rain tickles and tingles your body in a thousand places from the back of your neck to your heels. This arouses you more, and you transfer that excitement to your mate.

After a while, you exchange places, and let the other feel the rain massage.

Soon you are rolling in the warm rain, splashing in puddles, making wild, crazy love in complete abandon. You are engulfed in your own water world with streams of rainwater pouring over your face and body. Your thirst builds high, and the rain feeds it.

You wind up wet, dirty and totally fulfilled.

Inclement weather has always been a turn-on for me. Rain, snow, thunder and lightning, wind, arouse me to no end.

Let it do the same for you.

In the Rain in the Water

It's a warm, cloudy day. You are swimming together in your private cove at camp. Neither of you have suits, so you can feel the water everywhere on your body as you swim.

You are splashing, playing tag, wrestling, kissing, touching. Rain starts coming down in buckets. You can feel the cool downpour pelting your face, while your body is being caressed by warm water. The contrast is invigorating.

You walk out of the water to feel the stinging torrents on every inch of your body. It's eroticism that is found nowhere but in nature. You shiver a little and hug as the rain batters your bodies.

To warm up again, you fall back into the welcoming water together. You become oral with each other sheltered by navel high water, then heat up to making love in shoulder deep water.

Relaxed, almost woozy, and a little chilly, you go back to camp for a warm drink.

For a real experience, try this in a hail storm--small hail only.

NEVER do this in a lightning storm.

In a Thunderstorm

You are sitting on the camp porch loveseat, watching the evening rain.

As you hold each other and kiss, the weather picks up. You begin to kiss more passionately; the rain and wind become more intense. The weather seems to reflect your increasing torridity..

You touch and caress, your desires spiraling while the storm becomes torrential. Blazing eyes strike yours. Throbbing lips bond together in the strong wind. As you undress each other and the love sighs become louder, you are both encased in a capsule of light, followed by earth-shaking thunder.

You seem beckoned to the grove of hemlock surrounding your birch-covered lawn. You lie on the grass under the hemlock and kiss your invisible, then luminous partner. You are coupled in a fiery blinding light; then, as the thunder roars, you make blazing love in the dark. You come together as the entire sky is a blinding flashbulb.

The storm ebbs as the fervor slows. You stumble into the camp and warm yourselves with hot tea and warm blankets.

In a Snowstorm

You are drinking tea at camp and discussing the forthcoming hike. It is November, and the foliage is past its peak. The autumn day is bright and it is a crisp forty-five degrees.

You plan to hike to the south face of the mountain, climb up to the big ledge facing the valley, and picnic overlooking the mountains.

...The hike was easy; the climb an aphrodisiac. You spread your blanket before a panoramic view and begin lunch. You are munching on apples, cheese and crackers, and sipping fruit juice while savoring the heavenly surroundings.

After lunch, you hold each other on the blanket as you slowly progress to your loving dessert. You kiss quietly, almost reverently, and enjoy being alive in the velvet setting. Because you are out of the wind and facing south, the sun is keeping you warm. Your internal fire climbs higher than the summit as you come together against the mountain ledge.

At the peak of your volcanic heat, with no warning, snow quarters start kissing your backside. It's snowing in November, and it drifts your rapture even higher.

The snow stings, burns and cools as it melts on your body. It shrouds both your heated bodies in a cold envelope, doubling the pleasure as you both erupt.

Satiated and slightly chilled, you hold hands on the way back to camp. Baileys, coffee and snuggly blankets end a perfect day.

Since this type of weather is hard to find, an alternative is to make love in the falling snow near the camp. This allows you to run in and get warm quickly afterward. Pick a day with no wind and lazy fluttering snow. Try late fall or early spring if winter is too cold.

Besides lunch, you need a tarp to place on the snow or ground, and blankets to put over the tarp.

If it gets too cold, you might get a snowball fight going!

After an Ice Storm

There was an ice storm last night. The morning sun is sparkling on the trees as you drink your morning coffee. Before the sun melts the ice, you go out for a walk and some morning delight in the shimmering sunlight.

The woodscape before you is completely encased in glittering ice. Every branch, every twig is a jewel glistening and sparkling for the two of you. No diamond can match this beauty.

You lie in the cozy sleeping bag to take in the surrounding exhibit, then turn to your real treasure—and kiss the most valuable jewel anyone can have. As you undress each other, the vision of that sensuous body in the shimmering prisms steals your breath.

You are on the ground and looking up at your lover's shining eyes, with a thousand prisms of light fighting for your attention. You make slow, easy love in the midst of the gemlight.

Back at camp, you cuddle with hot toddies and blankets.

This requires a tarp to place on the snow, and blankets, a sleeping bag or a bedroll to put over the tarp.

Safety Considerations:

After an ice storm, don't bed down beneath any branches or trees which might fall down on you. The weight of the ice on the tree limbs makes being under any trees a risky undertaking.

Know all about frostbite and its symptoms. Watch each other for signs of them. Don't get too chilled. Know the stages of hypothermia, and get inside when either is in the early stage. If you are doing your job as a lover, your stormmate should never be cold at all.

Use mulled wine, brandy, hot cocoa, soup or buttered rum to take any chill off after you get back into camp. Get into warm blankets.

It's easy to slip and fall in rain, snow and ice. Walk carefully.

Know and take the standard precautions in lightning storms. Keep away from an open expanse of ground, stay out of water. Don't be near a tall tree or trees that are higher than the surrounding woods. A low wooded area is generally safe. Stay close to the ground while crossing the grass. You don't want to be the highest thing around. Get a set of instructions for safety in lightning storms from a state agency.

Chapter Five: THE LAKE OR POND

INTRODUCTION

Swimming Sans Suits

You have been hiking. You're both hot and sweaty. The cove is secluded, no boats pass through here, and the crystal clear water is inviting. You disrobe and enter a cool haven. The water is sensually caressing your naked bodies as you swim and watch each other, both above and below the water. You play like teenagers, touching and chasing one another; kissing, then falling back into the shimmering coolness. Is there a better time or place to make love?

For me, the spectacle of my lover's naked body bouncing in and out of the water is one of the most erotic sights I have experienced. It's a portrait I have forever stamped in my mind. I envision it when I'm away from her and am instantly aroused.

Loveplay in the water is the most exciting I have experienced. And for me, making love in the water is the biggest turn-on of all.

It may be the same for you.

In Navel-high Water

You found an isolated little bay perfect for swimming. It's secluded enough to go topless. You enjoy the sensation of the water caressing your naked upper body, while your mate appreciates the moving scenery.

After swimming and chasing each other for a while in complete solitude, you decide that bottoms are also optional. In playful nakedness, you splash each other, wrestle, tease each other's responsive areas, and are kissing warm, moist lips.

The sky has no clouds, the warm water strokes your bodies as you play, chase and tantalize each other. The sand massages your feet as you bound through the crystal water. You are removed from the universe in your waterworld love fantasy.

Each notices that the other is very aroused. Since you are both truly oral, and in a water setting, you try something new.

Your love stands in navel-high water with legs spread far apart. You take a breath, go under water and give oral pleasure. After twenty seconds or so, you slowly raise your head, get another breath, and go under again. This goes on for ten to fifteen minutes.

Then you exchange roles, with you standing in water at navel level, and your playmate becoming oral.

You can alternate back and forth for differing time periods, depending on breath control and your partner's arousal level.

This requires breath control. You don't hold your breath for as long as you can. You hold it until you feel the need to breathe, then slowly pull away, raise your mouth above water, breathe out, then in, and continue. The interruption for air should only take a few seconds. Move your head slowly so as not to take away from your partner's pleasure. Jerky, quick, hard breaths will ruin the mood, and have you gasping for air. Done properly, you can keep this up for hours.

Only breathe when your head is above water!

Both in Shoulder-high Water

You are still in that isolated little bay and are both ready to explode!. The oral teasing that you did in the water has each of you quivering in anticipation.

Neither of you wants to lose the mood by walking the two miles back to camp. Your arousal is at its peak. Only lovemaking in the water can calm and cool its burning, so you continue on.

You come together in your private, snuggly water bed....

You stand in water up to your nipples and find a flat, solid area to plant your feet onto. You stand firmly with your feet spread the width of your shoulders, knees slightly bent. If you lose your balance during this session, it could dampen the burning fire by falling in the water too soon.

Your lady wraps her arms around your neck, and her legs around your hips from the front. As the loving becomes more intense, you have to move your arms back and forth through the water just to keep your balance, and occasionally take a step forward or backward so as not to fall.

At the time of mutual ecstacy, you fall backward into the water. Embracing each other as you hold your breath, you float apart, then emerge in a daze.

Let your partner go after a few seconds underwater. You may have taken a good breath, while he or she did not.

Lying on the Beach, Waves Lapping Body

You are exploring the area near your camp away from the trails. You stop at a tiny sandy spot on the lake. The area is less than twelve feet wide with eight feet of sand reaching to the water. It is straddled by pine on three sides, with branches hanging waist-high over the sand.

The canopied sand invites you to lie down and take in the sun beaming from across the lake. As it gets really hot, you take off each other's shirts. Kissing and stroking each other, the rest of the clothes become a burden. As the early afternoon sun becomes sweltering, you lie with your lower bodies in the water, upper on the sand. The baby waves gently brush your bodies as you kiss and touch. Soon there's more heat than the sun is giving.

You lie with your back on the sand and your lower body kissed by the waves while your lover orally compliments the water motion. After a while, you change places.

Eventually, you join together in the loving, lapping water.

I suggest that you alternate being on top. The sensation of the waves supplements the love motions of your partner. With your back on the sand, as you look at your beachmate framed by pine boughs filtering the sun's rays, it seems more fantastic than real. Each of you should experience it.

Buried in the Sand Together Naked

Contributed by Patrick Hussey

This is an unusual entry, and may be more suited to the ocean's sand dunes than quiet beaches in the wilderness. But it could work on a beach with a lot of sand.

This requires another couple that you are very close to and trust completely. They will bury you alive, up to your chest. Then they will be watching out so that no one bothers you, and eventually release you from foreplay in your sand prison.

Dig a hole in the sand deep enough and wide enough for both of you to stand up in. Adjust the sand under your feet so that as you stand together, your lips are at the same level.

You excuse the couple for a while— tell them you'll call for them when you are ready. While still in your bathing suits, you begin necking thirstily. Soon you take your suits off and get into the hole. You face each other, put your hands on your sandmate's buttocks and kiss to make sure that your lips are aligned. Then you call the other couple.

Stark naked inches from each other, you ask the other couple to bury you in sand up to your chest. Put a little sand between the two of you so that you are barely touching at the chest. After checking that you both are all right, ask the other couple to leave for a while. They will check on you every so often.

You are completely immobile in the sand. All you can do is kiss and take in your surroundings. Your naked bodies are pressed near each other, but kissing is the only motion possible.

It's at once both beautiful and hellish. The kissing is your focus and it's wonderful. Enveloping lips capture yours. You can't move a muscle, and that's driving you mad.

This foreplay will drive you wild until the other couple releases you by digging you out. Then go off somewhere together. The other pair will probably go off elsewhere and do the same thing.

You may want to wrap a blanket around you both for modesty before being covered up with sand by the other couple.

When you are first covered up, if either of you feel claustrophobic, or have difficulty breathing, have the other couple dig you out.

When you are sure that you are both OK buried there, ask them to leave. Have the other couple check on you every fifteen minutes from a distance without being obvious and breaking your mood. They should always be in calling range.

In Water Over Your Head

You started out swimming at camp as most people do, wearing bathing suits. It's the middle of the week and the rest of the camps are deserted. First it's topless, with your top tucked into your suit bottom. Then realizing you are truly alone, you abandon suits altogether.

You play and chase each other in the water. Your partner swims underneath you and blows bubbles that touch you in the right places. Kissing, stroking each other, you fall into the water together while embracing.

Both of you are getting excited, when a wild idea pops into your head. You are both strong swimmers. Can you make love in deep water? You try, but it's too hard to stay afloat.

So you get your life jackets from camp, put them on over naked bodies and swim out to the deeper water. The support of the jackets allows you to join together.

You float on your back, place your legs over your partner's shoulders, and communicate love. After a while, you intertwine, your lips bonding above the water, your bodies joining below it.

The bobbing motion caused by the lovemaking is weird, sensual and a little scary.

Create your own set of waves!

This activity is more one of foreplay, rather than culmination. You have nothing to brace yourself against, so you can't move as much as you'd like. And you sometimes drift apart at the wrong time.

If it works for you, great. If not, it's wonderful teasing — swim to shore and attack each other there.

In A Tube

This scene is almost identical to the previous one, but adds the fun of bouncing around on an innertube.

You each grab an innertube, and float around, lazily basking in the sun, holding hands and sneaking an occasional kiss. It's a lazy, playful day.

You are alone. No boats have passed— it's a weekday. More kissing, followed by some tube-hugging. Soon a bathing suit top comes off. You begin petting while on separate tubes. The bottoms soon are gone. You dive down and seductively blow bubbles up toward the vulnerable, naked body draped within the tube. Your tongue brushes body parts as you swim underneath.

Then, somehow— you both are in the same tube.

You kneel on the tube above your partner, whose lips seek your body. Later, he lies across the tube, and straightens out his back as you straddle him with each knee braced on the tube.....

Because this is difficult to accomplish, it may be more fun for you than serious loving. Then, have *fun*. Play with your mate inside the tube, while you go underwater, blow bubbles, and tease orally.

Happy tubing.

For this love adventure, you need one sturdy, good-size truck innertube. Be sure that the valve is taped or covered in some way to protect yourself from being scratched. Two type 5 life jackets are also needed.

Don't dig your fingernails into the tube-- it might pop!

Hanging From a Rope in the Water

Like little kids, you have been swinging on a rope tied to a tree limb out into the water. Jumping and splashing, playing and touching, an occasional kiss makes time stand still.

You both grab the rope, swing out together, kiss, let go, and drop into the water, breaking the kiss.

When you emerge from the water, you kiss again. Your ropemate pulls upward on the rope, comes out of the water, and playfully places legs on your shoulders.

You oblige.

What else could you use this rope for?

You stand facing away from the shore in shoulder-high water holding onto the rope. Your feet are firmly planted about two feet apart. Your lady puts her arms around your neck, and legs around your hips.

Your lady then grasps the rope and pulls herself up, then lets herself down onto you as you hold onto that beautiful butt. Tongues intertwine, then unwind. Her exertion is not that great because she is buoyant in the water, and the up/down movement requires little travel. She can keep this up for quite a long time for a heightened arousal. You move your arms to help her, with your hands on her buttocks.

For this adventure, a lady with strong arms is a major asset— if she's a bodybuilder or a Champagne riddler, so much the better.

Safety Considerations

Don't get so involved in loveplay that you are exceeding your swimming ability. Stay close to shore. You may have to be able to make it back to land, for even more loving.

Stay out of fast moving, in fact, any current.

Wine and water don't mix. Skip the wine. The water is where the fun is.

The combination of sun, reflective water and sand can cause sunburn. Protect against it.

Deep Water Loving:

Keep out of any current, no matter how slow-moving. The only motions you want are your own, perhaps coupled with some wave action.

Both of you should be good swimmers who won't panic under any circumstances in deep water. The loving can cause some bobbing up and down, with occasional brief periods of several seconds where you have to hold your breath. You might occasionally swallow some water. If you are comfortable in water, this adds to the fun. If you aren't, I suggest you skip this scene.

This love scene requires some basic water safety equipment. Each of you should wear a Coast Guard rated Type 5 life jacket. This class jacket will keep you afloat through any activities you contrive. The collar of the jacket supports your head as you are lying on your back. Be sure that the jackets are adjusted snugly, so they don't slip up above your head.

Tubelove:

You both should be good swimmers who won't panic under any circumstances in deep water. You should be capable of saving one another.

It's important that neither of you will panic if the tube flips over. The likelihood is good that it will happen. It might even be fun to make it happen.

Keep out of any current, no matter how slow-moving. You don't want to be the focal float for a group of campers as you drift downstream intertwined in your parade of two.

Ropelove:

Never swing across land on a rope swing. From the second you are on that rope, you should be over unobstructed water. Always check the water for depth and underwater obstructions before using a rope swing.

The branch supporting the rope must be thick and strong. Never use a pine, poplar or willow tree as the base of a swing. Oak or hickory is best.

Make sure that the rope is new, strong and safe. Mountain climbing rope is best.

Footnote:

Olive oil can make joining in the water easier, if it's a problem.

Skip this chapter if you can't swim.

Chapter Six: THE STREAM

INTRODUCTION

Playing in a Stream

You are rock-hopping down a small rocky stream, when you suddenly come upon a bend with a beautiful sandbar in the slower moving current. Past the sandbar is a pool about four feet deep and fifteen feet long. Sun is slipping through the birches overhanging the stream, and suddenly you're really hot. You take off your shirt and wade into the coolness. Your streammate does the same.

The sun warms your skin as a gentle breeze caresses your chests. Walking downstream, your partner playfully splashes you with the cold water. It runs down your nipples and causes instant visible response. The sun quickly warms you up. You are a free, sun-worshiping half-naked couple. Wonder what the people back home would think?

Who cares?

You start splashing and playing, touching each other, kissing endlessly. As the water flows through your legs, you both are getting aroused. Where to go? Across the sparkling pool a warm, inviting sand bar beckons.....

For me, rock-hopping and wading in a stream is a return to childhood fun, as well as a turn-on.

When my lover undresses and jumps into a small pool, the sight of her body coming up from the water causes instant arousal. I begin to fantasize as that sandbar becomes a magnet for lovemaking.

Let it be yours.

Against a Big Rock in the Middle
of the Rushing Stream

Munching on crackers and cheese, you two are picnicking on a flat bank overlooking a creek. Downstream, a dozen small rocks seek your attention by splashing water upwards. They look like little haystacks sparkling in the sun. Below them is a big, flat rock that the small flow seems to be raging against and around.

You sip Merlot, and become lovingly lazy; kiss, touch and tease. After an hour of this foreplay in the warming sun, the heat of your passion grows intense. You fantasize about making love in the flowing water.

As you think about the loving, that big rock again comes into view. What would it be like making love against that rock with the water gushing all around your bodies?

Your love has the same idea. You playfully take off each other's clothes, then splash down to the rock holding hands....

The water enhances and stimulates every slight movement. It is a pulsating excitement that changes each time you move...

Your lover sits in the water with his back against the rock, facing the flowing water. He now has water forcing against him and flowing around both sides. You join facing him at first, then turn around, feeling the stream flow compliment your lover's movement in different ways.

Since the flow is not too strong, you decide to lean back against the rock, with your lover above. You experience the sensuality of the water as it whirls around and through.

Don't attempt this in too great a flow— you might be sitting against that rock until there is a dry spell.

Lying on Sand, Partially Immersed

You are picnicking on a sand bar adjoining a friendly, gurgling stream. While you open the Burgundy, a chorus of birds is singing a love song for your private performance. Biting the cheese causes you to drool, the red wine mingles with it to titillate your taste buds, and the warm sand is relaxing.

After you pour the second glass, you lie down and hold each other. Whispers of love float above the soft bubbling of the stream. You each turn full attention to caressing silken skin on that bed of sand.

The sand bar gently slopes into the moving current of that little stream. What an erotic love bed, with water running through it!

You lie on the sand with your hips barely covered by flowing water, as your partner is oral. As you are reciprocating, your sandmate throws your back down upon the sand, and you make love, joining in the moving water.

Lying on the sand, you have the sensation of your lover's caress, with the sand massaging your backside. You are immersed in water with the flow of the stream caressing your body. All the while, you are looking through the trees at the sky and smelling the fragrance of the nearby woods.

The heat of the sand contrasts with the coolness of dancing water. It's a sensual combination you will never forget.

Take turns being on the bottom..

Under a Small Waterfall

You are on a small path, close to a ledgy little creek. Every so often, you leave the path to rest by the stream. Funny how both body and senses are revitalized by viewing the little brook from its banks.

At one of your restful pauses, you spot an eight foot waterfall with a small flow cascading into a shallow pool. The sun pours through the misty trees, warming the entire setting.

Your streammate sheds all but underwear and steps under the falling water-- forward, out of the water, then back into, and behind. The sight of water pouring over that beautiful body instantly arouses you.

You strip and join in, each viewing the other in various positions in the falls. You sneak a touch. Later a kiss. Soon it is all kissing and touching as the turbulence tumbles over your bodies. Your skin is jubilant with stimulation from the pulsing water. You both sit and experience unique sensations as water gushes onto your loins. As your lover becomes oral, you realize that you have never felt anything like this before.

While you make love in the pool, the water flowing over the falls runs over your faces and all over your bodies. You kiss as the pourover washes both your faces and your moving loins at the same time.

If the waterfall is so powerful that it prevents lovemaking, use the pool that accepts the cascading mist as your waterbed.

In Small Rapids

Canoeing down a river, you stop for lunch at a charming little watery staircase of a brook where it meets the river.

You cool yourself by reclining in the water pouring over some rocks. This feels better than a jacuzzi! The water gushes over the rocks, hits the stream water, then bounces upward and backward. It's like a washing machine turned on its side. You are tumbled a little sideways by the watery turbulence. The water flows around the rocks and stimulates your backside, chest and loins at the same time.

A kiss in nature's whirlpool bath turns into many. The noise of the small rapids makes romantic music as *I love you* drifts into your ears. Taking a cue from the tingling water, you stroke here, then there. Soon you are complementing the water flow with your lips and tongues all over each other's bodies.

You decide to make love in this natural whirlpool bath. The whirling water raises sensations to new heights.

You sit in the rocky jacuzzi facing the flowing water. You align yourself so you and your partner can feel the washing machine action of the small rapid. Your lady kneels over you, first facing you, showering kisses, then turns around to enjoy the churning water on her lower body. You move together in love while caressing her with your hands.

Water over a foot deep might wash you and your fervor away downstream! Then you'll have to walk back upstream to your clothes.

On a Log that Bridges the Stream

As you follow the banks of a brook, you come to a steep section that prohibits your further passage. You scout around for a place to cross to the other, level side.

One hundred yards to the south, a bark-faced log spans the gully where the creek is shallow. You decide not to take the chance of slipping off the log if the bark comes off under your weight. So you ford the stream, bracing yourself against the hip-level log.

You wade together alongside the log, lean your logmate against it and kiss... for a long while. The water flows around your legs and your head is whirling as your lips meet again in another marathon embrace....

The log eventually becomes a vehicle for something better than stream crossing:

You bend over forward, bracing yourself on the log, as your partner caresses from behind. Both your legs are soothed by the current while you make love.

You change to face each other and kiss. Your lover leans against the log with his feet in the tickling water. You put your arms around his neck, climb up, dangle your legs over the other side of the log and wrap your lips in his....

Make sure the log is sturdy, else your flaming desires will get washed away in the stream.

On the Slippery Flat Stone of the Brook Bed

As you are following the brook upstream, the contour of the land and the creek characteristics change dramatically. The land becomes steep and hilly, while the stream transforms from a rocky, winding flow to ledgy, gushing, tiered platforms of waterfalls.

After playing in the little pool at the bottom, you climb above the falls to view a tranquil, softly moving pond of clear liquid. Although it's the same brook, it changed again, this time to a wide pool with a flat shale bottom.

The bottom is very slippery, and soon you are running and sliding on the flat shale. It's like skating on ice.

You sit and kiss, then roll around together in the shallow water, and kiss again. After the last slow, sensual bonding of your lips, you begin to think about making love on this slick slide.

As you become aroused, you lower yourselves down to the slippery bed and make wild love— facing each other while lying both upstream and downstream. Then you try facing upstream while your partner faces downstream, and vice-versa. You're in for the ride of your life on that slippery stone surface.

Don't slide down over that waterfall!

Safety Considerations

Never stand, walk, or make love in moving water that is above your knees. Use your good judgement. Depending on the speed of the stream flow, the water should be six inches to eighteen inches deep. Never over eighteen inches in depth. If the flow is too strong, you'll experience what it's like being inside a washing machine.

Don't walk through streams barefoot. Watch for sharp rocks and slippery rocks. If you turn your ankle, the mood can disappear, then getting back to camp will be no fun.

Protect the body parts above the water from sunburn.

Possible Equipment:

Stream adventuring requires whitewater sandals, reef runners, or whitewater booties to protect your feet and prevent you from slipping.

Another good idea is to have a pack or cushion, something to protect your back from the waterfall ledge and rocks or logs.

You can use a daypack to carry the food, wine and equipment.

Kneepads take up little space in your daypack. They can protect your knees from rocks in the stream.

Bring bug spray for your stream venture. It can prevent unnecessary irritation and a bad experience.

Chapter Seven: WATER CRAFT

INTRODUCTION

Candlelight, Wine in a Canoe or Boat under the Stars

The sun set long ago, and the mosquitoes have gone to bed. You are drinking wine with your campmate at the outside picnic table and gazing across the lake. The moon reveals the soft, shadowy silhouettes of the trees and mountains upon the still lake.

You want to be a part of that watery mirror image. You pick up the Pinot Noir, the glasses, and a candle, then beckon your partner into the bow. The moonlight on the mountains frames the portrait of a twinkly sky as you paddle out past the cove. A million stars are performing just for the two of you.

You stop, pour the wine and drink in the beauty of your love couched in the heavenly light. The vision takes your breath away. You quietly sip the wine, and taste the warm evening air.

To better feel the balmy whisper of a breeze, you both take off your T-shirts. You set up the candles in tho boat so that you can get glimpses of each other in its flickering light. Paddling again, you feast on the curves of your first mate's neck, shoulders and chest, radiant in the candlelight, then hidden again with each stroke.

You alternately drift, face each other, sip wine, then paddle for a little bit. Your love has the freedom and sensation of toplessness, the air fondling her chest as you paddle. You enjoy the teasing candlelit view. Your love is enjoying her nudity as you become aroused.

Since this trip is meant to be foreplay, don't allow yourself to touch each other.

When you can't stand the teasing candlelight any longer, it's back to shore for an evening of love...

A moonlit evening in a boat with my love provides one of the most romantic moments for me. The water lapping at the boat, the sound of the crickets, and the fresh evening air join with the enchanting lighting to enthrall me.

I trust it will do the same for you.

In an Open Boat at Night

When it's pitch dark and the mosquitoes subside, you build a campfire to use as a beacon and set up the candle, but don't light it. You arrange the air mattress or cushions in the center of the boat floor, placing one cushion against the center thwart/seat as a backrest.

Now the fun begins. In the dancing firelight, you take off each other's shirt and partially unzip each other's denim shorts. A long kiss, as you caress each other's upper body with oil. You slowly rub the olive oil wherever it feels good on your lover as the same is being done to you. You sensuously slide your hands over your playmate's body, occasionally squeezing and lightly pinching, then letting the flesh slip through your fingers. The fire warms the oil on your bodies as volcanic heat begins to boil.

When you can take it no longer, you light the candle and get into the boat. Your heart is pounding and your loins are shaking in anticipation, as you paddle out to a quiet spot near shore. By the time you get there, you have ebbed a bit. The anchor is set.

You meet in the center of the boat and pour the Pouilly Fuisse. You sip, kiss, touch and titillate each other slowly and easily. The renewed arousal is greater than by the campfire.

When your mate is burning far hotter than the candle, the boat becomes your floating lovebed.

If your lady has good muscle control, she can please both of you without ever rocking the boat. It may not work the first time, but after practice....

In an Open Craft During the Day

Paddling together around the lake, you spot a completely secluded cove. The entrance is so narrow that the canoe barely fits through. Once inside, you are in a pond-sized pool of your own. The water is deep and clear, and the shoreline birch reflect in its surface. No one would ever find you here.

As you anchor, a lone heron walks a few steps away to give you privacy. Pairs of red-winged blackbirds don't seem to mind your presence— you're just another couple.

Your paddling partner's arms are sore, so you kiss where it hurts, and massage the muscles. Looking around at birds, trees, water and sky, you feel true concert with nature. Kissing and massaging drifts to other parts, then turns to stronger natural urges.

...Keeping a blanket nearby, you let nature take its course.

The birds approve.

Afterwards, holding one another, you sip on Chianti Classico. Many kisses and several sips later, you love in the water, holding on to the boat.

In a Sailboat at Anchor (Maybe in a Storm)

You rented a sailboat for several days and completed your first day of sailing. The anchor is set in a quiet cove with a treed mountainous view. You're sipping Zinfandel and holding your first mate in the bow pulpit. After the sun sets, you adjourn to the cabin and turn on soft lights.

The boat has a huge V-berth forward and a quarter berth on each side in the main cabin.

You cuddle on a quarter berth and begin loving. You lie in the side berth, kiss and sway with the boat. The side to side motion heightens the kisses and the stroking. You touch and press together, sometimes unintentionally. The water movement is a turn-on.

When the play becomes more serious, it's not only the waves rocking the boat.

On the quarter berth, you make love in every position possible— with the added feature of the bed rocking.

Later you go out on the bow of the boat and love in the open. You become creative in the sturdy bow pulpit. Then there's the cabin rise, the mast, the cockpit, even tho transom.

If not in a storm, you can be in the water, holding on to the boat.

The next morning, you wake up looking at the ceiling in the V-berth. Feeling that warm, silky body against yours, you begin to get ideas. You get and give long kisses, play with each other under your blanket tent, and tease each other orally. As you begin to make love, your mate looks up with a twinkle in her eyes. She plants her feet up onto the low ceiling of the V-berth and has a movement and control that she never had before.

A storm can add even more sensation to your adventure. The rain is pounding on the deck, the waves are rolling the boat from side to side, and you are in for a ride you won't soon forget.

You can probably rock the boat all you want. Most larger sailboats are very stable.

In a Raft Down a Class I to III River (Daytime)

You two are fantasizing about the forthcoming adventure. While making the morning coffee, you kiss and touch each other a lot in private. Over breakfast it continues. Hours of teasing build up mutual anticipation before you get into the boat. But you each hold back. You are both ready to explode when you step into the raft.

The raft is all set; the guiding couple smile knowingly — you are guiding for them next week. You get under the tarp and undress. They push off into a slow moving current while you embrace. The river builds along with your ardor. You begin making love as you hit the rapids. It's the ride of your life!

The reality is more than you fantasized! Occasionally the waves splash onto your naked bodies. The cool water contrasts with the moist warmth of your raftmate, building your ardor. The motion of the raft down the river, the wave effects, and violence of the rapids while lovemaking have to be experienced to be believed.

If you get tossed around too much to focus, then play and tease each other. If the thought of class III whitewater scares you, find a slow-moving river.

If the thought of doing this on any moving river scares you, go on to the next setting. Only a few people will ever attempt this.

For this truly exceptional venture you need a whitewater raft with enough floor space to make love and a tarp tied over it to ensure your decency. An outfitter quality whitewater raft in good shape is best.

The raft floor space that you're using for a bed should protect your bodies from any rocks. A smooth piece of marine plywood with no sharp edges is good. You can put an air mattress or foam on top of that.

A good self-bailing raft would be the best, with the floor blown up hard and more cushioning on the floor.

You should enjoy this on a class I to III whitewater rated river with very few rocks that can jar the floor. Anything higher than III is too dangerous.

The couple guiding and paddling the raft need to be good friends who are private, unnosey and discrete.

Both couples should have an intimate knowledge of whitewater and guiding rafts.

Notes: You're entrusting your lives to the couple guiding and paddling the raft. It's best if they are licensed river guides who know this river well.

You can skip the wine before or on the river — it will be an omnitheatre for your senses without it. Alcohol blended with whitewater is a dangerous drink.

Everyone should wear Type 5 Life preservers—kept on at all times.

Don't fall out of the raft. It's no fun swimming whitewater.

Safety Considerations

If you use a raft rather than a boat, you can make every kind of foreplay or love in any or all of the positions that the raft provides. Since bigger rafts are very steady, there is little danger of tipping, unless you do something really crazy on a side tube.

If paddling a raft, DON'T bring a candle. Instead, use a flashlight that emits soft lighting 360 degrees around the handle when set straight up on its face. It has a soft lamp effect.

Canoes tip easily. If you're not used to moving around in a canoe, practice before trying this. In a moment of excitement, we once flipped the canoe, and wound up laughing while swimming back to camp, each blaming it on the other.

Have a red/green light on the bow of the boat, so that other boaters can see your craft while you are out at night. Tape a flashlight there, if necessary.

Have life preservers for safety. Both seat cushions and vests are a good idea. Some states require that you wear the life vest while you are in the boat.

During the daylight hours, protect yourself from sunburn.

Anchor, as an additional safety measure, to avoid drifting.

Too much boat rocking could really dampen your ardor!

Skip this chapter if you can't swim.

Possible equipment:

An air mattress protects your back from beatings by the boat and waves.

For evening boat escapades, place a candle seated in sand or rocks within a metal pan. It won't tip, and if the candle falls, there's no problem.

Bug spray is a good precaution.

Bring extra batteries for the bow light on your boat, or for the flashlight lamp. When you are loving, you lose track of time, and maybe the battery power for the lights.

Bring extra candles for that same reason.

Kneepads may be needed for the one on top.

Carry a blanket to cover yourselves with, especially if it's an open boat.

And, maybe, sweatshirts and loose shorts in case you need to dress quickly.

Last, an anchor, to avoid drifting too far toward, or away from shore.

Chapter Eight: AT CAMP

INTRODUCTION

Simple, Relaxed Moments

While camp may not seem to be the most romantic spot in the world, picture this:

You left your watch in the car, the radio and TV are at home. There is no time. There is no phone. You have no appointments to keep. You have absolutely nothing to do but relax, eat, sleep and make love. Let the world slip away as you spend quality time together. Talk, dream, make plans, hold each other and get passionate whenever the mood strikes. Morning, afternoon, early evening and at night.

My little, rustic camp is my haven. I sleep better there than anywhere else. I have experienced some of the highest romantic moments, as well as the most torrid lovemaking, in and around it.

Find your haven and forget the world.

In a Land Rover

You rent a Land Rover so that you can make it to your isolated camp with gear and food.

You unload your belongings, set up camp, then set out to explore the nearby trails. Several romantic spots pause your travels for a quiet moment together.

When you return perspiring and invigorated from the hiking, you take a bottle of Bordeaux from the Land Rover and share it. Both your T-shirts are wet, nearly transparent, and showing stimulation. You sip the wine and admire each other's protruding shirts.

Your companion slips out of the wet T-shirt. You do the same. A balsamy breeze fans your chests. Cooling down one way, you warm in another as you kiss and touch. Lips caress your chest, then thirstily seek yours. After more wine, a nutty thought creeps into your mind — what an outrageous commercial this would be for a four-wheeler! As the exhilaration becomes more intense, you fall together on the seat.

Looking up at the padded rollbars, you get some erotic ideas —

You sit atop the roll bar with your feet on the windshield while your partner obliges hungrily. Then your lover stands with one foot on each seat, picks you up and braces himself against the roll bar.

Later, as he tires, you step to the ground, bend down toward the bumper and pull your lover to you. The passion mounts as you move together, and you can hardly hold onto the bumper.

Then there is that padded side frame...

On the Camp Stairs

You arrive at camp early on Friday evening and are waiting for your campmate. You haven't seen each other all week, with very busy schedules. Late as usual!

You open some Blanc de Blanc, get two glasses, pour a drink and go out on the porch to wait. Your hummingbird neighbor buzzes by to say hello and hovers for a bit at the feeder as you sip the Champagne.

You sit on top of the stairs, then see a beautiful head of hair above a long coat coming down the path. The beauty ascends the stairs and bends to kiss you. Intoxicating aroma fills your senses. You pass the wine, still sitting. Next your love straightens up, straddles your legs, and opens the coat to present you with a naked, scented body.

You reach your lips to that sexy, inviting body, thinking— What a nice surprise greeting!

After kissing all over each other's bodies, you recline on the top of the stairs while your stairmate moves in your lap.

Later, she faces upstairs, bends over and holds on to the stairs and railing while you love her from one step down.

Hold onto the railing and position or strap yourselves in, so that your movements don't include bouncing down the stairs!

Candlelit Dinner at Camp

You are meeting your mate at camp. Exhausted from the week's craziness, you can't wait to get away from the world together. It's rainy and windy.

Opening the camp door, you are greeted by a half-naked partner, wearing only shorts and cowboy boots, illuminated by candlelight. The denim shorts are unzipped halfway. Dinner is on the table.

You remove your coat, take off your shirt and sit down to eat. The shrimp and pasta are delicious, but you keep forgetting to put food in your mouth as you devour that nakedness. Somehow you finish eating.

As the rain tickles the tin roof, your chef gets up and begins a slow, seductive dance. The wind is rustling the leaves, the rain is pounding the roof, and that beautiful body is swaying gracefully.

You can't wait for dessert!

The entire dinner, then the loving dessert is viewed only by candles — all night...

On the Picnic Table

What more appropriate place to make love than the location where you enjoy each other's company over food and wine?

You and your companion are supping at the lakeside picnic table, complete with grilled salmon, fresh corn and just-picked strawberries. Ironically, a huge bass jumps, then splashes into the lake directly in front of the table.

You feed the strawberries to your tablemate, kiss, then they're fed to you. You each accentuate lip and tongue movement as you accept the berry. Other juices start flowing through your system.

The setting sun frames your partner's face and hair in a tangerine light— what beauty! A mama mallard and her eight ducklings swim by, quacking away. Frogs across the lake have begun their medley, and the crickets provide accompaniment to your ears. What restaurant can provide this ambience?

After dining, you sip the Brut and begin thinking about the dessert course sitting on the bench. You hold your love, kiss and whisper.

Hungry lips feast on yours. Looking into ravenous eyes, you ease your tablemate down onto the bench for the first tasty dessert. The second dessert course becomes more than oral. You clear the top of the table and put it to better use...

You may need knee cushioning for the one on top, and a blanket to cover yourselves with. A tablecloth covers the table, a blanket on the bench prevents slivers.

And how about natural toppings for your real dessert? Maybe some cream or maple syrup? Or honey to complement your lover's? You can both decide on the flavors you want.

Pick a sturdy table that won't break.

On the Dock

Your dock is hidden from neighbors' view and distant from the eyes of passing boaters.

You spread the blankets and towels onto the dock. There is an air mattress to protect your backsides. The blanket is between the mattress and the dock to prevent puncture.

It's a lazy day. Fish are jumping, crows are cawing, a butterfly floats by, and the sparrows are flying back and forth.

You lie in the sun in your suits, relaxing, kissing, touching. The top of a suit comes off as the warmth penetrates. You rub each other with suntan lotion. A never ending kiss, along with sensuous stroking causes the suit bottoms to fall onto the dock. You savor each other's nakedness in the hot sun.

You progress to whatever comes naturally. If the scene is too bright and open, you can always adjourn to the cabin. Or simmer slowly until evening.

Here's an exciting variation— As pulsating lips request satisfaction, fall off the dock at just the right time. Select a side of the dock, where the water is at least four feet deep in the shallowest place, and there are no rocks, logs, ropes, rings or dock parts to hit if you fall in.

Use a tarp to protect yourselves and the air mattress from scraping the side of the dock as you fall in. Cover the dock with the tarp and let it hang down to the water on the side you selected. Place the double air/foam mattress on the dock, with one side extending out an extra foot over the water on the side you picked.

Then put the mattress to work. As the magic moment mounts for both of you, say NOW, hold your breath, roll into the water and into ecstacy! Make sure you let go after a few moments. Both should be good swimmers to avoid any panic.

P.S. Don't roll around too much too early. In one wild session, we fell off twice before the climactic finale.

You may want a blanket to cover yourselves with.

On the Beach

If there is a sandy, secluded beach near your camp, you have a perfect daytime lovespot. Hot sand and hotter desire!

You spread your blanket on the sand. Relaxing in the sun, you slowly kiss and stroke. Gradually you remove suits and rub each other with lotion. The hot, sunlit nakedness builds a roaring fire within. Sun is penetrating every fibre of your body. The heat is intense as you kiss and massage. Intense eyes lock with yours, communicating a need. Only one way to cool down...

You roll off the towels and make fiery love directly on the scalding sand.

....Afterwards, you jump into the water, letting the wet coolness slowly dissipate the heat.

Back on the towels you relax completely and doze peacefully as you tan.

Much later, you creatively mound the sand to make parts of the body project upwards or at different angles. It takes hours to test your work.

In the Water, Holding onto the Dock

Your dock is hidden from neighbors and passing boaters. Sunbathing on the dock, you tease each other and begin love games while still in bathing suits. The slow massaging of oil and touching of lips builds your craving.

Now you begin lubricating each other's bodies with olive oil. The stimulation drives you wild!

When you can't take it any longer, only the bottoms of the suits stay on the dock as you enter the water. You play, kiss and incite each other more until the water around you seems almost boiling. You come together easily in the water with the help of the olive oil.

You brace your feet against the flotation underneath the dock and hold onto the dock frame with your hands. Your lady floats onto you, sometimes facing you to kiss, others facing away.

This is a difficult position to maintain, but well worth the effort— hold on as long as you can. Enjoy the magical sensation of your dockmate's warmth as you move together, then the cool water as you move slowly away.

Fire and Ice

It's Spring, the wildflowers are blooming, the sun is shining, and you're in love.

The days are warm, the nights cool, and the lake is even cooler.

It's evening and dinner is over. You build a campfire to while away the evening. You two are warming near the blazing logs and sharing a bottle of Port. A blanket keeps the back warm, while the fire handles the front. A long kiss follows each sip of wine.

The fire is too big, you're getting hotter and hotter. Oh well, it'll burn down soon. It doesn't happen. You are both perspiring. Go into the camp? No, you want to enjoy the evening.

You decide to jump into the lake to cool off. You both drop the blanket, disrobe, then run in. The water is like melted ice on your skin — instant goosebumps. You scream and giggle a little from the shock. Then run out faster than you ran in.

In the firelight, you view your partner's naked body reacting to the cold— what a turn on. You embrace under the blanket and rewarm yourselves by the fire. You kiss and stroke, sip wine, and are soon again boiling.

Back into the lake! More visual firelit stimulation, more petting and Port. Again, too much heat.

When the foreplay has you quivering, you run to camp and make love. It's hotter than the fire ever was.

In a Sun Shower

You return to camp after an afternoon of hot hiking.

Your companion goes into the portable sun shower to freshen up. The shower curtain is hanging off a branch of the big hemlock.

You start fantasizing about that body, and decide to join in, carrying a bottle of olive oil. The water gets shut off, then on, then off and back on to arouse the skin along with the oil. Long, heated kissing, slow massaging and fooling, then the water goes off for a long while.

First you take turns loving with your mouths. Then the shower becomes as hot as a sauna! Only birds on the swaying branches above see the heated love celebration.

Your exceptionally strong lover picks you up onto him. When he tires, you step down and bend forward, grasping the hemlock, as he holds you from behind. You alternate the water off and on for more excitement.

For this, you need an outdoor shower with a lot of water.

If you get too involved and fall through the shower curtain without getting hurt, just keep on loving.

Of Plants, Feathers and Fur

(From a Suggestion by Mark, bowman on my best crew ever, West River, Fall 1996)

You decide to surprise your love this evening. During the day you gather a twig of spruce, a dried oak leaf, a pine twig, a piece of birch bark, a live maple leaf, some moss, some daisy petals and a feather. You remember that there is a fur hat in the camp.

That evening, you ask your campmate to undress and put on a blindfold. As he/she lies there, you caress your partner's naked body, starting with the fur. While your slave writhes in ecstacy, you slowly progress from soft to rough teasing, continuing with the feather and ending with the spruce.

You complete the session by exploring your captive's silken skin with your tongue.

After thirty minutes of this, your hostage rips off the blindfold and attacks you...

You may want to reverse the order, going from rough to soft.

If you or your captive is losing excitement because things are moving too slowly or a particular plant isn't exciting, then skip it and go to the next. Skip two, if you like. It all depends on you and your lover. This is a totally individual, personal foreplay. Only YOU can tailor it.

If you can't find all the plants, substitute, or skip those. If it seems like too many different plants are involved, reduce the number.

And don't limit yourself. Find your own plants.

On the Flat Camp Roof

You get a sturdy ladder, put it up against the roof, carry up a blanket, fruit juice and oatmeal cookies, and prepare for an afternoon of lofty lovemaking. You spread the blanket, undress, lie down and take in your aerial surroundings. It's a fall day with lots of sunshine, the temperature almost seventy. Up here your view of everything seems more clear because it's less obstructed. Even the cloudless sky reveals itself more from here.

You hear honking in the distance and turn to see not one, but three small convoys of geese flying in flawed *V* formations. Down below, the bees are gathering the last of the pollen from tiny wildflowers and the blueberry patch.

The sun is magnitudes brighter and warmer, as you apply lotion to each other's naked bodies. You quietly gaze down upon swaying branches, with the wind caressing your naked bodies.

Your perspective of the world is very different. You two are alone and above. Naked to the sun, you massage each other all over with the help of the slippery lotion...

At the peak of pleasure, the wind gusts and a flurry of leaves prickles your naked bodies.

Or you can do this at night under a full moon — a giant candle of soft light for safety and sensuality.

There is something about being up on a roof that has enthralled me since I was a child. Even as an adult, everything is magical, especially the lovemaking.

You'll see. Don't roll off!

You need a camp with a relatively flat slope, less than 20 degrees. Any more is too steep and dangerous. Make sure that the roof is not slate, asbestos, wood, or metal of any kind — that's too slippery. An asphalt roof is best.

After you get onto the roof, tie a brick to one end of a short rope, and the top rung of the ladder to the other end. Set the brick up on the roof so that the rope is snug, and the wind doesn't blow the ladder down.

Be in the center of the roof. If you get too involved and roll off the roof, you might get hurt. For sure it will break the mood.

You will likely need suntan lotion for this venture. Sunburn is a big factor here. Use a sunblock with a high number. Don't get it on your feet or the roof—you could slip.

Wine is probably not a good idea. It's too dangerous to be on a roof when you are a little tipsy.

Under the Camp

Now we go from the heat of the roof to the coolness of the earth under the cabin.

A lot of cabins are built on wood posts or stone piers with the sides left open so creatures don't take up housekeeping. You can use the area underneath as your love den. Clear the area so that you have enough space for a blanket.

On a rainy day that you would otherwise spend inside, get a tarp, blankets and a pillow along with some Madeira, take your denmate by the hand, and crawl into your lair. The two of you while away that rainy day in your snug little retreat.

You can smell the rain cascading off the roof, as the dampness sends a small shiver down your spine. You cuddle closer, entwining each other's legs, kissing and caressing.

Between those warm blankets, you kiss and pet until the heat causes you to throw off the top blanket, slow down, and sip the wine.... You've got all day, and you are going to take your time.

You make slow, lazy love in your warm sanctuary as the rain is dropping inches from your eyes.

On a Bench by the Campfire

This is far better than cooking marshmallows, I guarantee you.

You sit together on a bench by the evening fire with the blanket covering your backs, sip Bardelino and caress. The frogs are crooning, the crickets singing. An owl starts hooting away. Night sounds surround your ears and everything is right with the world.

Cooked in front, you turn around to warm your backs, and put the blanket in front. You feel like a chicken on a rotisserie. The fire is blazing hotter and hotter, as your lips burn more with every kiss. You wind up naked under the blanket.

You can't take the heated passion any longer. Flaming eyes demand to be quenched. Your partner pushes you down onto the bench and attacks. You come together and let the blanket fall to the ground. You make love with firelight dancing all over your perspiring, naked bodies.

The blistering heat from the fire has one part of your body flush, while the night coolness is goosebumping the other part. It's a matchless sensation as you feel your lover's moving warmth.

The bench should be strong and ought to have a cushion.

On a Mound of Freshly Dug Earth

Shades of Dracula!

You pick a night when the moon is full. After sunset, when the soil has become cool, you turn over a patch of ground the size of a coffin. The roots and big rocks get pulled out and put into a separate gravestone pile at one end.

Now, it's time for Bull's Blood wine. Of course! You sip, kiss and tease inside the camp. Between the hours of bothering and the wine, you two are very aroused.

The clock tolls midnight. By now the earth is cool and you are hot. A slight chill goes down your spine as you open the camp door— the intense moonlight illuminates the dug earth and gravestone pile. A coyote's eerie howl echoes from a distant mountain.

You undress on the porch, enjoying the moonlight view of each other's near-naked body. You can see everything in the full moonbeams— it's like daytime, only a little dimmer. No flashlights here!

The earth feels very cold to your feet, then your back as you lie down together. Soon you are immersed in each other. Frenzied lips seek yours. Hands massage, then squeeze.

You make intense, a little hurried, love on the fresh earth with an occasional chill here and there. You bite each other lightly on the neck, causing a shiver. You are very excited and a little scared.

The cool earth warms up with your body heat.

Later, you warm up with hot cocoa and blankets.

Drac says:

You can mound the earth to change the angle of the hips.

Dancing Naked by the Campfire

It's a warm summer night, with crickets and frogs trying to outdo each other. You built a little campfire for the evening cuddling.

You are both gazing into the fire, mesmerized by the radiating coals as they pulse bright, then dimmed orange light. Your mind is completely at rest, you are thinking of nothing. You kiss as you both realize that you were blanking out.

Suddenly your companion jumps up, goes into the camp, and returns with a bottle of olive oil. Your partner's shirt comes off and he/she begins a primitive dance in the firelight. Slowly rubbing the oil over selective areas, your love teases and tantalizes you, sometimes in shadow, then in the firelight.

Aroused, you remove your shirt and reciprocate. Soon the shorts fall off, followed by underwear, with more oil below. As you rub the oil on to arouse your partner, you are stimulating yourself with that slippery massage. The results are visual.

You each are dancing for the other, your bodies glistening in the flickering light. Two primates in an erotic mating dance.

Lips begin caressing the oil. You are almost in a frenzy! Two pairs of fiery eyes ignite together. With the fire and oil raging on your skin, you go hand in hand to the camp....

In a Bed of Freshly Cut Evergreen Boughs

You are trimming the evergreen trees around camp. The branches hang down to the ground, and you are cutting all branches below eye level so the earth will be less damp.

Or maybe you found a newly downed spruce tree.

The smell of those limbs reminds you of the Christmas tree you had last year. It would be a shame to waste them by burning.

Imagine making love, enveloped in the fragrance of that heavenly scent, as you crush the boughs. The needles caress your body through the tarp, rub together, and the fragrance builds as you move in ecstasy. Your fever intensifies, you move harder and faster. There's more massaging by needles, increasing friction of branches, and a building bouquet to heighten your senses.

You are breathing harder, more frequently, inhaling that scent, getting close. At the peak of passion, you both explode, as does the perfumed grenade of evergreen aroma.

You two lie relaxing in the boughs, tickling your nose and filling your lungs with the sweet breath of nature.

You need freshly cut evergreen boughs, preferably hemlock, spruce, or balsam — a stack two feet high and six feet in diameter. Plus a tarp to put over those sharp needles, and a blanket to put over the tarp. Wine is also a good idea.

If you get tar on your body, it is easily removed with cold cream, lotions, butter, or any oil.

Safety Considerations

Neighbors and passing boats can ruin things for you and them. Pick the right time and locale for your celebration.

Watch for poison ivy, oak and sumac.

Keep away from ant hills, bee hives/nests, and animal holes.

Be extra careful at night not to walk right into a tree in the dark. A tree branch could scratch you, or poke your eye.

Any time you are making love on or near wood structures, watch for slivers, projecting nail and screw heads.

Protect yourself from sunburn during the day.

Ladies, don't get sand or dirt into the wrong places! Play on top, or spread a small towel.

Chapter Nine: OUTDOOR SPORTS

INTRODUCTION

Doing it Outdoors

Sports in the outdoors is basic, simple and blood pumping. The fresh air and scenery charge your lungs, gladden your eyes and your spirits.

Relaxing with my love in nature's bed after a session of exertion, a cool breeze feels like a breath from heaven. The scenery and natural music couple in an environment unmatched in man's artificial world.

In these restful moments, gentle, slow kisses with your precious one seem the natural thing to do. If the kissing graduates to intense passion, lovemaking in nature's boudoir is a gift to be cherished.

I am both reverent and romantic in this setting. Come to the wilderness and share the experience as I do.

Hiking

The sunshine winds through the trees, forming an uneven checkerboard of light-dark patterns to your right, while the brook on the left is humming soft music. You are aerobically exercising, burning off calories, conditioning your heart and lungs.

That's how I see hiking and why I love it.

Hiking is the one sport that anyone can do at any age. It can also be the easiest and the most enjoyable, because of the immediate presence of nature surrounding you.

You make hiking easy by slowing the pace and traversing smooth, level ground. For more strenuous exercise, select a jaunt though irregular, hilly terrain. You can trek on any day according to your mood, level of energy and the surroundings you seek. It can be a one mile stroll or a twenty mile venture. It can begin as a one mile walk, then changed to five miles, as your disposition improves along the way.

Hiking puts me in a romantic mood when the scene around me is reason to pause, hold my lover, and absorb the cinerama that surrounds me. It offers all the lovemaking possibilities of the woods, ground, water, and bad weather.

When I think of hiking in more open areas and making love, I picture a couple on a secluded stone bridge overlooking a stream.

You embrace, then study the landscape. Another, longer hug ending with a kiss. Then another, each more heated and passionate than the previous. Probing tongues mate. Soon clothing is an obstruction...

You bend over and hold onto the stone railing. Your lover, kissing the back of your neck, caresses your chest as he joins. You make love while looking out on the bridge.

On another occasion, sneak off the path behind some large boulders and use the stones in sensual seclusion.

There are tens of thousands of these abandoned bridges, originally built for roads that no longer exist. If you can't find one, maybe an old bridge over a quiet country road is your lovespot.

Confirm that the bridge and the rail are solid and safe. You don't want to wind up flying through the air into that stream. If in doubt, love elsewhere.

Jogging

Jogging is something that I always hate to get started doing alone. I find an axe to sharpen, some brush to clear, anything to put it off for a little while. Eventually, though, I have to get running. I moan and groan for the first mile, then settle down and really enjoy the jogging.

But the thought of running on a path through the woods gets me moving immediately. The beauty, pure air, and coolness are so enjoyable to me that I run much further than normal without realizing it. Time stands still while I'm threading down a pretty wooded path.

The other circumstance that gets my running shoes on right away is the company of my lady. The vision of her calves flexing as her pony tail bounces in front of me— with those hips and behind dancing back and forth— is my best jogging incentive.

Combine these two catalysts, and running is pure pleasure, one I can't wait to do. The beauty of my lady on a winding path in a birch grove can keep me running for miles without being aware of exertion.

After a while, she makes me run ahead so she can watch me. It's only fair!

For us, jogging is a turn-on that slowly develops over the miles. When we stop for a water break, we sometimes use the opportunity to cool ourselves by spraying each other. I begin to fantasize about that beautiful body, so visible through that wet, clingy shirt. Often, that fantasy becomes real as I begin to caress the transparency. We kiss and touch, then escalate into lovemaking.

Because you can jog almost anywhere; by streams, rivers, lakes, mountains, you can also make love at any and all these locations.

The one place that stands out for me is a shaded, grassy hillside along a quiet road. The wind is caressing the grass, moving it like waves on the lake. You sit down to drink water. Mesmerized by the swaying waves, you slowly embrace, kiss and stroke. As pleading lips mate with a quiver, you progress to making love. The motion of the grass lovemat becomes that of a hurricane from your passion.

The grass is about eighteen inches tall, so no one can really see your loving activities as the wind ripples over your skin.

See if this works for you as it does for me.

Mountain Biking

For us, mountain biking is a way to speed up through boring, plain landscapes, then dawdle in panoramic places. It's great exercise, and the dallying is pure enjoyment.

Sometimes these idle, quiet moments are spent holding hands and looking around. Others add stroking and kissing; some go much further.

You see that we aren't die-hard mountain bikers, that go up and down terrain that experts would think twice about. We stick pretty much to old dirt roads, logging roads, and regular paths. It's a workout, but not an extreme test of the body's or the bike's limits. We stop often to cool down, talk and touch, sometimes kissing, for hours.

When your petting turns the rest period into torrid passion, you can find a loving/cooling off spot in a tiny stream under a bridge in the road. Or perhaps a splashing stream tumbling down a nearby hill. Look for water barely eight inches deep, cool and flowing slowly.

You start out playing and splashing each other. Shirts become transparent. Then the kissing and touching starts. You slowly pull the wet shirt off your partner and begin caressing. Soon the only way to satisfy your passion is to make swirling love in the flowing stream. Maybe kneepads and a small air mattress are used.

Because you can go almost anywhere with a mountain bike and bring equipment with you, the lovesites are unlimited. The woods, ground, streams, lakes and mountains are all available.

Make sure that your bikes are well concealed.

Rock Climbing

Here is a sport where you can watch most every muscle in your companion's body, maneuvering up a rock face. But make sure that while climbing, you concentrate on the holds and route.

This is an activity where you can't be thinking about anything else while you're climbing— you have to focus on the line upward. But when you're belaying and watching that beautiful body ascending, you can make plans for activities on the top.

If you are climbing in an area where no one else is, why not make love at the end of the climb? Can you think of a better way to celebrate?

You begin by rubbing each other's feet, calves, then thighs. As this raises your eroticism, other touching activities naturally follow. Slow kissing, hugging and touching. As you view your flushed beauty framed in the surrounding panorama, the ecstasy builds to a peak.

If it's only the two of you, climb at least two levels below what you would normally do with a group. Be conservative, and use safety gear where you normally wouldn't.

If you are not already a rated rock climber, skip this setting.

Cross-Country Skiing

The beauty of the woods in winter is something few people ever get to appreciate. The virgin white blanket, the quiet, the sun sparkling through snow-laden branches, the solitude— are all waiting for you. Chickadees will keep you company, flying from branch to branch, as you glide through the woods.

Cross-country skiing opens this world for your pleasure. It allows you to easily travel miles through the woods, following a path that few take in the winter.

Though you've been on this path several times in the summer, the landscape seems very different. You study the white setting in awe, and give thanks for being alive.

...There is an evergreen corral that shields you from other eyes. You lay out the tarp, pad and, sleeping bag. Then you crawl in and enjoy wine, cheese and stroking. If it develops, the lovemaking in the snowy solitude will be mystical. Or else enjoy the picnic surrounded by the white wilderness. But leave enough time to return before dark.

If it is a warm, sunny day and you are within one mile of the return site so that there is little possibility of hypothermia, here's a thought:

As blazing eyes ignite yours, roll off into the snow together. It's at once shocking, exhilarating and orgasmic. You might even create a giant coupled snowball!

You could substitute hot chocolate or coffee with Baileys for the wine.

Snowshoeing

Cross-country skiing can get you into parts of the woods. But only snowshoeing will take you anywhere you want to go in the winter.

The deep woods are yours alone. You can picnic, photograph and make love almost anywhere. You will see splendor that can't be expressed, only appreciated.

This seclusion and stark beauty is there only for the two of you. A white, velvet tapestry adorns everything in sight. You feel so reverent, so much in awe at your surroundings, that you speak in hushed tones. What a primal setting for making love!

For your primitive lovemaking, bring a tarp, air mattress and some real or artificial fur. Cheese and Beaujolais-Villages are a good addition that the Indians didn't have. You are making love in the fashion of the Indians and Eskimos, and the sensation of the fur on your body is an aphrodisiac.

The snowshoes lie on the snow to help support your bed, with the tarp, mattress and fur on top of the snowshoes. Then your loving bodies. If it is a warm day with a short return trek so that hypothermia is not a worry, roll off into the snow together at the right time. It's a titillating shock!

If it is too cold and windy, tease away, then finish your snow seduction at camp.

Safety Considerations

Stay out of the woods during the big game hunting season.

Always leave your route with someone in case of emergency.

In the Winter:

Know all about frostbite and its symptoms. Watch each other for signs of them. The same for hypothermia.

It's a good idea to leave in the morning, so that you can enjoy a morning of activity, a loving lunch, and an early afternoon coming back.

Because of the isolation, you should always have a compass, energy food, maps, matches, a sleeping bag, a tarp, a space blanket, and a first aid kit in your daypack.

Know your route well and memorize the landmarks on the way. The weather can change quickly and cover your inbound trail. Unless you have traveled the route before and weather is not a factor in returning, you probably should not stop for an extended picnic. If a storm is coming, you should be going.

Allow plenty of time to return before dark.

Please reread the general Safety Considerations at the end of the chapters on the Ground, the Mountain, the Woods, the Lake and the Stream so you know better what to avoid, and what to bring.

Easing Into Outdoor Love

For a gradual introduction into outdoor life and love, try this:

One or two days at a rustic cabin or tenting, making love at or around camp.

Then one or two days at the Hilton. You still can be hiking or biking, and celebrating love in the outdoors. Later, you can encore in a giant bed. The difference is, you dine in a fine restaurant, sleep in bed and have hot showers in your room.

Now one or two more days at camp, either tenting or in a cabin. More exploring and torrid outdoor lovemaking........

It's a nice mix and a way to ease into the outdoor lovelife. We did it in Las Cruces while on vacation in the Southwest. Our tenting meant no showers, while the hotel offered unlimited bathing, followed by 48 ounce Margaritas and a luxurious king-size bed. It works great!

Footnote — How do you find all of these places?

There is a stream 5 miles from a major city in New York. It flows under a busy interstate highway and is flanked by woods. One day I walked up the stream, passed underneath the road via the stream tunnels, walked a mile, and found a lover's paradise.

Pools to swim and make love in, waterfalls to love under, rapids to play in, flat rocks, trees and hills to experience. No one ever goes there, because the tunnels under the highway appear to be a barrier. It has become one of my favorite hideaways.

Any clean stream that flows under the road is a potential lovesite, especially if it disappears into woods. Look around.

Search for a camp at the extreme end of a lake. During spring, autumn and winter you frequently can prance around outside naked, and no one is near to disturb the frivolity. Activity on northern lakes slows to almost nothing after Labor Day.

During the summer, on weekdays, it's often the same. No one is around. You can celebrate anywhere you like.

The New York State Thruway, I-88, I-87, I-81 and a host of major state highways pass through sections of woods. Get off at the nearest exit and backtrack to find a future lovenest. This is workable in any state.

After the fall hunting season, follow some little-traveled, out-of-the-way state trails for a couple of miles. Keep looking off to the side of the trail for spots that could be perfect. You may find a haven that never has company.

During the summer season, check it several times to ensure that you won't be disturbed. It's a little time consuming, but it gets you outdoors and hiking, so it's a healthy use of time.

DeLorme makes topographical maps of a more than a dozen states. They show elevation, woodsy areas, streams, lakes, and road detail. It even shows dirt roads and some paths. Get a map of your state from them, or a similar one from another company. You can also find topographical maps at your friendly state government agency, Fish & Wildlife, Encon, one of those.

One of the best ways is to spend more time outdoors— don't drive everywhere. Bike, hike or jog around. You will see things you would miss by motorized vehicle, and find playareas under your nose.

Make love in the wild and unleash your passion!

With Love,
Chuck

NOTES:

NOTES:

NOTES:

NOTES:

NOTES:

Making Love in the Wild
ORDER FORM

Mail to :

Chuck Butkus
PO Box 4931
Schenectady, NY 12304

________		$10 (Canada $14)	__________
Quantity	@	Price Each	Subtotal

NY residents
add 8% tax __________

Shipping & Handling Charges

1 book	$3
2 books	$5
3 books	$6

(Add $1 for each book over 3)

Shipping __________

Total Order __________

PAYMENT:

Check (US funds only) written to Chuck Butkus

Allow up to 3 weeks for delivery. Thank you.

PRAISE FOR *THE LONGEVITY DIET*

"This book is a valuable tool for those interested in living a longer, healthier life. My research with laboratory animals has shown that a nutrient-rich, calorically reduced diet slows the aging process, decreases age-associated mortality, and increases longevity. Delaney and Walford translate the results of my and others' research into practical terms that are easy to understand and easy to put into practice. This is not a rigid 'diet book.' It is a flexible program that guides the reader towards a healthier way of eating and living. Follow the advice in this book and you will very likely see many extra years of health and vigor."

—STEPHEN R. SPINDLER, PHD,
Professor of Biochemistry,
University of California, Riverside

"*The Longevity Diet* offers a new way of living. It helps readers mull over a commitment to themselves to live long and healthy and how to achieve it. You can take baby steps at first if you aren't ready to change every eating habit, and charts help you choose nutrient-dense foods that are still filling and satisfying. The book addresses the deleterious effects of stress that often induce humans to overeat. Forget the idea of eating to lose weight, or even to feel better. Trade calories for years of healthy living. That's the Longevity Diet."

—BILL SARDI, Knowledge of Health, Inc.,
author of *The Anti-Aging Pill* and
How to Live 100 Years without Growing Old

ABOUT THE AUTHORS

LISA WALFORD has the fortunate distinction of having flesh and blood kinship to the late Dr. Roy Walford, who pioneered research on the effects of a low-calorie diet on aging. Lisa is the producer of Dr. Walford's Interactive Diet Planner and worked alongside him for eighteen years. They are both coauthors of *The Anti-Aging Plan*.

Lisa's main inspirations in life lie with Iyengar yoga, which she has studied for over twenty years. Now a senior intermediate certified instructor, she served on the faculty of the National Iyengar Yoga Association's North American conventions in 1993, 1996, and 2004. She currently directs the teacher training programs at Yoga Works in Santa Monica, California, and continues her studies annually with the Iyengar family at the Iyengar Yoga Institute in Pune, India.

BRIAN M. DELANEY has written numerous articles on health and longevity. He co-founded the Calorie Restriction Society with, among others, Lisa Walford and Roy Walford, and has been the society's president since 2002. He is currently completing his doctoral work in social thought at the University of Chicago and is a guest lecturer in philosophy, life extension, and health in the United States and Sweden.

with gratitude David; from the beginning you have supported the CR society, & its members. Thank you. Lisa Walford June 2005

ALSO BY LISA WALFORD

The Anti-Aging Plan
(with Dr. Roy Walford)

BRIAN M. DELANEY and **LISA WALFORD**

Foreword by Roy Walford, MD

the longevity diet

DISCOVER CALORIE RESTRICTION—
THE ONLY PROVEN WAY
TO SLOW THE AGING PROCESS
AND MAINTAIN PEAK VITALITY

MARLOWE & COMPANY
NEW YORK

THE LONGEVITY DIET: *Discover Calorie Restriction—the Only Proven Way to Slow the Aging Process and Maintain Peak Vitality*

Published by
Marlowe & Company
An Imprint of Avalon Publishing Group Incorporated
245 West 17th Street • 11th floor
New York, NY 10011

AVALON
publishing group incorporated

Library of Congress Cataloging-in-Publication Data is available.

ISBN 1-56858-309-5

9 8 7 6 5 4 3 2 1

Designed by Pauline Neuwirth, Neuwirth and Associates, Inc.
Printed in the United States of America

This book is dedicated to the memory of
Professor Roy L. Walford, whose work followed
the Enlightenment motto: *dare to know!* and whose life
followed his own motto: *dare to live!*

CONTENTS

Foreword by Dr. Roy Walford xi

PART I—THE LONGEVITY DIET: SCIENTIFIC BACKGROUND

1 What is the Longevity Diet? 13
2 How the Longevity Diet Can Change Your Life 19
3 ABCs of Nutrition 40
4 Your Calories, Your Life 67
5 Your Life, Your Decision 87

PART II—THE LONGEVITY LIFESTYLE

6 The Longevity Diet as a Way of Life 99
7 Your Daily Food Diary 119
8 Parenting the Longevity Diet Lifestyle 157
9 Monitoring the Longevity Diet Lifestyle 165
10 The Longevity Diet and Exercise 181
11 Optimal Living from a Few Veteran CR Practitioners 197

Glossary 205
Resources 215
Notes 219
Acknowledgments 225
Index 227

FOREWORD

BY DR. ROY WALFORD

I HAVE SPENT most of my professional life researching the relationship between level of caloric intake and longevity.

Year after year I would witness the dramatic results of calorie restriction in my laboratory at the University of California–Los Angeles. The animals eating a normal diet would start turning gray, their hair would start falling out, their bones would get brittle, they would start moving more and more slowly, and then they would stop moving forever. While these changes were taking place in the one group, there was a group of mice next to them going through something entirely different. This other group was on the CR (calorie restriction) diet. These animals retained an astonishing youth and vitality. At an age when most of the mice eating the normal diet were dead—a human equivalent of eighty-five or ninety years—nearly all of the mice on the CR diet were alive and, indeed, thriving! The females were even able to conceive! The aging process was slowed so dramatically that many of the mice on the CR diet lived to be a human equivalent of over 140 years, some even beyond 150 years!

I was well aware of Clive McKay's seminal research on dietary restriction, in the 1930s at Cornell University. His rodents were put on their regime early in life, one in which they were severely and abruptly restricted. Much has transpired since Dr. Richard Weindruch and I postulated and proved in my laboratory that adult-onset CR in mice, if done gradually, would trigger the health benefits described above.

At that time, I started writing books explaining the scientific principles behind CR, making the case that CR, even when started in adulthood, will almost certainly have the same effects in people as those seen in laboratory animals. We are compelled to say "almost" because the studies needed to prove this would of course take more than a century to conclude. But, as so far tested, CR works across nearly the whole animal kingdom, so it would indeed be surprising if it did not work in humans. Moreover, studies on monkeys currently underway in three laboratories in the United States very clearly show that the extensive physiologic and biochemical changes seen in CR rodents are also found in CR monkeys, to whom we are extremely closely related. In addition, the human studies I personally participated in, monitored, and published results upon, while the medical officer inside the experimental habitat Biosphere 2, also show the same changes.

More studies are underway, and preliminary results all point in the same direction: the CR effect appears to be universal in the animal kingdom. Researchers at Washington University, for example, have just published a report in the journal *Nature* showing that people on CR manifest the same changes in cholesterol, fasting glucose, insulin levels, and other parameters of health as those seen in nonhuman animals on CR. The question is: how can people best put this diet into practice?

My daughter, Lisa Walford, and Brian M. Delaney, have written this book with just that practical question in mind. Lisa has extensive experience with CR. She codesigned a software program that helps the user track nutrients in the diet, and coauthored a book on CR with me several years ago, called *The Anti-Aging Plan*. Brian was the founder of the first Internet-based life-extension group, Sci.life-extension, and is the president of the CR Society, a nonprofit group whose purpose is to support people practicing CR and participating in CR research.

The Longevity Diet is a multipurpose book. If you want to aim for six or seven score vital years, this book will explain how. If you have a less radical goal and simply want to reduce your chances of being felled by the heart attacks or cancer that struck many of your ancestors, this book will explain how.

And even if your principal motivation is "vanity"—and there's nothing wrong with that!—this book will provide what is probably the best way to look better and keep looking better. People who "go on a diet" in the normal sense, i.e., people who are simply trying to lose weight because they want to look good, have a "recidivism" rate of around 95 percent. That means that, after one year, 95 percent of the people who have gone on a weight-loss diet are back at the weight they started with. On the Longevity Diet, success rates are much, much higher. This may simply have to do with the difference in motivation. A desire to be healthy may have more staying power than a desire to be thin. But it probably has more to do with the diet itself. Instead of strange, unnatural-seeming levels of fats and proteins that we find in fad diets, the Longevity Diet, especially in its milder forms, is a diet focused simply on fruits and vegetables and other nutrient rich foods that "make sense." In addition, the selection of more healthful foods leads naturally to mild to moderate weight loss, which produces health benefits that reinforce these new dietary choices.

This book presents the practical knowledge gleaned from years of collective experience with CR. It is an invaluable guide for those who want to put the principles of the Longevity Diet into practice in their own lives. And giving this diet a try is something that I, as a physician, and as a researcher with decades of research under my belt, would very strongly recommend. It's a shame to die so young, because it takes so long to learn how to live.

Your health is now in your hands.

Roy L. Walford, md, (1924–2004) was a gerontologist who pioneered research on the effects of a low-calorie diet on aging. He was also the author of the bestsellers *Maximum Life Span* and *The 120 Year Diet,* and *Beyond the 120-Year Diet*. He is still considered one of America's leading experts on gerontology.

the longevity diet

■ PART 1 ■

THE longevity DIET

Scientific Background

1 WHAT IS THE LONGEVITY DIET?

INTRODUCTION

THE LONGEVITY DIET is a way of eating that will radically lessen your chances of suffering from the vast majority of diseases and other ailments that may afflict us as we age. It is a highly flexible program that emphasizes healthy, nutrient-rich foods and the reduction of empty calories. It can be implemented in whatever way suits your lifestyle. In milder forms it will significantly improve your health, and more rigorous adherence to the program will literally slow the effects of aging, and, in some ways, even turn back the hands of time. If you consistently follow the principles outlined in this book, in your sixties you will feel as most people do in their forties and, when you reach your eighties, nineties, and beyond, you will still be physically vigorous and mentally agile.

The principles of the Longevity Diet are based upon an enormous body of research into the relation between diet and aging. It is now clear that a reduction in the calorie content of a diet that is otherwise healthy and nutrient-rich will dramatically improve your health, and maintain youthfulness far longer than any pill or potion. This is why scientists generally refer to the diet simply as "CR," for calorie restriction. This diet has been the primary research tool used to study aging since the 1930s. Since then, over one thousand studies in a wide variety of laboratory animals have confirmed the dramatic results of longevity-enhancing, calorie reduced diets. Now the results from studies on humans are pouring in, confirming that the benefits of such a diet may indeed extend up the "food chain" to humans. These results have been so impressive that even the U.S. government, which tends to be conservative when turning research results into recommendations, is changing its tune on caloric intake. For years, official government agencies emphasized that "it's okay to gain weight as you age."[1] Now, government experts have realized that it is very likely *not* okay, and may even be harmful. Indeed, the version of the government's "Dietary Guidelines for Americans" that was published in the year 2000 says precisely the opposite of the conventional wisdom: "To be at their best, adults need to avoid gaining weight, and many need to lose weight." Indeed, maintaining a healthy weight is described as "key to a long, healthy life."[2] And the next edition of "Dietary Guidelines for Americans," released in early 2005, in the words of the Executive Summary, "places stronger emphasis on reducing calorie consumption."[3] Moreover, the hundreds of dramatic CR studies in laboratory animals that researchers have amassed, as well as the growing number of studies of short-term CR in humans, have finally convinced the government to fund studies of long-term, very strict CR diets in humans. This research project, known as CALERIE (Comprehensive Assessment of Long-Term Effects of Reducing Intake of Energy), is now underway at Duke University, Tufts University, Washington University in St. Louis, and Pennington Biomedical Research Center in Baton Rouge.

Long before the recent surge in media coverage of the new human CR studies, a few dedicated pioneers began following the CR-based Longevity Diet. They were inspired to do so by the research and writings of Roy L. Walford, MD, who was the world's most prominent CR and **gerontology** researcher until his death in 2004, and author of two best-selling books, *Maximum Life Span* and *Beyond the 120-Year Diet,* among other titles. Following Professor Walford's recommendations, these individuals went to their physicians, explained that they wanted to give this diet a try, had their cholesterol levels and a few other **biomarkers** measured, started the diet, came back to their physicians after a few months, got retested, and *voilà*! Even in that brief time, the diet had had a positive effect upon virtually every biomarker of every individual. Each shift was not only measurable, but dramatic. Their delight in the sheer look of astonishment on their physicians' faces was a major motivation to keep these people on the diet, as were their own observations that they were becoming trim and fit, and felt much better. But the support provided by concrete numerical measurements of their biomarkers has been, for most of these pioneers, the most important carrot keeping them moving forward on the path of health and longevity. Put yourself in their place: If after just three months on the Longevity Diet you have lost weight that will *stay* off, your total cholesterol goes from 220 to 170, your blood pressure from 140/90 to 120/70, and your doctor says, "Amazing! Keep going! I might even have to try this diet myself!" it should be easy for you to maintain the desire to make the Longevity Diet a permanent part of your life. If you have become disappointed with other health regimens that don't deliver or that have only temporary or imperceptible results—the Longevity Diet is for you!

BIOMARKERS

A biomarker is an indicator of some aspect of your state of health. Some biomarkers are simple, like your pulse rate, or the length of time you can stand on one foot with your eyes closed. You can measure these biomarkers yourself, and test your own longevity diet program! Others are measurements of substances found in your blood, such as cholesterol or fasting glucose. These can be ordered by your physician. See Table 1.1 for a list of biomarkers associated with health and aging that have been used by researchers over the years.

TABLE 1.1

THREE CATEGORIES OF HUMAN BIOMARKERS

(adapted from *Beyond the 120-Year Diet,*[4] page 32).

1. "Functional" Age

Vital capacity, breath-holding time, maximal oxygen consumption (VO_2 max), kidney function (creatine clearance), diameter of pupil of eye, visual accommodation, hearing, level of DHEA hormone in blood, tests of mental function.

2. Predictive Value for Remaining Life Expectancy

Vital capacity, heart size, systolic blood pressure, hand-grip strength, presence or absence of autoantibodies in blood, immune-function tests, reaction time.

3. Segmental Aging (Aging of individual parts of, or systems in, the body) and/or Disease Susceptibility

Glucose-tolerance test; levels of blood cholesterol, LDL, HDL, triglycerides, and homocysteine; systolic blood pressure; blood level of parathyroid hormone.

This regimen is not a trendy flash in the pan. We are among those who started the Longevity Diet many years ago, fourteen years ago in Lisa's case, twelve in Brian's. Both of us have been involved in the CR and longevity "movement" in various ways for a long time—Lisa, through her writing and work with her father, Professor Walford; and Brian, through his involvement in the creation of Internet-based health groups, and, above all, in his work as president of the nonprofit **CR Society**.

We are writing this book to share what we have learned over the years, so that others can benefit from the Longevity Diet.

THE LONGEVITY DIET IN A NUTSHELL

The Longevity Diet is a low-calorie, generally **low-GI** (glycemic index) diet that is rich in flavor and maximizes the natural benefits of foods high in vitamins and minerals. It does not involve unnatural quantities or the elimination of fat or carbohydrates or protein, or special potions, powders, or pills. There are no complicated, inflexible meal plans. The Longevity Diet is a prudent way of eating that focuses directly on what matters most for health: reducing your caloric intake while eating plentifully of foods that pack a concentrated goodness.

WHAT'S IN A NAME?

The diet we describe in this book has had nearly as many names as it has had practitioners. Since you will be hearing more and more about the diet from the press as research results from an increasing number of studies are released, it will be useful to know the various names the diet goes by. But don't let the plethora of names confuse you. These are all the same diet.

- **The High-Low Diet**—Named after the principle that the diet is high in essential nutrients, but low in calories.
- **The Walford Diet**—Named, of course, after the researcher who advocated the diet for human health.
- **Calorie Restriction** (or **CR**, or **The CR Diet**)—Captures the essence of the diet, but misses the *purpose* for which people

would want to follow the diet. (We will nonetheless often use "CR" to describe the diet because so many practitioners use that term, as do nearly all scientists.)

- **CRON**—Calorie Restriction with Optimal Nutrition. A bit too hubristic for our taste. People following the Longevity Diet are scientifically minded, and want to stress that we actually don't know what's absolutely optimal.
- **CRAN**—Calorie Restriction with Adequate Nutrition. A bit redundant: eating a CR diet for the purposes of increasing health and longevity *is* eating with nutritional adequacy.
- **CRL**—Calorie Restriction for Longevity. Makes sense, and captures the purpose of the diet, but aren't we getting tired of these obscure initials?
- **The Longevity Diet**—Captures the purpose of the diet, which we believe is the best way to keep people motivated to stick with it.

Since its principles are so straightforward and simple, you can implement the diet in whatever way best suits you, with regard to mealtimes and food choices. You can also pursue the diet to varying degrees, much like an exercise regimen: there are moderate, "relaxed" versions of the program that will still result in both immediate and long-term benefits, and more rigorous versions of the program that will provide more dramatic results. Which version of the Longevity Diet is best for you to follow is a matter that should be decided by you and your physician.

THE RANGE OF CR LONGEVITY REGIMENS

Both of us have experimented with different variations of the Longevity Diet over the years, and have learned from the experience of hundreds of other CR practitioners. Here are a few brief examples of how we and several others have put CR into practice.

lisa walford, 50—

VETERAN YOGA INSTRUCTOR, WRITER, AND OWNER OF NUTRITIONAL SOFTWARE COMPANY

Lisa's history with CR has taken many turns over the past fourteen years. She first experimented with an all-raw diet for a year, then a predominately vegetarian diet (for ethical rather than nutritional reasons).

From 1991 to 1993 her father, Professor Walford, was sealed inside the Biosphere 2 enclosure in Tucson Arizona. Eight people lived in a virtual mini-world, growing, harvesting, and recycling all of their own food. The El Niño weather pattern robbed them of the amount of sunlight they expected, and in fact needed, to produce a normal amount of food for eight people. They all thus survived on a limited food supply; yet Roy vicariously savored oysters and champagne through Lisa's descriptions of her weekly indulgences in these delicacies. Rather than entertain living with so extreme a degree of dietary exclusions embraced by her father in the interest of science, Lisa felt it more appropriate to explore different combinations of foods that would satisfy both her senses and her body's nutritional needs, as well as her principles.

Now a vegan, she eats very little for breakfast or lunch: juice in the morning, a light soy-protein lunch, and green tea midafternoon are sufficient to keep her alert and sated. Lisa's daily indulgence is a large evening meal featuring plenty of vegetables, soy protein, and a few nuts, prepared with pesto, peanut, or pasta sauce. She fasts one day a week, and notes that those hours comprise the most restful day in her week.

Lisa's petite frame belies her strength and CR-enhanced stamina, as Washington University CR and nutrition researcher Luigi Fontana commented at the second CR Society conference in 2003, at the University of Wisconsin in Madison. As Lisa has a low **Body Mass Index** of 15 (fashion models generally have BMIs of 17), he was surprised to see such strong bones in a CR body. Lisa currently balances her longevity diet with an exercise regimen that strengthens her heart, bones, and peace of mind, in total enabling her to live a full, multidisciplined, and potentially long life.

BODY MASS INDEX

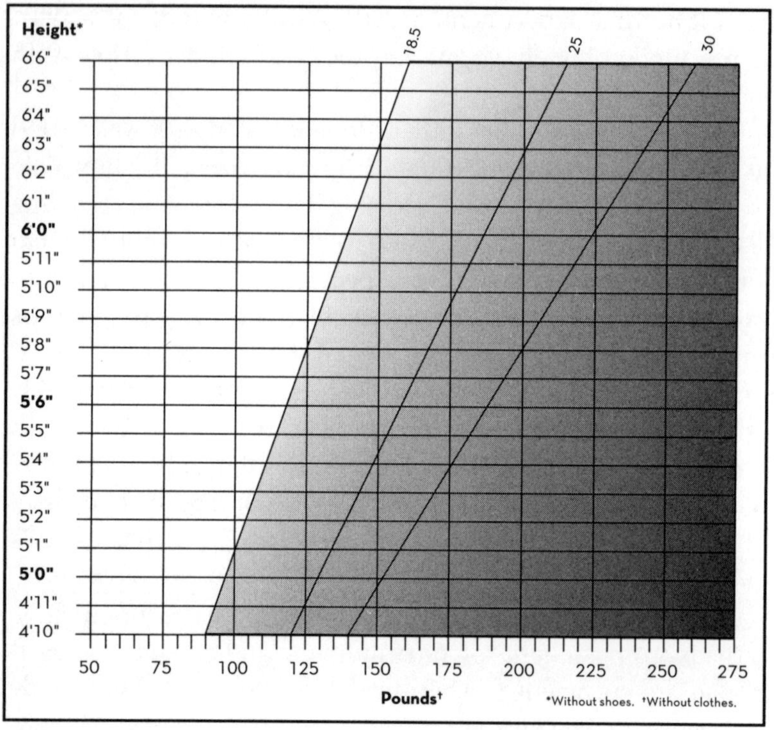

(Adapted from *Nutrition and Your Health: Dietary Guidelines For Americans,* 2000, 5th Edition, USDA.) Note: most people on CR have BMIs between 16 and 20.

brian m. delaney, 41—

PHILOSOPHY INSTRUCTOR, WRITER, AND PRESIDENT OF THE CALORIE RESTRICTION SOCIETY

Brian now follows a very simple version of the Longevity Diet: he eats whole-grain cereal with fruit, soymilk, and nonfat yogurt for breakfast; skips lunch; and, like Lisa, enjoys a substantial dinner of primarily vegetables. When eating with friends, he also enjoys a glass or two of wine. Someone commenting on his diet would probably say that he follows a standard, mostly vegetarian "health food" diet, but just doesn't eat lunch. Brian is not a strict vegetarian, however: his caloric allotment allows for a moderate portion of steak if a friend happens to serve one (he doesn't believe in troubling dinner hosts with his dietary requirements). If that "moderate portion" turned out to be immoderate, he would enjoy the steak, and make up the difference in calories with a lighter breakfast the next day, so that his caloric intake would average out the same across a twenty-four hour or so period. According to research, the occasional "cheat," rebalanced as quickly as possible with a skipped or lighter meal, is fine. In the long run, what matters is the average caloric count per day (that is, as averaged across several days—a slightly heavier day followed by a slightly lighter day is fine), not the caloric content of a single meal or snack. Consuming, for example, precisely 850 calories twice a day does not yield any CR benefits beyond what a diet of, on average, 1,700 calories per day would produce. Likewise, you may consume around 1,900 calories one day and 1,500 or so the next, divided among two meals one day, and three or four meals the next day, to produce an average intake of 1,700.

During his first years on the Longevity Diet, Brian was very rigorous in the way he ate, the results of which were extraordinarily healthy biomarkers his blood pressure, for example, was around 100/55. However, this version of the Longevity Diet requires a dedication to meal planning that Brian didn't have time for, and, more important, since he was already fairly trim to begin with, he felt he was becoming a bit *too* thin on so extreme a diet. Because, from the standpoint of disease prevention, he was doing even better than needed on the rigorous version, he decided it was safe to switch to the "skip lunch and eat normal-size breakfasts and dinners" version of the Longevity Diet, which continues to maintain his health. On this more moderate version of CR, Brian's blood pressure is on average 115/60. That is still, of course, excellent. Brian's physician and researcher friends all agree that he is in peak form and is probably aging a bit more slowly than he would otherwise be. Will he live to be 130 or 140 on this moderate version of the diet? Most likely not. Vanity and convenience have their price . . . but this is a plan that works for him on a day-to-day basis, and many readers would be happy to achieve his results with so easy a regimen as this moderate version of CR.

dean pomerleau, 39—

ENTREPRENEUR, ENGINEER, AND INVENTOR

In contrast to Brian, Dean is an example of an "extreme CR practitioner." Think of "extreme CR" like "extreme sports": it's a very tough challenge, but the rewards can be immense. While Dean hopes the Longevity Diet may allow him to live considerably longer than he otherwise might, he considers the other benefits of such a rigorous lifestyle to be paramount. These include physical health, emotional stability, and clarity of mind. The sheer adventure of pursuing a lifestyle different from most is also a strong motivating factor for Dean, in keeping with his visionary temperament and career.

Dean started the Longevity Diet at the turn of the millennium, at the age of thirty-five. Taking stock of his life, he didn't like the direction his health was headed in. Although still young and active, he already foresaw the writing on the wall: slightly weaker joints, a mild forgetfulness, fatigue, and a lack of energy lay in the future. Dean was not premature in his feelings of trepidation: Neural transmission time indeed starts decreasing when we are in our twenties. In our thirties, this and other health problems are of course only minor, and for many completely undetectable during everyday life, but Dean wanted to nip them in the bud.

Dean is a family man, and one of his biggest concerns when he started the diet was the impact his diet would have on his non-CR wife and kids. Dean began by trying to construct individual "optimal" CR meals for himself, while his family ate regular fare. But he soon realized that the actions required to create a single meal at a time were consuming too much of his time and energy: his family would be sitting down to a dinner of pizza while he was still chopping and washing vegetables.

Being an engineer and inventor, Dean cleverly developed a system by which he does all his food preparation in the mornings before his family wakes up. This way, he can sit down at the table alongside his family to enjoy what he considers to be an "optimal" diet.

For simplicity and ease of preparation, Dean eats two identical meals every day, in the morning and evening, like Brian omitting lunch. Like Lisa, Dean is a vegan for ethical reasons. Obviously, his meals are not literally identical throughout the calendar year. His standard meal consists of a large salad topped with a dressing of tomato sauce, olive oil, and several sources of vegetarian protein. For "dessert," he has a large serving of mixed fruit and nuts. In the middle of the day, Dean drinks several cups of green tea. Dean subscribes to a local organic food co-op. Every week during the growing season, he receives a bounty of wonderful produce delivered right to his door.

While his friends and family are astonished that he can contentedly eat the same kind of meal every day, it works for Dean; he savors the rich variety of fruits and vegetables that his regimen makes available to him, rather than finding his reliance upon one food group boring or restrictive. His solution demonstrates yet another way that one may integrate the Longevity Diet into one's life.

ed sullivan, 72—

FORMER BROADCAST ADVERTISING WRITER AND PRODUCER, AMONG MANY OTHER THINGS

After many years of equivocation, Ed started CR in earnest just before the Thanksgiving holiday in 1996. According to Ed, he weighed in at 233 pounds, and was five foot eight inches tall ("Waist measurement confidential," he noted). His triglycerides were over 1,000; his cholesterol, over 400 with HDLs in the 20s; his blood pressure, 160–180 over approximately 110. He chose the Dean Ornish program diet, and also followed the exercise, yoga, and meditation aspects of the program, although not consistently.

Via this regimen, Ed lost fifty pounds over the next two years. He did experience some discomfort: his hands were cold, and he was hungry much of the time. However, his blood pressure went down to high normal and his blood lipids improved—but not enough. He began using fish oil, and eating some salmon as well. This subsequently lowered his triglycerides to the 50s and 60s, and they've stayed there. Still basically following this regimen, he has regained some weight, and still is about twelve pounds above his lowest weight.

Ed has varied his diet greatly over the years. However, he has consistently kept his saturated fat intake between 3 and 10 grams per day, usually about 4 grams. The program includes six to ten daily servings of low-calorie vegetables, and one to three daily servings of fruit. Sweet potatoes, brown rice, and oats are Ed's heavy carbohydrate mainstays. He uses Take Control (a soy-based margarine-like spread used in the Lyon Mediterranean Diet study), canola oil, and olive oil. He sautés foods sometimes. He rarely eats poultry and never eats beef, lamb, or pork. He tries to restrict his calories to about 1,600 a day, but the nutrition software on his computer tells him he's actually averaging a little over 1,800. He does not preplan or prepare meals in advance ("Unless that's what you call preparing leftovers," he adds).

Ed says that while he is on his version of the Longevity Diet, which he calls "CREN" (Calorie Restriction with Excellent Nutrition), he feels well, and is well. No colds, no flu, no colon polyps. No problems. With a moderate amount of aerobic exercise weekly—perhaps six to fifteen miles of running—Ed's energy is good, and his mood is good. When he does a little weightlifting a couple of times per week, he feels strong, flexible, and pain free. In contrast, while he was off the program, he was sick most of the time: he ached, he was stiff, so much so that it was actually difficult for him to get out of his chair . . . sometimes painful just to walk across the room.

He wants to stress that, much of the time during the past eight years, he did not restrict his calories with a particular goal of losing more weight than he has, yet has eaten significantly less than the average-weight person of his height would eat, (almost . . .) all of it highly nutritious. All of the day-to-day health benefits of CR continue to be realized as long as he doesn't regain any weight.

So, he's a little hungry, eats carefully, and gets a little exercise, and the result is that he's healthier than he was in his forties, and nearly as strong.

jen, 30—
UNION ORGANIZER

Jen starts the day with coffee because she loves coffee, has always drunk coffee, and always will. *Then* she thinks about food. She and her husband have eggs together, but she just has a little bit, which she puts on her thick, whole-grain toast. On another slice of toast she'll have a high-protein spread: perhaps a low-fat hummus dip. Her breakfast concludes with an orange or another piece of fruit, a small glass of nonfat milk, and then she's off for the day!

Jen eats a small salad for lunch at work. Sometimes she brings it with her, sometimes she'll manage with what she can buy at one of the small cafés in the neighborhood.

For dinner, she'll make a rice dish or stuffed vegetables, sometimes fish; and she and her husband usually each have a glass of wine with dinner.

Jen, like Brian, is at the opposite end of the spectrum from Dean: her meals appear to follow a generally healthy diet, without any obvious exclusions. Most people around her don't even know she's following a moderate CR regimen. What they will notice, however, is her long-term good health.

HOW TO USE THIS BOOK

THIS BOOK IS intended to be a source of both information and inspiration. The pages that follow will enable you to tailor your CR program to your own life and needs.

Of all the diets currently being discussed and debated among experts, lay food faddists, and the media, the Longevity Diet is probably the easiest to implement in a safe way. But we suggest reading the whole book through at least once before making any changes in your diet or to your exercise program. And there is one more thing we strongly advise: **see a health-care professional before making *any* changes to your diet or exercise program.*** One particular advantage to having a complete medical checkup before changing your health regimen is that the practitioner will likely order a few simple tests, such as your cholesterol and fasting glucose levels, or at the very least weigh you and take your blood pressure and pulse. These test results will provide you with a series of measurements indicating the general state of your health.

Several months after you begin the Longevity Diet, ask your

* Indeed, you should see a health-care professional before making any decision at all about your diet, including the decision not to change a thing!

By the way, we will sometimes just say "doctor" or "physician" when we mean "health-care professional," but we are aware that some of you might have a health-care professional who technically is not a doctor, for example, a nurse practitioner or a practitioner of alternative medicine.

practitioner to retest you. Having objective evidence of the benefits of this diet is more valuable than you might imagine. First, starting the program with baseline hard data against which to compare your improvements will help keep you motivated: you'll be working with your own personalized "before and after" statistics, not those drawn from studies of other people. In addition, these numbers will give you a sense of how well you are doing over time compared with the goals of other diet plans. But also, you will have concrete information to show your spouse or other loved ones who may be skeptical about your desire to follow the Longevity Diet. Most important, your improved health and well-being, and follow-up test results, may soon encourage your friends and family to have their biomarkers tested as well, and perhaps even to try the diet themselves. Think of all the additional years you will have together! Last, consider beginning the program with CR "buddies" with whom to share your regimen. As you keep abreast of your respective and remarkable results, it will make it all the easier for you all to stay on the diet in the long term.

Of course, even within the same family or among peers, different degrees of calorie restriction might be advisable, depending upon each person's health, lifestyle, and goals. The great panoply of humanity lives in a broad range of circumstances that are sometimes beyond individuals' control. For a multitude of reasons, people may need or desire to dine in ways that differ fundamentally from what scientific research prescribes as optimal to health; for example, in many cultures certain foods and meal plans uphold revered traditions, and it is socially or even religiously important for members of that community to perpetuate those traditions. The Longevity Diet provides you with realistic options adaptable to a large range of personal tastes and habits, and community practices. This book has been written to help you understand how the dietary choices you make may affect your body, and to guide you toward choosing an achievable health regimen that would best fit your unique body and environment.

LEARNING MORE ABOUT CR AND LIFE-EXTENSION

ALONG WITH OUTLINING the Longevity Diet regimen, this book will explain a few basic principles that will make it easier for you to interpret the broad deluge of information about health, diet, and medicine with which we all are constantly being bombarded.

If after reading *The Longevity Diet* you have questions about CR, turn to the Resources section of this book, in which you'll find a list of additional sources of information. When exploring new paths in health or medical topics, we have found that the best source of help is other people already successfully following a health regimen. The CR Society, for example, sponsors discussion forums at which one can pose questions about the Longevity Diet and obtain extremely useful advice. Indeed, this book occasionally quotes or reiterates material from the society's Web site. Another informational tool would be membership in a health-oriented discussion group (Internet-based or not; check local newspapers for "live" discussion/support groups and seminars in your area), since the human contact and encouragement provided by others who may be having the same experiences as you could be as useful as advice from scientific experts. Especially as you begin our program, the sheer morale-building presence of such feedback-focused sites may be as useful to you as our book's concrete tips and menu plans.

Successfully following any health regimen involves more than just choosing the recommended foods or gear. Your mind and feelings need to be engaged, too. So, what have you got to gain by extra reading and intrapersonal networking, you may wonder? Only every good reason to desire a tasty, healthy diet; an improved robustness and strength of mind, body, and spirit; and a youthful appearance that belies your long, *long* years.

2

HOW THE LONGEVITY DIET CAN CHANGE YOUR LIFE

OF MICE AND MEN

THE RESULTS OF CR research in hundreds upon hundreds of studies in a wide variety of laboratory animals up and down nearly the whole animal kingdom are truly astonishing (see table 2.1). Studies of different exercise regimens, **antioxidants**, and so on, don't even come close to producing the same improvements in longevity and health.

Over the last few years, mainstream researchers have finally begun to realize that calorie restriction—a concept that existed for decades in the laboratory as merely a research tool—could also be applied outside the laboratory to improve the health of human beings. Even the conservative U.S. National Institutes of Health has recently recommended, in "Aim for a Healthy Weight,"[5] that people improve their health by lowering their overall caloric intake, in a diet rich in nutrients, rather than by reducing protein or fat consumption. And the National Cancer Institute, the American Diabetes Association, and the National Institute of Aging have all given long-term funding to study CR in humans. After all, given that its effects have been observed in so many different creatures, from simple worms through fish and flies and rodents all the way to dogs, *and* there is already evidence of greater longevity in human cultures where a mild version of the Longevity Diet is followed, it would naturally follow that the Longevity Diet would be beneficial in humans.

TABLE 2.1

EXAMPLES OF CR-INDUCED LIFE-SPAN CHANGES OBSERVED IN A FEW DIFFERENT SPECIES.

	NORMALLY FED		ON CR	
	Avg. life span	***Longest lived***	***Avg. life span***	***Longest lived***
PROTOZOA[6]	7 days	14 days	13 days	25 days
WATER FLEA[7]	30 days	42 days	51 days	60 days
SPIDER[8]	50 days	100 days	90 days	139 days
GUPPY[9]	33 months	54 months	46 months	59 months
RATS[10]	N/A	36 months	N/A	56 months

Of the many different species on which we have experimental data on life-span change via CR, it is mice on which we have the most precise data. Mice have the distinction of being the research animal of choice for modern biological research. Thus, literally *hundreds* of CR studies on mice have been performed.

The results are simply too stunning to be left inside medical research journals. Look at the following graph:

Survival of Normally Fed Mice and Mice on Varying Degrees of CR

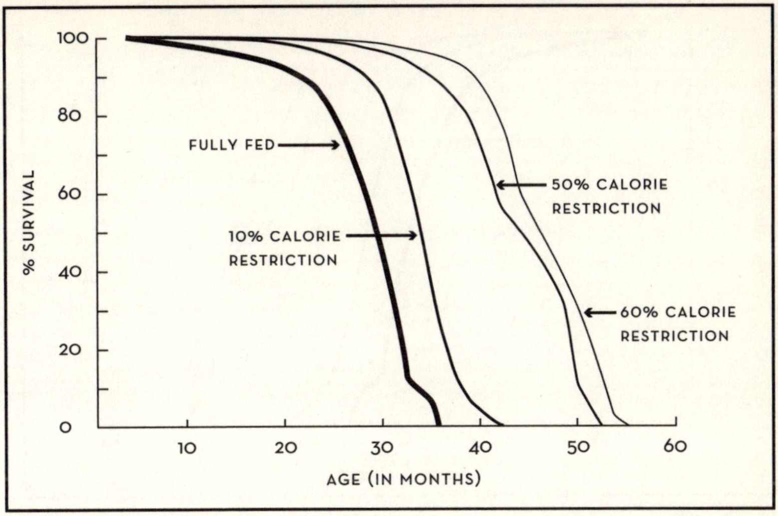

(From *Beyond the 120-Year Diet.*)

The above graph is typical of the results of CR studies, and has been repeated time and time again over the course of the last two and half decades, in many different animal species. CR can increase **maximum life span** of all the creatures in which it's been tested, by anywhere from 40 to 60 percent on extreme versions of CR. Several studies in humans commenced in 2002, and even the short-term changes in the subjects' biomarkers already match those observed in other animal species that have been studied at length, which strongly suggests that the CR effect is truly universal in the animal kingdom. This would mean that we could translate the above graph into human terms, and get approximately the following:

SURVIVAL OF NORMALLY FED HUMANS AND HUMANS ON VARYING DEGREES OF CR

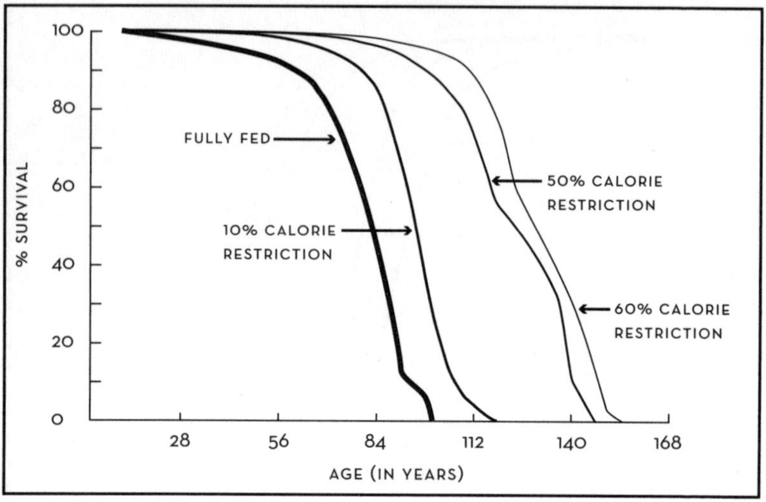

(Adapted from *Beyond the 120-Year Diet.*)

We must stress that this second graph is only an extrapolation. Since CR was not being studied during the early 1900s, obviously the maximum achievable life span of humans on a CR diet has not yet been able to be determined. But based on all the evidence we currently have, the graph gives a very realistic picture of the results we might expect if we had four groups of people, one group eating normally, one on a very mild CR program, one on a stricter CR program, and one on a *extremely* severe program.

HOW THE LONGEVITY DIET MAY EXTEND YOUR YEARS

LET US THINK about what the extrapolated graph might mean in concrete terms. First, keep in mind that no health regimen is perfect. Some people have extraordinarily bad genes, or will simply have extraordinarily bad luck while crossing a street—accidents happen. But CR, started early in life, can be expected to prevent many unusually early deaths. In our extrapolated graph, we see a dip in the non-CR group very early on, when the subjects are in their teens and twenties, and the dip continues downward, though still very slowly, when we move to their next decade or so of life. If you had a group of fifty or so people, that might be just what you'd expect: you'd see maybe one or two very early deaths, as in the situation with which many of us are familiar, of a schoolmate dying of cancer or in a car crash—a rare, but nonetheless statistically expected phenomenon. As we move into the next age group, people in their thirties and early forties, another death we would still consider quite premature might be that of someone we know who has bad genes for cholesterol production and who dies of a heart attack in his late thirties, although deaths by heart attack after two score years are, unfortunately, not at all uncommon, especially among men in the United States.

TABLE 2.2

LEADING CAUSES OF DEATHS IN THE UNITED STATES, BY AGE AND CAUSE, 2001.[11]

	HEART DISEASE	CANCER	CEREBRO-VASCULAR DISEASE	CHRONIC LOWER RESPIRATORY DISEASE
1-24	1,496	1,786	330	318
25-44	16,486	20,563	3,092	1,259
45-64	98,885	139,785	15,518	14,490
65 and over	582,730	390,214	144,486	106,904

Animal studies have shown that CR radically alters biomarkers associated with heart disease. Here, when it comes to humans, we have more than epidemiological data. We also have much direct evidence from human studies, such as Professor Walford's Biosphere 2 data,[12] and, more recently, the ongoing study at Washington University in St. Louis, to name just two.[13] Such studies have shown that people with the healthy cholesterol levels that result from CR have a much, much lower risk of cardiovascular disease. Thus the person in the non-CR group who dies of a heart attack at age forty or so would very likely live much longer—perhaps an additional two or three or even more decades—on even a relatively mild CR program.

We know also that CR dramatically reduces the incidence of cancer in laboratory animals,[14] and evidence has been mounting that CR, not surprisingly, reduces cancer risk in humans as well.[15] [16] [17] Thus, it's not at all unrealistic to suppose that CR, whether mild or severe, may prevent early deaths from cancer, or may at least radically push it back, as suggested by the extrapolated graph for human life expectancy.

As we follow our extrapolated graph over to the right, we see many more people in the non-CR group dying in their fifties and early sixties—and even a few in the mild CR group, as well, bearing out animal-study results that CR in its milder forms is not nearly as beneficial as a more stringent program. Once we get to the age of sixty-five or seventy, people in the non-CR group begin to dwindle dramatically, as disease strikes or organs fail. If human life-expectancy indeed follows that of animals placed on a CR diet, we would expect the threshold of what we now consider elderly to be pushed back nearly fifteen years for the group of people on the mild CR regimen, and that it would be pushed back even more for the subjects on rigorous CR.

And, as we move even further to the right on the timeline, we see that very few of the non-CR group are likely to be alive in their nineties. However, most of the mild-CR group will still be around then, as will the vast majority of the rigorous CR groups.

So what, then, is the ultimate effect of CR? Calorie restriction shifts the survival curve to the right, and it does so in such a way that *everything* is pushed to the right. People on CR will not become senile and crippled at the same age as others, and then be forced to live an extra few decades in this state of decrepitude. Quite the contrary; CR promises that *youthfulness itself* will be preserved. Thus, for the group on more rigorous CR programs, the cycle of life and death would look very different indeed from what we picture as the normal life cycle. If you go on even a moderate CR program, you can expect to live, on average, at least a decade longer than you otherwise would—and perhaps several decades longer, if cancer or a stroke is averted. And it's not just that your life span is extended, your **youth span** will also be extended. Aged laboratory rats[18] [19] and mice[20] [21] on CR run mazes just as quickly and intelligently as they did when they were in the equivalent of their "teens." They also have sex at an age when the animals in their studies' **control group**—those creatures that, given the mortality of non-CR rodents, are lucky enough still to be alive—don't even remember what sex is.

FROM THE LAB TO YOUR LIFE: CR RESEARCH THROUGH THE AGES

prehistory

The notion that restricting one's diet could be salubrious in various ways is actually an ancient one. In the Middle Ages, for example, it was thought that tumors could be eliminated via restricted eating: Both the tumor and the body need food to thrive, but the body, being more virtuous, would survive a reduction in food longer than a malignant—and therefore evil—tumor, and thus the tumor would die before the body would. (Do not try this at home!)

So went the reasoning. At the beginning of the last century, a slightly more biologically enlightened version of this line of thought led to some scientific studies revealing a correlation between food consumption and tumor growth. As early as 1909, for example, it was shown by Carlo Moreschi, an Italian immunology researcher, that tumors transplanted into underfed mice did not grow as quickly as tumors transplanted into normally fed mice.[22] Over the next ten or so years, the development of tumors itself was shown to be to suppressed in underfed lab rodents.

While it is true that most types of cancer become more prevalent with age, establishing a relation between cancer growth and food intake is not the same as establishing a relation between rate of aging and food intake. That latter relationship only began to be explored two decades later, and even then partly as an unintended consequence of a Cornell University cancer researcher's experiment.

the modern period of CR research

Clive McKay, a researcher at Cornell University, was interested in the long-term effects of stunted growth upon mice, which in a study in the mid-1930s he induced via a drastic reduction in the lab animals' food intake.[23] A completely unexpected finding was that the rodents lived around a third longer than rodents on a normal lab diet! No one knew what to make of this finding, though some researchers tried to figure out what the crucial factor was—a particular component of the diet, or the mere quantity of food, or the total energy content of the laboratory meals. It was shown in the 1940s that it was indeed the energy content—which is to say, the caloric content—alone that made the difference. Indeed, by reducing the energy content only, and *not* any other components of the diet (such as critical vitamins and minerals), the benefits were even greater.

Despite that important breakthrough, little CR research was done until the 1970s, when the modern period of research into this regimen began. Knowledge of molecular biology had developed to the point where it was possible to investigate *how* CR exerted its effect. Over the next decades, CR research evolved into the standard, primary tool for investigating the fundamental mechanisms of aging, because it quickly emerged that calorie restriction is the *only* intervention that retards the rate at which organisms age. Understanding how and under what conditions CR works in laboratory animals has thus been viewed as tantamount to understanding the aging process itself. And because no other means of appreciably slowing the aging process has yet been discovered, CR has, since the 1970s, remained the primary laboratory model for understanding the mechanism, or perhaps *mechanisms,* of aging in laboratory animals.

The general research strategy is not complicated or overly technical. One approach is the following: A researcher first selects one of the myriad differences between CR animals and normally fed animals. He or she then tries to elicit the one change, be it a hormone that is expressed at a higher or lower level in CR animals, or even a particular gene whose function is not yet known, which is expressed at a different level in animals on CR. Then, the researcher tries to see whether the alteration of this one factor in normally fed animals can elicit the CR effect, or, conversely, whether an attempt to suppress this change in animals on CR might abolish the CR effect. For example, animals on CR typically have lower body temperatures than do their non-CR control group. Professor Roy Walford, along with some Japanese colleagues, showed that artificially raising the body temperature of animals on CR abolished at least certain aspects of the CR effect.[24] This suggested that this one change, a lowered body temperature, might be fundamental to the beneficial effects of the diet.

The most recent CR studies follow this same pattern, and scientists appear to be getting very close to understanding how CR works. Research at Brown University, Harvard University, and MIT has shown that forced expression of a particular gene can actually elicit the CR effect in yeast and fruit flies. This change in gene expression, more than hormones or body temperature, appears to be an essential factor, if not *the* essential factor, in the host of changes that lead to the greatly improved health seen in laboratory animals on CR. For more about this exciting new research, see chapter 4.

For now, let us summarize what we know about the consequences of CR in laboratory animals:

HOW CR AFFECTS YOUR HEALTH

CR PRODUCES A wide variety of positive effects upon laboratory animals. Many of these benefits have actually been confirmed, in short-term studies, in humans as well.

- **Improved insulin sensitivity**

  Insulin is a hormone secreted by the pancreas that enables your cells to use their most important fuel, glucose. As we age, cells tend to become less responsive to insulin. This leads to unnecessarily high levels of glucose, which can lead to type 2 diabetes, and maybe even accelerated aging.

  The effect of CR in lab animals on insulin sensitivity is one of the most well-documented CR research findings. One of Professor Walford's contemporaries, Edward J. Masoro, of the University of Texas Health Science Center in San Antonio, was one of the first to investigate the mechanism of the dramatic effect of CR on the age-associated decrease in insulin sensitivity.[25] Many others have expanded on this work.[26] [27]

  The data from the long-term studies of CR in nonhuman primates have been consistent with the findings in rodents. In the NIA (National Institute on Aging) Primate Study, the monkeys on CR have dramatically lower circulating insulin levels, which we know is an excellent measure of insulin sensitivity. (The more sensitive your cells are to insulin, the less your body needs to secrete insulin into the blood).[28]

And countless studies of short-term CR in overweight humans have shown conclusively that insulin sensitivity increases on CR.[29] [30] [31] While we don't yet have long-term data on CR in people who already are thin, those who already have type 2 diabetes can probably even improve their glucose metabolism with CR. The American Diabetes Association has begun stressing that reducing energy-intake, as part of a comprehensive program of diabetes management, can improve insulin resistance in diabetics.[32]

Even a conservative physician with no awareness of CR would agree that CR will most likely reduce your chances of developing type 2 diabetes, and, if you already are "prediabetic," CR will probably halt the march toward full-blown diabetes.

Lower average circulating levels of glucose

This change is, of course, directly connected to insulin sensitivity. The rodent studies show lowered levels of circulating glucose, just as they show lowered levels of circulating insulin, since the two go hand in hand. But in addition to being correlated with lowered insulin, a lowered glucose level is good thing in and of itself.

Glucose is your body's liquid fuel. Like your car's gasoline, it is an "energetic" chemical that can damage what it comes into contact with (see chapter 4 for more about this effect of glucose). In brief, superfluous glucose will needlessly harm the molecules, cells and tissues of your body. According to many theories of aging, this damage may well be a significant cause of aging. Thus, all your tissues, from brain tissue to skin tissue, will benefit from lower levels of circulating glucose in your blood: just enough to keep your body running smoothly, without "spills."

Increased maintenance of DNA

DNA (deoxyribonucleic acid) is the extremely long, intricate, fragile molecule that constitutes your body's blueprint. The design specs encoded in your DNA determine most of your biological characteristics as you grow into an adult, but they also guide ongoing repair and maintenance during your many (we hope!) decades of adult life. As we age our DNA becomes damaged, and not all of that damage can be repaired. This deterioration of your DNA slowly results in progressively worse functionality at all levels: your cells, organs, and your whole body.

The earliest studies of CR in laboratory animals could not measure the ability of CR to protect DNA against age-associated damage, since DNA hadn't even been discovered yet! But starting in the mid-1980s and early 1990s, new techniques made it possible to show that DNA damage is reduced in laboratory animals on CR,[33] although, not surprisingly, the effect is greater on DNA involved in the use of energy.[34 35] Interestingly, it isn't simply that DNA damage is reduced. There is an actual increase in DNA *repair*.[36 37]

Studies of the effect of CR on DNA damage in humans are ongoing, though there is already suggestive evidence that DNA damage is reduced in humans on CR.[38]

Whether or not damage to DNA has anything to do with aging per se, keeping your DNA intact is a good survival strategy! Changes in cellular DNA are implicated in many diseases, above all cancer.

Reduction in expression of oncogenes

On a CR regimen, you can expect that *oncogenes*—genes that lead to abnormal, unnecessary cell proliferation (which is all cancer really is)—will be less likely to be "switched on." This effect is very well established in laboratory mice.[39 40 41]

There is considerable epidemiological evidence that CR

in humans reduces cancer risk, and, amazingly enough, there is even evidence that mere "FR"—indiscriminate restriction of food, not a targeted restriction of calories in an otherwise healthy diet—reduces cancer risk.[42] Thus, when a proper CR program is instituted, we might expect an even greater reduction in risk of cancer.

Reduced decline in sexual activity with age

The sexual activity of laboratory animals on an extreme CR regimen actually decreases a bit in their younger years. This is consistent with theories of why CR would have evolved in the first place: resources get shifted away from reproduction and growth, toward repair and maintenance. But in animals on CR, sexuality does not decrease with age at the same rate as it does in their control group.[43] In fact, this was first noted over fifty years ago in studies by Maurice B. Visscher at the University of Minnesota.[44]

As Professor Walford noted in *Maximum Life Span,* there are astonishing studies showing that laboratory animals on CR not only still have sex and otherwise display sexual interest at an age beyond that of animals in the non-CR group that have died, but they can actually become pregnant and give birth to healthy babies when *all* of the control animals are dead![45]

Moreover, CR actually increases follicular reserves—meaning, in human terms, that menopause could be postponed by many years.[46]

Lowered blood pressure

This is of course good news for those of you who are worried about stroke or embolisms. This is also, by the way, something you can easily measure yourself at one of those blood pressure machines that many pharmacies and health-fair clinics provide for public use. Take advantage of these services. Again, hard evidence of your progress will increase your motivation.

- **Reduced risk of arthritis**

  Arthritis may not be life threatening—at least not while you're still in midlife—but it is extremely painful and restrictive. We know several artists and musicians who, only in their forties and fifties, will soon have to stop practicing their art because of this condition. In the lab, CR has been demonstrated to greatly delay the onset of arthritis.

- **Improved mental functioning**

  This is a lab finding that is perhaps most important to keep in mind if you're worried about CR simply prolonging old age. It most certainly does not—it prolongs and even restores youth, in many ways. That a mouse which in human years would be over one hundred years old can zip through a maze with the problem-solving skills of a young adult rodent may seem incredible, but this phenomenon has been documented repeatedly in research studies. The ability of calorie restriction to maintain youthful mental functions is believed to be the beneficial result of a very straightforward effect already discussed: because it strengthens and repairs the body's cells in general, CR prevents the brain cell death that normally occurs with age.[47]

THE 2004 WASHINGTON UNIVERSITY CR STUDY

Calorie restriction has grown far beyond the laboratory, and into layman practice. This is partly the result of the recently published study by a group at the Washington University in St. Louis (WUSTL). The 2004 WUSTL study presented powerful evidence of the dramatic results of long-term CR in humans. Again, we lack mortality data because, for these subjects, that material will not be assessed conclusively for many more decades to come. But the study clearly indicates positive shifts in those biomarkers that are associated with disease risk and that are thought to be associated with rate of aging.

The following table appeared in the very first research paper published by the WUSTL group concerning this groundbreaking discovery:

TABLE 2.2

	VALUE		
Parameter	**CR** ***(n = 18)***	**Controls** ***(n = 18)***	***P*** **value**
Tchol, mg/dl	158 ± 39	205 ± 40	0.001
LDL-C, mg/dl	86 ± 28	127 ± 35	0.0001
HDL-C, mg/dl	63 ± 19	48 ± 11	0.006
Tchol/HDL-C ratio	2.6 ± 0.5	4.5 ± 1.3	0.0001
TG, mg/dl	48 ± 15	147 ± 89	0.0001
TG/HDL-C ratio	0.8 ± 0.3	3.5 ± 2.8	0.0001
Systolic BP, mmHg	99 ± 10	129 ± 13	0.0001
Diastolic BP, mmHg	61 ± 6	79 ± 7	0.0001
Fasting glucose, mg/dl	81 ± 7	95 ± 8	0.0001
Fasting insulin, mIU/ml	1.4 ± 0.8	5.1 ± 2	0.0001
Hs-CRP, μg/ml	0.3 ± 0.2	1.6 ± 2.2	0.001

Values are means ± SD. IU, international unit; Hs-CRP, high-sensitivity CRP; 1 mmHg = 133 Pa.

(From *Proceedings of the National Academy of Sciences of the United States of America*.[48])

Key to some of the abbreviations in the table:

Tchol = total cholesterol.
TG = triglycerides.
Systolic BP = blood pressure when the heart pumps, e.g., the 120 in 120/80.
Diastolic BP = blood pressure between heart beats, e.g., the 80 in 120/80.
Hs-CRP = High-sensitivity C-reactive protein, a protein which is a marker of inflammation.
P value = a measure of the probability that the differences observed between the group on CR and the non-CR group occurred by chance. These are extremely low *P* values for a medical study.

The next time you go for a medical exam, bring this book with you and show your health practitioner that table. Tell her (or him) to go to a medical library and look at the actual research paper in which the table appears. Encourage her, while she is at the medical library, to look at all the other CR research that's been done. Once she will have finished reading, she will understand why there's nothing surprising, wrong, or faked about the numbers in the WUSTL paper. These kinds of impressive results are supported by all CR studies in lab animals, all shorter-term CR studies in humans, and indeed all theories of aging.

Based upon the numbers in the WUSTL report, your health practitioner would surely agree that the people on CR have, on average, a much lower risk of getting cardiovascular disease, a much lower risk of stroke, and a lower risk of arthritis; and that their risk of type 2 diabetes couldn't possibly be much lower.

SO, WHAT'S THE CATCH?

Q: Wait a minute, this sounds too good to be true. By simply reducing my calories, I can radically reduce my chances of getting cancer, heart disease, stroke, type 2 diabetes, and more, even slow my aging process—and live decades longer than my parents and grandparents? There's got to be a catch, right?

Well, that depends on you.

No serious scientist or physician who has taken the time to review the scientific basis for the Longevity Diet can deny its benefits. The documented results of CR research are more solid than many quasi-scientific claims about the relationship of diet, health, and longevity. But many health professionals do tell us this: "It's too hard for most people, because they'll be too hungry."

Here, it is vital to distinguish between a need for missing essential nutrients, and what most people generally *perceive* as a need to eat: a desire for food, regardless of whether the body has in fact been adequately fed. Indeed, all too often what is interpreted as hunger is merely the habit of eating automatically based upon external factors such as the setting sun or hour, as in, "It's noon, therefore I must eat lunch" or "I'm about to seat myself in a movie theater, therefore I need to buy popcorn."

The sudden adoption of an extreme version of the diet (or any diet in which particular foods are eliminated) may well produce, as a side effect, the *perception* that one "must" eat more. This is not at all surprising: at the beginning of the regimen, of course you'll be very aware that you are eating less than you have grown accustomed to; furthermore, it takes time for a body that is used to processing high levels of sugar, animal proteins, or fat to adjust itself to receiving less. This is not what many would call "true hunger"; rather, it is your body's confused way of signaling that its internal chemistry has been changed. Hang in there! Eventually, you will forget your old eating habits and, if you're like most CR followers, you will soon no longer view calorie restriction as "missing" something; meanwhile, trust that your metabolism will learn to feel sated by the correct amounts of the nutrients it needs to run, and will stop signaling you so urgently for more.

If you experience hunger, try drinking a non- or low-calorie beverage, such as sugarless tea or even just water. Diverting yourself with activities that hold your attention or busy your hands is another way to keep control. Do whatever you can to ignore those external markers that tell you it's time for a meal or snack. Instead, listen to your body, and that includes listening to its silence—if you *don't feel hungry,* you don't need to eat! Though you may find this hard to believe, some people who are not even trying to diet can become so wrapped up in work or other activities that they entirely forget to stop for lunch or dinner . . . they've technically missed a meal, yet don't "miss" it at all. Even a deliberate all-day fast becomes easier if you plan other activities for the day than watching the clock.

Here's what a few people who have been on CR say about hunger:

brian m. delaney

When I was on a more extreme version of the Longevity Diet than I'm on now, I was certainly hungry. I am onc of those unlucky people who suffers from extreme hunger when I haven't eaten for a few hours. My body tells me to stuff my face. A lot.

Still, after a while, the hunger lessened significantly. Partly this is because I knew CR was changing my life dramatically for the good. This made me feel better, and I was more productive, more excited about what I was doing, and thus, after a few months, I didn't even think about the hunger very often. Mind you, I was on very severe CR. I'm around five foot eleven, and by that point I weighed only 129 pounds. This was, for someone who ate constantly while growing up, an amazing achievement. And, of course, that is a case of the sort of extreme results that many people may not even be interested in achieving. The knowledge that I was eating astonishingly well made the hunger I did experience somehow "part of the whole package" of eating for excellent health in a culture that tells us to do just the opposite.

Now, on my somewhat milder, "skip lunch" version of the Longevity Diet, I may sometimes feel hungry during the mid- to late afternoon, once my breakfast calories have been digested. However, as had occurred before once my body had adjusted to a much lower caloric intake, I generally don't even think about it. If I happen to be in a boring phase of a work project, though, I certainly will notice the body-chemical kick-in of hunger in midafternoon. But then I just think: this means my stomach is empty, my glucose levels are low, my body has learned how to use glucose very efficiently (which is probably why I feel energetic, despite the low glucose levels), and my body is aging more slowly.

lisa walford I have always been a very slow eater. I savor every bite, but this does not mean that I take long lunch breaks or that I eat less food! As a consequence, my meals feel filling. I drink lime-flavored mineral water and green tea throughout the day, which takes care of any oral urges. I am also a grazer, so I nibble on a small amount of nuts or fruit if my stomach beckons my attention. But perhaps because I am so interested in the life beyond immediate workings of my own body that hunger rarely surfaces to distract me. I really find that I focus better and am much more productive by postponing my main meal until evening.

On my one-day-a-week fast, by late afternoon, I am definitely hungry! The abstinence actually makes me fill my hunger with other things, like watching a sunset or practicing my yoga. I satiate my senses other than taste. Strange, you might say, but I find it a rewarding reminder of the many, many ways that I can nourish myself. This focus upon nourishing my life puts CR into perspective, and yet CR has been the main avenue for developing this attitude—go figure!

harry—
AEROSPACE ENGINEER

I'm on a fairly severe version of the Longevity Diet, but I eat so many vegetables and other high-volume, low-calorie foods that my stomach feels pretty full most of the time. If the hunger is "there," I don't notice it! I am fortunate that the Longevity Diet is truly effortless for me.

natalie—
MARKET ANALYST

My secret is tea. I have been on the CR longevity diet for over five years. At times it's seemed effortless, other times, a challenge. The excitement of doing something that was improving my health so immensely was enough to forestall any hunger issues. But after a couple years I started to have "Difficult CR Days." Maybe I was just pushing my CR too hard, but there were times when it felt very difficult. My stomach was just empty, and seemed to "demand" to be filled.

That's where tea came in. I discovered that drinking green tea filled my stomach in a more effective way than water did, even when I didn't add any milk or honey or anything else with calories in it. When I'm hungry but my next meal is an hour or two away, a cup of warm green tea helps me feel satiated. My CR routine is now something I know I'll be able to stick with for a lifetime.

OBSTACLES AND CHALLENGES TO THE LONGEVITY DIET

We understand that one's relationship to food carries with it so many other issues that "just" eating less is of course not so easy for certain people. Aside from those who have a genetic predisposition toward overeating, many others grew up in families where food was used as part of a subtle, and in some cases extremely cruel, punishment-and-reward system. For these people, eating less can of course be a tremendous struggle. But it is important to separate as much as you can the actual nutritional purpose of food from whatever else you might feel about eating. If you are feeling blue because you've broken up with a lover, devouring an entire pint of ice cream in one sitting and then feeling guilty about it will not reunite the two of you. If you have just received a raise, you can find many other ways to celebrate than by going out for a lavish dinner. For any diet to work, you need to be aware of what kinds of issues trigger your food-related temptations, and break the pattern of emotional hunger by the deliberate substitution of something that will not "punish" or "reward" you with unnecessary calories.

SOME POSSIBLE SIDE EFFECTS

ASSUMING YOUR HEALTH-CARE practitioner has given you the go-ahead to begin the Longevity Diet, you may do so with little concern for side effects. There are only a few that we can think of, common to only the rigorous versions of the Longevity Diet.

One is that your body temperature will probably be a bit lower. This might best be understood as a consequence of the body's increased efficiency; *it is a healthy condition*. You may or may not even notice the difference in your everyday life . . . though, if you live in a very warm part of the world, it might even be a big plus!

Another "downside" for some people: if your baseline weight prior to your switch to an extreme form of CR is already relatively low, reducing your calories may result in extreme skinniness! If you don't like the way you look when you're so much thinner, then extreme CR might not be for you.

3

ABCs OF NUTRITION

EVEN IF YOU are thinking that the Longevity Diet is perhaps not right for you, please keep reading: This chapter contains information that *everyone* should know. It provides an easy-to-follow overview of the basics of human nutrition. This is important background information not just for those who will be following the Longevity Diet, but for anyone who wishes to have a better understanding of how foods interact with the human body.

THE KEY TO WEIGHT LOSS

NOTHING IS MORE frustrating than the endless, intricate, ever-changing flood of nutritional advice that streams past us in waves far too fast even to dream of being able to catch.

The August 2004 issue of *National Geographic* tried to cut through this miasma of confusion over diet and health. The cover story was actually not about CR, but rather about the more general phenomenon of obesity in the United States. The goal of losing weight is of course related to the goals of the Longevity Diet program. However, the article is written from a different perspective than our last chapter: its concerns about what has been called an obesity epidemic center upon getting you *away from* the most unhealthful end of the spectrum of caloric intake. There is a presumption that any benefits aside from weight loss will just fall into place, as long as you cease your intake of fatty (or carbs-laden), high-calorie foods. The Longevity Diet, in contrast, focuses on moving you *toward* the most healthful end, concentrating far more positively on trying to optimize your health, and not just trying to avoid the diseases of obesity.

The magazine article poses the question of why we're so fat. And then—one can almost hear a drumroll as one begins reading further—the answer to this seemingly mysterious problem is announced: "Because we eat a lot." It's that simple—whether your caloric intake is 5,000 calories/day or 3,500 calories/day, the culprit is not evil fast-food corporations, it's not your television set, it's not carbs. It's you. YOU ARE EATING TOO MUCH.

That might seem like bad news, but it's not. It's *great* news. Because the solution is just as simple: You just have to eat less.

We urge you to ignore those diet gurus who claim the consumption of huge amounts of protein or fat will magically trick your body into "thinking" it doesn't need more food. Indeed, recent research is showing that diets such as the Atkins diet are not at all effective in maintaining weight loss. As Dr. Ernst Schaefer of Tufts University, one of the researchers now investigating the claims of these diet gurus, recently put it, "despite all the controversy about diet . . . a calorie is a calorie is a calorie."[49]

Just eat less . . . and eat real food.

WHAT IS REAL FOOD?

HEALTHIER EATING ISN'T simply about consuming *less food*, it's about consuming *fewer empty calories*. This is the key to the Longevity Diet. If your diet currently consists of, let's say,

4,000 calories/day of potato chips, bacon, and beer, making the change to 2,000 calories/day of potato chips, bacon, and beer will certainly make you lose weight, and *certain* aspects of your health may well improve, but the bottom line is that such a diet is not CR, it's merely FR—food reduction. You are lessening your intake of what your body doesn't need, true, but without the necessary step of substituting the nutrients your body—in part via hunger—signals that it craves. This is why so many other diets fail; your body feels hungry because it is experiencing a "true" need: a need for real food. In extreme forms, dietary restriction characterized by unhealthy obsessions about food can result in **bulimia** and/or **anorexia nervosa**, wherein you deny your body the fuel essential for it to function. A nutrient-empty FR diet definitely sabotages your health and longevity!

TABLE 3.1
THE LONGEVITY DIET VS. ANOREXIA

LONGEVITY DIET	ANOREXIA
The goal is health	***The goal is denial***
Someone on the Longevity Diet is motivated by the desire to have a long, healthy life. People on the Longevity Diet want to be around for a while to come! They want to be *present*!	Anorectics often describe their motivation as, "I want to control my diet, my health, my life," while the subconscious reality may be one of worthlessness. Hence the internal dialogue: "I want to be less 'present,' less 'visible.'" They often view their body as being larger than it is, and work to achieve as skeletal an appearance as possible. Often, they don't realize until it's too late that such a regimen can be fatal—

LONGEVITY DIET	ANOREXIA
	that rather than controlling their life, they are virtually eliminating it.
A scientific, practical orientation toward life	***A dogmatic, Good vs. Evil approach to life***
Because the goal is health, those on the Longevity Diet tend to keep close tabs on discoveries in nutrition and medical research, and are always "tweaking" their own diets. The vast majority would give up the diet if the same effects could be obtained with a pill!	The anorectic believes that food is Evil, and that corporeal flesh is Evil. Thinness is Good. And the more thin the Better. That's it. This Good vs. Evil orientation literally consumes the anorectic's life. Research about a healthy means of achieving weight loss is utterly irrelevant to the anorectic, who is focused on the goal of not having a body, healthy or otherwise. (This is why anorectics are not cured by a nutritionist, but rather by a psychologist.)
The Longevity Diet means good nutrition	***Anorexia—"FR"—means bad nutrition***
If the goal is to reduce caloric intake, other important parts of the diet—such as vitamins and minerals—cannot also be reduced at the same time. This is why we call it the "Longevity Diet," and why others call it "CRON" (Calorie Restriction with Optimal Nutrition), or, with a bit less hubris: "CREN" (Calorie Restriction with Excellent Nutrition), or even "CRAN" (Calorie	Anorectics practice "FR": Food Restriction: eating as little as possible, of anything. In a bulimic anorectic, this takes the form of overeating but then removing food from the body, via self-induced vomiting or purgatives, as quickly as it is consumed, before its nutrients can be properly digested. The result of either regimen is extreme malnutrition, in which the body's

LONGEVITY DIET	ANOREXIA
Restriction with Adequate Nutrition). A proper longevity-enhancing diet regimen includes a range of highly nutritious foods that in many cases, such as green leafy vegetables, may be consumed without worrying about exceeding one's projected caloric intake for the day, since the stomach quite simply isn't large enough to permit this!	cells and organs are starved of the nutrients needed to function and rebuild.

Three meals a day of junk food can easily top out at 4,000 calories or more per day. And yet such meals usually constitute a kind of overfed form of malnutrition: a diet rich in fat, protein, salt, and sugar, but containing few vitamins and minerals. On the other hand, if you eat three meals of foods with fewer calories—whole-grain cereal for breakfast, lunches, and dinners featuring a range of vegetables, plus snacks consisting mostly of fruit—your caloric total will be much lower, while your intake of vitamins and minerals and other essential nutrients will be much, much higher. Besides such low-calorie meals being aesthetically satisfying (we've come a long way from the "mystery (fake-) meat" health foods you may have encountered in years past), most low-calorie foods are low on the glycemic index, meaning they'll digest slowly: you'll sustain your energy levels a lot longer than if you just grab a can of soda and some chocolate.

To put it simply, the Longevity Diet, especially in its milder variants, is based on *pure common sense*! If you're currently stuffing yourself with junk, STOP. Stop believing those articles that point out that this fast-food burger meal is healthier for you than that one. They are *all* loaded with empty calories. Instead, select nutrient-packed foods, and ideally as many fresh foods as you can. More extreme versions of the Longevity Diet might require careful meal planning to be successful, to be sure you are consuming the right proportions of all the necessary nutrients, but starting out with a mild version of the Longevity Diet simply involves replacing empty-calorie processed foods with healthy ones that have been prepackaged by nature to have their own panorama of delicious flavors, often beautiful colors, and always lots of vitamins and minerals. Or, as your parents probably told you, *eat your vegetables!*

WHAT YOU NEED TO KNOW ABOUT NUTRITION

Nutrition can be approached in many ways. If you want to educate yourself in depth about this subject, you may easily do so by enrolling in a nutrition program at your local college or by attending lectures at the community-education wing of your local hospital, or simply by going to a medical library and reading about the chemistry of food. While much of what you learn might not be easy to put into practice in your own diet, the subject is fascinating, and the knowledge you gain will be rewarding in and of itself.

Meanwhile, here are some of the fundamental principles of nutrition that are essential for everyone to keep in mind when thinking about what to eat:

THE BASICS: YOUR BODY'S ESSENTIAL NEEDS

Your body needs to get a certain amount of **protein**, **lipids**, **vitamins**, **minerals**, and, yes, **calories**, from the diet. Your body also needs a steady supply of two other items: oxygen and water. For the purposes of this book, we'll assume you know how to breathe and know that it's important to drink enough water (at least six glasses a day, which can include juices, teas, and broths). Let's take those other necessities from the top:

PROTEIN

PROTEIN IS A general term for a whole class of molecules built up from smaller, nitrogen-rich chemical units known as **amino acids**. Amino acids link together to form all the proteins and protein complexes in your body. For example, the principal protein of your hair is keratin, while the principle protein of your skin is collagen. They are built up from different combinations of amino acids.

Your body puts proteins to use in a variety of ways. Protein is an essential component of tissues in your body, which are not static substances but need lifelong replenishment by means of additional protein. Another example of proteins are enzymes, molecules that control certain chemical reactions in your body by speeding up those responses that need speeding up, and slowing down others. Protein is also found in hormones, and can be used as a source of energy (calories).

Fortunately, we do not need to eat keratin to get the protein we need for our hair, nor collagen to get what we need for our skin. Whatever proteins we eat—be they from animal products in the form of meat, poultry, fish, eggs, or dairy products; or from grains, legumes, vegetables, or nuts—are broken down by our digestive system (specifically, by pancreatic enzymes) into their component amino acids. The body then uses the amino acids it gets from these ingested proteins, along with the other amino acids the body can produce itself, to construct whichever proteins it requires.

In humans, twenty kinds of amino acid are used to build proteins. Your body can actually synthesize most of them itself, but adults need to obtain eight amino acids from dietary sources. These eight are called "essential amino acids," since it is essential that we include them in our diet.

ESSENTIAL AMINO ACIDS

isoleucine
leucine
lysine
methionine (and/or cysteine)
phenylalanine (and/or tyrosine)
threonine
tryptophan
valine

For people living in Western cultures, the risk of not getting enough of these eight amino acids is very, very low. The main exception is the careless, so-called "junk-food vegetarian" who, by eating a lot of say, potato chips, may have slight shortages of a few key amino acids. Another exception might be a person who, due to food allergies, lacks the enzyme to digest a particular food source of protein, for example, someone who cannot digest the casein in milk, or a celiac child who cannot digest gluten. Otherwise, the risk is rather that you're getting too *much* protein.

Take a look at table 3.2.

TABLE 3.2
PROTEIN NEEDS

Average man	65 g protein/day
Average woman	55 g protein/day

If you want to keep it *really* simple, table 3.2 is *all* you have to think about. If you're a man, make sure you get at least 65 grams (about 2½ ounces) of protein each day; if you're a woman, 55 grams (about 2 ounces). If you eat a varied diet, as you should, you don't need to worry about whether you're getting the exact number of grams of tryptophan, leucine, and the other eight essential amino acids that your body needs. Just think about your total grams of protein per day.

If you want a more exact formula for your daily requirement of protein based upon your body weight, use the following formula: 0.8 g protein per kilogram of body weight per day (or 0.36 g per pound of body weight per day—some experts suggest going a tiny bit higher: 0.4 g per pound of body weight per day). As your doctor will tell you, this may need to be adjusted slightly upward if you exercise a lot. A person who weighs 75 kilograms (165 pounds), will need around 60 grams of protein each day, if you're an average, healthy adult who is as physically active as most people are (and not pregnant or nursing). But, again, this amount of protein is so easy for the average person in the industrialized world to consume that you really don't need to worry about it, especially if you follow the Basic Guidelines at the end of this chapter.

Table 3.3

BODY WEIGHT (POUNDS)	PROTEIN/DAY (GRAMS)
100	40
110	44
120	48
130	52
140	56
150	60
160	64

BODY WEIGHT (POUNDS)	PROTEIN/DAY (GRAMS)
170	68
180	72
190	76
200	80
210	84
220	88
230	92
240	96
250	100

Some of you may have heard about there being different "qualities" of protein. For example, the protein in eggs is often considered the "best" kind (actually, the protein in human breast milk, not surprisingly, is even better, but you won't find it on supermarket shelves). All this means is that eggs contain nearly the exact ratios of essential amino acids that people need. But we don't need to consume precisely the right ratio of amino acids in each individual food item we eat. As long as we get the amino acids we need over the course of a meal, we'll be fine. Indeed, many nutritionists now say that getting the needed amino acids over the course of a whole day is sufficient.

LIPIDS

FATS HAVE GOTTEN a bad rap for many, many years, or, we should say, *had* gotten a bad rap. Over the last few years, some authors of diet books, such as Dr. Atkins, have gone in the opposite direction, claiming that a lot of fat (and a lot of protein) in the diet can ultimately be healthful. But one point on which all nutritionists would agree is that if we completely eliminated certain types of fats from our diet, we would die. In Western society, it is extremely difficult *not* to consume at least *some* fats, so there is little danger of your not having enough of them. Indeed, advocates of high-fat, high-protein diets notwithstanding, most of us probably consume *too much* fat. Fat tastes and feels good, adding to the "richness" of food; it is no coincidence that we tend to associate low-fat versions of normally high-fat foods—low-fat cottage cheese, low-fat milk, etc.—with feelings of deprivation. As with protein, Western diners do not seem (or want) to believe that a little truly goes a long way.

The fat situation is a bit trickier than that of protein, however. In the case of protein, if you're an average adult in the United States, Canada, Australia, New Zealand, Western Europe, or Japan, you almost certainly don't have to worry about suffering from protein malnutrition (known as *kwashiorkor*). But, in the case of dietary fat, most people in the West may well need to think more carefully about the *balance* of different types of fats in their diets. Danish physicians noted in the 1970s that natives of Greenland who ate large quantities of fish and other seafood had an unusually low incidence of heart disease and arthritis. And, of course, these Greenlanders consumed essentially no corn oil, safflower oil, or other vegetable oils of the sort that one can scarcely avoid in the United States. This led to research that forced a major rewrite of nutrition textbooks' chapters on dietary fats: it's the *ratio* of the kinds of fatty acids that are found mostly in fish (though also in many nuts and seeds) to those found in most vegetable oils, which matters for health. And this ratio tends to be far too low in the West, especially in the United States.[50]

While you may need to think more about your fat consumption than you do about your protein consumption, any imbalances in your intake of dietary fats are, fortunately, very easy to correct.

what are fats?

What most of us call fats are referred to as *lipids* by nutritionists and others in the scientific community. Lipids include fatty acids, triglycerides, sterols, and waxes (though we don't eat a lot of wax!), as well as so-called "compound lipids"—lipids complexed with another kind of molecule—such as phospholipids and lipoproteins. Lipids are the primary component of cell walls, and are used to make sex hormones, several adrenal hormones, and most eicosanoids (small signaling molecules that help regulate basic bodily functions like blood pressure and inflammation; see page 53). Lipids are also found in abundance in the brain, especially as the covering, or "sheath," around nerve fibers.

Sterols are, technically speaking, a kind of alcohol containing a fused four-ring structure. Cholesterol and steroids, as the names suggest, are examples of sterols.

Fatty acids, on the other hand, are generally smaller molecules that usually consist simply of a chain of carbon atoms with a carboxylic acid group at the end. The chain of carbon atoms can be completed surrounded by ("saturated" with) hydrogen atoms, in which case it is a **saturated fatty acid** (SFA), surrounded by hydrogen atoms except for one "hole" or "unsaturated" spot, in which case it is a **monounsaturated fatty acid** (MUFA), or there can be more than one unsaturated spot, in which case the fatty acid is a **polyunsaturated fatty acid** (PUFA). (See figure 3.1.) A common saturated fatty acid is stearic acid, found in beef and many other foods. There is only one common dietary monounsaturated fatty acid, oleic acid, which is the primary constituent of olive oil and canola oil, and is present in high quantities in avocados and many nuts. There are many different polyunsaturated fatty acids. Arachidonic acid, shown in figure 3.1, is found in meat, and EPA is abundant in cold water fish.

FIGURE 3.1

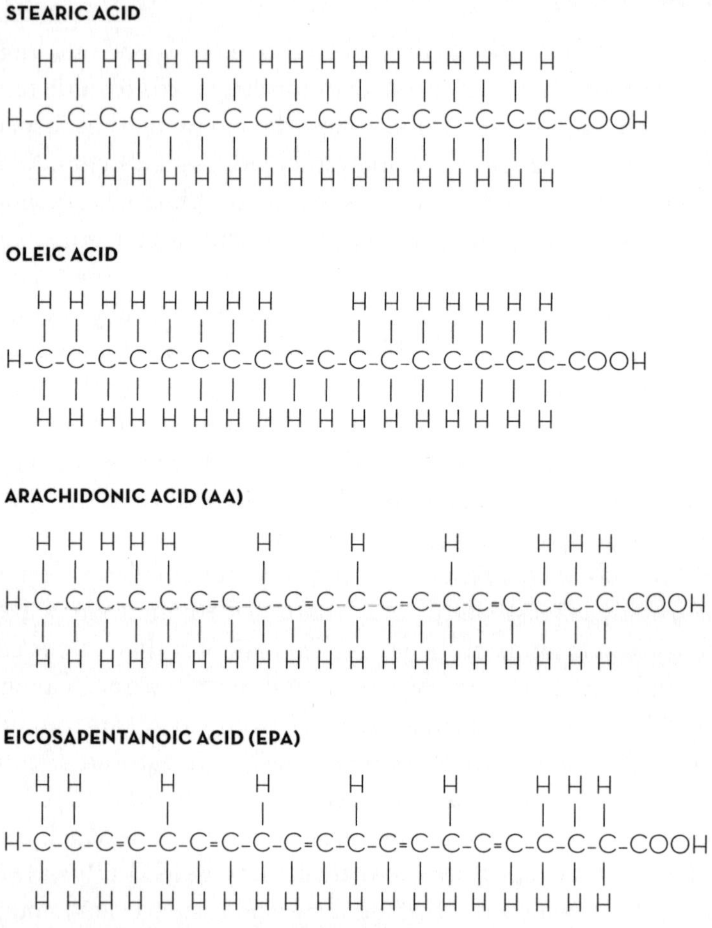

Triglycerides are esters of three (thus "tri") molecules of fatty acids linked with one molecule of glycerol, a syrupy alcohol that gives fat its greasiness. When we talk of body fat, it is triglycerides that we are speaking of, since this is the form that lipids take in our body when we put on the pounds. Most phospholipids are just like triglycerides, except there are only two fatty acids, and in place of the third fatty acid is a small group of atoms containing a phosphorous atom.

A balanced proportion and reasonable amount of lipids are necessary for the very structure of the body itself, such the walls of your trillions of cells, as well as for critical elements of the body's signaling system. In addition, lipids are terrific sources of energy, comparable to the petroleum-based oil or other substances burned to run machinery (how many calories a food has is an expression of how much fuel it can provide).

omega-3 and omega-6

After our whirlwind tour of the complex chemistry of lipids, the following will be reassuring: *Every single lipid the body needs can be made by the body itself,* with only two exceptions: n-3 and n-6 fatty acids, popularly known, respectively, as the **omega-3** and **omega-6** fatty acids. Two common variants of omega-3 are linolenic acid and eicosapentaenoic acid (EPA); two common omega-6 fatty acids are linoleic acid and arachidonic acid (AA).

The omega fatty acids are essential to our bodies because of their use in the creation of hormonelike prostaglandins and leukotrienes. These substances are produced in essentially all cells, and, in contrast to most hormones, tend to act locally and have very short half-lives, sometimes as short as only a few minutes. They are involved in the regulation of blood pressure, inflammation, smooth muscle contraction, reproduction (including even the process of labor in pregnancy), and many other vital biological processes. Because there are twenty carbon atoms in the molecular backbone of these substances, they are often grouped together under the term *eicosanoids,* which literally means "things of which there are twenty (*eicosa*)." There are different classes of eicosanoids, such as one that regulates inflammation. To function properly, some eicosanoids need to be "oiled" with omega-3 fatty acids, and some require omega-6.

Note: the body cannot "interconvert" omega-3 and omega-6 fatty acids, that's why both are needed in the diet. If you look at figure 3.1, you'll see that arachidonic acid has its first double bond (represented by the two horizontal lines between the Cs, which represent carbon atoms) between the sixth and the seventh carbon atoms, counting from the left. The left end of the molecule is the "omega end" of the molecule, that's why it's called an "omega-6" fatty acid: its first double bond begins after the sixth atom from the omega end. EPA, on the other hand, has its first double bond between its third and fourth carbon atoms from the omega end. That's why it's called an omega-3 fatty acid.

Omega-3 and omega-6 are needed in very, very small amounts, and cases of deficiency leading to the death of healthy people are nearly nonexistent. Indeed, it is usually only when placed on completely artificial diets that entirely omit one or both of these two fatty acids that people can suffer from a deficiency; and even then it takes some time before any symptoms appear.

Beyond the exceedingly rare cases of genuine deficiency, there is an additional potential problem involving these essential fatty acids, and that arises because the functions of eicosanoids made from omega-3 fatty acids are often opposed to those of eicosanoids made from omega-6. Generally speaking, those derived from the omega-6 promote inflammation, cell growth, and blood clotting, whereas those derived from omega-3 tend to diminish these effects or even have the opposite effects. Maintaining the correct balance between the two types of fatty acids is crucial to good health.

The body has some control over how many eicosanoids of each type get produced, but its regulation of such production is strongly affected by the omega-6 to omega-3 ratio in our diet, increasingly so as we age. If we consume a lopsided ratio of omega-6 to omega-3 fatty acids, our bodies will have a lopsided balance of eicosanoids, and this can lead to problems. For example, because many types of arthritis often begin with an excessive inflammatory response, a high omega-6:omega-3 ratio in the diet can lead to an increased risk of arthritis. Indeed, a low incidence of arthritis in Greenlanders' diet is one of the things observed by the Danish physicians who first got Western medicine thinking about dietary omega-6:omega-3 ratios.

Because in industrialized countries, especially the United States, food production has changed in such a way that omega-6 fatty acids are abundant in the foods most widely available to us, we are at risk for an overproduction of those eicosanoids made from omega-6 fatty acids. Look at food labels and note how often you see "vegetable oil" listed. Most vegetable oils contain a huge quantity of omega-6 fatty acids—one that is (a) greater than our bodies even need but also, more dangerously, (b) difficult for our typical diet to counterbalance with the appropriate quantity of omega-3.

However, balancing your omega-6 to omega-3 ratio is very easy, regardless of whether you decide to follow the Longevity Diet. Just eat less of those foods containing omega-6, and eat more of those containing omega-3 (see chapter 6). Omega-3 fish oil capsules are another simple means to introduce the fatty acid to your body, apart from diet, although it's so easy to get omega-3 from one's diet that there is little reason for the average, healthy person to resort to fish oil capsules.

There is one slight wrinkle to the omega fatty acid story that should be mentioned before proceeding. We mentioned above that there are "variants" of omega-3s, and "variants" of omega-6s, and that there are several dietary omega-3s that will fulfill the need for the eicosanoid produced from the omega-3 class of fatty acids; likewise for omega-6 fatty acids. Nevertheless, fatty acids that already have twenty carbon atoms in their "backbone" are one step closer to being converted to the biologically active eicosanoids than those that don't have twenty, since the latter first have to be "eicosan-ized"—i.e., made into the twenty-carbon-atom variant—before they can be turned into the biologically active regulating molecule. This, in fact, is the difference between the plant-based omega-3 and -6 fatty acids versus the animal-based ones: the PUFAs found in animals (and fish) tend to be of the twenty-carbon variety, those that are very readily converted to prostaglandins and other eicosanoids. This is part of why it is often recommended that therapeutic PUFA supplementation—for arthritis, Crohn's disease, bipolar disorder, and many other conditions for which omega-3s are often given as treatment—be in the form of fish oil, since it has lots of EPA, the omega-3 fatty acid that readily gets converted to the omega-3 eicosanoids.

But, we repeat, unless your health-care practitioner directs you to supplement your diet with fish oil capsules, going easy on common vegetable oils and occasionally eating the omega-3 foods listed in chapter 6, should suffice to keep your omega fatty acids in balance.

saturated vs. unsaturated fats

Another worry about fat—at least if you're not on a rigorous version of the Longevity Diet—is whether you are consuming too much saturated fat, and/or too much partially hydrogenated vegetable oil. Both, especially the latter, have been correlated with increased risk of cardiovascular disease. The saturated fat in our diets comes mostly from animal products. Partially hydrogenated vegetable oils (which contain the infamous **trans fatty acids**, a form of fatty acid not often found in nature, but which is produced by the **hydrogenation**, or hardening, process, and is especially dangerous to your health) are found in many processed foods. Some of the worst culprits are supposed "low-fat" spreads and commercially prepared salad dressings (see table 3.5).

Another lipid common in the West, especially in southern Europe, is monounsaturated fat. Monounsaturated fats are liquid at room temperature—that is, they are oils. The most common example is the main fat in olive oil. These are thought to be an important factor in the reduced risk of cardiovascular disease in Mediterranean countries, and are an excellent means by which to raise your **HDL** levels. Another source of monounsaturated fat is avocado. Adding monounsaturated fat to your diet is not as big a concern if you're on a rigorous version of the Longevity Diet, since your cardiac risk profile will almost certainly be excellent. But if you do not follow a CR regimen, replacing saturated or partially hydrogenated fats with monounsaturated ones is a wise idea.

TABLE 3.4

HEALTHY ALTERNATIVES TO SATURATED FAT

SATURATED FAT	MONOUNSATURATED FAT
Butter on bread	Olive oil on bread
Brazil nuts, macadamia nuts	Almonds
Cheese dip	Avocado dip
Cream cheese (on a bagel, for example)	Hummus, lox
Typical commercial salad dressing	Simple homemade dressing with vinegar, olive oil, and spices

MICRONUTRIENTS: VITAMINS AND MINERALS

VITAMINS AND MINERALS are, together, generally referred to as "micronutrients" because most of them are needed in exceedingly small quantities. This is why many people are able to fulfill their daily need for them with a pill. Compared with this, the amount of protein you need every day, if you're an average-size adult, would be about the size of a your thumb, while your daily requirement of the essential fatty acids would be a very small puddle in the palm of your hand. The amount of *certain* vitamins, like vitamin C, and *certain* minerals, like calcium, could rest with a generous margin on the tip of your pinkie. But some minerals would be nearly invisible specks. These latter are called "trace minerals," because we need them in only trace amounts.

One characteristic that marks vitamins and minerals as different from protein and fat is that they never are used as fuel. They play purely structural and/or functional roles in our body. One of the most important roles of calcium concerns bone and tooth formation and maintenance. And many minerals and vitamins are parts of enzymes, or are used as cofactors in enzymatic processes. Selenium, for example, influences the "p-450" enzymes that help the body expel chemical toxins.

Do you have to worry about getting too few or too many vitamins and minerals? Well, the picture here is not at all as simple as with protein and lipids. If you are a fairly typical adult, and eat a varied, non-high-fat (that is, not necessarily low-fat, but not really fatty) diet of mostly unprocessed foods, and are sure to include several servings (some experts say five, some say seven, some nine) of fruits and vegetables every day, both your macronutrient and your micronutrient intakes will probably be fine. But most people, especially most Americans, don't eat that way. Thus, the popularity of multivitamin and mineral supplements. These can be useful, but only up to a point. For one thing, they do not preclude eating sensibly; lab-produced vitamin compounds omit many other important food-derived nutrients. For example, if you don't like vegetables, a small capsule cannot possibly replace the fiber of dark, leafy greens. Even more important, however, is that there may well be nutrients of whose essentiality we aren't yet even aware! As it is, strictly essential or not, there are many nutrients that are, at a minimum, *beneficial*—for example many of the hundreds of chemicals that give fruits and vegetables their varying colors, such as lutein, found in green bell peppers and other green vegetables, which protects against macular degeneration,[51] or lycopene, found in tomatoes and other red fruits and vegetables, which protects against several forms of cancer.[52] No pill can account for all the nutrients that science will later tell us are essential, nor those hundreds which we already know are useful.

WHAT'S A SERVING?

- 1 piece of fruit the size of an apple or orange
- ½ cup cut-up canned, frozen, or fresh fruits (in 100% juice) or vegetables
- ¼ cup dried fruit
- ¾ cup 100% fruit or vegetable juice
- 1 cup raw leafy greens
- 1 small potato
- ½ cup of cooked legumes (lentils, red beans, navy beans)
- 1 cup of ready-to-eat breakfast cereal
- ½ cup of cooked rice, pasta, or cereal
- a smallish bagel (i.e., about the size of a hockey puck, not the huge bagels that have become popular)
- 1 cup of yogurt or milk
- 1 ½ ounces of natural cheese
- 2 ounces of processed cheese
- 3 ounces cooked meat (about the size of a deck of cards)

Also, beware of the facile assumption that, if achieving the **RDA** (recommended daily allowance) of a micronutrient is good for you, taking megadoses is even better. It is indeed possible to overdose on vitamins and minerals; vitamin A, for example, while beneficial to skin and bones, can actually cause skin and bone disorders if taken in high doses. Likewise, a recently published meta-analysis conducted by researchers at the Johns Hopkins

School of Medicine concluded that even supplemental vitamin E, long thought to be helpful in preventing cardiac problems, and "essentially safe even when taken at extremely high amounts," increases overall mortality.[53] Please consult your doctor before taking *any* high-dosage dietary supplement.

Whatever diet you choose to follow, tracking the nutrient content of your meals over the course of a few days with nutrition tables or even a computer program (see *Resources*), just to see whether you might be running short on certain vitamins and minerals, is probably a good idea, and can even be fun! See chapter 7 for more on how to do this.

calories

Your body needs energy, measured in **calories**, to run . . . in fact, you burn calories even while you are completely relaxed and lying still. Without a minimum average calorie content in your diet every day, you would die.

Unlike the other essential nutrients, a calorie is not a particular molecule or group of molecules. This is because many different substances can be used as fuel. Two of the previously mentioned essential nutrients, protein and (some) lipids, for example, are excellent fuels. A calorie is therefore not a specific substance, rather a measurement of energy.

The dietary sources of calories are carbohydrates, lipids, protein, and alcohol.

Of those, certain things we eat can *only* be used as fuel. This category is carbohydrates. There are two principal groups of carbohydrates: sugars and starches. Starches are simply groups of sugars linked together into long chains. Starches are very readily broken down in the stomach to yield their component sugars. Some carbohydrates, however, cannot be broken down by the digestive tract to be used as energy; they are called **dietary fiber** (see page 62).

Carbohydrates in and of themselves cannot be considered essential nutrients, since their function—serving as an energy source—can be filled by other macronutrients. But a diet where all the energy came from fat and protein (or, for that matter, alcohol, which is not a carbohydrate, though can be used as a source of energy) would be literally heavy and not very healthy, simply because it would be loaded with far too much fat and protein. Too much dietary fat—especially saturated fat—is of course associated with increased risk of cardiovascular disease. But, as indicated, too much protein can also pose a health risk: it puts a strain on the kidneys, and can even cause urinary calcium excretion, which could increase your risk of osteoporosis. We thus recommend that you be cautious with diets containing high levels of fat or protein, and, unless directed otherwise by your doctor, try to meet a substantial amount of your energy needs with carbohydrates in the form of fruits and whole grains.

THE ESSENTIALS

essential macronutrients

Protein (or amino acids), which is used in building and maintaining body tissues and bones; as enzymes and hormones; and as fuel.

Lipids, which are used in building functions, in signaling functions, and as fuel.

Carbohydrates, which are used as fuel.

essential micronutrients

Vitamins, which are complex molecules needed by the body in various ways, often as "cofactors" used by enzymes to facilitate the enzymes' job.

Minerals, which are inorganic substances used in building functions and, like vitamins, are often cofactors or components of enzymes. They can also have signaling functions, especially in nerve cells.

DIETARY PLUSES

MANY DIFFERENT COMPONENTS of a healthy diet are regarded as beneficial, but not essential. Let us just consider two major categories: **dietary fiber** and **phytochemicals**.

dietary fiber

Dietary fiber is of great importance because of its role in disease prevention. We know that diets high in fiber reduce the risk of diverticulitis and certain types of cancer—above all cancer of the bowel—in humans, lower cholesterol levels, and improve sugar metabolism. And, of course, there's the uncomfortable, if not life-threatening condition of "irregularity," as laxative ads delicately put it. (The Irish physician, Denis Burkitt, who first discovered the importance of dietary fiber, noted: "The only reason you have a laxative industry is because you've taken fiber out of your diet.")

Fiber is often divided into two types: *soluble* and *insoluble*. (See table 3.5.) Soluble fiber is the kind thought to be best at lowering cholesterol levels, and insoluble fiber is thought to be best at improving bowel function and decreasing your risk for colon cancer. There are many different types of each kind of fiber. As with much in human nutrition, given how little we know about fiber to date, variety is the safest bet. You should try to consume at least 40 to 60 grams of fiber each day, split among whole grains (individual grains, such as barley or brown rice, as well as whole-meal breads, bran, and other high-fiber cereals), legumes (lentils, black beans, garbanzos), and high-pectin fruits (apples, pears, peaches, oranges) and vegetables (artichokes, shiitake mushrooms, broccoli). Seaweed contains important nutrients and is spectacularly high in fiber, too.

TABLE 3.5
FOODS CONTAINING SOLUBLE AND INSOLUBLE FIBER

SOURCES OF SOLUBLE FIBER	SOURCES OF INSOLUBLE FIBER
Corn	Whole wheat
Pears	Brown rice
Apples	Other whole grain products
Prunes	Most vegetables
Nuts	Popcorn
Oat bran	
Dried beans and peas	
Carrots	
Sweet potatoes	
Citrus fruits	

(Note, many of those foods listed, for example nuts, contain ample amounts of both types of fiber.)

phytochemicals

The word *phytochemical* just means "plant chemical." Phytochemicals are the thousands of chemicals in plants that are thought to play a role in human health when they are ingested. They are also sometimes called "phytonutrients," especially where a health role for a phytochemical has been established. Many of these, such as the many different pigments found in richly colored plants, are antioxidants; while others have hormonelike properties.

Scientists have known for a very long time that fruits and vegetables are good for you: they contain many essential vitamins and minerals, and they also contain a lot of fiber. More recently, however, numerous other substances in plants have been identified that play a role in the body's defense against such diseases as cancer. We *know* we'll die fairly quickly if we don't get enough vitamin C or magnesium or protein. However, the situation is different with phytonutrients. It is now thought that anthocyanins, for example, which are abundant in blueberries, protect brain cells from age-related damage; and lycopene, which is found in such foods as tomato sauce, protects against cancer. Will we die if we don't consume these nutrients? Some people might, but we don't know yet. How much of these should we consume? We don't yet know that either. There are no immediate indications of phytonutrient deficiencies, as comparable to vitamin or mineral deficiencies, this is why such nutrients aren't yet considered essential. But the tomato you eat today might well prevent a carcinogenic molecule from being able to damage your DNA, damage that would otherwise have led to cancer a decade from now. It is of course *exceedingly* unlikely that one meal will have an effect on your health! But a lifetime of a phytochemical-rich diet will greatly improve your health, and reduce your risk of dying prematurely of cancer or heart disease. Green tea and a range of brightly colored vegetables (especially green, leafy ones, carrots, and beets) and fruits are excellent sources of phytochemicals.

COOKED VEGETABLES AND NUTRIENT AVAILABILITY

Cooking breaks down the cell walls of plants, which makes some nutrients more available to you. This is particularly true in the case of many nutrients in carrots and tomatoes.

Yet heat, over time, also can destroy some of the nutrients in vegetables, especially vitamin C, certain B vitamins, and many phytonutrients.

What to do? A few simple guidelines:

- Steam vegetables until they have become slightly soft.
- A little bit of fat can aid in the absorption of fat-soluble nutrients, which are found in abundance in vegetables—but don't go overboard. If you will be eating nuts with dinner or within a few hours of dinner, or will be having a slice of avocado, a typical salad dressing on your salad, or a serving of fish, then you're getting plenty of fat to ensure the optimal absorption of the fat-soluble nutrients in your meal.
- Why not mix and match? Have *both* steamed and raw vegetables. If science discovers that a few key phytonutrients are far more susceptible to heat damage than we realized, you'll be covered!

SOME BASIC GUIDELINES

Reducing your calorie intake is easier than you might think, and its benefits are so powerful that any other non-CR diet that has been advocated for health will seem both ineffectual and needlessly persnickety, as Katherine Tallmadge, the author of a fine book called *Diet Simple,* has pointed out in a *Washington Post* article about the CR study being conducted at Washington University (WUSTL): "I believe that one of the real benefits of the low-calorie approach is that it places important emphasis on the central issue: reducing calories, rather than getting diverted into seemingly important, but in fact, peripheral matters, such as carbohydrate and fat counting."[54]

But if you decide not to try the Longevity Diet, read on. A few simple principles will suffice:

Include as many unprocessed foods (whole-grain bread instead of white bread, corn instead of corn chips, etc.) as would be practical in your diet.

Eat several servings (at least five, preferably more) of fruit and vegetables every day.
Don't eat a lot of meat, particularly fatty meat.
If you want to avoid meat altogether, make sure you get some legumes (pinto beans, navy beans, lentils, nuts, etc.) every day, as well as some grains (pasta, bread, rice, etc.).
Get at least twenty minutes of aerobic exercise at least three times a week. *This is especially important if you're not going to go on the Longevity Diet.*
Check with a health-care professional before making *any* decisions about your diet or exercise regimen (including even the decision *not* to change anything). Get a few tests done, just to learn your baseline biomarkers. Having some data on a few basic parameters of health—for example, your cholesterol or fasting glucose levels—will be extraordinarily helpful to you in the future.

You may want to simplify things even further. Not everybody wants to devote a lot of thought to food or health, and we understand that. So, the short version of this advice to is make sure you eat a varied diet that includes less processed food and more fruits and vegetables, and try to run or swim or dance or play tennis or football or soccer (or any other physical activity that will be pleasurable and yet raise a sweat) a few times a week. If you don't want to try the Longevity Diet now, please tuck this book away where you can find it, should you someday be more concerned about becoming more proactive about your health.

4 YOUR CALORIES, YOUR LIFE

THE TRADITIONAL VIEW OF CALORIES

CALORIES ARE A much more controversial nutrient than the other principal essential nutrients in your diet. Scientists have long had a pretty clear idea of how much protein your body needs each day. This is the basis for the standards set by nutritionists and governmental health organizations. The case is the same with vitamins, minerals, and lipids. Such standards place particular stress upon the *minimum* you need of any nutrient for your body to function properly.

In contrast, we know that when you consume *fewer* calories than mainstream nutritionists think is optimal, your health actually *improves* (up to a point, of course). So why do most recommended calorie requirements remain so high?

One answer might be that nutritionists, governmental health agencies, and most physicians simply have not heard of CR. Moreover, many gerontology researchers are still unconvinced of the potential clinical application of CR despite such extraordinary results in laboratory studies of its effects upon animals, and growing evidence that we may expect no less spectacular results in humans.

But also, notions of the relationship between quantity of food consumed and health have been so deeply ingrained across the centuries that top-of-the-line modern CR researchers still have a hard time convincing even other scientists and doctors that eating a minimal diet may be healthy. On an evolutionary time-scale, it has only been in the blink of an eye that CR studies have started, ever so slowly, to change people's minds. And this is because it has only been in the blink of an eye that food shortages have ceased to be a serious threat to the average citizen of Western countries. Though, most unfortunately, situations of starvation or malnutrition still exist in third world nations, in industrialized areas of the world we no longer see calamities like the potato famines that swept Ireland during the mid-nineteenth century. And when was the last time you met someone with beriberi (a severe deficiency of vitamin B_1, often seen in diets that are heavily dependent upon rice) or rickets (of vitamin D, largely stamped out now by fortified dairy products) or scurvy (of vitamin C, which for centuries affected not only sailors but mainland dwellers who did not eat sufficient fruit and vegetables). If anything, we are surrounded by an overabundance of food that, like the little cake in *Alice's Adventures in Wonderland,* ever beckons us with the temptation, "Eat me."

From the standpoint of traditional medicine, CR represents a radical departure downward from a norm that has existed in the West for centuries upon centuries: "The more the better!" "If there's food, eat! You never know when there might *not* be food around!" Your body has the ability to convert and store energy in the form of fat. This ability was crucial to the survival of your ancestors. In the wild, food availability varies, of course, wildly. Therefore we humans, along with the vast majority of life on the planet, have developed the ability to convert stored energy to useable fuel when external sources of energy cannot be found. That way, if there's a famine, you can live off the fat of your belly when you can't live off the fat of the land.

Having a lot of body fat has traditionally been a marker of success even in other animal species: Think about the science programs you've probably seen on TV, where the alpha male gorilla is leaning against the tree with his two or three female companions. Compared with these companions and the other male gorillas, he is fat. And yet the alpha male is not viewed as a failure, as one who "hasn't been able to keep off the pounds." On the contrary, any other gorilla just has to glance at him to know he is the alpha male. Enemies approaching from the distance spot him and think twice about attacking. It is understood even cross-species that you don't mess with the alpha male. Until very recently, "alpha humans" also tended to be large. Napoleon notwithstanding, many emperors and kings were enormous.

Right up through the nineteenth century, in not only third world but Western cultures, plumpness was also considered a sign of a person's wealth and congeniality, even morality; it is no coincidence that our image of a beneficent Santa Claus is always of an exceptionally rotund man, while such evil figures as Satan, on the other hand, are always depicted as scrawny (though one would think, if food were so sinful, Satan would be first at the table . . .). In Victorian times, a common term for a vegetarian was a "crank." A commitment to such an alternative lifestyle was considered eccentric. Even gender enters into the equation: Throughout much of the twentieth century, many people thought there was something amusing or peculiar about a male who willingly made a meal of salad, considered a ladies' delicacy. It was *manly* to eat meat. And even our own twenty-first-century culture retains that phrase, a "meat and potatoes man," as one implying a fellow who is figuratively (and perhaps literally!) four-square and dependable. It is difficult for doctors and nutritionists to fight this kind of message that runs so deep in our collective history, even while in this last century it has become fashionable for *women* to be slender.

The association between rotundness and success has of course reversed over the last few generations, partly because of the wide availability of extremely cheap food; in our own culture far too many people who don't have the income or time to prepare nutritious meals from scratch, have become overweight or even obese due to a steady diet of fast foods and processed foods high in fat and carbohydrates. But the notion that a bit of pudge is healthy is still widespread, despite the utter absence of evidence for it.

Some people, for example, feel that they need "bodily reserves" in case they get cancer or some other wasting disease. There may, indeed, be some truth to the notion that with *certain* diseases, a bit of pudge might at least help you get through treatment, such as chemotherapy. But it would be far wiser to try not to get those diseases in the first place. The Longevity Diet is one of the best ways to ensure that your chances of becoming ill or dying prematurely are minimized.

THE GENETIC FACTOR

As humans and animals evolved through periods of want, the message to overeat became encoded into our very genes, as a safety net to ensure the continuation of our species. The body itself—some bodies more than others—seems ever to crave more calories than it needs. Your body doesn't immediately start crying out for more foods containing, say, vitamin B_{12} when you get less of the vitamin than its RDA; the effects of such deprivation can only be measured by a blood test, or by symptoms that develop over a period of time. But calories are different: the body cries out for energy-rich food when even a few hours go by without a meal. There are many interlinked though independently operating signaling systems that control hunger. Emptiness of the digestive system and low blood sugar levels lead the hypothalamus in the brain to send "Eat!" messages that are far more internally insistent than the inviting message written on Alice's cake. It's difficult for nutritionists to ignore so powerful a physiological reaction when setting standards for caloric intake. To them, the fact that such a "symptom" exists means it must be responded to.

Table 4.1 contains the standard wisdom about caloric intake. For even reasonably active adults, these recommendations are extraordinarily high compared with the calorie intake of people on the Longevity Diet.

TABLE 4.1

Moderately active men of average size	2,500 calories/day
Moderately active women of average size	2,000 calories/day

SURVIVAL OF THE FITTEST?

EXACTLY HOW DID this internal calorie meter develop? For the answer to that, we must step into the footprints of our ancestors:

When food is plentiful, it would make sense for you and your "tribemates" to eat a lot, make a lot of babies, stay around long enough to teach your young how to survive and start making babies of their own, and then fade away. But when food is scarce, during a drought, or a hard winter, or a period of blight-induced famine, it would *not* make sense to make babies. It would make sense to wait until more food is available, and *then* make babies. Otherwise precious resources are being used up in a venture that is itself going to demand even more resources than simple sustenance. And here is the key point: *It is critical that your body conserve its resources to survive the times that are tough*. You must be youthful enough, virile enough, and fertile enough, to be able to have children and live long enough to rear them. This means, in essence, that the aging process has to slow down during a food shortage. Resources need to be shifted towards the survival of the individual, not toward reproduction (the survival of the species). When evolution was sculpting us, what would have been available during difficult times would have been small quantities of seeds, nuts, berries, vegetables, and the occasional very lean meat (*very* lean, since the game available during a food shortage would itself have had slim pickings).

Evolution built into the genes of our most ancient ancestors a valuable tool for survival: when food is scarce, the body undergoes changes that permit it to survive, with all its vital functions intact, longer—much longer—than when it's "well fed" (in the old-fashioned sense). And there is considerable evidence to support this.

From an evolutionary standpoint, the Longevity Diet is about making your body "think" there's a shortage of food—how *much* of a shortage, is up to you! Think of it as a gift from your ancestors.

YOUR BODY IN ITS FINEST FORM: LEAN AND EFFICIENT

From a purely evolutionary standpoint, reducing your calorie intake will ensure you will last a long time. But what does this process look like from the standpoint of biology? What is happening at the level of hormones and cholesterol and DNA? While, of course, there is much more for researchers to understand about the biology of CR, we have learned a lot over even the last decade.

There are many theories of just what happens to our bodies as we age, and why it happens. Each deals with a different "system," so to speak: both the large-scale evolutionary systems just discussed, and systems as small as your enzymes, hormones, and the tiniest molecules within your cells. Each theory has predictions about what kind of changes we would expect to see if that theory is correct. Interestingly, animals on CR indicate the changes predicted by *all* the major theories of aging.

As noted, we do not yet have data on life expectancies for people following the CR regimen, because experiments in humans have only recently begun. But we have **life-span studies** from animals from widely different parts of the evolution tree showing that CR slows aging, and, in the short-term CR studies in humans, the biomarkers so far measured—such as fasting glucose levels, body temperature, etc.—match those observed in the long-term animal studies where greatly extended life spans were observed. Thus, it is very likely that the CR effect will be present in humans on the diet. Moreover, even if we can't yet prove that you can live to be 140 or more on CR, we *can* be certain that CR will reduce the probability that you will get diseases associated with aging, and that you will live longer than you would otherwise expect to on a non-CR regimen.

So goes the reasoning of more and more researchers who have been so impressed by the effects of CR upon animals that they have gone on the diet themselves. For example, a senior researcher at the U.S. National Institute of Aging, Mark P. Mattson, PhD, has placed himself on CR. So has James Greenberg, at the Health and Nutrition Sciences Department of Brooklyn College. And Richard Weindruch, a student and former colleague of Roy Walford, has also tried the diet.

THE AGING PROCESS

Let us now turn to the various body systems and parameters that change as we age, as viewed through the lens of several common theories of aging. Interestingly, every one of these parameters is altered by CR.

These theories are of course by no means mutually exclusive. Indeed, each may capture a piece of the puzzle, or even be simply a different way of describing the same puzzle piece. Most of the controversy in the research community surrounds the question of which theory is fundamental, and which rather just describes a consequence of another theory. What is important to our discussion is that *none* of these theories has proved to be inconsistent with the biomarker changes seen so far in humans on CR. This provides yet more evidence that CR not only reduces disease risk in humans, it actually slows the aging process itself, just as it does in nonhuman species in which the anti-aging effect of CR has been roundly tested.

We'll begin with the broad, evolution-based biological theories of aging.

disposable soma

The *disposable soma* theory of aging is, in essence, the technical name given to the evolutionary logic of the CR effect explained above. It is not so much about what is happening on a biological level when we age, as about *why* we age at all.

Soma means "body." The disposable soma theory holds that individual bodies are, well, disposable. What matters is reproduction: individuals can be "disposed" of, so long as the species survives. This explains why signs of aging start to appear very rapidly once we are no longer able to reproduce.

If the disposable soma theory of aging is correct—and it almost certainly is—we would expect to see exactly what we see in laboratory animals on CR: during times of famine (artificially induced in the lab), the survival of the species is threatened, and thus individuals, or "somata," need to remain youthful enough to reproduce and care for their young once the famine is over.

antagonistic pleiotropy

Yes, that word is "antagonistic": what this theory means is that the very genes which are beneficial to us early in life turn against us later on. "Pleiotropy" is the characteristic of having more than one effect, or one or more forms of expression. The immunological theory of aging (see next page) is actually just a concrete application of antagonistic pleiotropy. And the ability of cells to "commit suicide" to prevent runaway cell growth (cancer) early in life is the very same *inability* of cells to continue to survive and thrive much later in life. In other words, the genes leading to cell death are helpful to the individual when he or she is young, but less so as time passes. Even menopause has been theorized to be a consequence of antagonistic pleiotropy: depletion of the number of follicles in ovaries is thought to be important for the maintenance of regular cycles. Yet, in later decades, it leads to infertility.[55]

Antagonistic pleiotropy is of course related to the disposable soma theory, since genes that are useful for the species earlier in life become damaging to the individual (soma) later, once the individual has passed on her genes, and thus is, from the standpoint of the species, "disposable."

"SYSTEM" THEORIES OF AGING

System theories of aging look at the body as a system, that is, as a systematic whole. We will only mention a couple of them here.

rate of living

This is a theory that says if you live "faster," you'll die sooner or, as the proverb goes, "If you burn the candle at both ends, the candle won't last long." This theory makes intuitive sense, and has been around for a very, very long time in various forms.

The rate-of-living theory is also consistent with longevity studies in the laboratory and in short-term CR studies performed on humans. Animals and humans alike, on a CR diet, use their body's energy more efficiently. That means you buy more time. It's as if you have fifteen gallons of gasoline and you tune up your car so that it's running more effectively: the car with the tune-up will go farther.

However, there is an interesting twist here. CR actually seems to give the body more "living allotment." That is, it's not that the candle is simply burning more slowly, or only at one end. With CR, it begins to grow more wax. On CR, your body will use energy more effectively, your heart will beat more slowly, your body temperature will be a little bit lower. But also, the very amount of extra energy available to you will increase beyond merely the amount those markers of metabolic efficiency conserve.

immunological

The *immunological theory* of aging was developed at UCLA by Professor Roy Walford. It is an example of antagonistic pleiotropy, mentioned above. According to this theory, your immune system, which is of course vital to your survival, starts to turn against you as you age. This can easily be observed in laboratory animals: **autoantibodies**, antibodies that attack parts of the body instead of defending it against germs, tend to multiply with age. These autoantibodies can easily be measured in humans. However, animals started on CR before they get too old stave off this rise in autoantibodies, and consequently live longer, healthier lives. Thus far, the CR effect upon autoantibodies has been firmly established in studies in animals, and will very likely be seen in humans as well.

neuroendocrine

The *neuroendocrine system* is a complicated network of brain cells (neurons), hormones, and glands that govern, broadly speaking, **homeostasis**: the overall stability of the body's functions. A central component of the neuroendocrine system is the hypothalamus gland, located in the brain. The hypothalamus has a "master controller" function, monitoring and troubleshooting the state of the body. When the hypothalamus is working well, it reacts to the body's needs by changing the hormones it sends out into the bloodstream to deal with any problems.

The hypothalamus becomes increasingly damaged and dysfunctional as we age, as well as less in tune with its bodily environment. Once it is impaired, it regulates our hormone levels less and less effectively, which in turn damages the hypothalamus itself (above all, via excessive cortisol). Laboratory rodents on CR have youthful hormonal regulation much, much longer than normally fed laboratory animals. The evidence we have so far from the long-term nonhuman primate studies of CR shows the same changes seen in other laboratory animals.[56] Moreover, humans on short-term CR have so far shown the same preservation of overall endocrine function.[57]

CELLULAR THEORIES OF AGING

CELLULAR THEORIES FOCUS, as the name suggests, on changes that occur with age at the cellular level. There has been considerable focus on these over the last few years, although the basic idea that when your cells age, you age, has been around for many decades.

cellular senescence

In 1961, at the Wistar Institute in Philadelphia, biologists Leonard Hayflick and Paul Moorhead observed that normal human cells only divide fifty or so times in a Petri dish. This limit is now known as the "Hayflick Limit." In the 1970s, a likely molecular basis for this limit was discovered: *telomeres*. Telomeres are "caps" at the end of DNA molecules that become shorter with each cell division. When a cell's telomeres reduce to a certain length, the cell stops dividing, and eventually dies. Interestingly, cancer cells (and a very few noncancerous human cells, such as germ cells) have an enzyme, *telomerase,* that puts a bit of the telomere back after each cell division, which is why cancer cells are essentially immortal.

Most of the cells in our body will not have divided fifty times by the time we die, even if we die in our nineties. While the Hayflick Limit cannot directly explain aging, just what role it does play is still being studied. It is conceivable that relatively short telomeres, even those long enough to permit additional cell divisions, are nonetheless deleterious in some way. Interestingly, recent research shows that lab animals on CR experience less telomere shortening than those in control groups.[58]

wear and tear

This is perhaps one of the most obvious theories of why we age and, in part because it's so obvious, it has been around for a while, indeed for centuries. The wear-and-tear theory says, in essence, that aging in organisms is a lot like the aging of inanimate objects: like inanimate objects, living bodies wear out over time.

It is, however, a relatively weak theory, strangely enough. Despite its intuitive appeal, it can't account for why your body's response rate of self-repair decreases with age. Wear and tear is a side effect of life; aside from any external damage you might be aware of, your body is constantly repairing and replacing your tissues, cell walls, and DNA. This mechanism is not, in and of itself, aging. Indeed, it makes more sense to say that what *ages* you is the decrease, with time, of your body's natural ability to repair itself.

CR slows that decline in your body's response to general wear and tear, continuing its strengthening and revitalizing functions as it ages.

glycemic

When it comes to calorie restriction, this is the most important theory of aging, since calorie restriction means energy reduction, and glucose is the most important source of energy for most of the cells in your body.

Glucose is a sugar that is ideal as a fuel source because it contains, in its very molecular structure, a lot of energy. Glucose is constantly present in our bloodstream, ready to be taken in as needed by cells all over the body.

It is in part because of its molecular structure that glucose can also cause collateral damage as it circulates around the body. According to the *glycemic theory of aging,* it is this damage caused by circulating glucose that leads to the pathological changes which occur as we age.

How can your body's primary fuel be bad? Too much of a good thing—any good thing—tends to be bad. The problem here lies in the ease with which the glucose molecule spontaneously binds to amino acids in proteins, changing the structure and function of the proteins. These *advanced glycation end-products (AGEs)* are thought to be responsible for most of the symptoms seen in diabetes, and, according to the glycemic theory of aging, for at least some of the changes in the body as it ages.

We know that CR lowers average levels of circulating glucose. CR may therefore slow aging simply by retarding the damage caused by excessive blood glucose levels.

Let's take a brief look at what happens to the glucose levels in your blood when you eat a meal. First, glucose levels rise. They rise faster and higher if you've eaten a **high-GI** meal but, even when eating a low-GI meal, glucose levels will rise. In response to this, the pancreas releases insulin. The job of insulin is to allow your cells to utilize the glucose for energy (though some cells, such as brain and liver cells, do not need insulin to use glucose). Some of the glucose is immediately used as fuel, and some is conserved for later use, either as glycogen (which is stored in the liver) or as fat (which is stored, well, you know where!). Slowly glucose levels in the blood decrease, until you eat your next meal, and the cycle starts over again.

The glycemic index has increasingly drawn attention from the medical community because of its relevance in the prevention of type 2 diabetes. Most physicians now recommend that you select your foods with care to avoid causing a high "glucose spike," which taxes your pancreas, and, after time, can make your cells less sensitive to insulin, thus creating a downward spiral in which the pancreas is taxed even more, since more insulin is needed to do the same job, eventually leading to insulin resistance, and then type 2 diabetes. For most people, a sensible goal is to eat only small amounts of high-GI foods and to have a diet centered on low-GI foods, whose sugars burn slowly: a candle-flame is all you need, not a blowtorch. This is why one often hears that "grazing" is better than eating just two or three huge meals every day.

Interestingly, a rigorous CR diet may make concerns with the GI of foods irrelevant. In CR studies in laboratory animals, neither different feeding schedules—eating twice a day, once a day, or, the ultimate in "nongrazing," every other day—nor variations in the GI values of foods used in the experiments, makes much of a difference in the resulting life-span extension.

In insulin resistance, the downward spiral of inefficient insulin has led to higher average levels of circulating glucose in the blood, since more is needed to achieve the same level of transport from the blood into cells. Basically, the collateral damage caused by all that glucose zipping around your body increases as the amount of glucose in your blood increases.

In a sense, the glycemic theory of aging could be seen as explaining both why people with insulin resistance and/or type 2 diabetes develop so many health problems and generally don't live very long, *and* why all people, not just those with type 2 diabetes, develop health problems as they age.

INSULIN AND AGING

INTERESTINGLY, THERE IS considerable evidence that insulin is itself central to the aging process. Indeed, studies of centenarians have shown that low average levels of circulating insulin are one of the very few things they all have in common.[59] This may at least in part be a different way of saying they have low average-circulating glucose levels—and these centenarians do indeed also have relatively low blood glucose levels—but it appears that insulin plays a role in aging that is independent of that of glucose.

While much more research needs to be done, Cynthia Kenyon at the University of California–San Francisco, and Marc Tatar at Brown University, to name just a few of the researchers investigating insulin pathways, are starting to unravel the mysteries of the relationship between insulin and aging.[60] [61]

Whether or not insulin is fundamental in the aging process, or is merely a marker for some other fundamental process, we already know there is a correlation between lowered insulin levels and a reduced rate of aging. CR lowers circulating insulin levels in all creatures in which it's been tested, including humans.

CR IN A PILL? CR IN A BOTTLE OF WINE?

Fascinating new research is beginning to unlock the mysteries of precisely how CR actually slows aging. The hope in many quarters—a potentially trillion-dollar hope, of course—is that a "CR-mimetic" pill can be created that will enable everyone, even those who don't want to change their eating habits, to live an extra two or three decades.

The research centers on the question of how cells sense that glucose availability is low, and how that translates into the changes that result in longer life. It appears that a substance known as **resveratrol** can increase the expression of genes that, at least in lower animals, are also switched on when these animals are on CR. We know now that resveratrol can increase maximum life span of the roundworm[62] and yeast,[63] although more research is definitely needed: one recent study could not reproduce these effects.[64] Studies on mice have just commenced. Much more study is required before we know whether resveratrol will lengthen life in such higher organisms as humans. But resveratrol, or a compound like it, may, someday, allow us to have "CR in a pill." Resveratrol is, in fact, already available as a dietary supplement. The chemical is very unstable, and breaks down easily; according to David Sinclair, a researcher at Harvard who researches the effects of resveratrol, almost all resveratrol compounds on the market have essentially no resveratrol in them (although one exception appears to be Longevinex).

Another way to get resveratrol is in red wine—in particular, in Pinot Noirs made from grapes grown in cooler, moister climates, such as northern California, Oregon, Washington State, upstate New York, the Burgundy region in France, and Tasmania. Keep in mind that, however much many of us might love a good Pinot Noir, alcohol is, among many other things, a potentially highly addictive poison. If you're able to drink alcohol in moderation, and don't want to stop (at least one of the authors of this book has no plans to stop), then shifting toward Pinot Noir instead of gin or vodka might be a smart health move.

Keep an eye on the CR-mimetic research, but in the meantime eat sensibly. The "I'll continue to eat fast food and just wait for the pill to come out" strategy might be a big gamble. We don't know how long it will take for CR-mimetic research to pay off.

free radical

If there's any theory of aging that you've heard about it's probably the *free radical* theory of aging. This has nothing to do with anarchistic political movements. **Free radicals** are, rather, highly reactive chemical fragments that can cause damage to vital molecules and tissues in your body. We need to go into some detail here, since this theory of aging is so often discussed, and, unfortunately, has so often been the basis of highly simplistic, deceptive ads for "miracle" cures.

To put it simply, a free radical is an atom or group of atoms with the wrong number of electrons. Free radicals *really want* to get the right number of electrons. You might remember something about "electron spin" from a high school or college chemistry class. Electrons with "up" spin need to pair with electrons with "down" spin in order for the molecule they orbit to become balanced.

Free radicals grab the nearest available electron they find in order to get the right electron balance. There are two ways this can happen. One is that a free radical finds another free radical, and they share their electrons in a way that both become satisfied. This is how stable chemical bonds are formed. It is like playing dominoes: the basic technique places bars flat on the table end to end against each another, pairing quantities of dots, like with like. But the other way is that a free radical will steal an electron, which in turn creates another free radical: the molecule from which the electron was stolen. Once *that* molecule is a free radical, it might steal an electron from yet another molecule, in a crashing *domino effect* that can go on for quite some time. This latter process is a dangerous chain-reaction of molecular malfunctions.

Free radicals also play a useful function, of course, such as in the destruction of bacteria by the immune system. But the body needs a way to arrest the activities of free radicals where they aren't needed. We have enzyme systems that can neutralize them very well. But also, antioxidants can neutralize (or actually "trap") free radicals. More about those in a moment.

Most of the damage done by free radicals can very quickly be repaired, but a little bit remains after each free radical "strike." The damage that even this small amount can do is known to play a role in a number of illnesses, especially cancer. Free radical damage to DNA molecules causes mutations, which can lead to out-of-control growth—cancer—of the kind of cell whose DNA was damaged.

It is also postulated that free radical damage causes the overall decline in body functions that leads to, or, rather simply *is,* aging. Here, of course, is where the supplement industry has seen a golden opportunity.

The free radical theory of aging, at least in its broadest outlines, is legitimate and pretty straightforward: free radicals are "bad guys" that do bad things; if there were "good guys" to lasso and get rid of them, we wouldn't age as quickly. However, beware of the methods of over-the-counter antioxidant packagers, who are very sophisticated and slick . . . and simplistic, not unlike the snake-oil salesmen of yesteryear. In health food stores, for example, one brochure we've seen features a picture of a young woman's face, with a small part of her cheek expanded into a close-up view showing a few delicate-seeming collagen molecules and some small red circles representing free radicals. The red circles are little, fanged devil faces getting ready to chomp on the fragile molecules. Then there are some green circles with smiley faces, representing antioxidants. They are positioned to look as though they are guarding the woman's collagen against the devils. The next picture shows shiny new bottles of vitamins C and E (two vitamins that also happen to be antioxidants), whose manufacturer's icon—surprise!—bears a striking resemblance to an antioxidant smiley face.

What could be more compelling than such a simple view of health, one that matches our notions that the world is divided into Good and Evil, Virtue and Vice? Yet, for better or worse, the human body is not simple. The putative virtues of antioxidant supplements cannot make up for bad eating habits.

The fact is, *no* studies to date with antioxidant supplements of *any kind* have demonstrated a significant slowing of the aging process in laboratory animals. There do appear to be some health benefits to antioxidant supplementation, but so far, in the laboratory, the aging process per se has not been altered by supplemental antioxidants. Does this mean the free radical theory of aging is incorrect? Not at all! The more reasonable conclusion is that your body actually requires a certain level of free radicals—free radicals, after all, play an important physiological role, especially in the immune system. Thus the body may simply alter production of its own antioxidants in order to maintain the right balance of free radicals and antioxidants in the face of the onslaught of vitamin C or E that you're consuming in the form of a pill.

Unlike regimens reliant upon supplements, the Longevity Diet, via the shift in resources required under conditions of reduced energy-intake, actually lowers free radical production.

The less free radicals you have to wreak havoc upon your cells, the less your body will be damaged by instances of their domino effect. The result may be a longer life.

MISCELLANEOUS THEORIES

THERE ARE MANY other theories of aging, some focusing on even smaller components of the body, such as the DNA inside your *mitochondria,* the small components of cells that produce energy. We find that CR in lab animals produces changes consistent with a slowing of the aging process as defined in these theories of aging as well. For example, CR greatly reduces the age-associated increase in damage to mitochondrial DNA.[65] Another DNA-related theory focuses on the decline with age of the organism's ability to regulate gene expression—CR also mitigates this decline.[66]

The fact that there are so many competing theories of aging makes it clear how far we have to go in understanding the aging process. But the facts that the effects of CR are consistent with *all* of these theories, and that all changes so far observed in humans on short-term CR are *also* consistent with these theories, strongly suggest that CR will greatly improve your health, and will most likely slow your rate of aging appreciably.

5 YOUR LIFE, YOUR DECISION

We are constantly amazed at how many people we speak with get hung up on the question of whether the Longevity Diet "really works," given the lack of any present evidence of regimen-followers living a record-breaking number of years. True, we won't know with *absolute certainty* until after the year 2100 or so whether the Longevity Diet in humans genuinely slows the aging process itself as has been projected, if the studies that have recently commenced even continue that long. But while the gold standard of anti-aging studies—which is to say, animals (human or otherwise) living past the age of the longest known member of his or her species—can't be achieved for another century or so, there is nonetheless overwhelming evidence that such a diet will indeed slow the aging process, and the facts are even more solid when it comes to the effect of the Longevity Diet on diseases associated with aging, such as type 2 diabetes and heart disease.

Imagine that no long-term, controlled study had ever been done specifically on the relation between smoking and health in humans. Imagine that we "only" have hundreds of studies showing that smoking shortens the lives of a wide variety of lab animals; that we have short-term studies in humans showing that smoking increases plaque formation in blood vessels, damages tissue in the mouth, throat, and lungs, damages skin on the face, and in many other ways appears to be extremely deleterious to your health. In addition, imagine that we also have many theories about *how* smoking shortens the life of the animals in the lab studies: about the effects of carbon monoxide in their blood, and of the high temperature of the smoke upon their oral passages and respiratory system, and of tar in their lungs; and so on. Now imagine that we can actually measure increased carbon monoxide in humans who smoke, the effects of the high temperature smoke on the tissue in their mouths and throats, the presence of tar and other chemicals in their lung tissue, etc. And that not only do we see the lab animals that are exposed to smoke over the course of a lifetime often coughing up disgusting black stuff from their lungs shortly before they are going to die; we see humans who smoke for many years coughing up disgusting black stuff from their lungs. Would it make sense to say, "Gee, I don't know whether I'm going to quit smoking. I need to wait until the long-term, carefully controlled studies with humans are completed." Of course it would not make sense! When it comes to your health, waiting for 99.5 percent certainty to go up to 99.9 percent would be silly.

But it would not be silly in the slightest to say that you don't want to quit smoking because you love smoking. That's an entirely different matter! Same thing with deciding that you don't want to give up your current eating habits.

You may decide you just don't want to change the way you eat. The pleasure of dining on rich, fatty foods, the intense pleasure of *excess,* is delightful, and may quite simply be something you do not want to give up. We're not on any kind of moralistic crusade against obesity. Indeed, there's far too much moralizing about food and weight as it is—food guilt has in of itself become a huge problem in our society. We should not make people feel bad because of the way they choose to eat (and certainly not because of the way they look).

You should feel good about yourself, about whatever decisions you make in life. But if you have decided that living a long, youthful life is important to you, try the Longevity Diet!

Our only caveats: if you are pregnant or trying to become pregnant; are not yet fully grown; have a history of eating disorders; or have not been to a health-care professional about beginning this diet, do not proceed with the diet. But, even if you fit one of these special situations, please keep reading, as we still have much to say concerning basic nutrition and health.

- **If you are pregnant, or even thinking about getting pregnant, don't try the Longevity Diet**

  CR during pregnancy has not been studied extensively. Either way, CR during pregnancy is a risk—to mother and child—not worth taking. Given what we know about the evolutionary role of the CR effect, it would make sense that the Longevity Diet could also make it more difficult to get pregnant.

- **If you are not fully grown, don't try the Longevity Diet.**

  When begun before the animals have physically matured, severe CR stunts the growth of laboratory animals. Don't try the Longevity Diet if you're not fully grown!

- **If you have a history of eating disorders, we would suggest avoiding the Longevity Diet.**

  People with eating disorders, or those who have had an eating disorder, are severely at risk of slipping into another episode if they attempt this diet, because they have a predisposition toward an unhealthy body image and/or unhealthy obsessions about food. If you have or have had an eating disorder, you should not eat fewer calories than have been prescribed by your doctor.

- **If you haven't spoken with a health-care professional, don't try the Longevity Diet—indeed, don't try any diet!**

  Talk with your doctor before making any significant changes to your diet. Always! We should all have good, long-term relationships with our physicians. Your doctor knows you, your medical needs, your habits, and so on.

If you want to start the Longevity Diet, and your doctor agrees it's a good idea, you will probably have a lot of questions about precisely *how* to put its principles into practice. Part II of this book will explain the various forms of the regimen.

Before we turn to the Part II, however, there are still a few remaining technical matters that we need to address.

HOW MUCH TO REDUCE YOUR INTAKE OF CALORIES

THE CONCEPT OF the Longevity Diet is simple: reduce your caloric intake, while being certain not to fall short on essential vitamins and other nutrients, and your health will be greatly improved, and your body will almost certainly age more slowly.

But reduce from *what*? This question is one of the trickiest in the application of CR to humans. There is at least as much art as science here. We will offer three different approaches: (1) "weight watching," (2) calorie counting, and (3) health markers (which can be combined with the first two).

Key to determining how much to restrict your energy intake is the notion of **set point**. Set point is, technically speaking, difficult to define, yet intuitively it makes a lot of sense: it is how much your body "wants" to weigh, the weight your body tends toward if you make no special effort to lose or gain weight. We all have met people who find it extremely difficult to lose weight. Even if they are moderately active, and if they eat what and when their body tells them to, and not more, they end up very heavy. Their bodies still seem to "defend" a higher weight than other bodies do. And then there are those extremely scrawny people who have to "remember to eat" in order not to become even scrawnier. The first kind of person is one with a high set point, the other, with a low set point.

Laboratory animals, of course, also have set points. One species of mouse known as the "ob/ob" mouse (yes, "ob" stands for obesity, and this mouse has two copies of this particular obesity gene) has an extraordinarily high set point. An ob/ob mouse is so fat it almost looks like a "mouse puddle"—a flattened, circular, fluid blob with a tail on one end and little ears and eyes on the other. These mice have *really* bad genes! On a very severe CR regimen, begun early in life, these mice still do not end up particularly scrawny, yet they live 40 to 50 percent longer on this regimen. They can't be taken to much more extreme levels of CR without endangering their health, even though they are not at all emaciated.

Remember, CR is not about trying to be thin. Weight loss is of course a side effect, but it is not the goal. The goal is putting your body into a state where its energy economy is altered such that maintenance and repair are prioritized. This state is achieved when the body is given less energy than it normally "wants," which will result in the body weighing less than it normally would "want" to weigh.

Technically, set point is often defined as what you weighed during relatively normal periods of your life in your mid- to late twenties. If you were training for a marathon when you were twenty-seven, ignore what you weighed then. If you had to gain fifty pounds to play the part of Henry VIII in your local community theater when you were twenty-nine, ignore what you weighed during that time. Just think of what your "normal weight" during your early adult years was. That's your set point, at least as is often defined by scientists.

Where the art of set point comes in, is that many of us have to make some adjustments to that scientific definition. If you were *always* training for a marathon in your mid- to late twenties, and, especially, if you are significantly thinner than everyone in your family, your set point is probably higher than what you weighed during that period. Your body probably "wanted" to weigh more, to receive more calories, than it did during that period, but wasn't able to because of your training program. And, of course, you may be above your set point for cultural, subcultural, or psychological reasons. Set point, in so far as it is genetically determined, can't have changed in the course of one or two generations. Yet in the U.S., and increasingly, many other countries, average weight has gone way, way up. Determining whether or not your typical weight during your young adult years was the result of your genetic program or cultural influences can thus sometimes be a tricky matter. But once you've got a good idea what your set point is, you'll be ready to start determining your Longevity Diet target weight.

THE "WEIGHT WATCHER" STRATEGY

WITH THE "WEIGHT watcher" strategy, you will plan to lower your body weight by 10 to 25 percent, slowly, over the course of many months, if not a year or two. Early studies of extreme CR initiated in adulthood did not lengthen life, and in some cases even shortened it.[67] The adult body needs time to adjust, at least for more extreme versions of CR. We will explain more about the "caloric descent" in Part II.

If your set point is relatively high, you can probably aim for a 25 percent reduction in weight, perhaps even more, if you're very overweight to begin with. If your set point is very low, reducing your body weight by more than 10 percent could be risky, since there are health problems sometimes associated with extremely low body weight (more specifically, with a BMI below 14 or 15).

Remember, of course, to talk with your health care professional about any significant decisions you make about your health, and to get a few basic tests of the state of your health done before changing your diet. Tests of your health, along with a basic checkup from your doctor make questions of set point and percentage weight loss irrelevant. See sidebar below for some tests you should take. Some of these, such as blood pressure and cholesterol levels, are very likely familiar to you. Others might seem a bit obscure, but your doctor can explain them to you.

Tests you can easily do at home

- Body weight (taken under same conditions each day; upon waking is best).
- Resting pulse (taken the same time each day, under the same conditions, preferably upon waking).
- Body temperature (and save thermometer, in case it is calibrated incorrectly).

Relatively simple, generally cheap tests your health-care professional can order for you

- Standard metabolic panel (includes sodium, potassium, calcium, chloride, carbon dioxide, fasting glucose, blood urea nitrogen [BUN], creatine).
- Liver function panel (includes ALT, AST, Albumin, AP, Bilirubin, and Total Protein).
- Lipids panel (includes total cholesterol, HDL, LDL, and triglycerides).
- Blood pressure (ask for this at every doctor's appointment; also, ask for weight and temperature, for comparison with your own measurements).
- Complete blood-cell count (CBC), including white blood cell with differential and red blood cell.

Slightly more expensive (listed roughly in order of importance)

- T3
- Insulin
- rT3
- Cortisol
- Glycated hemoglobin
- DHEA-S
- Free testosterone
- IGF-1
- Albumin

THE CALORIE COUNTER STRATEGY

ANOTHER APPROACH IS to focus more on how many calories you currently eat, instead of your weight. If you or your doctor thinks you may be overweight, then pick a reasonable target for reduction in calories. For adults in their fifties or sixties or older, reducing energy intake by more than 20 to 30 percent for the long haul is about as far as you should go, unless you're very overweight. But start slow! If you're forty, and currently eat around 3,000 calories/day, and if you simply replace high energy-dense foods with low energy-dense foods, you'll very likely naturally eat less than 3,000 calories/day. And you'll lose weight. If you track what you eat, you'll probably see you're eating 2,500 or 2,600 calories/day. Stay at that level for a few months. Enjoy you new way of eating. Then check with your doctor, discuss your plan to go down to 2,300 or 2,400 calories a day, get a few simple tests of your health done, and proceed. If you feel good, aren't too hungry, and want to get even more CR benefits, check in again with your doctor after a few more months, get a few tests done, and discuss your plan to go further on your caloric descent, shooting maybe for 2,000 calories/day. As long as your health is being tracked by a doctor, and remains strong (and it will probably improve greatly), reducing your caloric intake to 2,000 will almost certainly improve your health further, and poses no risks.

THE HEALTH MARKER STRATEGY

SOME PEOPLE HAVE the time and money to get *lots* of tests done very frequently—once every two or three months. One of our friends on CR puts it this way:

> I don't really know what my set point is. I'm a 5'10", 37- year-old man who weighed around 170 pounds in my twenties, I have a somewhat thick bone structure, so I wasn't at all overweight at 170 pounds, I just had some "love handles." Two years ago when I decided to try the Longevity Diet I more or less guessed that ending up at 145–150 pounds would be a good "CR level" for me. I'm not even sure what reduction in calories that translates to. But I didn't care. I got my cholesterol levels and fasting glucose levels tested (both of which were not so great), and focused first on eating more healthy foods. It wasn't really consciously following CR or the Longevity Diet, I was just eating more "health food." I naturally lost eight pounds very quickly. Then I got more tests done after around two months, and saw that my health had improved. I stuck with that approach for another few months, then started consciously eating less. I still wasn't counting calories, but I weighed myself a few times a week. I started to read food labels to make sure I was getting enough protein. I knew I was getting enough vitamin A and C because of all the veggies and fruit I was eating. Same thing with

> essential fatty acids. And I was almost certainly getting enough B vitamins, but I took a multivitamin pill just to be safe. After a while I had to have a few simple rules to keep my weight from going above 150, such as not eating after 9:00 PM, and not snacking between lunch and dinner. It was hard at first, but I kept thinking about the lowered glucose levels in my blood, the lowered levels of free radical damage, DNA damage, etc. It made it fairly easy to think of the last few hours of the evening as non-snacking hours. They were my "hours of freedom from free radicals." And I pop in to my doctor's to get tests done every 2–3 months. He says my health is excellent, so, even though I'm being kind of "loose" about my CR, it seems to be working extremely well. I may drop down a few more pounds, but I'm going to wait another year or so, just to make sure my current plan "sticks."

THE ELDERLY AND CR

OLDER SOULS MAY be wise and strong, but older bodies tend to be wizened and weakened. We know from animal studies that older animals often don't adapt well to extreme reductions in energy intake. There is of course evidence that those who are over sixty and obese will live longer if they lose weight, but if you're over sixty and not grossly overweight, you should be especially cautious with your Longevity Diet program. You have a huge amount to gain, maybe many extra decades, but don't risk that gain by rushing headlong into an extreme dietary change. Readers over sixty or so (this is a somewhat arbitrary cutoff point, since the relevant studies have not yet been done) should discuss this program thoroughly with their health-care professional, and proceed slowly.

PART 2

THE longevity DIET

The Longevity Lifestyle

6

THE LONGEVITY DIET AS A WAY OF LIFE

READY—SET—WAIT

Remember how, in school, you had to address five key points when writing a review or paper: who, what, when, where, how? Let's do the same thing here.

who?

You, and the rapidly growing number of people who have decided that the Longevity Diet is the most sensible way to improve health and vitality. But primarily, and most importantly, *you*. As you begin to explore and design a healthier life, remember that it is you, yourself that you live with. While that may sound rather trite, the life you move toward should be filled with things *you* love. And this includes what you eat: your dietary choices need to reflect the kinds of meals you want to sit down to, not a rigid regimen of foods you don't enjoy. Using our simple guidelines, you'll be able to tailor the Longevity Diet to suit your individual taste.

Remember, this is not a "Simon Says" diet. And that is a good thing! The probability of sticking with a cookie-cutter regimen of foods you don't like is low. Most dieters fall off the bandwagon of programs that require them to eat only specific foods or entirely shun others, or that impose upon them particular mealtimes regardless of how unnatural those may feel. Keep in mind that the Longevity Diet is, in fact, far more than just a diet. It is a lifestyle program that enables you to take control of your body's health and longevity.

what?

The Longevity Diet, of course!

The Longevity Diet is based on extensive research in a wide variety of disciplines, and is now gaining popularity among open-minded physicians, especially specialists in diabetes, Alzheimer's disease, autoimmune diseases such as lupus, and inflammatory diseases such as rheumatoid arthritis.

The Longevity Diet is often described by its practitioners as the "thinking person's" health program: You will learn about health, you will learn about food, and you will learn about yourself. This knowledge—or rather this lifelong path of learning—will enable you to modify your regimen over the years, as new research results become available, and your body responds to the program. Flexibility is key to success.

when?

Why not start now? Animal studies have shown that, the sooner a CR regimen is adopted, the greater the overall benefits, including an extended, vigorous life span. As Ashley Montagu, (1905–), anthropologist and author of *On Being Human,* said, "The idea is to die young as late in life as possible." Sounds good to us. And remember Dr. Walford's words: "It's a shame to die so young, because it takes so long to learn how to live." You have many,

many years ahead, and potentially more youthful ones, if you start the Longevity Diet now.

where?

Whether you eat at home, in restaurants, at the office, in social situations, or during travel, even to other cultures, you can adapt the Longevity Diet to wherever you are. The diet is easy to assimilate into everyday life and special occasions alike. And there are no absolutes, as with many other health programs; as noted in our introduction, the occasional "cheat" does not derail the regimen, provided you get back on track as soon as you can. Kim Sandstrom notes that "the times I eat off plan are actually more deliberate than a 'letting down of my guard,' and it is easy now, after a year and a half, to get back on the plan at the next meal."

> The first CR Society Conference was held in Las Vegas in 2001. Who showed up? Finally fixing faces with names that we had seen on our e-mail lists and discussion forums, we realized that CR enthusiasts were an eager and motley group of all ages and professions who did not need to wait for a centuries-long human life span study to believe in and begin a health-promoting diet that could potentially ensure a very long life. We had already come to know intimately such details as our complete blood counts, lipid profiles, and food preferences, as well as the effects of calorie restriction on our respective lifestyles. By way of introduction at the conference, we stated our name, age, and occupation, followed by—just for fun—what we each preferred to eat for breakfast. "Oatmeal with a few almonds" started off the rounds, "grapefruit juice and coffee," said another participant. The variety continued, from egg-white omelets with rye toast and a side of applesauce; to kitchen-sink smoothies; to an oddly precise eight almonds, one

brazil nut, three hazelnuts, and four to five macadamia nuts over low-fat cottage cheese.

After a day of presentations on biology, nutrition, longevity, and CR strategies, we were hungry! With such a range of eating strategies, we had a hard time choosing a restaurant: one person was a vegetarian, another preferred raw food, one simply felt like having salmon. In the end, we proceeded to a typical Las Vegas buffet, thinking that there we would each find something that would suit us, and in a way we did—the salad-eaters gathered garnishes from other dishes; the protein-seekers managed with poached salmon. But those were slim pickings from the general fare, and we refrained from protesting to anyone but one another.

In Las Vegas, arguably the adult entertainment capital of the Western world, we thus experienced firsthand the difficulties even in the supposedly enlightened third millennium, of dining healthily in public. Obviously, the Longevity Diet message had yet to reach such restaurateurs . . . or their typical clientele. And so began our mission. Determined to wave the red flag and offer alternatives, we find now that current statistics on obesity, cancer, diabetes, and heart disease indicate that we didn't make quite enough noise back in 2001.

how?

Chapters 7 and 8 will spell out strategies to help you adjust your health habits and guide you through a gradual makeover. And it *should* be a gradual shift; we do not recommend the most extreme Longevity Diet regimen for beginners, even if losing a lot of weight is for you a significant goal. Here is your agenda, in brief: (a) consult your health-care practitioner before you start; (b) learn as much as you can about your own baseline biomarkers and nutrition before you make *any* changes to your diet;

(c) use the worksheets provided for you in chapter 8 to track your progress as you proceed with the diet; (d) sign up with an online group for pointers (see *Resources*), so you will have a support system that you know is on a parallel track with you and will be in touch with CR followers if you have any dietary questions we haven't been able to answer in this book; and (e) stay current on the latest research, via news media, the Internet, and your personal health community.

REMEMBER, THE LONGEVITY DIET WORKS WITH *YOUR* LIFESTYLE

- You can mix and match what you eat—protein, carbohydrate, and fat ratios—as long as you consume a variety of vegetables on a regular basis and observe the nutritional guidelines recommended.
- You can mix and match how you schedule your meals. Depending on your lifestyle, you may prefer to eat your main meal in the morning, or perhaps at night. It is the total caloric content of what you consume across an entire day that counts. Variations in your caloric intake from day to day are okay, as long as the average daily caloric intake remains relatively stable.
- You can mix and match how many times per day you eat, according to your lifestyle and appetite: three regular-size meals a day, one large main meal, or grazing on small meals throughout the day.
- You will discover which foods best fill you up. Some find that protein and fats defer hunger. Others find that low energy-density foods with a high water content satiate them. It's up to you how to balance each meal with your appetite and energy needs.

Q: But, what, exactly, should I eat?

Focus first and foremost on vegetables and fruits. Think of them as a rainbow from which you will obtain a broad range of nutrients:

- **blue**—blueberries
- **purple**—red cabbage, kalamata and black olives, Concord grapes, currants, plums, blackberries, figs, eggplants
- **red**—beets, tomatoes (especially cooked tomatoes and tomato sauces), red peppers, red-skinned onions, apples, cherries, red grapes, watermelon, cranberries, strawberries, raspberries, pomegranates, rhubarb
- **orange**—carrots, winter squash, sweet potatoes, cantaloupe and other orange melons, oranges, clementines, tangerines, apricots, peaches, nectarines, mangoes, persimmons, papayas
- **yellow**—summer squash, corn, yellow-skinned onions, bananas, lemons, grapefruit, pineapple, star fruit
- **green**—especially cabbage and Chinese (Napa) cabbage, romaine lettuce, bok choy, broccoli, Brussels sprouts, kale, collards, Swiss chard, spinach, beet greens, mustard greens, and turnip greens; but also asparagus, okra, cucumbers, zucchini, scallions and leeks, green peppers, celery, green olives, avocados, pears, green grapes, green apples, kiwis, honeydew and other green melons, limes (remember, wax or green beans and peas are actually legumes—and good for you, too)
- **white**—cauliflower, turnips, rutabagas, white potatoes, garlic, mushrooms, jicama, lychee

While many phytonutrients have been synthesized and made available in supplement form, we do not recommend them: such supplements leave out important, if not essential, nutrients found only in genuine foods.

Plants won't be the *only* thing you'll be eating, but should and indeed shall form the "bulk" of your diet: Plants are low in calories so you can eat a lot of them, and they provide the fiber to keep your digestive system moving. They also have a low **energy density**, which means that their water and/or fiber content is high and hence they will satiate you more than the equivalent volume of most nonvegetable foods.

Vegetables can be enjoyed in many different ways—raw as finger-foods (the only notable exceptions: potatoes, sweet potatoes, artichokes, okra, and Brussels sprouts), in soups or salads, extracted as juices, steamed, or stir-fried. Fruit can be eaten out of hand or in a salad, but also incorporated into gelled or baked desserts, drunk as juice or blended into smoothies, or frozen as sorbets and granitas. If you've always hated a particular vegetable or fruit when prepared a particular way, give it another chance in another form or two before rejecting it entirely—and, if you have never sampled some of the above foods at all, buy them in small quantities and experiment. Discover the heady delights of flavored mustards, nut oils, and herb- or fruit-steeped vinegars; stock your pantry with a variety of spices, low-fat dips, and light sauces. Read vegetarian and vegan cookbooks and magazines for inspiration—but if you like to eat meat; just lessen the quantity of it that you consume, while upping the vegetable count. For example, if you love old-fashioned chicken soup, prepare a potful with only one chicken breast and lots of root vegetables, rather than using a whole chicken plus only one carrot, celery rib, and onion. Substitute more flavorful, nutrient-rich fruits or vegetables than celery, when preparing a poultry or fish salad (plain old tuna salad takes on a whole new dimension when paired with grated carrots, chopped red cabbage, chopped fresh cranberries or raspberries, or chopped apple and walnuts). See what happens if you mix various fruit juices with various flavors of soy milk (an amazing combination is mango juice mixed one part to two with chocolate-flavored soy). Play with your food!

> When asked for advice on initiating a plant-based Longevity Diet, Dean suggested: "Buy one of everything in the produce aisle, and start chopping and chomping!"

Q: When should I eat?

Peter Voss, a CR practitioner of seven years, eats many small meals per day. Lisa does not eat until noon, when she will drink fruit or vegetable juice and have a light protein snack. Dean Pomerleau, an active participant in the CR Society, eats two square meals a day, in the morning and the evening, just as Brian does. And April Smith, a savvy twenty-nine-year-old still new to the Longevity Diet, eats differently every day.

Explore what the best time of day may be for you to eat a protein-rich meal. Some people on the Longevity Diet find that protein is what satiates them the most. If your stomach yells at you in the afternoon, it might make sense to have protein at noon. Or, if you refrain from eating after 7:00 p.m., a strategy adopted by some people on strict versions of the diet, then a high-protein breakfast may be an important meal for you.

Many studies show that most people will be more alert throughout the day if they've begun with a nutritious meal. But even though most nutrition and diet books insist that breakfast is the most important meal of the day, it might not work for you. So if you simply don't like breakfast, and you don't feel any worse for the wear without it, don't feel compelled to eat it. Or, if you simply can't face solids at that hour, a smoothie combining milk or soy milk, such fruit as bananas or blueberries, and a little flaxseed oil might be the perfect compromise.

Q: Wait: won't I be hungry?

You may be hungry, at least at first. But we encourage you to experiment and learn which foods fill you up the most, what kinds of foods deter your hunger the most, and which of your hunger cues actually don't relate to food at all, but to particular settings or emotions. (Technically, these are, in fact, three separate issues.) Each of the major elements that make up foods—protein, fats, carbohydrates, fiber, sugar, and water—has a specific effect on satiety, both short-term (degree of fullness) and long-term (degree of hunger deterrence).

Let's place two meals side by side: One is piled high with a large assortment of vegetables, including spinach, broccoli, cabbage, red pepper, mushrooms, sweet potato, plus some cooked grains, a glass of milk, and a slender piece of meat. This meal is mostly vegetables with 3 ounces (85 grams) of protein. It totals 650 calories and is roughly 28 percent protein, 49 percent carbohydrates, and 23 percent healthy fats.

The other meal includes a generous (3.5 ounce) piece of salmon, 1 tablespoon of olive oil–sautéed red pepper fajitas, broccoli, carrots, a sauce made of tomato paste and ricotta cheese, and a glass of milk. This meal totals 640 calories, but the protein and carbohydrate totals are 33 and 32 percent respectively while the fat content is 35 percent.

Which meal would you prefer? Nutritionally, they actually differ only slightly: The veggie-based meal is lower in cholesterol and sodium, and it is higher in fiber and has a much higher water content. The salmon- and fajitas-based meal is higher in some vitamins. They are both healthy, nutritious meals. But which would fill you up the most?

The vegetable dish is based on one of Dr. Walford's weekly salad recipes. Vegetables have a high water content, plenty of fiber, and are low in calories, hence you can eat a lot of them. This meal will make you feel more immediately full. The fajitas, sautéed in heart-healthy olive oil, along with the additional omega-3 fatty acids in the salmon and the fat content of the ricotta cheese sauce, will take longer to digest, and this may sustain you through your hunger and your stomach through its fantasies. You see, both methods work, see which one works best for you!

Q. How much protein should I eat?

Some people following on the Longevity Diet believe it is important to eat extra protein. There is actually little solid empirical evidence for this, but there are some theoretical reasons why this might be wise. Peter, for example, is especially careful to get lots of protein. According to U.S. government recommendations, he would only need 52 grams of protein for his current weight of 130 pounds. Yet, three years into his CR program, he actually increased his protein intake by 10 grams per day, from 75, already more than the government recommendations would indicate, to 85 grams. We don't yet know whether unusual increases in protein intake are indicated for most people on CR, but anyone on CR, especially very severe CR, should, of course, be followed by a physician. Based on your exercise habits and other needs peculiar to your own life and body, you and your physician can determine a level of protein intake that makes sense for you

Note, however, that during the weight loss phase of the diet, as opposed to the "maintenance phase," it might be important to get a more protein than you otherwise might need. Whether you prefer fish, lean meats, poultry, legumes, or soy products, this is, fortunately, very easy to do!

If you are a vegetarian, low-fat dairy products, legumes, nuts, soy, and perhaps tempeh are already your primary protein sources. Include smaller amounts of grains, brown rice, quinoa, rye, wheat berries, and such whole cereals as amaranth, to build complementary protein sources. If you eat eggs, omelets made with more egg whites than yolks are an excellent source of protein, as are soufflés. These protein recommendations may seem difficult to attain if you are a vegan, that is, if you eat no animal products whatsoever, not even cheese or milk. But Lisa has been a vegan for six years, and has had no adverse effects from her diet.

Q. What kind of fats should I eat?

An oil is an oil when it comes to calories—100 percent fat.

But when it comes to nutritional benefits, all oils are not equal. Consume predominantly monounsaturated fats, avoid saturated fats, and aim for more of the omega-3 form of polyunsaturated fats than the omega-6 form. Most oils consist almost entirely of these four types of fat, in different combinations. The most commonly available and healthy monounsaturated fats are olive and canola oils. Canola oil is preferable for baking, and is less expensive than olive oil; it also has more omega-3 than all other commonly available cooking oils. We prefer the taste, however, of olive oil in stir-fries. And there is nothing like the fragrance of a good olive oil in salads!

Olive oil is rich in antioxidants and a substance called *squalene,* that has anti-inflammatory properties. Produced in the liver, squalene helps keep your skin moist and is an intermediary in the biosynthesis of cholesterol, hence it helps somewhat to lower cholesterol. The antioxidant polyphenols found in extra-virgin olive oil help protect against heart disease and lower blood pressure.

Recent evidence suggests that olive oil may protect against breast cancer.[68] A study conducted by the Harvard School of Public Health and the Athens School of Public Health on over 2,000 women indicated a 25 percent reduction in breast cancer for women who ate more than a single serving of olive oil a day. But remember, be moderate—even olive oil is still 100 percent fat.

Olive oils are pressed from the whole, ripe fruit of the olive, and are hence "fruit" oils, as compared to "seed oils," such as flax or walnut. *Virgin* olive oils are the only unrefined oil available to the mass market. By the time an oil is bleached, processed, and deodorized, it is robbed of its natural antioxidants, phytosterols, (found in pigment), and other nutrients. *Pure* olive oils have been refined, despite the contradiction in the name! *Light* or *extra-light* olive oils refer to color and flavor, not calories! This olive oil is also refined, stripped of its olive taste and color. Avoid the refined oils, and select extra-virgin or virgin olive oil.

Olive oils are also classified by acidity, color, flavor, and aroma. Their taste varies according to the climate, soil, variety of tree, and ripeness of the fruit when picked. Similar to wine, the etiquette of the lofty olive, called "liquid gold" by Homer, has become quite sophisticated. Oils are graded according to their bitterness, whether they are pungent, fruity, musty, or oxidized (another term for a rancid flavor). *Consumer Reports* defines fruity as "a high-quality oil that may have the flavor and aroma of ripe olives—nutty, buttery, or floral. Or it can have a 'green olive' character, with flavors and aromas reminiscent of grass, vegetables, herbs, green banana, green apple, eucalyptus, or mint."[69]

Extra-virgin is the prima donna of olive oils. Generally used in smaller amounts on salads and pasta, a quality extra-virgin olive oil may cost more, but its robust flavor can virtually make the dish. Olive oils that are rich in color are generally more pungent, while the lighter varieties may be mild or even taste-free.

You may prefer a richer extra-virgin olive oil for salads, roasted vegetables and pasta, but a milder, less expensive virgin olive oil for stir-fries and sauteing.

Flaxseed oil is the richest source of omega-3 fatty acids, among the vegetable oils. We always add a little flaxseed oil to salads. You may also grind flaxseed (available at health food stores) in a coffee grinder and add the ground seeds, rich with their freshly released oil, to your salad, smoothie, or vegetables. Take care never to heat flaxseed oil, though it may be sprinkled on cooked foods. This is the only oil that needs to be kept cool to remain fresh; find it in the refrigerator case at your health food store, and pop it into your fridge as soon as you bring it home.

Walnut and hemp oils are runners-up after olive, canola, and flaxseed oils. They contain a higher percentage of omega-6 fatty acid than the omega-3, but are still healthier than other mainstream fats and oils (butter, soy, safflower); and will offer variety to your meals. Hemp oil has a rich, lightly nutty taste that nicely complements a steamed vegetable salad.

FOODS HIGH IN OMEGA-3

- salmon, sardines, herring (other fish from very cold waters)
- canola, olive, flaxseed, hemp, and walnut oils
- flaxseeds, walnuts
- kale, collard greens (other green leafy vegetables)

FOODS HIGH IN OMEGA-6

- corn, safflower, cottonseed, and sunflower oils

ORAC FOODS

THE **OXYGEN RADICAL Absorbance Capacity (ORAC)** assay is a test-tube analysis that measures the total antioxidant power of foods. The assay could in theory be applied to all foodstuffs and ingredients, but initial testing has focused solely on fruits and vegetables, since these contain the most antioxidants. According to research conducted by the USDA Agricultural Research Service Human Research Center at Tufts University in Boston, eating foods rated high on this scale has been shown to increase the antioxidant levels in human blood by as much as 25 percent.[70] These foods are good free radical scavengers and will protect against natural age-related oxidative stress.

By the middle of this century, nearly one-third of the U.S. population is expected to be over the age of sixty-five. If further research supports these early findings, millions of aging people may be able to guard against diseases or dementia simply by adding high-ORAC foods to their diets, even without the Longevity Diet. "It may be that combinations of nutrients found in foods have greater protective effects than each nutrient taken alone," said Guohua (Howard) Cao, a physician and chemist who developed the ORAC assay.[71]

Many CR practitioners favor vegetables over grains, since they are foods with low energy density. In addition, vegetables and fruits rate highest on the ORAC scale. Of course whole grains are also extremely healthy; they are rich in fiber and contain many minerals, and, together with vegetables, can form a complete protein. The Longevity Diet favors vegetables over grains, so you would benefit by switching from a dish of predominantly grain plus a few vegetables to a dish with many vegetables and only a little grain. Pasta Primavera made with lots of vegetables and less than a standard portion of whole-wheat pasta will fill you up, give you ample phytonutrients and antioxidants, and is low in calories. The foods in Table 6.1 are the best ORAC foods you can eat; see pages 136–155 for a table showing the ORAC levels of other foods.

TABLE 6.1

TOP-SCORING ORAC FOODS PER 100 GRAMS (3.5 OUNCES)

Eat at least 3,000 units daily

FRUITS		VEGETABLES	
Prunes	5770	Kale	1770
Raisins	2830	Spinach	1260
Blueberries	2400	Brussels sprouts	980
Blackberries	2036	Alfalfa sprouts	930
Strawberries	1540	Broccoli florets	890
Raspberries	1220	Beets	840
Plums	949	Red bell pepper	710
Oranges	750	Onion	450
Red Grapes	739	Corn	400
Cherries	670	Eggplant	390
Kiwi	602	Sweet potato	301
Grapefruit, pink	483	Peas	300

ENERGY DENSITY

ENERGY DENSITY IN food is a relative newcomer to many of us, familiar as we are with other measures of nutrition in food, such as RDAs, Daily Food Values, and percentage of calories from protein and fat. Many people on the Longevity Diet simply aim for foods that have high nutrient density. If you are trying to eat fewer calories (i.e., are trying to take in less energy), what matters most is that you get more nutrients *per calorie*; focusing on foods with high nutrient density is simply a way of achieving that goal.

Energy density is an entirely different measurement of food. And it isn't precisely the inverse of nutrient density. Energy density concerns the amount of calories in a set measurement of a particular food versus the quantity you should reasonably eat of that food. For example, 1 ounce of grapes has 20 calories, while 1 ounce of raisins has 84. What is the difference? Water content. And it's the water content that helps fill you up. Foods that provide many calories in a small portion of food, like the raisins, are high energy-dense foods; while foods that feature fewer calories for the same weight of food, the grapes, are low energy-dense.

NUTRIENT DENSITY

High nutrient-dense foods are healthy, nutritious foods, packed with vitamins, minerals, and other essential nutrients. Foods can be nutrient-dense and be low in calories, or, surprisingly, nutrient dense and high in calories. The staples of the Longevity Diet are foods that are both nutrient dense and low in calories.

ENERGY DENSITY

Low energy-dense foods are high in volume and low in calories. Since water has an energy density of zero, foods with a high water content are low energy-dense foods, and therefore high in volume.

> Eating these foods means you eat more food yet fewer calories. High energy density means that the energy in the food is dense, and thus smaller; less filling portions contain more calories.

To get the best of both worlds, we should try to eat nutrient-dense/low-calorie meals that are composed of low energy-dense foods. Now that is a tongue twister! But it's not that complicated: choose foods that are high in essential nutrients, but low in calories, and high in volume (fiber, which is indigestible, or water), and you'll feel sated yet won't have eaten a high-calorie meal. A few simple changes to your diet are a good way to start. For example, use whole-grain pasta instead of noodles made from bleached flour, and add lots of vegetables to the dish. You will have a nutrient-rich low calorie and low energy-dense meal. Or, using our grapes and raisins example, a small bunch of red grapes will make you feel fuller, at a cost of far less calories, than will a handful of raisins.

At the other extreme: cheese, chocolate, nuts, and chips are high energy-dense foods; their fat content is much higher than that of fresh fruit and vegetables. Some of these foods are nutrient-dense, and in some instances you should chose high energy-dense foods for their nutritional value. The trick is that you need to eat them in small portions. The avocado is a fine example, rich in healthy monounsaturated fats; the 45 calories in one ounce of succulent avocado flesh (roughly a half-inch slice from a medium-size avocado) will provide vitamin E and fiber. It is, however, a high energy-dense food; hence, guacamole is energy-dense (and we never stop with just one tablespoon on two chips, do we? Try extending guacamole with chopped tomatoes or cooked mashed asparagus to dilute the density).

See the Food Data table on pages 136–155 for the energy density of foods. Keep in mind that what fills you up in the moment may not defer your hunger over a day as effectively as other types of foods. That is the challenge. Fats may take as long as five to seven hours to digest, proteins take up to four hours, and whole foods or complex carbohydrates take about two hours. Refined sugars pass through really quickly, in only thirty minutes. You will have to experiment a bit to see what suits your particular metabolism and lifestyle. For example, although fats log twice as many calories as carbohydrates, including them in your meals will slow the absorption of other foods, and will therefore help to stave off hunger. Likewise, adding a little protein to a largely carbohydrate meal will deter hunger longer. If you are a night owl who works deep into the wee hours, perhaps your dinnertime should be kicked back to a later hour if that meal is primarily carbs, to provide you with the energy you need to keep going.

THE CALORIE COUNTDOWN

If you feel burdened by numbers and calculations, then proceed to the Weight Watcher section of this book, page 173. However, if you are a numbers person or a whiz on the computer, you just hit a home run: following your natural inclination here will reward you with a satisfying transition into life on the Longevity Diet. Some members of the CR Society have designed their own interface to the USDA food database using Excel spreadsheets. Others make use of commercially available nutrition software programs.

what should you track? and how often?

The following chapter will explain how to keep a journal of your meals and how to figure their calorie content. The calories, as well as nutritional content, of what you eat can be averaged over several days—the Longevity Diet is not about a struggle to get *precisely* 100 percent of *all* vitamins and minerals every single day. Beyond reducing your intake of calories, your priorities should be:

1. to eat enough protein for your body weight and level of CR (especially if you are a vegetarian)
2. to get adequate amounts of omega-3 fatty acids
3. to eliminate processed foods from your diet

Beyond that, eating enough fiber, low-GI carbohydrates, and foods rich in antioxidants should all be key elements of your Longevity Diet program. But these latter goals can make slow entrances, as you learn to eliminate unhealthy foods from your diet.

In the beginning, do your best to jettison all junk food, all empty calories. However, be compassionate with those moments of surrender to temptation, or the occasional meaningful splurge like a slice of birthday cake. The Longevity Diet is about saying yes to life; you can always make up for a cheese-and-wine sampler the next day with an especially high-nutrition, low-calorie meal. Indeed, in time you will find that a plate of colorful veggies is as much a yes to life as is a celebratory piece of cake with friends. Ultimately, CR can be seen as extending your food options, not restricting them. And it certainly extends your life!

It does help, if you are new to watching calories, to read the labels on everything. Brand names, and even similar products produced by the same company, can vary widely in nutrient, fat, sodium, and sugar content. West Soy, for example, markets regular soy milk, enriched soy milk, and low-fat soy milk. If you include packaged foods in whatever CR program you use, compare the labels occasionally to see whether the manufacturer has changed any elements, particularly if a product has been repackaged as "improved."

STRIKING THE RIGHT BALANCE

- Phytonutrient-rich foods *must* be included. Eat at least seven to nine servings of colorful fruits and vegetables per day, as described on page 104.

- If you're not a vegetarian, and you don't want to try a very extreme version of CR, it is a good idea to eat at least two servings per week of a fatty fish, in particular wild Atlantic or canned salmon, sardines, and herring. (As strange as it might sound, mash and eat the bones of canned salmon or sardines along with the fish, for extra calcium.) If you eat meat, choose 100 percent meat in low-fat cuts: lean red meats and pork, the light meat of poultry; avoid deli meats, frankfurters, "mystery meat" fast-food hamburgers, and bacon, all of which are rife with filler, chemicals, and fat. And eat some nuts (but not handfuls at one sitting!), especially walnuts, Brazil nuts, and almonds, which are rich in healthy oils as well as important minerals.
- When you cook with oils, use primarily monounsaturated fats, such as olive or canola oil. Eliminate trans fatty acids from your diet; these are found in margarines, dressings, and deep-fried foods. (If you see "hydrogenated" in an ingredients list, the food has trans fatty acids in it.)
- Adequate calcium is especially important in the Longevity Diet; consider supplements, particularly if you avoid dairy products. Get into the habit of using skim or 2% milk rather than whole milk, and choose low-fat yogurts and cheeses. When selecting soy milks and yogurts, remember to read the ingredients label showing the vitamin and mineral content: some (even made by the same company) are more enriched than others.
- Choose whole grains over enriched grains: whole wheat or multigrain artisan breads, brown rice rather than white rice, whole-grain pasta. Add legumes to your diet in the form of beans and peas, legume-based soups, peanut butter, hummus, soy products, and bean sprouts.
- Don't neglect plant proteins, if you're a vegetarian. Vegetarians can consider eating tempeh, seitan, calcium-fortified tofu, and low-fat soy products.

- Adequate fiber is important: choose whole foods over processed or refined foods, and do not overcook your grains and vegetables.
- Avoid foods high in refined sugar (watch out for corn syrup, pervasive in sweetened soft drinks and juices, even those sold in health food stores). Remember that, though natural, honey, maple syrup, brown rice syrup, and other sweeteners are essentially just sugar.
- Watch your ORAC and energy-density levels: keep the first high and the second low.

RODNEY SAYS

CR doesn't seem to be particularly difficult so far. Perhaps snacking after 7:00 PM is something I would like to get better under control. An automatic timed lock on the refrigerator door that unlocks at 6:00 AM and locks at 7:00 PM might help? Sounds a bit Draconian, but might be worth trying!

I started CR quite gradually, by exerting marginally more control over my caloric intake than I was used to. The result has been a weight loss of about half a pound a week. The quality of my diet has always been good, so I tried to cut back on calories by eating fewer starches. I learned what I could to further improve the quality of my meals: I started eating lots of soups, especially homemade, containing all the foods believed to be the healthiest, whether or not the conventional wisdom believes they belong in soup! Multiple vegetable; tomato; miso; commercial chicken noodle with green vegetables added; bean and pea. I avoid fats in general, trans fats and cancer-implicated oils in particular. And I eat at least some fish pretty much every day, 90 percent of it canned—salmon, mackerel, sardines, tuna, or herring.

7

YOUR DAILY FOOD DIARY

LET'S FACE IT, your relationship to food is one of the most basic relationships that you have. In the very first phase of your life, the milk in your mother's breast was the simple answer to your body's most pressing nutritional needs. Not long thereafter, life became much more complicated. With life's complications came food on the run, food from machines, instant or processed food, school cafeteria and restaurant food, and party food.

Food can calm you when you are under duress; it can also relate powerful feelings to others—cooking something sensual for a romantic partner, generously providing a magnificent spread for family or friends. To many people, food represents bonding with the people closest to you, a literal reassertion of how well you understand each other's tastes. From the moment you left your mother's milk behind, food has been about far more than simply satisfying your hunger.

In this chapter you will learn to separate what you eat from all the extra meanings and circumstances that surround it, by keeping a diary that makes you conscious of what you are ingesting, and when. Unlike life, there is nothing complicated about it: this diary is intentionally straightforward, to enable you to use it unhesitatingly and, though consciously, un*self*-consciously. When you know that you will be reviewing later what you write down today, this awareness shall eventually inspire you to make better food choices—or, at least more thoughtful ones. Be patient with yourself—you will be the only person reading this diary, and if you slip every so often with a large meal or sugary snack, consider such slips useful information about behaviors that could still use some attention.

While you record what you eat and drink, think about (perhaps even jot down) the influences that may have affected your dining decisions: emotional triggers, what people were eating in your presence, and other situations that tend to push you into reactive or mechanical patterns. For example, consider restaurant dining: do you habitually fill up on bread as you wait for the meal you ordered to be prepared for you, even if it means taking home a "doggy bag" of a main dish you then cannot finish? Do you feel obligated to have an appetizer if not ordering one would make you the only person at the table without one? As you notice such tendencies, your diary will help prepare you to change your dietary behaviors to saying no or making substitutions, ultimately consuming only those foods that will do your body the most good.

Do not think about calories at this point. If you get obsessed about numerical details in the beginning, you may overlook the sensory pleasures of eating wholesome foods, which is what this diet is all about. A week after you begin the diary, you will consider the nutritional content of what you normally consume, and then finally its caloric content. But for now, for one week you will simply write down your meals and snacks . . . your baseline diet.

Start by writing down everything you eat and drink. Yes, *everything*, even if it's just a cracker with your soup or a glass of milk before bedtime. There is no rigid format as to how to keep your diary; if you are a grazer rather than a three-meals-per-day person, ignore the meal/snack headings in the chart that follows and just write down what you eat at what hour. The important thing is to remember to write everything down. The times of day do become an important factor later along, as they will help you figure out which mealtimes or snack times are more habitual than nutrient-necessary for you, as well as which kinds of nutrients your body seems to crave at certain hours.

DAILY FOOD DIARY

DAY OF THE WEEK: **TIME**

BREAKFAST

MORNING SNACK

LUNCH

AFTERNOON SNACK

DINNER

EVENING SNACK

A typical day's jottings might look like this:

DAILY FOOD DIARY

DAY OF THE WEEK:	TIME
BREAKFAST	*7:30*
2 scrambled eggs with 2 slices bacon	
1 cup orange juice	
English muffin with 2 tablespoons butter	
black coffee	
MORNING SNACK	*11:00*
Starbucks maple scone	
Starbucks coffee Frappuccino	
LUNCH	*1:00*
hamburger (single patty on bun) with slice of tomato, ketchup, and mayo	
3 oz. French fries	
10 oz. Coca-Cola	
AFTERNOON SNACK	*4:00*
1 oz. peanuts	
banana	
black coffee	
DINNER	*8:00*
cocktail; 12 oz. beer	
6 crackers with cheese	
1 cup lentil soup	
dinner roll with butter	
1 glass (8 oz.) white wine	
3 oz. broiled salmon with tartar sauce	
1/2 cup carrots	
3/4 cup mashed potatoes	
EVENING SNACK	*10:30*
apple pie with 1 scoop ice cream	
1 cup milk	

TRACKING YOUR NUTRIENTS

ONCE YOU HAVE recorded a week's worth of meals, transfer your diary notations into the Nutrition Tracker that follows, using our breakdown below to note which nutritional factors, such as protein or calcium, comprise each of the foods and beverages you have recorded. Some individual foods or a dish involving several ingredients may bridge more than one category, in which case you will need to check off all appropriate categories for that food. For instance, salmon contains both protein and omega-3; if you have lentil soup and crackers, you would check off both protein and whole grains (lentils), and enriched grains (crackers). If you have a nutrition software program (see *Resources*), use it to help you monitor the nutritional value of your selected foods and beverages.

how to list foods and beverages in the nutrient tracker

1. **Vegetables and Fruits:** vegetables and fruits, 100 percent vegetable and fruit juices, and vegetable products, such as tomato sauce.
2. **Whole Grains:** whole grains and whole-grain products, legumes.
3. **Protein:** eggs, poultry, fish, meat, nuts, soy products, legumes, cheese.
4. **Omega-3:** salmon, sardines, and coldwater fish; olive or canola oil; flaxseeds; walnuts; Brazil nuts; avocados.
5. **Fats:** hydrogenated polyunsaturated fats (most margarines and dressings); monounsaturated fats from meat, poultry, or dairy sources (such as butter); rich sauces.
6. **Calcium:** dairy products, soy and tofu, dark green leafy vegetables, fish eaten with their soft bones (such as canned salmon or sardines).

7. **Enriched Foods and Sweets:** enriched grains such as white rice, and enriched-grain products: most cereals, crackers, pasta, breads, processed and fast foods—any food high in corn syrup, which is pervasive in commercial brands—most dairy desserts and baked desserts, granulated sugar and honey, jams and jellies, candy, soft drinks and non-100 percent juice drinks such as cranberry juice cocktail and spritzers.
8. **Miscellaneous:** condiments such as catsup, prepared mustard, salsa, jam; beverages such as tea, coffee, seltzer water, and water.

NUTRITION TRACKER

List each food from your daily food journal and place it in the proper column(s)

TODAY'S DATE:

FOODS YOU ATE TODAY	VEGETABLES & FRUIT	WHOLE GRAINS & WHOLE GRAIN PRODUCTS	PROTEIN	OMEGA-3 FOODS & FATS

FATS	CALCIUM FOODS	ENRICHED OR FAST FOODS & SWEETS	MISC.	CALORIES

Here's how our meal example would add up:

NUTRITION TRACKER

List each food from your daily food journal and place it in the proper column(s)

TODAY'S DATE:

FOODS YOU ATE TODAY	VEGETABLES & FRUIT	WHOLE GRAINS & WHOLE GRAIN PRODUCTS	PROTEIN	OMEGA-3 FOODS & FATS
Breakfast, 7:30	*8 oz. orange juice*	*English muffin*	*2 scrambled eggs* *2 slices bacon*	
Morning Snack, 11:00		*Starbucks maple scone*		
Lunch, 1:00	*slice tomato*		*hamburger patty*	
Afternoon Snack, 4:00	*banana*		*1 oz. peanuts*	
Cocktail, 7:15			*cheese*	
Dinner, 8:00	*¾ cup mashed potatoes* *½ cup carrots* *lentil soup*		*1 cup lentil soup* *3 oz. salmon*	
Evening Snack	*apple pie*			

BUT WHAT ABOUT CALORIES?

THE FINAL STEP in structuring your food diary—once you have become familiar with the nutrients of the foods you eat, and have perhaps already begun selecting foods that can be listed in the healthier categories—is to begin calculating how many calories you are consuming per portion size. Packaged foods usually include the calorie count per serving on the area

FATS	CALCIUM FOODS	ENRICHED OR FAST FOODS & SWEETS	MISC.	CALORIES
2 tsp. butter			*coffee*	
			Starbucks coffee Frappuccino	
mayonnaise		*white bread bun* *3 oz. French fries* *ketchup (sugar)* *10 oz. Coca-Cola*		
			coffee	
		12 oz. beer *crackers*		
2 tsp. butter *tartar sauce* *¼ cup milk (in potatoes)*	*2 tsp. butter*	*dinner roll with butter*	*8 oz. white wine*	
	1 scoop ice cream	*apple pie* *1 scoop ice cream*		

of the package that contains ingredient information. Do take portion size seriously: a cup of a particular fresh vegetable, such as steamed kale, may be considerably more than you are accustomed to eating, and if you eat less, the calories you list for it need to be lowered accordingly; on the other hand, when you fill your bowl with breakfast cereal, you may be eating far more than the serving size suggested on the side box panel that contains its calorie information. This goes for every food down the list: if you've never actually measured your servings, it might be helpful for you to weigh in grams on a food scale or pour into a measuring cup the amounts that the calorie chart or package label specifies as a serving. Don't worry, you won't be measuring food your whole life! After a while you will be able to eyeball the correct amount. You'll get used to the idea that a healthy serving of fish, poultry, or meat should not exceed the size of the palm of your hand.

NUTRITION TRACKER

List each food from your daily food journal and place it in the proper column(s)

TODAY'S DATE:

FOODS YOU ATE TODAY	VEGETABLES & FRUIT	WHOLE GRAINS & WHOLE GRAIN PRODUCTS	PROTEIN	OMEGA-3 FOODS & FATS
Breakfast, 7:30	*8 oz. orange juice*	*English muffin*	*2 scrambled eggs* *2 slices bacon*	
Morning Snack, 11:00		*Starbucks maple scone*		
Lunch, 1:00	*slice tomato*		*hamburger patty*	
Afternoon Snack, 4:00	*banana*		*1 oz. peanuts*	
Cocktail, 7:15			*cheese*	
Dinner, 8:00	*¾ cup mashed potatoes* *½ cup carrots* *lentil soup*		*1 cup lentil soup* *3 oz. salmon*	
Evening Snack	*apple pie*			

Once you become familiar with what constitutes a portion and standardize how much you typically consume, filling the calories into your Nutrient Tracker will become a simple matter of looking up what calories you listed for that food when you last ate it.

When you are ready to include the calorie count of your foods, begin fill in the last column on the Nutrient Tracker on pages 126–127. Our sample meal would add up as follows:

FATS	CALCIUM FOODS	ENRICHED OR FAST FOODS & SWEETS	MISC.	CALORIES
2 tsp. butter			*coffee*	630
			Starbucks coffee Frappuccino	550
mayonnaise		*white bread bun* *3 oz. French fries* *ketchup (sugar)* *10 oz. Coca-Cola*		1,000
			coffee	240
		12 oz. beer *crackers*		460
2 tsp. butter *tartar sauce* *¼ cup milk (in potatoes)*	*2 tsp. butter*	*dinner roll with butter*	*8 oz. white wine*	850
	1 scoop ice cream	*apple pie* *1 scoop ice cream*		500
			TOTAL	4,233

WHAT A CR DAILY FOOD DIARY MIGHT LOOK LIKE

As you will see from the following example, Lisa eats her main meal at night. She is a vegan, meaning that she eats no animal or dairy products, not even cheese. From the list below, she made the assessment that her diet was a little low in protein, and was

LISA'S NUTRITION TRACKER

List each food from your daily food journal and place it in the proper column(s)

TODAY'S DATE:

FOODS YOU ATE TODAY	VEGETABLES & FRUIT	WHOLE GRAINS & WHOLE GRAIN PRODUCTS	PROTEIN	OMEGA-3 FOODS & FATS
breakfast			*4 walnuts, 6 almonds, 10 peanuts*	*walnuts*
morning snack	*1" avocado slice*	*½ slice whole wheat toast*	*2 tbsp. hummus spread (chickpeas)*	*1" avocado slice*
midafternoon snack	*16 oz. apple/beet/carrot juice*			
dinner	*Steamed: broccoli, red pepper, kale, tomato, squash, sweet potato, onions, cauliflower* *½ cup tomato sauce*		*2 oz. baked tofu*	*1 tsp. olive oil* *1 tsp. flax oil*
evening snack			*10 toasted almonds*	

high in heart-healthy fats. You will see she recorded everything she ate, even if it was only a light snack.

Lisa's food list includes these servings totals by category: approximately 10 servings of veggies and fruits; protein, 3 servings; omega-3, 2 servings; fats, 2 servings; calcium, 1 serving. She takes calcium and B_{12} supplements.

FATS	CALCIUM FOODS	ENRICHED OR FAST FOODS & SWEETS	MISC.	CALORIES
			black tea	
	2 oz. baked tofu		*black pepper* *marjoram*	

AS YOU BEGIN THE LONGEVITY DIET

Now that you understand how to keep a Daily Food Diary, use it (page 122), along with the Nutrient Tracker on pages 126–127 to record the foods and beverages that you consume. Refer to chapter 6 for ways to improve the nutritional content of your intake while reducing such unhealthy elements as processed carbs, and chart your progress.

Don't despair if the record-keeping feels complicated at first; once you become accustomed to viewing your foods with an eye toward their categories, keeping the lists will become much easier. Indeed, as you become comfortable with what constitutes healthy foods, you will enjoy finding ever more creative ways to keep clear of the "unhealthy" columns, as well as to nip and tuck your calorie intake. Think of making substitutions as playing a game in which the lowest scores advance you toward the winner's box: each week, try to beat last week's low calorie count, or to keep from eating anything that would require you to place a check in an "unhealthy" column. For instance, if you find yourself at a food court, opting for sushi or all-veggie fajitas would be the way to go, rather than heading for the burger counter—bing! you won that round! Remember to eat something super-nutritious to make up for any slips into the high-yet-nutritionally-empty-calorie columns. Whatever you do, keep in mind that your goal is not to write down less and less *food,* but to eat a satisfying quantity and range of nutritious, low-calorie foods fitting into as many *healthy* categories as possible.

Following is a table of foods and beverages, listing their calories per serving size, and also the degree to which they are nutritious (ORAC and Energy Density). Again, don't be intimidated by this degree of information. In time, you will learn which foods have similar numbers, and will be able to make healthy everyday dining selections without always needing to consult the charts. For more information, you might also wish to visit these Web sites:

http://yarrow.best.vwh.net/Usda_data/foods_db.html: A companion piece to this book, attached to Dr. Walford's Web site. It is a search engine that delivers almost everything you need to know about more than five thousand foods—vitamins, minerals, and the percentage of calories from fat, protein, and carbohydrates are all listed in an accessible format.

http://yarrow.best.vwh.net/Usda_data/foods.cgi?state_num=5: A highly informative extension of the basic search engine on Walford.com that allows you to compare and identify foods that are highest or lowest in twenty-eight nutrient categories. However, please note that it does not feature many name-brand foods.

www.calorieking.com/: A very user-friendly site. Its nutrient data are limited to nutrition label material, but there are many name brands listed. If you are looking for nutritional information about commercially packaged and processed foods and fast foods, this is the place.

www.nal.usda.gov/fnic/foodcomp/search/index.html: The most comprehensive site, albeit a bit unwieldy to use. Even includes a complete lipid breakdown, i.e., what kinds of fats are in each food.

FOOD DATA TABLE

FOOD	SERVING SIZE	CALORIES	GRAMS	ORAC Choose high values	ENERGY DENSITY (cal/gr) Choose low values
Vegetables					
Artichokes	Base ends & leaves	26	100	26	0.3
Asparagus	4 large spears	24	100		0.2
Beet Greens	1 cup, cooked	40	150		0.3
Beets	1 cup, diced	60	140	715	0.4
Broccoli	1 medium stalk	50	180	817	0.3
Brussels Sprouts	2 large	59	140	412	0.4
Cabbage	1 cup, finely shredded	23	90	380	0.3
Cabbage, Chinese (Napa)	1 cup, 1-inch pieces	9	75		0.1
Cabbage, Red	1 cup, shredded	27	100	210	0.3
Carrots	1 carrot (7½″ × 1⅛″)	35	80	160	0.4
Cauliflower	1 cup florets	25	100		0.3
Celeriac	¼ of one large	42	100		0.4
Celery	1 cup, chopped	19	120	120	0.2
Chard	¼ lb.	21	115		0.2
Corn	kernels of 1 cob (5″ × 1¾″)	110	140	320	0.8
Corn	½ cup frozen prepared	65	82	65	0.8
Cucumber	1 small (6″ × 1½″)	21	180	60	0.1
Eggplant	1 cup, diced	56	200	95	0.3
Garlic	1 clove (1⅓″ × ½″ × ⅓″)	5	3	58	1.7
Kale	¼ lb.	32	115	1500	0.3
Leeks	3 to 4 (5″)	31	100		0.3
Lettuce, Iceberg	Wedge ⅛ of head	10	90	200	0.1

FOOD	SERVING SIZE	CALORIES	GRAMS	**ORAC** *Choose high values*	**ENERGY DENSITY** *(cal/gr) Choose low values*
Lettuce, Romaine	1 cup, chopped	8	55		0.2
Mushrooms, Button	1 cup, sliced or diced	17	70		0.2
Mushrooms, Shiitake	2 oz. dried	162	55		0.3
Onions	1 cup, chopped	60	160	720	0.4
Parsley	1 teaspoon, chopped	2	4		0.5
Pepper, Green Bell	1 cup, strips	27	100		0.3
Pepper, Red Bell	1 large or 1 cup, strips	27	100	700	0.3
Potato, White	2¾″ × 4¼″	220	202	200	1.1
Potato, Sweet	5″ × 2″	117	114		1.0
Potato, Baked (new white or sweet)	1 potato	145		145	0.7
Radishes, Red	10 small (1″ diam.)	20	100		0.2
Spinach	1 cup, chopped, raw	6	30	1150	0.2
Spinach	1 cup, cooked	41	180		0.2
Squash, Summer	1 cup, cubed	26	130	360	0.2
Squash, Winter	1 cup, baked	75	205		0.4
Tomato	2½″ diam.	21	100	233	0.2
Turnip Greens	¼ lb.	34	115		0.3
Water Chestnuts	4 chestnuts	12	25		0.5
Yams	¼ lb.	133	115		1.2

FRUIT

Apples	1 medium (2¾″ diam.)	59	100	300	0.6
Applesauce, Unsweetened	½ cup	43	100		0.4

FOOD	SERVING SIZE	CALORIES	GRAMS	ORAC *Choose high values*	ENERGY DENSITY *(cal/gr) Choose low values*
Apricots	1 medium	19	40	58	0.5
Avocado	1 medium	360	170	300	2.1
Banana	1 medium	108	118	252	0.9
Blueberries	1 cup	81	140	3240	0.6
Cantaloupe	½ medium	96	270	620	0.4
Cranberries	1 cup	49	100	1660	0.5
Dates, Fresh or Dried	5	114	40		2.9
Figs, Raw	2 medium	74	100		0.7
Fig, Dry	1 fig	45	19		2.4
Grapefruit	½ medium	39	120	580	0.3
Grapes	1 cup	61	90	27	0.7
Lemon (peeled)	1 medium	24	85		0.3
Lime	1 medium	30	90		0.3
Nectarine	1 medium	33	70		0.5
Orange	1 medium	64	140	982	0.5
Papaya	⅓ medium	39	100		0.4
Peach	1 medium	42	100	137	0.4
Pear	1 small	82	135	200	0.6
Persimmon, Native	1 medium	60	50		1.2
Pineapple	1 cup, diced	76	155		0.5
Plums	2 medium	36	65	1200	0.6
Raisins	2 tablespoons	54	18	900	3.0
Raspberries, Red	¾ cup	50	100	1130	0.5
Strawberries	1 cup	50	150	1200	0.3
Watermelon	1 cup, diced	52	160	501	0.3
Apple Juice	1 cup, bottled	116	248		0.5
Grape Juice	1 cup, bottled	154	248		0.6
Grapefruit Juice	1 cup, fresh squeezed	93	248		0.4
Prune Juice	1 cup, bottled	181	253		0.7

FOOD	SERVING SIZE	CALORIES	GRAMS	ORAC *Choose high values*	ENERGY DENSITY *(cal/gr) Choose low values*
Vegetable Juice	1 cup	46	240		0.2
Orange Juice	1 cup	111	248		0.5

Legumes

Beans, Garbanzo	¼ cup	60	50		1.2
Beans, Green	1 cup	31	100	250	0.3
Beans, Lima	½ cup	71	100	115	0.7
Beans, Pinto	½ cup	86	100	640	0.9
Cowpeas	½ cup	92	70		1.3
Lentils, Brown	½ cup	116	100		1.2
Peas	1 cup	72	140	530	0.5
Soybeans (Mature)	¼ cup	77	50		1.5
Soybean Curd (Tofu)	1 piece (2½″ × 1″ × 2¾″)	115	120	195	1.0
Split Peas	½ cup	115	100		1.2
Burger, Veggie, Boca	1 burger	110			
Chili,Vegetarian, Fat-Free	½ cup	80			

Healthy Carbs: Whole Grains

Cereals, Grains, Breads

Amaranth	1 cup, cooked	182	80		2.3
Buckwheat	1 cup, cooked	194	100		1.9
Bulgur	1 cup, cooked	151	182		10.8
Couscous	1 cup, cooked	175	157		1.1
Millet	1 cup, cooked	207	174		1.2
Quinoa	1 cup, cooked	211	170		1.2
Cereal–Rolled Oats	1 cup	311	80		3.9
Cereal–Rye	1 cup	260	80		3.3

FOOD	SERVING SIZE	CALORIES	GRAMS	ORAC Choose *high values*	ENERGY DENSITY *(cal/gr) Choose low values*
Shredded Wheat	1 biscuit	90	25		3.6
Oat Bran	1 cup, cooked	88	219		0.4
Oatmeal	1 cup, cooked	145	123		1.2
Wheat Flakes	1 cup	100	30		3.3
Wheat Germ	1 tablespoon	21	6		3.5
Wheat Bran	½ cup	60	24		2.5
Bread, Rye (American)	1 slice	89	32		2.8
Bread, Pumpernickel	1 slice	80	32		2.5
Bread, Mixed Grain	1 slice	80	32		2.5
Bread, Oat Bran	1 slice	70	32		2.2
Bread, Pita, Whole Wheat	1 small pita	74	28		2.6
Crackers, Health Valley, Whole Wheat, Low-Fat	6 crackers	60			3.6
Crispbread, Wasa, Light Rye, Fat-Free	1 slice	25			3.6

Other Grains and Flours, Pasta

Barley, Pearl	1 cup, cooked	193	157		1.2
Cornmeal	¼ cup	300	30		10.0
Gluten Flour	1 cup	378	140		2.7
Rice, Brown, Short-grain	¼ cup	171	50		3.4
Rye Flour	1 cup sifted	357	100		3.6
Wheat Bran	1 tablespoon	13	6		2.2
Wheat Flour, Enriched	½ cup sifted	203	60		3.4
Wheat Flour, Whole	½ cup sifted	203	60		3.4

FOOD	SERVING SIZE	CALORIES	GRAMS	ORAC Choose high values	ENERGY DENSITY (cal/gr) Choose low values
Wild Rice	1/4 cup	41	40		1.0
Noodles, Soba	1 cup cooked	112	114		1.0
Macaroni, Whole Wheat	1 cup, cooked	173	140		1.2
Spaghetti, Whole Wheat	1 cup, cooked	173	140		1.2
Popcorn, Plain-popped	3 cups	97	24		4.0
Popcorn, Microwave, Weight Watchers, Smart Snackers	1 package	100	28		3.6

UNHEALTHY CARBS : BAKED GOODS AND SNACKS

Bagel, Egg	1 bagel (3″ diam.)	247	89		2.8
Bagel, Whole-grain	1 bagel (3″ diam.)	226	89		2.5
Biscuit, Butter-milk (refrigerator)	1 biscuit	93	27		3.4
Bread, Italian	1 piece	54	20		2.7
Bread, Raisin	1 slice	71	26		2.7
Cake, Angel Food	1 piece, 1/12 of 12 oz. cake	73	28		2.6
Cake, Carrot (no frosting)	1 piece, 1/[illegible] of 18 oz. cake	176	42		4.2
Cake, Chocolate (with frosting)	1 piece, 1/18 of 18-oz. cake	234	64		3.7
Cake, Pound, Fat-Free	1 slice (1 oz.)	80	28		2.9
Cake, Pound (made with butter)	1 slice (1 oz.)	110	28		3.9
Cheesecake	1 piece, 1/6 of 17-oz. cake	257	80		3.2

FOOD	SERVING SIZE	CALORIES	GRAMS	ORAC Choose high values	ENERGY DENSITY (cal/gr) Choose low values
Chips, Potato, "Lite"	1¼-oz. bag	166	35		4.7
Chips, Potato, Barbecue	1¼-oz. bag	174	35		5.0
Chips, Potato, Salted Plain	1-oz. bag	115	28		4.1
Chips, Tortilla, Plain	1 oz. (about 15 chips)	142	28		5.1
Cinnabon Caramel Pecanbon	1 (8 oz.)	890	224		4.0
Coffeecake, Cheese	1 piece, ⅙ of 16-oz. cake	257	76		3.4
Cookie, Chocolate Chip	1 soft type	69	15		4.6
Cookie, Fig Newton	1 cookie	55	16		3.4
Cookie, Nabisco Oreos	1 cookie	52	11		4.7
Cookie, Oatmeal	1 big cookie, 3″ × 4″	112	25		4.5
Cookie, Oatmeal, Fat-Free	1 big cookie, 3″ × 4″	92	28		3.3
Cookie, Sandwich (with chocolate creme filling)	1 cookie	47	10		4.7
Cookie, Sugar	1 cookie	71	15		4.7
Cornbread	1 piece (about 2 oz.)	173	65		2.7
Cracker, Ritz	2 crackers	78	16		4.9
Cracker, Saltines	1 large round	43	10		4.3
Cracker, Sandwich (with cheese filling)	1 sandwich cracker	34	7		4.9
Cracker, Wheat Thin	1 cracker	14	3		4.7
Croissant, Au Bon Pain, Almond	1 (5 oz.)	630	140		4.5

FOOD	SERVING SIZE	CALORIES	GRAMS	ORAC *Choose high values*	ENERGY DENSITY *(cal/gr) Choose low values*
Danish Pastry	1 pastry	265	71		3.7
Doughnut, Chocolate (cake type, sugared)	1 doughnut	250	60		4.2
Doughnuts, Jelly	1 doughnut	289	85		3.4
English Muffin, Sourdough	1 muffin	133	57		2.3
English Muffin, Whole Wheat	1 muffin	134	66		2.0
Melba Toast	1 slice	19	4		4.8
Muffin, Au Bon Pain Carrot Pecan	1 (5 oz.)	480	140		3.4
Muffin, Blueberry	1 muffin	196	71		2.8
Pie, Apple	1 slice, ⅛ of 9-inch pie	296	125		2.4
Pie, Blueberry	1 slice, ⅛ of 9-inch pie	290	125		2.3
Pie, Coconut Cream	1 slice, ⅙ of 7-inch pie	190	64		3.0
Pie, Lemon Meringue	1 slice, ⅙ of 7-inch pie	302	113		2.7
Pie, Pecan	1 slice, ⅙ of 7-inch pie	452	113		4.0
Popcorn, Cheese Flavor	1 cup	57	11		5.2
Popcorn, Oil-Popped	1 cup	55	11		5.0
Pretzels, Salted Plain	10 twists	228	60		3.8
Pretzels, Whole Wheat	2 oz.	205	56		3.7
Rice Cakes	2 cakes	68	18		3.8
Scone, Starbucks Maple Nut	1 scone	570			
Strudel, Apple	1 piece	194	71		2.7

FOOD	SERVING SIZE	CALORIES	GRAMS	ORAC Choose high values	ENERGY DENSITY (cal/gr) Choose low values
Trail Mix (with chocolate chips)	1 oz.	137	28		4.9
Turnover, Pepperidge Farm Apple	1 turnover	284	89		3.2
Waffle, Plain	1 waffle	88	28		3.1

PROTEIN

Eggs					
Egg, White	1 medium	17	33		0.5
Egg, Whole	1 medium	77	50		1.5
Egg, Yolk	1 medium	59	16		3.7

Seaweed					
Hijiki	⅛ cup	5	8		0.6
Kombu	⅛ cup	6	8		0.8
Nori	⅛ cup	6	8		0.8
Wakami	⅛ cup	5	8		0.6

Nuts & Seeds					
Almonds	14 medium	98	28		3.5
Almond Butter	1 tablespoon	101	16		6.3
Brazil Nuts	1 nut	18	3		6.0
Cashews	14 large	162	28		5.8
Chestnuts, Fresh Roasted	2 large	50	35		1.4
Filberts (Hazelnuts)	10 nuts	88	14		6.3
Macadamia Nuts	11 nuts (1 oz.)	199	28		7.1
Peanuts, Dry Roasted	1 tablespoon chopped, or 15 whole	165	28		5.9
Peanut Butter	1 tablespoon	94	16		5.9

FOOD	SERVING SIZE	CALORIES	GRAMS	ORAC Choose high values	ENERGY DENSITY (cal/gr) Choose low values
Pecans	10 large	189	28		6.8
Walnuts	1 oz.	172	28		6.1
Pumpkin Seeds	1/8 cup	90	17		5.3
Sunflower Seeds	1/8 cup	102	18		5.7
Tahini	1 tablespoon	85	15		5.7

Fish

Bass, Black Sea	3½ oz.	124	100		1.2
Bass, White Sea	3½ oz.	124	100		1.2
Catfish	3½ oz.	103	100		1.0
Clams	4 cherrystone	51	70		0.7
Cod	3½ oz.	105	100		1.1
Crab (steamed)	3½ oz.	97	100		1.0
Haddock	3½ oz.	112	100		1.1
Halibut	3½ oz.	140	100		1.4
Herring, Pacific	1 herring	100	50		2.0
Lobster	1 cup cubed	142	145		1.0
Mackerel, Atlantic	3½ oz.	262	100		2.6
Ocean Perch	3½ oz.	121	100		1.2
Oysters	medium, 2 selects	66	25		2.6
Perch, White	3½ oz.	121	100		1.2
Red Snapper	3½ oz.	128	100		1.3
Salmon, Atlantic	3½ oz.	206	100		2.1
Salmon, Atlantic (canned)	1 small can (6½ oz.)	283	185		1.5
Sardines, Pacific	3½ oz.	208	100		2.1
Sardines, Atlantic (canned)	3½ oz.	208	100		2.1
Scallop, Raw	1 large	22	25		0.9
Scallop (breaded and fried)	1 large	66	31		2.1
Shark	3½ oz.	130	100		1.3

FOOD	SERVING SIZE	CALORIES	GRAMS	ORAC *Choose high values*	ENERGY DENSITY *(cal/gr) Choose low values*
Shrimp (raw)	3½ oz	99	100		1.0
Shrimp (cooked)	4 large	21	22		1.0
Sole	3½ oz.	117	100		1.2
Squid	3½ oz.	92	100		0.9
Swordfish	3½ oz.	155	100		1.6
Tuna (canned)	½ cup	213	115		1.9
Sushi, Salmon	4 small pieces on rice with nori wrapper	160	N/A		

Meat & Poultry

Bacon, Regular	3 medium slices	109	20		5.5
Bacon, Canadian-style	2 slices	86	45		1.9
Beef, Flank Steak (no visible fat)	3 oz	224	85		2.6
Beef, Ground (extra-lean)	3 oz.	218	85		2.6
Beef, Ground (lean)	3 oz.	231	85		2.7
Beef, Ground (regular)	3 oz.	245	85		2.9
Beef, Loin/Sirloin	3½ oz.	226	100		2.3
Beef, Porterhouse Steak (lean)	3 oz.	190	85		2.2
Beef, T-Bone Steak	3 oz.	262	85		3.1
Beef, Top Sirloin	3 oz.	228	85		2.7
Beef, Round	3½ oz.	265	100		2.7
Beef Liver	3 oz.	136	85		1.6
Buffalo	3 oz.	111	85		1.3
Calves' Liver	3½ oz.	165	100		1.7
Chicken, Dark Meat	3½ oz.	192	100		1.9

FOOD	SERVING SIZE	CALORIES	GRAMS	ORAC Choose high values	ENERGY DENSITY (cal/gr) Choose low values
Chicken, Light Meat	3½ oz.	153	100		1.5
Chicken, Drum-stick (medium-size, with skin)	1	112	52		2.2
Chicken, Drum-stick (medium-size, skinless)	1	75	44		1.7
Ham, Canned	3½ oz.	239	100		2.4
Cured Ham	3 oz.	140	85		1.7
Hamburger Meat	3½ oz.	235	100		2.4
Lamb (cubed for kabobs)	3 oz.	158	85		1.9
Lamb, Rib	3 oz.	305	85		3.6
Lamb, Sirloin	3 oz.	248	85		2.9
Pork Chop, Loin (bone-in)	3 oz.	205	83		2.5
Pork, Sirloin Roast (bone-in)	3 oz.	221	85		2.6
Rabbit, Domestic	3½ oz.	197	100		2.0
Turkey, Thigh (with skin)	1 thigh	492	314		1.6
Turkey, Light Meat	3½ oz.	157	100		1.6
Turkey, Dark Meat	3½ oz.	187	100		1.9
Veal, Breast (boneless)	3 oz.	226	85		2.7
Veal, Loin	3½ oz.	217	100		2.2

Calcium-Rich Foods

Milk and Soy Milk Products					
Buttermilk	1 cup	99	244		0.4
Low-Fat Milk (2%)	1 cup	102	244		0.4
Skim Milk	1 cup	85	244		0.4
Whole Milk	1 cup	159	244		0.7

FOOD	SERVING SIZE	CALORIES	GRAMS	**ORAC** *Choose high values*	**ENERGY DENSITY** *(cal/gr) Choose low values*
Sour Cream, Nonfat	1 tablespoon	31	14		2.2
Yogurt, Low-Fat, Plain	1 container (8 oz.)	231	240		1.0
Yogurt, Low-Fat (containing fruit)	1 container (8 oz.)	220	240		0.9
Yogurt, Nonfat, Plain	1 container (8 oz.)	100–120	240		
Yogurt, Low-Fat, Plain	1 container (6 oz.)	170–180	168		
Yogurt, Nonfat, Plain	1 container (6 oz.)	80–100	168		
Yogurt, Whole Soy, Plain	1 container (8 oz.)	140	240		0.6

Cheese

American	1 slice (2¼″ square)	106	28		3.8
Blue Cheese	1″ cube	61	17		3.6
Camembert	1″ cube	50	17		2.9
Cheddar	1″ cube	114	28		4.1
Cottage (dry)	1 cup	85	200		0.4
Cottage (1% fat)	¼ cup	40	60		0.7
Cream Cheese	1 tablespoon	50	14		3.6
Cream Cheese, Fat-Free	1 tablespoon	13	14		0.9
Feta	1″ cube	44	17		2.6
Goat Cheese, Semisoft	1 oz.	100	28		3.6
Monterey Jack	1″ cube	64	17		3.8
Mozzarella, Part-Skim	1″ cube	72	28		2.6
Parmesan	1 tablespoon	22	12		1.8
Ricotta, Part-Skim	½ cup	171	124		1.4

FOOD	SERVING SIZE	CALORIES	GRAMS	ORAC Choose high values	ENERGY DENSITY (cal/gr) Choose low values
Soy Cheese	1 oz.	70	28		2.5
Soy Cheese, Fat-Free	1 oz.	40	28		1.4
Swiss	1″ cube	56	15		3.7

Frozen Confections

Ice Cream, Low-Fat	½ cup	178	120		1.5
Ice Cream, Sugar-Free	½ cup	98	120		0.8
Ice Cream, Chocolate	½ cup	142	120		1.2
Ice Cream, Eskimo Pie	1 bar	166	50		3.3
Ice Cream, Häagen-Dazs	½ cup	280	120		2.3
Ice Cream, Ben & Jerry's	½ cup	275	120		2.3
Ice Cream, Cascadian Farm Sorbet & Cream	½ cup	110	120		0.9
Ice Milk, Weight Watchers, Fat-Free	½ cup	82	120		0.7
Ice Milk, Healthy Choice	½ cup	124	120		1.0
Yogurt, Frozen	½ cup	115	120		1.0
Yogurt, Frozen, Stonyfield Farm	½ cup	125	120		1.0
Soy "Ice Cream," Turtle Mountain It's Delicious	½ cup	120	112		1.1
Rice Dream	½ cup	120	112		1.1
Tofutti	½ cup	215	112		1.9
Sorbet, Dole	½ cup	50	112		0.5

FOOD	SERVING SIZE	CALORIES	GRAMS	ORAC Choose high values	ENERGY DENSITY (cal/gr) Choose low values
Sorbet, Häagen-Dazs	½ cup	170	112		1.5

Healthy Oils

Canola Oil	1 tablespoon	120	14		8.6
Flaxseed Oil	1 tablespoon	120	14		8.6
Mayonnaise, Light	1 tablespoon	35	14		2.5
Olive Oil	1 tablespoon	120	14		8.6
Rape Seed	1 tablespoon	120	14		8.6
Safflower Oil	1 tablespoon	120	14		8.6
Sesame Oil	1 tablespoon	120	14		8.6
Walnut Oil	1 tablespoon	120	14		8.6

Unhealthy Oils

Butter, Salted	1 tablespoon	100	14		7.1
Margarine, Tub-Style, 48% Fat	1 tablespoon	50	14		3.6
Margarine, Parkay	1 tablespoon	70	14		5.0
Margarine, Trader Joe's	1 tablespoon	100	14		7.1
Margarine, Whipped Light	1 tablespoon	23	14		1.6
Mayonnaise, Regular	1 tablespoon	100	14		7.1
Mayonnaise, Reduced Fat	1 tablespoon	50	14		3.6
Mayonnaise, Fat-Free	1 tablespoon	10	14		0.7
Mayonnaise, Canola Harvest	1 tablespoon	100	14		7.1
Corn Oil	1 tablespoon	120	14		8.6

FOOD	SERVING SIZE	CALORIES	GRAMS	ORAC Choose high values	ENERGY DENSITY (cal/gr) Choose low values
MISCELLANEOUS					
Dressing, Hidden Valley, Fat-Free (all flavors)	2 tablespoons	30	28		1.1
Dressing, Kraft, Light (all flavors)	2 tablespoons	50-60	28		
Dressing, Kraft Honey Dijon	2 tablespoons	100	28		3.6
Dressing, Kraft Thousand Island Bacon	2 tablespoons	130	28		4.6
Dressing, Kraft Cucumber Ranch	2 tablespoons	140	28		5.0
Dressing, Naturally Fresh Blue Cheese	2 tablespoons	170	28		6.1
Dressing, Naturally Fresh, Poppyseed	2 tablespoons	140	28		5.0
Dressing, Newman's Own, Ranch	2 tablespoons	140	28		5.0
Dressing, Wishbone, Fat-Free (all flavors)	2 tablespoons	40	28		1.4
Dressing, Wishbone Classic Caesar	2 tablespoons	110	28		3.9
Dressing, Wishbone Deluxe French	2 tablespoons	120	28		4.3
Dressing, Wishbone Ranch	2 tablespoons	160	28		5.7
Ketchup	1 tablespoon	15	15		1.0
Mustard	1 teaspoon	15	5		3.0
Salsa, Tomato	¼ cup	18	N/A		

FOOD	SERVING SIZE	CALORIES	GRAMS	ORAC Choose high values	ENERGY DENSITY (cal/gr) Choose low values
Yeast	1 tablespoon	14	5		2.8
Jell-O, Sugar-Free, Low-Calorie	½ cup	7	N/A		0.1
Gelatin desserts, Non-Sugar-Free	½ cup	79	N/A		
Ice Pops	1 bar (1.8 fluid oz.)	37	N/A		
Orange Marmalade	1 tablespoon	49	N/A		

HEALTHY SNACKS

Soup					
Soup, Miso with Noodles, Low-Fat	1 cup	130	240		0.5
Soup, Black Bean, Fat-Free	1 cup	100	240		0.4
Soup, Health Valley Lentil	1 cup	130	240		0.5
Soup, Health Valley Pasta Parmesan	1 cup	100	240		0.4
Soup, Health Valley 14 Garden Vegetable	1 cup	80	240		0.3
Soup, Progresso Manhattan Clam Chowder	1 cup	110	240		0.5

FAST FOODS

Biscuit, Egg & Sausage	1 biscuit	580	180		3.2
Biscuit, Egg & Bacon	1 biscuit	458	150		3.1
Burrito, with Beans & Cheese	1 large	377	196		1.9

FOOD	SERVING SIZE	CALORIES	GRAMS	ORAC *Choose high values*	ENERGY DENSITY *(cal/gr) Choose low values*
Burrito, with Beans, Cheese & Beef	1 large	331	203		1.9
Cheeseburger (large double patty plus condiments)	1 serving	704	258		1.6
Cheeseburger (large single patty plus condiments)	1 serving	562	219		2.7
Cheeseburger (regular double patty plus condiments)	1 serving	460	160		2.9
Chicken Fillet Sandwich	1 sandwich	515	182		2.8
Chicken Nuggets, Plain (breaded and fried)	1 serving	287	106		2.7
Chicken Nuggets, with Barbecue Sauce (breaded and fried)	1 serving	330	130		2.5
Chicken, Dark Meat (breaded and fried)	2 drumsticks	430	148		2.9
Chicken, White Meat (breaded and fried)	1 breast	494	163		3.0
Chimichanga, Beef & Cheese	1 serving	443	183		2.4
Cookie: Chocolate Chip	1 box	232	55		4.2
Croissant, Egg & Cheese	1 croissant	368	127		2.9
Danish Pastry, Cheese	1 serving	353	91		3.9

FOOD	SERVING SIZE	CALORIES	GRAMS	**ORAC** *Choose high values*	**ENERGY DENSITY** *(cal/gr) Choose low values*
Danish Pastry, Fruit	1 serving	335	94		3.6
Fish Sandwich (with tartar sauce)	1 sandwich	431	158		2.7
Fish Sandwich (with tartar sauce and cheese)	1 sandwich	523	183		2.9
French Toast (with butter)	2 slices	356	135		2.6
Hot Dog (on bun with chili)	1	296	114		2.6
Ice Cream Sundae, Chocolate	1 sundae	284	158		1.8
Nachos, with Cheese	6-8 nachos	345	113		3.1
Nachos, with Cheese, Beans, Beef & Chilis	6-8 nachos	568	255		2.2
Onion Rings	8-9 rings	275	83		3.3
Potato, Baked (with cheese)	1 potato	473	296		1.6
Potato, Baked (with sour cream)	1 potato	392	302		1.3
Potato Salad	⅓ cup	108	95		1.1
French Fries, McDonald's	small serving: 2.4 oz.	210	68		3.1
French Fries, McDonald's	super-size serving, 7.1 oz.	610	198		3.1
French Fries, Burger King	small serving: 2.6 oz.	230	72		3.2
French Fries, Wendy's	small serving 3.2 oz.	270	88		3.1
French Fries, Carl's Jr.	one serving, 3.3 oz	290	90		3.2
French Fries, Jack in the Box	regular serving, 4 oz.	350	112		3.1

FOOD	SERVING SIZE	CALORIES	GRAMS	ORAC *Choose high values*	ENERGY DENSITY *(cal/gr) Choose low values*
Pizza, with Cheese and Sausage	1 3″ slice	336	129		2.6
Pizza, with Cheese and Pepperoni	1 3″ slice	442	154		2.9
Shake, McDonald's McFlurry	small, 12 oz.	610	336		1.8
Shake, McDonald's Triple Thick	small, 16 oz.	570	480		1.2
Shake, McDonald's McFlurry	large, 16 oz.	890	480		1.9
Shake, McDonald's Triple Thick	large, 32 oz.	1140	896		1.3
Shake, Burger King, Old Fashioned	22 oz.	760	616		1.2
Submarine, Roast Beef	1 sandwich	410	216		1.9
Submarine, Tuna	1 sandwich	483	256		1.9
Taco	1 small	369	170		2.2
Taco Salad	1½ cups	279	198		1.4
Yogurt, Frozen, Vanilla	½ cup	114	72		1.6

8
PARENTING THE LONGEVITY DIET LIFESTYLE

ANY MAJOR LIFESTYLE change that you initiate involves several stages. First, you start to believe in the evidence that the change you are considering has actually had the desired effect in other people who have made that change. Next, you cultivate the belief that it will work for you. You tell yourself, "*I really need/want to do this; I know it will help me*," draw up a plan, and then work systematically from point A to point B and beyond; or maybe you just jump right in and build your path as you move along. Perhaps you enlist the aid of a buddy, or join a support group, to help keep you on track.

Next comes the trial-and-error stage, when your faith in the evidence, your resolve, your experiences as compared with your original expectations and your actual progress, and your support system (if applicable) will be tested. Finally, you assess the gains or sacrifices of your decision and either stay on board with your program or shift gears, subtly or otherwise.

Andrew went through this process several times:

> I tried diet after diet—the usual fruitless search, and classic yo-yo weight loss/gain. Some diets worked briefly, some didn't work at all, but even when they

> worked, the weight all went back on eventually whenever I stopped or got bored with whatever dietary restrictions were involved. I've been doing CR seriously for about fourteen months now. I've lost about thirty pounds. And why did CR stick? I suppose my need for long-term weight-control and good nutrition gave me the persistence to stick to it so that I could pursue my love of sports well into old age.

Andrew was convinced to begin the Longevity Diet by the scientific evidence for it, and the stories of others on the CR Society e-mail list. Or, as Andrew enthused,

> They're an amazing bunch of characters on the CR mailing list. This is the first time I've actually felt like I'm part of an exciting, real-time experiment with other real people who think and feel the same way I do. Long may we thrive!

HOW TO BEGIN

your contract

Once you decide that you are ready to try the Longevity Diet, make a contract with yourself. (Well, let's back up. Once again: Talk to you physician first!) Writing things down will help you clarify why you want to do this, and how you plan to go about it. For example, Andrew wants to be healthy enough to run a marathon well into old age. For him, the Longevity Diet is a means toward something that he loves.

What does a contract look like? It could be something very formal, or akin to a letter you might send a good friend. How detailed you may wish it to be, is purely up you. Here's an example:

From today onward and for at least the next ________ I choose to follow a longevity diet program that consists of selecting foods that nourish me. I will gradually eat fewer calories.

Today I weigh ____________. My goal will be to eat sensibly, not merely to reduce my weight, as I understand that too-fast weight-loss may present a hardship to my body. I plan on losing ____________ per week.

I respect what happens under my skin and want to learn as much as I can about the Longevity Diet. I understand that this is "CR," not "FR," mere food restriction. It is a longevity diet only if I'm eating foods replete with nutrients, like vegetables. A balanced diet is crucial for a successful experience.

I will consult my health care practitioner before beginning this program and, if I begin to doubt or have problems with my program, I will seek the advice of someone familiar with the Longevity Diet.

I plan to live long enough to see ________________ (the next century, a solar eclipse, a few great-great grandchildren, you can be creative here).

Signed and dated:

Set six months or longer as your trial period. It takes time for your taste buds to transform and for you to crave healthy foods, if you didn't before. Be patient. Anything really worth doing takes a while to master, particularly when it is something that is custom-fitted for you. Since you will design a program that best suits your lifestyle and food preferences, the road map to success is in your hands—while many others have traveled a similar path and will offer suggestions, ultimately your transition will be unique to you.

You may want to read your contract on a daily basis, or use it as a gauge to monitor your progress weekly.

Be prepared to have days when your particular emotional triggers or stressful events lead you to backslide into old habits. This is perfectly normal, and nothing to feel guilty about. Just try, at the beginning, to stick to your contract as best you can, resuming your healthful diet as soon as possible. You may want to buy or make a calendar and mark *G* for great days and *D* for difficult days. Note on the calendar what event challenged your resolve. Social issues? Work? Family? Then, knowing that you might be faced with another challenging event, prepare yourself mentally to handle that situation differently, to not use food as a solution to a circumstance that does not, at its core, even involve food. It could help to have a few sugar-free mints or your favorite tea on hand for emotional emergencies—a small, nondestructive yummy something going down your gullet may be all you need to feel better.

learn

Every veteran CR practitioner recommends that you learn as much as you can about good nutrition and healthy foods. This is especially important if you *really* want to extend your life span and pursue a more regimented Longevity Diet program. Fulfilling the nutritional requirements of someone with a low body mass index are essential for good health, especially in regards to sufficient consumption of protein and calcium.

When we on the Longevity Diet reach for an apple, the first thing we think of is its great taste. But by now we also know that it is an ORAC food, antioxidant rich, and that it is also contains a high level of a beneficial fiber, pectin. Before you make a financial investment, don't you research it? Isn't health your best investment? Read up on heart-healthy fats, antioxidant-rich foods, and phytonutrients, so that you, too, can appreciate what you eat not only as flavors and aromas, but as long-term sources of nutritional "dividends" for your body.

strategize

Set small achievable goals, like filling in the Daily Food Diary with every morsel of food, for a week, consciously substituting a low-calorie, healthy food for a high-calorie or processed choice. This activity by itself will put you in charge of minute-by-minute decisions that do not eliminate but merely exchange food, such as eating a banana instead of carrot cake, or having a cup of tea to help you make it through the mid-morning slump, rather than a bagel.

prepare

Prepare psychologically as well as physically. The contract, a buddy system, and a few pertinent questions about your habits and history with food and diets should help you. Take honest stock of where you're at: your emotional state, your ability to commit to things, and your natural proclivities. Have you tried to lose weight before? Was it difficult? If it was, you may need to set strong boundaries. We will give you some suggestions. Even if you know that you easily adapt to self-selected routines, it will still benefit you to prepare by learning as much as you can about CR and nutrition, as you may be unconsciously carrying the program of other diets' incorrect information about foods and your body's use of them.

> From an ancient Vedic text comes this pertinent idea:
>
> Watch your thoughts; they become words.
> Watch your words; they become actions.
> Watch your actions; they become habits.

find support

This may be posting motivational notes on the refrigerator, calling a friend, or even a "cr-onversation"—an imaginary dialogue with your self about health and the Longevity Diet, whenever you need an ally. Imagine yourself vital, alert, healthy. April has a great sense of humor—read her "cr-onversation with Myself at 4:30 AM":

> "Now, self, you know you have to eat your egg whites for breakfast before you leave for work."
>
> "But I don't want to! It's four thirty in the morning and you know I don't like to eat breakfast!"
>
> "I know you don't like to eat breakfast, but you barely ate anything yesterday because you stupidly ordered the dead fish after saying you wouldn't, took three bites of it, and decided to feed the rest to the cat. And it made you feel sick for the rest of the day. No more dead fish, self. But now you're low on energy, very low in protein, and you have a busy day ahead. You have to eat your egg whites."
>
> "Can't I just skip breakfast and promise to eat something later, when I'm not feeling so, well, four thirty a.m.-ish?"
>
> "Have you not understood anything that you've read in the last three months? Breakfast is important, and protein is even more important. If you don't eat your egg whites, which give you a 29 gram head start on your protein quota, you know you won't eat enough protein later to make up for it. Protein makes you strong! You want to live a long time and be healthy, not look like a waifish supermodel! If you don't eat your protein, you'll never be strong enough to live to 110, and you'll never get to be six feet tall."

"What if I eat a Dunkin' Donuts bagel instead? That's food. And I'm pretty sure that the Longevity Diet won't make me six feet tall, even if I do get enough protein."

"That's a big waste of calories for almost no nutrition! Remember, the last time you did that you were distinctly underwhelmed by the taste. You've grown out of such silliness, little self. You're right about the height thing, though. The Longevity Diet won't make you taller. I get confused. It's been a rough week."

"It's been a rough week. And yesterday was a bad eating day . . . FR, not CR, due to the unfortunate demise of our lunch. The cat sure liked the salmon."

"So are you going to eat those egg whites?"

"Okay, I'll eat my egg whites."

"How about a glass of skim milk with that? Remember, we're working on calcium."

"Don't push your luck."

Remember, the Longevity Diet is not "just another diet" nor is it, indeed, a weight-loss program. It is a quality-of-life program. It is not about deprivation or hunger. *You will, however, lose weight.* You should, therefore, savor, relish, and enjoy your life on the Longevity Diet. Think of everything you learn about nutrition and your unique metabolism as having a positive impact upon not only your body but your mind. Note that several comprehensive health programs, such as Dean Ornish's Life Choice and the Okinawa Program, specifically incorporate body-mind techniques to reinforce healthy choices. Your initial projection, day-by-day awareness, and growing appreciation of your improving behaviors are the fundamental building blocks to a successful lifestyle makeover.

As Andrew recommends,

> From one who has been through [the Longevity Diet]—learn about your body, its care and maintenance—it's

> the only one you have, so learn to love it. . . . Be aware of the stressors that might make you want to lose confidence in yourself, especially if that leads to overeating. Work, love life, daily commute; we all have them. Know yourself, and trick yourself into ignoring them. There are many such tricks; taking a few deep breaths, a few motivational words. With practice you can rise above these issues. And to help gain insight and control, try a course in meditation. If nothing else, you'll enjoy the time out.

And April says,

> My particular brand of the diet has evolved a lot over a short period of time. In the beginning, I was just cutting out most junk foods, eating less of what I had eaten before, and substituting salad for pasta and bagels. As I became more serious and went through a period of reading the CR Society Archives, I drastically changed the content of my diet and dropped my calorie levels. Throughout the process, I've had occasions when I've eaten more calories than usual, or eaten foods I now only rarely eat. This isn't "cheating" because the Longevity Diet is not a dictatorial diet in the normal sense . . . it's about eating as few calories as you can without eating less of other nutrients essential for health.

9 MONITORING THE LONGEVITY DIET LIFESTYLE

ARE YOU A WARRIOR OR AN EXPLORER?

the warrior's code

If there is a bag of chips on the counter, can you eat just a few? Do you have a hard time choosing between salad and creamed soup as an appetizer? Then following the Longevity Diet will call upon your finest resources to remain strong in your resolve to have a healthier body! As in the first step in any twelve-step recovery program, you first need to admit that you may have felt powerless to resist (in this case) the call of the refrigerator, or perhaps of your stomach. That does not mean you will fail on the Longevity Diet; quite the contrary. Eating for longevity gets you to become proactive against your inner wimp, by becoming knowledgeable about nutrition and imposing some behavioral rules that will tell your belly who's boss. Along with these strengths, you need to develop the flexibility to roll with life's punches in ways that will not derail your nutritional wagon.

As discussed earlier, we all have emotional triggers or other externally motivated behavioral patterns that may undermine our goals for health and well-being. When you begin the Longevity Diet, those triggers and patterns will at first raise their volume, begging for your attention, *precisely* because you have become so aware of your desire not to hear them. While your office mates snack at their desks before lunch hour, or your kids tear into an aromatic pizza, your inner dialogue may nag that you, too, really deserve a little treat. Be prepared with a counteroffensive: not to consume *nothing,* but to rethink your definition of a "treat": nibble on something healthy—a small handful of dried apricots or almonds, an apple, a big bowl of low-fat soup that has its own yummy fragrance. A large mug of green tea or just a glass of water with a squirt of citrus might even do the trick, if your mouth and then your stomach are contented by simply a feeling of being filled.

If temptation really rules in your roost, then you may need to clean out your kitchen and remove the seductive foods that lure you to give in. Don't order or cook the kinds of things that cause you to overeat. Cook with portion sizes in mind, storing or freezing the foods in individual servings. If you bring a "doggy bag" of food home from a restaurant, remember that it constitutes a second meal, not a second serving as soon as you are home. If hunger strikes, reach for any and every kind of fruit or vegetable, preferably one that takes a while to peel or chew. Try setting aside twenty minutes on a weekend to prepare vegetable snacks and small servings of nuts as snacks for the coming week. Store them in sandwich-size plastic bags so you can see what's in them and easily carry them with you.

Think of yourself as a warrior facing down an enemy—not food per se, but a simple yet pernicious thing: poor eating habits. Gluttony, one of the seven deadly sins, will initially fight for its right to control you, but forewarned is forearmed: now that you know your intention is to eat more wisely, you already have an argument ready for those moments when a pineapple Danish waves at you from the deli counter as you wait for your all-bran cereal. You may sometimes lose a battle, but you are determined to win the war.

You need strong weapons to combat everyday minefields. One solution may be as simple as reciting to yourself an affirmation, a mantra. In the 1920s, a well-being movement had followers telling themselves each morning, "Every day, in every way, I am getting better and better." April shared with us her own jingle: "We are Dr. Walford's mice, we find a longer life quite nice." You can image how surprised and warm this made us feel! And it worked for her. Focusing on the positive, on every refusal to give in being one more step toward your ultimate goal, will help to underscore that calorie restriction is *not* deprivation, but a honing down of your diet to the most healthful essentials.

Consider it a victory every time you stop yourself from reaching for a food your body does not even want, every time you recognize and tune out a trigger or external cue. After a while, you will automatically make the right choices, but as you begin the program you will need to consciously jog yourself into a state of nutritional awareness, one that reshapes your old, poor eating habits into good ones. Imagine, for instance, that you are having a dialogue with a sibling, your spouse, a mentor, or a Longevity Diet role model—with someone who cares about your well-being and who wants you to be around for a long, long time. Hear them say, as did April's "cr-onversation" partner, "Come on, does this food really nourish you? What about having some nice ___________ instead?"

A genuine in-the-flesh buddy system may help immensely, too. Phone an empathetic friend or drop by a colleague at work, to keep them abreast of what successes and failures you've had. The CR Society and its various support groups are great resources. Many people have celebrated weight loss, been warned of possible nutrition deficiencies or haphazard dieting, and found role models through these virtual groups. As we mentioned earlier, Andrew found a lot more than support from an online group.

The Warrior's Code will help you to harness your will power by reallocating your food choices and dealing with behaviors that undermine your health. Because you are probably going to find this program an uphill climb, with many questions, we recommend that you eat fairly structured meals and keep a Daily Food Diary along with a valiantly honest Nutrition Tracker, for as long as it takes to feel your new eating habits are second nature with you.

After six months juggling her routines, April recorded in her blog:

> Now I'm making different choices. I don't always get it right, but I'm glad that, as the work pressure goes up, I'm sticking with my resolve. I feel so much better on a daily basis than I did before. It's unfortunate that most people throw their healthy habits (if they ever had any) out the window the second life becomes stressful. It is when you're stressed that you most need your healthy habits!

the explorer's trail

Were you excited by the first half of this book? If you were, then you are the kind of person who wants to digest all the information you can and make a conscientious decision on how best to proceed. You believe that the evidence indicates that the Longevity Diet will be great for you, and accept that you will be fully in charge of how to go about implementing the diet. You already feel those creative juices flowing as you look forward to designing, coordinating, and navigating your way through our recommendations.

You already understand that it is all about wholesome food and fewer calories, and that the rest is just mix and match, according to what works for you. Some people, like Peter Voss, graze throughout the day. Others, like Lee Shurie, eat one main meal a day. Still others, like Lisa, juice-fast one day per week. Dean Pomerleau prepares and eats the same meal every day. Some, like Khurram Hashmi, weigh and record all their foods. April, on the other hand, went freestyle and just made conversational-in-tone entries online in a blog for her first six months.

Because you are already attuned to the mind-body connection, following the Longevity Diet may be easier for you than for the Warrior first learning to read his or her inner signals. In your case, use the Daily Food Diary to track not what causes you to eat, but how you feel while your body is using what you have consumed. We find, for example, that eating a light protein meal midday maintains even energy levels in the afternoon. Whole grains, veggies, nuts, dairy protein, in whatever combination you may enjoy eating at night, can constitute a large supper, as long as it is predominantly veggies. Remember, vegetables are highest on the ORAC scale, filled with phytonutrients, low energy-dense, and high in fiber. If you can feel energetic in the morning without eating a big breakfast, don't feel you need to eat one to start your day; Lisa does her yoga in the morning, with no breakfast before practice. And yet most nutritionists say that breakfast is the most important meal of the day. Brian has followed that dictate all his life, and the Longevity Diet hasn't changed that. Do what literally feels right for your body.

Since you are already of the mind-set to choose an apple over an apple turnover, you should be able to make the transition to a moderate Longevity Diet without needing to counteract detrimental eating habits. Peter Voss suggests, when you go shopping, to fill your cart with wholesome foods. Don't bring home anything you know you should not eat. No need to nix the snack food already on your shelves, it will be overwhelmed by your conscious substitution of healthy choices, and gradually you'll stop feeling any desire to replace an emptied unhealthy package with another of the same product.

Lee's story

It was not the Longevity Diet that salvaged what could have been a difficult life for Lee. It was his own ingenuity and persistence. There is nothing that dramatic about the Longevity Diet lifestyle, no secrets, no special food combinations, just good common sense. Highly motivated and savvy as he was, Lee rescued himself from a potentially life-debilitating disease and serendipitously found that he was actually on CR. He then became an inspiration to many on the CR Society mailing lists.

> When I was in my mid-forties I was diagnosed as diabetic. The slow miserable decline associated with long-term diabetes presented a grim future for me, and I vowed to somehow find a cure—or at least a management program that would permanently keep the disease at bay. Because the medical profession does not have such a cure, I was determined to find one myself.
>
> I spent the first year refining my diet and kept a daily journal of everything I ate, including quantities, time of day, calories, protein, carbs, fat, and fiber content. The journal also records exercise, blood sugar level, weight, and notes about my mental and physical condition. The journal helped me to successfully design a program to normalize my blood sugar levels. I now don't need any medication. I followed a strict regimen for months and months, during which time I ate only low-glycemic-index foods and lost approximately 15 pounds. Unfortunately, the switch to low-glycemic foods and the weight loss was not sufficient

to fully counteract the disease. My blood sugar levels improved approximately 5 percent, but there was still work to be done. The next item I worked on was exercise. This wasn't easy, because I have two young children, social obligations, and am president of my own company. But it was absolutely necessary! Unfortunately, the switch to a vigorous exercise program was not sufficient to fully counteract the disease. My blood sugar levels improved another 5 percent, there was still work to be done.

As I continued my diet regimen I found that I was naturally consuming far fewer calories than before. I realized how important it was to choose highly nutritious foods. After experimenting and adjusting, I ended up on a low-calorie, nutrient-dense diet. Later I learned there is a scientific basis for the Longevity Diet: the decades of research into CR. And that one benefit of CR appears to be the improvement in blood sugar levels that I had stumbled upon. As I researched CR and longevity further, I found that many of the biometric and quality-of-life improvements that I had experienced were associated with the CR dietary approach. I now follow the diet with my own modifications regarding meal timing. I believe each person on this diet must tailor their own eating plan and schedule, and follow what works in their body and with their lifestyle. I am quite active athletically and often go all day at high energy levels while those who've eaten breakfast and lunch or energy snacks fall behind. This routine works well for me, with my lifestyle, and you will see from the graph that it has stabilized my blood sugar levels dramatically.

Effect of Diet and Exercise on Blood Sugar Levels

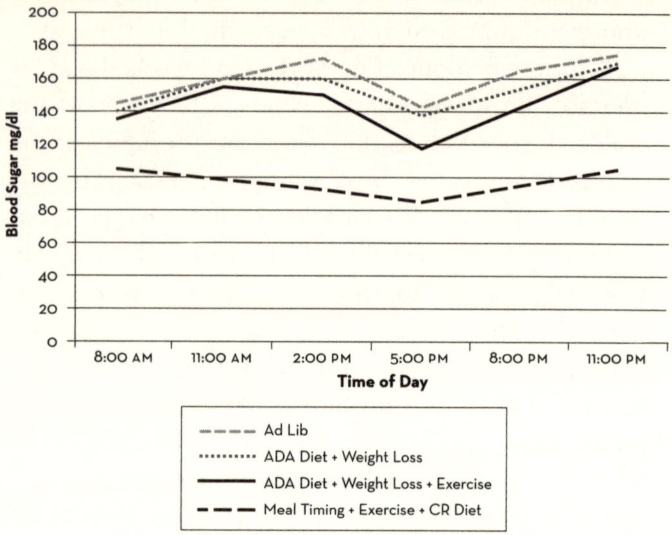

ADA Diet = American Diabetes Association recommended diet.

Above graphs based on personal journal records and reflect the experience of one individual only.

Normal fasting blood glucose levels are typically defined as 80–100. Prediabetes diagnosis begins at 126, and full diabetes is 145 or above.

I don't eat until 6:00 p.m., when I have a large salad with quite a variety of goodies. With a foundation of fresh green and cruciferous vegetables, tomatoes, and onions, I accessorize it from day to day depending on the ingredients I have available. If it is to be my only meal, then I may add an ounce of low-fat mozzarella cheese, an ounce or two of leftover baked chicken breast, 1 hard-boiled egg, and 8 or 10 nuts (mixture of almonds, cashews, and hazelnuts). The dressing is a homemade balsamic vinaigrette with extra-virgin olive oil. I often add a couple tablespoons of fresh salsa to spice things up, and sometimes a bit of prepared horse-radish. At times, I'll alternate with 3 ounces of chicken breast, a two-egg omelet, 1 ounce of low-fat mozzarella cheese, or 3 ounces of fish (preferably sashimi). Note there are *no* breads, pastas, or grain/flour products whatsoever in my diet. Fruit is an occasional treat but not a staple. If you look at the USDA food guide pyramid, I've completely wiped out the bottom row. I never ever consume sugars or sweetened drinks—other than an occasional diet soft drink. I do make use of Splenda in my salad dressing—or if I need an occasional beverage sweetener.

For me, this regimen is very easy to maintain. It fits with my lifestyle and my natural hunger patterns. Now I seldom get hungry during the day, even when I'm involved in strenuous sports activities. Prior to CR I ate the traditional three hearty meals a day plus snacks, but was nevertheless *always* desperately hungry. What I do advocate is to keep a journal when you experiment with new foods or eating patterns. This way you can learn exactly what works for *you*, regardless of the confusing and often incorrect literature and advice floating around on the subject of nutrition.

ARE YOU A CALORIE COUNTER OR A WEIGHT WATCHER?

other approaches to monitoring the lifestyle changeover

In the process of writing this book, we realized that some people like to improvise and others prefer to have a structured game plan. Both styles are effective, as long as you stick with the program. Whether you like to count calories or not is less important than eating healthy foods and very gradually eating less of them, which will reduce your weight.

After a week or two of watching what you eat and filling your plate with ample amounts of colorful and whole, rather than processed, foods, the simplest way to begin the next phase of the Longevity Diet is to watch your weight. You don't need to be obsessive about weighing yourself, especially if you don't feel that you need to be on an extreme version of the Longevity Diet. Weighing yourself once or twice a week might suffice. There will be daily fluctuations in your weight, of course, but these won't matter at the beginning, especially if you're not radically restricting your caloric intake.

The ratio of protein to carbohydrates or fat is not as relevant as eating healthy foods and eating fewer calories. You don't need to eat smaller volumes of food. It depends on what kind of foods you choose to indulge in. If you prefer foods with low energy density, then your plate will be piled high with vegetables and whole grains, and topped with a smaller portion of protein. If you prefer a higher percentage of protein in your diet, then you will need to serve smaller portions. Both methods are health conscious; both work. You can decide which method *you* like.

Then, settle in for a few years of *very gradual* weight loss. This is not a deprivation diet. You should not have to go out and buy a new wardrobe in a few months. Losing weight quickly is counterproductive and will stress your body physiologically, possibly releasing toxins into the blood that were stored in fatty tissue. A life-extension diet is really a life maintenance diet, and hence not a reducing "diet" at all.

JW's story—a calorie counter

JW's high blood pressure story attests to the dictate that calories count. When we first read about his initial days on the Longevity Diet, we weren't sure we could use the details of his experiences. White rice? For the short run, JW's diet worked quickly and effectively to lower his blood pressure. He then conscientiously designed a wholesome diet. But it really demonstrates that it is the calories that will launch *your* healing journey as well.

> In 2000 I was coerced into beginning CR. I depended on my beta-blockers and calcium channel-blockers to hold hypertension at bay. And I could not see my toes. . . . I woke up one morning disgusted with the ineptitude of doctors and nutritionists and decided to eat nothing. That quickly migrated to eating something "bland," so I opted for steamed rice, fat-free milk, and sugar. My blood pressure started dropping that day. At lunch I ate rice, strawberries, and fat-free milk. By suppertime, my BP was low enough I could skip the evening beta-blocker. This rice-based, low-sodium, low-protein diet continued for several weeks. My wife also went on this diet.
>
> We had a diet that worked and I wasn't hungry. At about two months into the diet, my wife asked if that was all *we* were ever going to eat. She had lost from 185 to a beautiful 150. We started adding steamed veggies one at a time to test for allergies. I found I could eat almost any veggie steamed, and almost any fruit. We were lacto-vegetarian. I once said I would eat no meat forever, but since then I found I could eat a little meat as long as I did it without using salt. I leave off flavoring on veggies as well, so I can taste the true veggie taste. But my diet remains 95 percent lacto-veggie with a little fish, usually shellfish. Beef, and pork is rare. Turkey maybe once per year, chicken breast salad maybe six times per year. Most pork, chicken, and turkey today is soaked in salt.
>
> My weight didn't fall that much at first, it took about six weeks to drop down to 172 pounds from 206 pounds. At my roundest I weighed 234 pounds

> and it took me six years to work it down and up and down to 206 pounds. But rather than my new slender frame, my low blood pressure is what kept me on CR; and the looks for my wife. She's sixty-seven and looks maybe fifty years old. The effect was overwhelming for me. Practically all my wife's family have now lost weight and we have not pressured them at all. All are older than we are. Her bro-in-law is down from about 260 to maybe 190 now.
>
> I developed a spreadsheet to keep track of foods I ate so that I could correlate it with blood pressure. I wrote a Basic program to massage the USDA database into a spreadsheet. That tool is basic to knowing what and how many calories I eat. Now I can judge the calories by eyeball. I now weigh 172.5 to 177.5. A key point I think is to cycle the weight up maybe five pounds, then down seven pounds, to maintain control. I plan to control it downward as I get older, maybe 165 next year, scaling down to 125 at age 100.

Peter Voss's story—a weight watcher

Peter Voss is one of our longtime CR Society members. He and his partner, marathon runner Louise, frequently visited the late Dr. Roy Walford at his Venice Beach studio in California to discuss the Longevity Diet, as well as more "out there" futuristic topics like cryonics. Peter has perhaps the most flexible and well-adjusted attitude of any longtime practitioner of the Longevity Diet. Once well-established with a routine that works for you, he says, "Most important, if CR becomes difficult, or if it makes you unhappy, relax and eat a little more!" Perhaps Peter's success can be attributed to his motto: "Rationality, give me the strength to change the things I can, the serenity to accept those that I can't, and the wisdom to know the difference."

When I started CR in 1997, I weighed 155 pounds. Now, seven years into this lifestyle, I have hit my cruise control and, with less than 5 percent body fat I don't think that I want to lose any more weight! The 1,800 to 1,850 calories a day I need to maintain my weight, satisfies me; I feel strong and don't suffer from the frequent colds I used to before starting CR. Hunger was a problem in the beginning (I restricted fairly rapidly—more than I would recommend), but now I manage fine (it almost seems that my stomach has shrunk)! At first, I regularly monitored, recorded, and analyzed *all* the food I would eat for periods of about four weeks, and then go for two to three months without monitoring (other than my morning weight); but with the same eating habits. I lost weight slowly, not more than one pound per month. My blood pressure declined over the first two years to around 105/70.

I very gradually, over several years, cut back the serving sizes of high-calorie ingredients. For example, from one-half slice of full-fat cheese per cracker I cut back to one-eighth slice low-fat cheese, and I would use one tablespoon of salad dressing rather than two. Strangely, I've found that my taste buds adjusted and food seems even tastier now. I'm now able to discern more subtle textures and flavors.

I am a grazer, so many small meals savored throughout the day helped me maintain my energy. I have lots of desirable food readily available, with fruit on my countertop and veggies in the fridge. Green, black, and rooibos tea along with lots of water help keep me hydrated and full.

This is just background to the main point that I hardly ever cook, buy virtually all my food at the local supermarket chain store, and go out to eat frequently (I order with care: both what I select and changes I request. Minor adjustments can make a huge nutritional difference). I love strawberries, broccoli, spinach—veggies and more veggies, often with pasta sauce—salmon, chicken breast, almonds, steel-cut oats, yogurt (including frozen), hot chocolate (diet), and nonfat crackers with a little peanut butter and banana. I really love the food I now eat, and miss it when I can't get it.

April's story—calorie counting plus weight watching

We discovered April, with her contagious enthusiasm, and the many great stories she has contributed via her blog at http://blog.calorierestriction.org. She lost weight a little too quickly at first, but learned to regulate her diet to a more healthy level of calories.

I have been working on changing the composition of my diet to increase protein and good fats, replacing junky carbs, and that's a constant struggle. I think I can reach lower calorie levels, but I have to put much more effort into the content of those calories in order to do so with optimal nutrition. When I first started playing with the lower calorie levels, I was seduced by the high feeling that I got from very low cal days, and I lost weight too fast. I got scared when I saw that five pounds had come off in only two weeks. The life-extension benefits seem to evaporate in animals that lose weight too fast, and I don't want to be one of those dead rats! So I broke down and bought a scale and am monitoring my weight.

OTHER TECHNIQUES FOR THE LONGEVITY DIET

fasting

There have been many discussions amongst our group regarding the benefits and efficacy of fasting. A true fast consists of consuming only water. This strict, and potentially therapeutic, approach to ameliorating some disease warrants further research, and is beyond the scope of this book.

However, less stringent definitions of fasting are plentiful. Lisa abstains from food one day a week, drinking plenty of water and twelve ounces of diluted fruit or vegetable juice. While this is technically not a fast, it does shear 1,000 calories off of her weekly average, and gives her a day of rest from food anticipation, food prep, food consumption, cleanup, and digestion. These are her most productive days. Not only does Lisa ingest less food on her fasting days but food consumes less of her time that she can then funnel into other activities.

Fasting can be mentally strengthening as well as an easy way to cut calories. If you choose this strategy, we suggest that you pursue short fasts—do not fast for more than one or two days at a time—and drink plenty of fluids. If you have a serious health problem do not attempt to fast unless you are under the care of a physician. This includes diabetics, and anyone taking prescription medicines.

10

THE LONGEVITY DIET AND EXERCISE

WHILE EXERCISE, IN and of itself, does not slow the aging process, for many people it can be an important element in a successful longevity program.

AGING AND CELLS

DO YOU RUN, pedal, swim, lift weights, or do yoga or T'ai Chi? The truth is, although such activities will add life to your years, they will not necessarily add years to your life. Exercise can mitigate the effects of an unhealthy lifestyle: it can lower blood pressure, slow down or reverse arteriosclerosis, lower cholesterol, improve insulin metabolism, maintain and improve bone density, release endorphins, and reduce stress. However, while exercise helps extend the average life span of groups studied, virtually no studies have proven that such regimens improve the maximum life span of any species studied. That is, only the Longevity Diet will slow the aging process itself.

Calorie-restricted sedentary mice were compared to non-CR sedentary mice that could eat as much as they wanted, with

CR mice who exercised, and with non-CR mice that exercised but could eat as much as they wanted. As expected, the non-CR sedentary mice became heavy, developed various cancers, diabetes, and grayed more quickly. Surprisingly, the CR mice that did not exercise looked like the non-CR mice that exercised and ate as much as they wanted—except that the CR mice that didn't exercise lived even longer![72]

Lifelong, committed, long-distance runners generally don't die young. But they don't live extraordinarily long lives either. Serious aerobic exercise is great for you. We all know that! It reduces your odds of getting many of the disease associated with aging. But it doesn't slow the aging process itself. But even if your goal of reduced risk of heart disease, type 2 diabetes, stroke, and other diseases of aging is achieved via the Longevity Diet, and not aerobic exercise, aerobic exercise can still make you feel good. It reduces the deleterious effects of stress, can help stave of depression, and can be a lot of fun!

AEROBICS: GOOD FOR THE HEART AND BRAIN

IF YOU'RE NOT on a rigorous Longevity Diet program, the traditional benefits of aerobic exercise are very much worth keeping in mind.

The American College of Sport's Medicine defines *aerobic exercise* as "any activity that uses large muscle groups, can be maintained continuously, and is rhythmic in nature." *Aerobic fitness* refers to your body's ability to get oxygen to your muscles. When your heart is strong, more oxygen-rich blood is pumped with each heartbeat. When you are not aerobically fit, your heart must beat faster and work harder to provide the oxygen required for any physical exertion. Hence, people who are not in good shape get out of breath quickly. Just like your biceps, the heart is a muscle, and it will respond and reward you when you work out diligently over a period of time.

Aerobic exercise, as with CR, also improves the brain's agility, that is, your ability to problem solve and reason things out. The brain, just like your muscles and organs, needs oxygen. With age, the oxidative decline throughout the body also largely affects front-brain activities. With our rapidly changing world, lifelong learning is essential, and you will need an agile mind. Brain health is best maintained by a rigorous Longevity Diet program. But for those not on rigorous diet, evidence is pouring in that regular exercise maintains brain health. Researchers at the University of Illinois at Urbana–Champaign have shown that those who are fit perform significantly better on tests of cognitive function.[73]

Brisk walking, running, swimming, cycling, cross-country skiing, dancing, rollerblading, and stair climbing are a few common forms of an aerobic workout. If you are new to aerobic exercise, build up to twenty minutes gradually. Familiar theme? As with easing into the Longevity Diet, moderation will help trigger the body's adaptive process more effectively than the compulsive "new lease on life" that often sabotages a true lifestyle change. In addition, if you push too hard in the beginning you may get frustrated and strain muscles. Begin with brisk walking, a treadmill, or whatever is convenient, until you are a little short of breath, and slowly lengthen your sessions. If you begin to feel too comfortable while working out, this is a sign that you need to increase the relative difficulty of your regimen. For example, if walking one mile in twenty minutes has become easy, up your pace to cut the time to fifteen minutes. You need to feel your body reaching toward its goal, for the exercise to have an effect. Being slightly winded is good: it indicates that you are engaging your body's vital systems enough to build stamina and improve fitness, but not so much as to wear yourself out.

The effect of exercise is cumulative. If you have been aerobically active all your life, the cardiac benefits are greater than if you begin later on. However some benefits depend on repeated and regular exercise. Increased sensitivity to insulin, for instance, declines only a few days after you stop exercising. If you are ill or injured, ease back into a lighter exercise routine as soon as you can; and get into the habit of raising a sweat at least briefly on a lazy day.

Resist overdoing it. Much more than thrice-weekly twenty-minute aerobic sets may run contrary to optimal health. The demands imposed on the body by, for example, a marathon run can cause damaging oxidative stress (free radical production) that is counterproductive to its otherwise favorable effects on your heart. Be mindful not to adopt an exercise regimen that exhausts your energy rather than enhances it. Learn to distinguish between stretching and strengthening your body, and straining it. Addictive zeal may lead to a sport therapy clinic, arthritic knees, or worse.

WEIGHT-BEARING EXERCISES AND RESISTANCE TRAINING: GOOD FOR THE BONES

WEIGHT-BEARING EXERCISE AND resistance training are important for everyone, even those on more rigorous versions of CR.

The disease **osteoporosis**, or "porous bones," currently affects 8 million women, and 2 million men, with an additional 34 million at risk for low bone density, and fractured hips, wrists, or vertebrae. The statistics are scary; in people over the age of fifty, 1 in 2 women and 1 in 4 men will experience some osteoporosis-related fracture in their remaining lifetime. Additional risk factors include being thin, having a small frame, low testosterone levels in men, long-term treatment with corticosteroids, lack of exercise, and a low calcium intake (common with a vegan or milk-free diet). In particular, Caucasian menopausal women undergo hormonal changes that can weaken their bones.

Your bones are living tissues, constantly being renewed. As a normal part of its life cycle, old bone is broken down and reabsorbed into the body and new bone is formed. This process is called *remodeling*. When you are about thirty years of age, your bones will begin to absorb bone mass at a rate that outpaces your body's ability to generate new bone. This process is normal, whether you drank your milk as a child or not. The good news is: bones do respond to outside stimuli, such as weight-bearing exercise or resistance training. In fact, if you x-ray the arm of a tennis player, you will see that the bones in the playing arm are thicker and denser than the bones in the other arm.

> An exercise routine for the bones should include weight-bearing and resistance-training exercises.

weight-bearing exercise

The term *weight-bearing exercise* is quite literal: an activity in which you bear weight and resist gravity. This does not mean you need to lift weights. In such exercises, you are in fact carrying your *own* weight. Examples of weight-bearing exercises are walking, running, and stair climbing. On the other hand, swimming (in which water supports your weight) and bicycling (in which the bicycle itself does) may be among your aerobic favorites and are excellent for the heart, but they will not benefit your bones. So whether you choose a health spa with its treadmills and NordicTrack machines, or twenty minutes jogging outdoors in the fresh air and sunshine, your bones will bear testimony to your efforts and reward you with good density. Keep in mind that, while weight-bearing activities will strengthen the bones to the legs and hips, they are not as effective on the upper body, unless you pursue such activities as rock climbing or ball-hitting sports that create an interplay between your body's weight and the muscles of your arms.

resistance training

Resistance training, also known as *bone-loading exercise,* stresses the bones in another way, by exerting the pressure of muscular contraction. As your muscles contract and extend, the tendons that connect muscle to bone pull on the bone, and this pressure stimulates the tissues in the bones themselves. Hence, in a well-designed sequence, you would use all the major muscle groups in your arms, legs, and torso to reinforce a balance to the flexor and extensor muscles and an even distribution of pressure on the bones.

> Some in our CR community have reported a loss of bone density disproportionate to their age. Whether you lift weights, practice Iyengar yoga or Pilates, bone loading exercise is probably a must for serious practitioners of the Longevity Diet.

Proper technique, good posture, and sequencing are vital for safety, and to target specific muscles and bones. In sequencing a routine, it is important to warm up the body sufficiently before you start and to proceed through the exercises in the correct order, so find an instructor, a class, a video, or a good book on the subject before you begin. Health clubs are a valuable resource for equipment and expertise. Usually they have posters with safety tips and recommendations for using their weights and machines hanging on the walls, and they should have staff on hand to advise you on posture and technique. For convenience, various kinds of weights may also be purchased to be used at home.

getting started

For your arms, shoulders, and upper back, select a weight that you can lift easily eight times and practice repetitions until the muscle fatigues after ten to twelve cycles. Increase the weight by no more than ten percent after you can comfortably practice with your beginning weights. Too much weight will increase any risk of injury, so take your time. Research indicates that *a single set* of a dozen repetitions with the proper weight is just as effective for bone mass as three sets. Again, less, when done properly, is more.

Do not underestimate the importance of good posture. Lift and lower weights slowly, this will minimize any risk of injury and maximize the strength building and bone loading effects. Sore muscles or a little stiffness the day after exercise is normal, but throbbing or searing pain is a sign of nerve impingement or aggravation to tendon, ligament, muscle, or joint. With a brief period of complete rest, the body will usually recover on its own. When you do resume your routine, reduce the amount of weight you lift and build back with fewer repetitions. If pain persists, or interrupts your sleep, see a doctor. And be patient—strength training is a slow process. Begin slowly and gradually build up a longer, more heavily weighted practice over a period of several months.

EXERCISE AND CALORIES

Regular exercise not only burns calories, it also builds lean muscle mass and thus raises the *resting metabolic rate* (RMR). How? Remember that metabolism is the process that extracts and utilizes energy from food. Your resting metabolic rate is the amount of energy required to maintain your most basic body functions, such as respiration and cell repair. The minimum number of calories you need to eat while you are doing *absolutely nothing* is your RMR. This accounts for approximately 70 percent of the energy you use every day. Lean muscle requires more energy (much like how a high-performance car engine prefers supreme gasoline) and burns more calories than fat, even at rest. If your primary goal is weight-loss, this is particularly important.

Q. So if I am a power lifter or run daily, and am on the Longevity Diet, should I eat more?

If you are physically fit and thin, you will have a greater percentage of lean muscle and will have a higher resting metabolic rate, and hence you may need to eat more calories than a heavier person who does not exercise. It is precisely for this reason that too much exercise is counterproductive to the Longevity Diet. Regardless of your exercise routine, your current weight, and your daily caloric intake; remember that your overall weight and moderation in all CR-related physical activities are key to good health.

YOGA: THE NEW WAVE

YOGA IS GOOD for more than just your peace of mind.

Yoga postures can also "stress" bone while stretching muscles, presumably the perfect combination. In fact, certain styles of yoga qualify as both weight-bearing and resistance training; while stretching out your muscles and lubricating all your joints to boot. A yoga method where you stay in the posture for at least a minute, and in particular standing postures and inversions (such as the "Downward Facing Dog" pose) offer the most in weight-bearing and bone-loading benefits.

Yoga is largely an isotonic form of exercise, wherein you strengthen muscle by using controlled movement and the resistance of the muscles themselves to hold the posture. Rather than the singular flexing action in a particular muscle from lifting a weight, which isolates and strengthens that muscle, yoga poses encourage a coordinated effort among all body parts, muscle, joint, and bone, legs, torso, and arms, to target a particular area. Rather than twelve repetitions that target a particular muscle and bone (the recommended form of weightlifting for people on the Longevity Diet), yoga uses your own body weight by holding the poses for longer periods of time, which stimulates the bone[74] while increasing flexibility in the muscles.

The vocabulary of yoga poses includes standing poses, twists, forward and backward bending poses and inversions, and upside-down poses. In a good class, every major body part will be addressed to strengthen, stretch, and increase the range of motion in the joints.

The standing poses provide a full range of movement for the legs and hips, and thus will help to maintain both the stability and flexibility required for a healthy back, strong hips, and limber knees. Twists encourage circulation to the intervertebral discs, help to relieve backaches, and will improve elimination. Yoga also releases the muscular tension so often faulted for headaches, indigestion, sleep difficulties, and backaches.

Over time you may be introduced to inversions, the infamous headstand and shoulder stand poses. These postures become weight-bearing exercises for the upper body and, in particular, the spine. Since the vertebral column is very susceptible to fractures, and is difficult to isolate in exercise, these postures may be able to stimulate bone density in the spine itself. There are, however, many contra-indications to both the headstand and shoulder stand, so it is imperative that you seek out a qualified instructor and to begin gradually before attempting to go upside down!

not all yoga is created equal

Today there are as many schools of yoga as there are types of running shoes. Buyer beware: you will find power yoga, yogaerobics, hot yoga—anything that will sell the image of a lean muscle machine. Our purpose here is to build bone strength, improve flexibility, and reduce stress. Trendy styles of nontraditional yoga lack cohesive standards, so your chance of finding a teacher who understands good alignment is hit or miss.

In addition, these popular classes tend to be large and are conducted in overheated rooms. We suggest you avoid yoga teachers or venues that do not support relaxation. Also, Integral yoga, Sivananda yoga, and the Viniyoga systems place more emphasis on meditation and relaxation so, while they may calm your mind, they will not benefit your bones.

The Iyengar and Anusara systems of yoga have certified teachers trained in good alignment. In particular, instructors teaching under the Iyengar trademark are skilled in both remedial applications of yoga (injuries from other exercise programs) and in overall good form. Even when pursuing these systems, be sure you work with a certified instructor in a supportive space.

STRESS— THE SILENT BUT INSIDIOUS MOLE

WITH SO MANY well-documented ill effects of stress, we are continually amazed at how few people actively pursue relaxation techniques. While exercise is currently a marketer's dream, with the proliferation of fitness studios, gyms, equipment, videos, clothes, and trainers, relaxation is relegated to an afternoon by the pool or a massage. And while increased interest in exercise is a welcome counterpoint to the dire statistics underlining the rise in sedentary lifestyles, including diabetes, hypertension, and obesity, it omits the powerful mind-over-body effect for which conscious relaxation is well known.

Everyone would agree that less stress leads to better health; and that sleep, eating, and mood disorders are often associated with anxiety. Studies show that chronic stress decreases the body's ability to heal, from minor cuts to major surgery. Chronic psychological stress can lead to an accelerated shortening of telomeres (cellular aging; see page 77), as recently reported in a PNAS (Proceedings of the National Academy of Sciences) article.[75] Stress quadruples the risk of asthma attacks in children,[76] and stress is seen as a cause of some miscarriages. The National Institute of Mental Health distributes a handbook entitled *Stress and the Developing Brain,* alerting parents to the dangers of a stressful household to children. Researchers at the Boston School of Medicine contend that acute and chronic stress induces a chronic inflammatory process that culminates in atherosclerosis. These findings may account for up to 40 percent of diagnosed cases that cite no other attributable causes. The list is quite extensive, and covers everything from irritable bowel syndrome to exacerbating the painful effects of rheumatoid arthritis and multiple sclerosis.

In addition to supporting the physical healing process, relaxation techniques help reinforce a person's resolve to stick with a healthy lifestyle makeover and to cope with life's changes.

Some stresses are beneficial and others harmful. How can stress be beneficial? Mikhail Baryshnikov once said that he was nervous before each dance performance. Perhaps this is what gave him the edge that made his leaps so breathtaking. Similarly, the intoxication before a romantic evening or the anticipation before a job interview produces the aroused, or heightened, state of consciousness we associate with performance anxiety, and this in turn sharpens our senses. Our adrenaline flows. We become more alert. We are stressed by looking forward to something we want to accomplish, and that very stress can be the boost that helps us achieve it.

Purely physical stress can also be beneficial: In physics, stress is the internal resistance of a body to an applied force or system of forces. As in resistance-training practices and in aerobic exercise, this productive stress triggers the adaptive mechanisms in the body to strengthen internal structures—bones and such systems as the cardiac and respiratory.

But we most commonly associate stress with this *American Heritage Dictionary* (2000) definition: "A mentally or emotionally disruptive or upsetting condition occurring in response to adverse external influences capable of affecting physical health, usually characterized by increased heart rate, raised blood pressure, muscular tension, irritability, and depression." Now, that sure doesn't sound beneficial, does it?

Take care that your attempts to relax do not actually produce additional stress. Some people say that they find prolonged exercise relaxes them, that it solicits a natural high, like "entering the zone." This is different from *choosing to practice a* centering method or relaxation technique that helps you to cope with any increase in pressure, be it from external circumstances or internal issues. To go for a run when you are stressed-out may indeed help calm you, but it may wear your resources thin if your anxiety level has persisted for a period of time; you may be more prone to injury and you may lower immunity against illness. How? Stress hormones, along with other deleterious consequences, have a strong anti-inflammatory effect on tissues, muscles and joints. Hence, you might actually feel like you can do more, and that the exercise is enabling you to tune out your feelings, but you are acting *under the influence* of a strong chemical effect, that of excessive adrenaline. If the adrenal glands continue to pump adrenaline into the body, over time they become exhausted, and the neurotransmitters that deliver messages of well-being and restore internal equilibrium become muted. Your immune system then shuts down, and you become vulnerable to physical accidents, even to infection.

Thoughts are food to the mind; and they can nourish or poison you. Every state of mind affects the body, even if you are not conscious of their doing so. If your body pipes up with stress-related symptoms, you need to listen, and to find a safe means of releasing your stress. While adequate family and community support or psychological maturity is helpful, for a long and healthy life we encourage you to seek out and practice some relaxation technique, be it meditation, keeping a journal, visualization, or biofeedback.

True relaxation techniques enable the mind to let go of obsessive thought patterns and replace them with a composed perspective. In our opinion, the most advantageous thing that you take from this chapter is this understanding of conscious relaxation.

> In a pinch, you can quickly realign your runaway reactions before acting impulsively. Try the following:
>
> Close your eyes. Take a gentle but deep breath in, imagine the air nourishing every cell in your body with tranquility, composure. As you exhale, open your mouth slightly and let a satisfying sigh escape your lips. Or you might prefer to relax all the muscles in your face as you exhale, especially the jaw, like chocolate melting in the sunlight.

the relaxation response

The relaxation response, a state of deep physiological relaxation, is characterized by a reduction in heart rate, blood pressure, respiratory rate, and muscular tension; many of the effects are similar to those of calorie restriction.

There are many methods that induce this effect. Some of us are more visually inclined, so guided imagery may be effective. Some are more kinesthetic, or physically oriented. Progressive relaxation emphasizes the gradual release of all voluntary muscular tension until you experience a deep state of inner peace. Various meditative schools use awareness of the breath as a focal point to shift into an **alpha**, or a heightened state of consciousness. Pain-management programs often begin with exercises, which first bring awareness to the movement of the breath, and then to deepening the exhalation. Prayer is effective for many; or the repetition of a simple yet meaningful phrase, which helps train you to shift your mind from scattered thinking to purposeful, controlled, and quiet thought.

As important as what you choose is *how often* you do it. A few minutes every day will be far more effective than a class you take once a week. So begin with something simple, something that you can practice preferably at home. There are many good tapes available, or, if you do find a class, practice! The cumulative effect and skills you reap from this work will help support your commitment to the Longevity Diet lifestyle.

HOW DO I BEGIN MY LONGEVITY EXERCISE REGIMEN?

WHETHER YOU WORK out with a trainer, go to a gym to use the equipment, or exercise on your own, practice your aerobic and resistance-training programs on alternate days. This will allow your muscles, tendons, ligaments, and joints to recover from any potential excessive practice. And remember, aerobic activities, weight-bearing or resistance training, and stress reduction are *all* important elements of a healthy lifestyle, although a serious and mature practitioner of the Longevity Diet may not need the benefits of the aerobic routine. Do not do only a single kind of action exclusively. Here is a sample weekly schedule to help you visualize how these programs can all work together:

Sunday: Aerobic activity: walk, hike, skate, run, swim twenty to thirty minutes

Monday: Resistance workout or Iyengar yoga class (or any form that holds standing poses and inversions)

Tuesday, AM: Twenty to thirty minutes of aerobics; PM: thirty minutes of stretching

Wednesday: Resistance workout or Iyengar yoga class

Thursday: Aerobics: a fun, social activity like skating or biking, to counteract any midweek slump

Friday, AM: Twenty to thirty minutes of aerobics; thirty minutes of stretching or resistance work

Saturday: Resistance workout or Iyengar yoga class, or alternate your activities with yet another kind of aerobic activity or stretching class.

Your present or projected schedule may look quite different, depending on your preferred routines and available time. If you already practice yoga, add an aerobic activity (unless your style of yoga is aerobic). Perhaps, especially if you run, the kinds of warm-up stretches you already do may not be enough to strengthen all your bones nor will they help with your tight hamstrings and upper back; seek out a stretch or yoga class. Whatever you do, be sure to choose activities that you enjoy, in a setting you like. If formally structured exercise is difficult to fit into your lifestyle, remember that active sports, dancing, and even just twenty-minutes spent walking up and down the stairs at home or an office building (find a colleague willing to go "buddies" with you during a break), are all exercise.

As with your food choices, if you enjoy your physical activities, you will more likely to stick with your goals. If you exercise solely because it is good for you, and not because you like to, your chances of maintaining a well-balanced program over the long haul are slim. Perhaps you multitask by reading the newspaper while using a stationary bicycle or by watching the evening news while stretching. That's fine. But don't use such tactics to block from your consciousness what you are actually doing with your body. If you really see and appreciate the trees, the sky, and the people around you while you work out; or use your exercise period to tune in to the world inside yourself, with its sensations of breath, warmth, the release of a tight muscle, or the stimulation of a spine unfolding and lengthening, then your exercise regimen will feel gratifying in of itself and will become an integral part of your life.

11 OPTIMAL LIVING FROM A FEW VETERAN PRACTITIONERS OF THE LONGEVITY DIET

peter In addition to being an advocate of CR, Peter Voss exemplifies the integration of thought and action that Dr. Walford referred to in his preface to *Maximum Life Span*: "I believe that the effects of life-span extension will be outstandingly positive for mankind as both social and individual animals, will help solve many of our dilemmas, and revolutionize human potential." A longevity diet is but one facet of Peter's vision to enhance what it means to be alive.

> Contrary to popular opinion, I see the impending dramatic improvement in longevity as a tremendous boon for mankind. Not only for the obvious selfish benefit of living a vastly extended vital life, but more generally for the advantage of having more wise people active in society. Today, just as we learn how to live life—you know, after three careers and two marriages. . . . well, seriously—having learned to be in touch with our emotions; how to effectively communicate with others; how to make and keep money; having raised children; having had the time and interest to study

some psychology, philosophy, and science; having developed an appreciation for art, and so on—we find ourselves out of circulation. As our active years are extended, I expect that many more dynamic, wise and able people will experience and demonstrate Optimal Living—and will thereby positively contribute to society. My passion is for exploring what I call Optimal Living: maximizing both the quantity and quality of life. Optimal Living is not one single, "perfect" version of life. *Optimal* means "best or most favorable under a given set of circumstances." The circumstances and contexts of our lives are also in a continual state of flux. Specific values optimal to one person at a given time may be detrimental in a different context.

Hence, there are many ways to coordinate the factors in CR. CR is a lifestyle change, it is not a diet, and will therefore be unique to each individual. It can be a positive experience—I would focus on finding new and delicious foods and food preparations rather than on what I "shouldn't eat," and I would not beat myself up if I thought I had failed. I made a point of discovering ready-to-eat and easy-to-prepare healthy low-cal foods that I really enjoy—often this simply meant improving the meal by changing the type of dressing used (delicious fat-free versus conventional mayonnaise), or the quantity of some ingredients (half the rice).

As I see it, the basics are simple: Subject to certain limits, the fewer calories you consume, the better your health and longevity, and the benefits are proportional. The primary payoff is avoiding, or vastly delaying, the major killer diseases: heart, stroke, diabetes, cancer; but other benefits include a stronger immune system, increased fitness, and a greater appreciation of food.

In the context of my philosophy of Optimal Living, this also implies that I must enjoy my CR lifestyle—in addition to striving for vastly increased longevity and vitality. Good nutrition and exercise are complemented with strategies for improving mental and financial well-being, and reducing risk of accidental death—plus the ultimate safety net (of unknown fabric): cryonics.

Let's work towards overcoming life's current limitations. Let's have the option of enjoying a fuller, healthier, and much longer life. Who knows what new heights we may reach. . . .

dean

In the formative years of the virtual CR Society, Lisa and Roy Walford regularly observed the CR list while refraining from posting, to avoid any semblance of influencing the generally friendly but sometimes heated milieu of these extremely bright people with strong opinions.

Inspired by the imaginative approaches many practitioners adopted for themselves, they were particularly drawn to the systematic way that Dean applied himself to the Longevity Diet. Dean's is a well-known voice on CR Society's mailing list, answering sophisticated questions as well as offering simple suggestions to the newcomers who frequent the community.

This diet has created a life for me here and now that I truly love and find incredibly fulfilling. Any health/longevity benefits that may accompany my practice of CR I consider to be "gravy."

Let me try to explain. As you may be aware, CR results in a number of physical and psychological changes in its practitioners. The usual focus in CR is on how the physical changes impact health/longevity.

The psychological changes are typically either ignored, or viewed as unfortunate side effects.

What are these psychological changes? I can only speak from personal experience, but I've been told by other people on CR that they've experienced some of these as well. Specifically, I've noticed changes in my brain's "reward centers"—I definitely receive more internally generated positive feedback from little things than I ever did prior to CR. For me, such appreciation of little things started with food.

For example, I eat and have been eating an identical, relatively simple meal three times a day for well over a year. Prior to CR, I could never have imagined such behavior. More interesting, I truly get pleasure from each and every one of these meals. In fact, I'm certain I enjoy my food more today than I ever did prior to CR, despite its monotony.

With some training, finding pleasure in simple things extends into other aspects of life. I would never have anticipated this from CR. It is as if the so-called deprivation in one area of my life (food), has fostered a sense of gratitude and appreciation in all areas, which may need to be experienced to be appreciated, but is a truly wonderful state. Suffice it to say that I hop out of bed each morning anxious to experience what the day has in store, despite the fact that quite often, today is very much like every other day.

CR is not like the Atkins diet or the South Beach diet or the Weight Watchers point system, where there's a very prescribed set of things you can and can't eat. You have to decide how many calories you need, how far you want to drop, what the easiest way to practice is. So your intention is important. Successful veteran CR folk tend to be in it for the adventure. We might think, "If I feed my body the right things, it will work better" as opposed to, "I want to look better." The science of it and the tweaking and tuning of it appeals to a different demographic.

In the beginning, CR did interfere with my enjoyment of life. Food clouded my thoughts for at least a year. Food obsession, long hours spent in food preparation, and thoughts about how to best avoid/delay my own mortality distracted me from things that are (or should have been) really important to me, like my family, and helping others. I am the sole practitioner of CR in my family (wife and two young children). I have worked very hard to optimize my practice of CR so as to reap the benefits without compromising my relationship with my family. Mostly this has meant streamlining my food preparation so as not to interfere with my family time.

You might ask: doesn't the hardship associated with my extreme form of CR detract from my quality of life? Let me try to explain. I've experienced a calming of the emotions and my appreciation of the little things in life started with the diet. Put together with the extraordinary health benefits, CR is well worth it.

francesca

A much-publicized *Washington Post* article did more to put CR on the map than former research reviews in the *Wall Street Journal* and even the *New York Times*. Why? The story featured two women, their trials and tribulations in life, and finally CR. Francesca was one of these women. Francesca has been an active member of the CR Society.

I'm Francesca Skelton, sixty-four years old and I started CRing in the spring of 2000.

For the vast majority of my life, I was very thin—one of those lucky people who could eat just about anything I wanted, and as much as I wanted, without gaining weight. And I took great advantage of that, often consuming vast amounts of food with no visible consequences!

That all changed in 1999, when my oldest brother died of cancer just six weeks after diagnosis. This was the latest in a string of losses of close relatives due to ill health. I was devastated and stopped eating in my usual hearty manner, and in fact, ate very little for several months as I grieved my brother's death and lost weight—weight which I could scarcely afford to lose. Thankfully, after a few months, I recovered from the grieving process, but my metabolism had completely changed. I started gaining weight for the first time in my life. I discovered I could no longer "pack it away" without gaining. When my 5'4" small-boned frame reached 138, or about twenty-two pounds over my usual lifetime adult weight, I was jolted into the realization that something had to be done. I now weighed more than I ever had in my life.

I turned to CR. Four years later, my weight is 110 to 112 (depending on whether I am soaking wet or not), but even more importantly, I am rarely ever sick. Previously, in a year, I would suffer two colds, and one or two bouts of miserable stomach viruses. These are now all history! My immune system is functioning at a level as never before. I constantly marvel at my resistance to illness.

But there's more. As a bonus, my skin looks great and my hair is full, healthy, and bouncy—this at an age when many woman are starting to experience thinning hair. Certainly CR is worth any small sacrifice for the beauty benefits alone!

Fortunately, I find it easy to stay on CR. If I stray a bit, I just get right back on the program. My "tips" and best catalysts for success are (1) online support; (2) reminding myself of my present good health and how awful it used to feel to be sick and (3) staying on a moderate program—one that is easy to stick to over the long haul.

GLOSSARY

alpha—Brain wave frequency indicative of a relaxed yet alert and reflective state. Brain wave frequencies are rhythmic fluctuations of voltage between parts of the brain resulting in a flow of electric current that can be monitored by an electroencephalograph (EEG).

amino acids—Small nitrogen-containing chemical units which link together to form **protein** molecules. The body can make some of the amino acids it needs to construct its proteins, but others must be obtained from the diet.

anorexia nervosa—Psychological disorder in which the afflicted person intentionally consumes dangerously low quantities of food because of a belief that it will improve his/her appearance or well-being. If untreated, can lead to death from malnutrition or from other complications. (See **bulimia**.) This is *not* a longevity diet! (See table 3.1 on page 42 for more on the differences between CR and anorexia nervosa.)

antioxidants—Molecules such as vitamin C and Vitamin E (and even food additives such as BHT ad BHA) that "mop up" or neutralize **free radicals**.

anti-aging medicine—Type of medicine practiced by health care professionals who seek to slow and where possible reverse the aging process of their patents. (See **life-extension** and **geriatrics**.)

average life span—Average age of death of a group of organisms, be it a group of organisms in a scientific experiment, or a group found in nature. (See **maximum life span**.)

autoantibody—*Antibodies* are proteins produced by the immune system that bind to and neutralize or help neutralize substances thought to be germs or anything else that doesn't belong in the body. *Autoantibodies* are antibodies that target and bind to normally functioning parts of the body itself, thus causing diseases known as *autoimmune diseases*.

biomarker—Indicator of some aspect of your state of health. Some biomarkers are simple, like your pulse rate, or the length of time you can balance on one foot with your eyes closed. Others are more sophisticated, for example tests of substances found in your blood, such as cholesterol or fasting glucose. (See page 5 for a fuller discussion.)

BMI (Body Mass Index)—Measure of thinness or fatness that takes into account height.

Some people (who for example are very tall) would not be overweight if they weighed 190 pounds. A very short person who weighed 190 pounds would, on the other hand, almost certainly be overweight. BMI makes it easier to distinguish between those two types of people.

Specifically, BMI is calculated as the your weight in kilograms divided by the square of your height in meters. The formula for BMI using height and weight in pounds and inches respectively is: 703 multiplied by weight in pounds divided by the square of height in inches. For example, if you weigh 170 lbs., and are 5'9" (69 inches) tall, your BMI is 170 divided by 69", which is 25.1.

Note: while BMI is a better measure of fitness than weight

alone, it is still not perfect, since a flabby 190 pounds on someone with thin bones who was six-feet tall would be far less healthy than a muscular 190 pounds on a person of the same height with a heavy bone structure.

bulimia—Psychological disorder related to anorexia nervosa in which the afflicted individual at times eats too little for good health, just as in anorexia, and at other times eats normal amounts of food (or perhaps even too much), but then forces himself or herself to vomit or in some other way—for example manic, compulsive exercise, or even laxative abuse—"get rid of" the consumed food that is perceived to have been excessive. The classic, clinical pattern of bulimia is a binge and purge cycle. (See **anorexia nervosa**.)

caloric allotment (**daily caloric allotment**)—Number of calories someone on CR allows himself or herself each day. For a large person on moderate CR, this might be as high as 2500 or so, for a small person on a very extreme CR program, it might be under 1500.

calorie—Unit of energy often used to measure the amount of energy in food. A calorie (not capitalized) is, technically, the amount of energy (or heat) needed to raise one gram of water by one degree Celsius (1.8 degrees Fahrenheit). The word "calorie," when used to refer to the energy content of food, is actually a kilocalorie, or one thousand calories. Sometimes this food calorie is capitalized, "Calorie," to distinguish it from the other calorie. In this book, when we use "calorie," we mean kilocalorie.

control group—In a scientific experiment testing the effect of a medicine, dietary regimen, lifestyle change, or any other variable, at least two groups of laboratory animals (or people or plants or whatever is being tested) are needed: (1) the group on which the medicine or regimen is tested, and (2) a group that doesn't take the medicine or undergo any other changes. The first group is called the **experimental group**, and the second is called the *control group*. The control group makes it possible to attribute changes in health observed in the experimental group to the intervention being tested, since everything else between the two groups was the same (that is, was "controlled").

CR Society (**Calorie Restriction Society**)—Nonprofit organization dedicated to helping people learn about and practice longevity diets, helping further CR research, and advancing the cause of anti-aging medicine in general. (See *Resources*.)

dietary fiber—Plant material built up from simple sugars. The human body can derive no energy from fiber because we, unlike cows and many other animal, lack the enzymes needed to break down the fiber into its component sugars.

energy-density—Measure of the amount of energy (or number of calories) in a given volume of food.

epidemiology—Study of disease patterns in (generally large) human populations.

epidemiological evidence—Scientific evidence based on assessments of the disease patterns and health observed in relatively large populations.

experimental group—(See **control group**.)

fatty acid—Type of lipid. Fatty acids are relatively small molecules that usually consist simply of a chain of carbon atoms with a *carboxylic acid group* (a carbon atom and an oxygen atom, joined to an oxygen atom and a hydrogen atom, often represented as "COOH") at the end.

fiber—(See **dietary fiber**.)

free radicals—Highly reactive chemical fragments that can cause damage to vital molecules with which they come into contact. Free radicals are highly reactive because they contain unpaired electrons, which results in their "stealing" electrons from nearby molecules.

gerontology—Scientific study of the biology of aging.

gerontologist (or **research gerontologist**)—Scientist who studies the biology of aging.

geriatrics—Medical specialty focused on the care of the elderly. (See **anti-aging mediation**.)

geriatrician—Physician whose specialty is **geriatrics**, i.e., a physician who treats the elderly.

GI—(See **glycemic index**.)

glucose—Simple sugar that is the body's main source of fuel.

glycemic index (**GI**)—Measurement of the extent to which a food raises blood glucose levels. Pure glucose is arbitrarily assigned the reference value of 100. Foods with a GI below around 45 are considered **low-GI** foods; those with a GI above 70 or so are considered **high-GI** foods.

HDL (**high density lipoprotein**)—Form of cholesterol that is thought to be healthful in part because it transports excess cholesterol to the liver, where it is eliminated. HDLs are often referred to as the "good cholesterol."

high-GI—(See **glycemic index**.)

homeostasis—Homeostasis is the physiological process by which various bodily systems (temperature, blood pressure, etc.) are maintained at in a state of equilibrium, despite varying external conditions.

hydrogenation—Addition of hydrogen molecules to an unsaturated fatty acid such that it becomes more saturated. This is a process generally applied to vegetable oils (liquids), which turns them into fats (solids). The process is also referred to as "hardening." The fatty acids that result from this process are **trans fatty acids**.

LDL (**low density lipoprotein**)—Form of cholesterol that contributes to the formation of plaque in the walls of arteries. It is often referred to as the "bad cholesterol."

life span—Length of life of an organism. (See **average life span** and **maximum life span**.)

life span study—Type of scientific study that measures the age of death of animals or subjects in a study, with the aim of determining which factors led to variations in mortality.

life-extension—Attempt to slow down and reverse the aging process. (See **anti-aging medicine.**)

lipids—Very broad, diverse category of compounds including fats, oils, steroids, waxes, that are generally insoluble in water. (See page 49 for a thorough discussion.)

low-GI—(See **glycemic index**.)

maximum life span—Length of life of the longest lived member of a given species. For statistical reasons, maximum life span in experimental studies of anti-aging interventions is sometimes measured not as the longest lived member, but rather as the average of the longest lived 10 percent, or 5 percent, etc. (See **average life span**.)

minerals—In the context of nutrition: inorganic substances of (ultimately) non-biologic origin that are essential for health.

monounsaturated fatty acid (MUFA)—Type of **fatty acid** with a chain of carbon atoms that is surrounded by ("saturated" with) hydrogen atoms except for just one "hole," or "unsaturated" spot along the carbon chain. There is only one common dietary monounsaturated fatty acid, *oleic acid,* which is the primary constituent of olive oil and canola oil, and is present in high quantities in avocados and many nuts.

MUFA—(See **monounsaturated fatty acid**.)

omega-3—Type of **polyunsaturated fatty acid** found in some nuts (for example walnuts) and seeds (for example flax seeds), and, abundantly, in many cold water fish such as salmon, with its first double bond (or "unsaturated spot") between the third and fourth carbon atoms from the *omega end* (also known as the *methyl end*) of the molecule.

omega-6—Type of **polyunsaturated fatty acid** like the *omega-3* fatty acids, except with the first double bond between the sixth and seventh carbon atoms from the omega end.

osteoporosis—Disease characterized by loss of calcium in bones which results in bone brittleness, and which leads to increased risk of fracture.

Oxygen Radical Absorbance Capacity (ORAC)—Test tube analysis that measures the total antioxidant power of foods.

phytochemicals—Literally: "plant chemical." Many of the hundreds that have been studied are thought to confer health benefits to those who consume them. Sometimes called *phytonutrients,* especially where a health role for a phytochemical has been solidly established.

phytonutrients—(See **phytochemicals**.)

polyunsaturated fatty acid (PUFA)—Type of **fatty acid** with a chain of carbon atoms that is surrounded by, or "saturated" with, hydrogen atoms, except for several "holes" or "unsaturated" spots along the carbon chain. (If there is only one unsaturated spot along the chain, the fatty acid is a *monounsaturated fatty acid*.)

prospective study (sometimes called *cohort studies*)—Type of scientific study in which certain independent variables such as caloric intake or exercise are measured at the beginning of the study, then the changes hypothesized to result from the independent variables are examined (longevity, incidence of cancer, diabetes, etc.). (See **retrospective studies**.)

protein—Structurally and physiologically vital molecule, built up from smaller, nitrogen-rich chemical units known as **amino acids**, with multiple roles in essentially all life forms.

PUFA—(See **polyunsaturated fatty acid**.)

RDA (Recommended Daily Allowance)—Widely used quantification, developed by the Food and Nutrition Board (a part of the National Academy of the Sciences), of the amount of each particular essential nutrient that the vast majority of healthy Americans (and others) should consume each day. Started being replaced by a more accurate set of several measurements, the Dietary Reference Intakes (DRI), in the mid-1990s.

resveratrol—Small chemical produced by certain plants such as grape plants, partly as a defense against mold. Thought by many researchers to have a variety of health benefits. May be able to produce effects similar to calorie restriction (though much more research is needed).

retrospective study (sometimes called *case-control studies*)—Type of scientific study in which a group with a certain pre-existing disease or condition is compared with a group (the control group) without the affliction, in order to discover what factors in the groups' respective histories might account for the difference in health between the groups. It is because researchers conducting this type of study are looking at the histories of the two groups that this kind of study is called *retrospective*. (See **prospective study**.)

saturated fatty acid—Type of **fatty acid** with a chain of carbon atoms that is entirely surrounded by ("saturated" with) hydrogen atoms. Common saturated fatty acids are solid at room temperature, as opposed to *unsaturated fatty acids* (both **polyunsaturated fatty acids** and **monounsaturated fatty acids**).

segmental aging—Name for the notion that different parts of the organism (different "segments") age at different rates. Some biomarkers might only measure the state of health or agedness of one or a few segments, not the whole organism. For example, one can have very high blood pressure, but very low fasting glucose.

set point—Weight your body "defends" when you are a young adult. That is, the weight your body tends toward if you make no special effort to lose or gain weight, don't exercise extraordinarily much or extraordinarily little. (See page 90 for a thorough discussion.)

trans fatty acids—**Fatty acid** with two particular hydrogen atoms linked to the adjoining carbon atoms in a double bond, and positioned farther away from each than in the nearly identical *cis* fatty acid, which is the form found much more often in nature. The *trans* form has a relatively straight molecular configuration, which makes it solid at room temperature. Trans fatty acids exist in nature, but the overwhelming majority of the trans fatty acid we consume was created by the **hydrogenation** process. This form of fatty acid is known to increase the risk for heart disease, and may damage health in other ways as well.

vitamins—Molecules that cannot be manufactured by the body and are essential for health. (Literally, "vital amine.")

youth span—Period of time during which the state of health of an organism is youthful.

RESOURCES

ORGANIZATIONS SUPPORTING CR AND RELATED LONGEVITY DIETS

Calorie Restriction Society (CR Society)
The Calorie Restriction Society
1827 W. 145th St, Suite 205
Gardena, CA 90249
USA
1-310-329-6511
www.crsociety.org

The CR Society is a nonprofit educational organization dedicated to teaching people about the Longevity Diet, supporting research into understanding how CR works and how it can best be implemented in humans, and critically exploring other health regimens that purport to offer similar benefits.

The CR Society is an essential resource for anyone interested in the Longevity Diet, and, indeed, is an important resource for anyone interested in health in general.

Changing your life takes work. A support group is an essential resource. The CR Society's Internet-based discussion forums, as well as its growing number of regional support groups that have regular meetings, provide essential support and guidance to those interested in trying rigorous versions of the Longevity Diet.

The discussion forums also provide an easy way to get feedback on your own longevity program from experienced practitioners of the Longevity Diet. No one book can speak to all the particular issues that each reader would want addressed. But among the 1,500 (and growing) members, you will likely find someone facing challenges similar to those you are facing.

In addition, because the group was founded by "life-extensionists"—those interested in slowing the aging process and living very, *very* long, healthy lives—there is a constant engagement with cutting-edge biological research. When relevant new research findings appear that could affect your health, you will probably hear about these findings first via the CR Society.

Membership in the CR Society includes many other benefits, a newsletter, discounts at our conferences, and more, which you can read about at the above Web site.

Walford Web Site

www.walford.com

Roy Walford's Web site contains pointers to a great number of resources for people interested in living longer, healthier lives. In addition, there is a lot of historical information about Roy Walford's extraordinary life. Take a look at this Web site if you simply want to get inspired about life and its manifold possibilities!

CRS Insider

The CRS Insider ("CRS" stands for Calorie Restriction Society) is the newsletter of the CR Society. Insider Editor-in-Chief, Bob Cavanaugh, puts out an informative and even entertaining newsletter four times a year. This is perfect for people who don't have the time our patience to log on to the Internet-based CR groups to find out what's new in the world of CR or gerontological research.

To subscribe to the newsletter, call 1-310-329-6511, or send an e-mail to subscriptions@calorierestriction.org. To contact the Editor directly, send an email to insideeditor@calorierestriction.org.

Dr. Walford's Interactive Diet Planner

Longbrook Company
903 Pacific Ave.
Venice, CA 90291
www.walford.com

Popularly known as DWIDP, this software program is a helpful companion to this book. Using the U.S. Department of Agriculture database of over 6,000 foods, including whole, name brand, processed, and fast foods, it is designed to allow you to put together optimal daily or weekly food combinations to achieve highest quality and full RDA values at lowest calorie intake. The unique powerhouse of DWIDP, not found like this in any other nutrition software program, is the Search Engine. It works like this: suppose you are on a 1,600 calorie diet and today's food list comes to 1,200 calories, 25 percent derived from fat, and DWIDP tells you the RDAs for selenium, vitamin B_6 and calcium are low. What single food or two foods can you add, 400 calories of which will make up the difference, and also be low in fat? DWIDP will tell you this, or any other combination of desires, and no other program will. You can maximize, minimize, or optimize one or many items, and at the same time. Twenty-eight nutrients are covered in the program. A Tutorial and Help program guide you through the interactive capabilities of DWIDP. Up to 99 users may each have a personal profile based on height, age, frame-size, and desired percentage of fat.

NutriBase Nutrition Software

www.nutribase.com

NutriBase is a nutrition software program with enough features to satisfy any techie, yet it's graphical interface makes navigation fairly easy and user friendly for home use. NutriBase uses the USDA R 14 nutrient database as well as name brand and restaurant entries and features over 31,000 food entries. Depending on which of the home use versions you choose, you can select from 51 nutrients to 88 nutrient to monitor. You can specify which nutrients you wish to use in your analysis, thus customizing your reports. It is easy to find the foods you need, and you can organize your recipes into 26 folders.

You can customize your toolbar and easily resize or re-sequence columns of data for ease of use. View meals, recipes, and foods in a spreadsheet that ranks them according to parameters that you select.

The fitness manager comes with all versions of NutriBase. Calorie expenditures are calculated according to your activity and weight loss can be charted and predicted with the fitness manager.

The Personal Edition tracks alcohol, caffeine, and sugars, and the Personal Plus edition also tracks vitamins.

While the home user versions of NutriBase are extremely rewarding, the NutriBase Clinical is a high-end program that was named the official dietary monitoring software for the "Calorie Restriction with Optimal Nutrition Effects Pilot Study." It is the obvious choice for professionals in the nutrition, fitness, and health industries. The Clinical edition tracks minerals and omega fatty acids.

For more information on the home editions of NutriBase please refer to: http://dietsoftware.com. And for the professional version visit: www.nutribase.com.

NOTES

1 U.S. Department of Agriculture, U.S. Department of Health and Human Services. *Dietary Guidelines for Americans.* Third Edition, 1990. (*Home and Garden Bulletin,* no. 232.)

2 U.S. Department of Agriculture, U.S. Department of Health and Human Services. *Nutrition and Your Health: Dietary Guidelines For Americans, 2000,* 5th Edition.

3 U.S. Department of Agriculture, U.S. Department of Health and Human Services. "New Dietary Guidelines Will Help Americans Make Better Food Choices, Live Healthier Lives." (Press release: www.hhs.gov/news/press/2005.html.)

4 Roy L. Walford, *Beyond the 120-Year Diet: How to Double Your Vital Years.* (New York: Four Walls Eight Windows, 2000). Previously published in 1986 as *The 120-Year Diet.*

5 www,nhlbi.nih.gov/health/public/heart/obesity/lose_wt/patmats.htmc.

6 E. B. Edney and R. W. Gill, "Evolution of Senescence and Specific Longevity," *Nature* (October 19, 1968) 220 (164): 281–2.

7 R. Weindruch, "Caloric Restriction and Aging," *Scientific American* (January 1996) 274 (1):46–52.

8 S. N. Austad, "Life Extension by Dietary Restriction in the Bowl and Doily Spider, *Frontinella pyramitela,*" *Experimental Gerontology* (1989) 24 (1): 83–92.

9 B. K. Patnaik, N. Mahapatro, and B. S. Jena, "Ageing in Fishes" *Gerontology* (1994) 40 (2–4): 113–32.

10 M. H. Ross, "Length of Life and Caloric Intake," *The American Journal of Clinical Nutrition* (August 25, 1972) 8:834–8.

11 Centers for Disease Control and Prevention, U.S. Department of Health and Human Services, *National Vital Statistics Reports,* 52 (9) (November 7, 2003).

12 R. L. Walford, D. Mock, R. Verdery, and T. MacCallum, "Calorie Restriction in Biosphere 2: Alterations in Physiologic, Hematologic, Hormonal, and Biochemical Parameters in Humans Restricted for a 2-Year Period." *The Journals of Gerontology. Series A, Biological Sciences and Medical Sciences* (June 2002) 57 (6): B211–24.

13 L. Fontana, T. E. Meyer, S. Klein, and J. O. Holloszy, "Long-term Calorie Restriction Is Highly Effective in Reducing the Risk for Atherosclerosis in Humans," *Proceedings of the National Academy of Sciences of the United States of America* (April 27, 2004) 101 (17): 6,659–63.

14 R. L. Walford and R. Weindruch. *The Retardation of Aging and Disease by Dietary Restriction* (Springfield, IL: Thomas, 1988).

15 M. T. Goodman, J. H. Hankin, L.R. Wilkens, L. C. Lyu, K. McDuffie, L. Q. Liu, and L. N. Kolonel, "Diet, Body Size, Physical Activity, and the Risk of Endometrial Cancer," *Cancer Research* (November 15, 1997) 57 (22): 5,077–85.

16 A. S. Furberg and I. Thune, "Metabolic Abnormalities (Hypertension, Hyperglycemia and Overweight), Lifestyle (High Energy Intake and Physical Inactivity) and Endometrial Cancer Risk in a Norwegian Cohort," *International Journal of Cancer. Journal International du Cancer* (May 10, 2003) 104 (6): 669–76.

17 A. Mellemgaard, J. K. McLaughlin, K. Overvad, and J. H. Olsen, "Dietary Risk Factors for Renal Cell Carcinoma in Denmark." *European Journal of Cancer* (April 1996) 32A (4): 673–82.

18 N. Pitsikas, M. Carli, S. Fidecka, and S. Algeri, "Effect of Life-long Hypocaloric Diet on Age-Related Changes in Motor and Cognitive Behavior in a Rat Population," *Neurobiology of Aging* (July–Aug 1990) 11 (4): 417–23.

19 C. L. Goodrick, "Effects of Lifelong Restricted Feeding on Complex Maze Performance in Rats." *AGE* 7:1–2.

20 L. W. Means, J. L. Higgins, and T. J. Fernandez, "Midlife Onset of Dietary Restriction Extends Life and Prolongs Cognitive Functioning," *Physiology & Behavior* (September 1993) 54 (3): 503–8.

21 F. Idrobo, K. Nandy, D. I. Mostofsky, L. Blatt, and L. Nandy, "Dietary Restriction: Effects on Radial Maze Learning and Lipofuscin Pigment Deposition in the Hippocampus and Frontal Cortex," *Archives of Gerontology and Geriatrics* (December 1987) 6 (4): 355–62.

22 C. Moreschi, *Beziehungen zwischen Ernährung und Tumorwachsen* [The connection between nutrition and tumor promotion]. *Zeitschrift für Immunitätsforsch* (1909) 2: 651–75.

23 C. M. McCay, M. F. Crowel, and L. A. Maynard, "The Effect of Retarded Growth upon the Length of the Life Span and upon the Ultimate Body Size," *The Journal of Nutrition* (1935) 10: 63–79.

24 A. Koizumi, Y. Wada, M. Tuskada, T. Kayo, M. Naruse, K. Horiuchi, T. Mogi, M. Yoshioka, M. Sasaki, Y. Miyamaura, T. Abe, K. Ohtomo, and R. L.

Walford, "A Tumor Preventive Effect of Dietary Restriction Is Antagonized by a High Housing Temperature through Deprivation of Torpor," *Mechanisms of Ageing and Development* (November 29, 1996) 92 (1): 67–82.

25 E. J. Masoro, "Antiaging Action of Caloric Restriction: Endocrine and Metabolic Aspects," *Obesity Research* (September 1995) 3, Suppl 2:241s–247s.

26 S. R. Spindler, J. M. Grizzle, R. L. Walford, and P. L. Mote, "Aging and Restriction of Dietary Calories Increases Insulin Receptor mRNA, and Aging Increases Glucocorticoid Receptor mRNA in the Liver of Female C3B10RF1 Mice," *Journal of Gerontology* (November 1991) 46 (6): B233–7.

27 B. C. Hansen, "Obesity, Diabetes, and Insulin Resistance: Implications from Molecular Biology, Epidemiology, and Experimental Studies in Humans and Animals," Synopsis of the American Diabetes Association's 29th Research Symposium and Satellite Conference of the 7th International Congress on Obesity, Boston, Massachusetts, *Diabetes Care* (June 1995) 18 (6):A2–9.

28 G. S. Roth, M. A. Lane, D. K. Ingram, et al., "Biomarkers of Caloric Restriction May Predict Longevity in Humans," *Science* (2002) 297:811.

29 T. A. Hughes, J. T. Gwynne, B. R. Switzer, C. Herbst, G. White, "Effects of Caloric Restriction and Weight Loss on Glycemic Control, Insulin Release and Resistance, and Atherosclerotic Risk an Obese Patients with Type II Diabetes Mellitus," *The American Journal of Medicine* (July 1984) 77 (1): 7–17.

30 R. I. Misbin, "Dietary Regulation of Insulin Receptors in Obesity," *The Journal of Nutrition* (March 1981) 111 (3): 475–9.

31 P. J. Savage, L. J. Bennion, and P. H. Bennett, "Normalization of Insulin and Glucagon Secretion in Ketosis-Resistant Diabetes Mellitus with Prolonged Diet Therapy," *The Journal of Clinical Endocrinology and Metabolism* (December 1979) 49 (6): 830–3.

32 American Diabetes Association, "Evidence-Based Nutrition Principles and Recommendations for the Treatment and Prevention of Diabetes and Related Complications," *Diabetes Care* (2002) 25:S50–S60.

33 J. M. Lipman, A. Turturro, and R. W. Hart, "The Influence of Dietary Restriction on DNA Repair in Rodents: A Preliminary Study," *Mechanisms of Ageing and Development* (May 1989) 48 (2): 135–43.

34 R. S. Sohal, S. Agarwal, M. Candas, M. J. Forster, and H. Lal, "Effect of Age and Caloric Restriction on DNA Oxidative Damage in Different Tissues of C57BL/6 Mice," *Mechanisms of Ageing and Development* (October 20, 1994) 76 (2–3): 215–24.

35 V. Haley-Zitlin and A. Richardson, "Effect of Dietary Restriction on DNA Repair and DNA Damage," *Mutation Research* (December 1993) 295 (4–6): 237–45.

36 C. M. Gedik, G. Grant, P. C. Morrice, S. G Wood, and A. R. Collins, "Effects of Age and Dietary Restriction on Oxidative DNA Damage, Antioxidant Protection and DNA Repair in Rats," *European Journal of Nutrition* (July 28, 2004).

37 D. C. Cabelof, S. Yanamadala, J. J. Raffoul, Z. Guo, A. Soofi, and A. R. Heydari, "Caloric Restriction Promotes Genomic Stability by Induction of

Base Excision Repair and Reversal of Its Age-Related Decline," *DNA Repair* (March 1, 2003) 2 (3): 295–307.

38 S. Loft, A. Fischer-Nielsen, I. B. Jeding, K. Vistisen, and H. E. Poulsen, "8-Hydroxydeoxyguanosine as a Urinary Biomarker of Oxidative DNA Damage," *Journal of Toxicology and Environmental Health* (October–November 1993) 40 (2–3): 391–404.

39 D. Kritchevsky, "Caloric Restriction and Cancer," *Journal of Nutritional Science and Vitaminology* (February 2001) 47 (1): 13–9.

40 S. D. Hursting and F. W. Kari, "The Anticarcinogenic Effects of Dietary Restriction: Mechanisms and Future Directions," *Mutation Research* (July 15, 1999) 43 (1–2): 235–49.

41 B. S. Hass, R. W. Hart, M. H. Lu, and B. D. Lyn-Cook, "Effects of Caloric Restriction in Animals on Cellular Function, Oncogene Expression, and DNA Methylation in Vitro," *Mutation Research* (December 1993) 295 (4–6): 281–9.

42 See, for example: K. B. Michels and A. Ekbom, "Caloric Restriction and Incidence of Breast Cancer," *JAMA: The Journal of the American Medical Association* (March 10, 2004) 291 (10): 1,226–30.

43 A. M. Holehan and B. J. Merry, "Modification of the Oestrous Cycle Hormonal Profile by Dietary Restriction," *Mechanisms of Ageing and Development* (October 14, 1985) 32 (1): 63–76.

44 C. J. Carr, J. T. King, and M. B. Visscher, "The Effects of Dietary Caloric Restriction on Maturity and Senescence, with Particular Reference to Fertility and Longevity," *The American Journal of Physiology* (1947) 15:511–519.

45 Roy L. Walford, *Maximum Life Span*. (New York: Norton, 1983): 90.

46 J. F. Nelson, R. G. Gosden, and L. S. Felicio, "Effect of Dietary Restriction on Estrous Cyclicity and Follicular Reserves in Aging C57BL/6J Mice," *Biology of Reproduction* (April 1985) 32 (3): 515–22.

47 A. Hiona, C. Leeuwenburgh, "Effects of Age and Caloric Restriction on Brain Neuronal Cell Death/Survival," *Annals of the New York Academy of Sciences* (June 2004) 1019: 96–105.

48 L. Fontana, T. E. Meyer, S. Klein, and J. O. Holloszy, "Long-term Calorie Restriction Is Highly Effective in Reducing the Risk for Atherosclerosis in Humans," *Proceedings of the National Academy of Sciences of the United States of America* (April 27, 2004) 101 (17): 6,659–63.

49 From an interview quoted by Reuters. Study: "Special Diets Don't Mean More Weight Loss." Reuters newsfeed (via www.yahoo.com), November 9, 2004.

The research was reported in: M. L. Dansinger, J. L. Gleason, J. L.Griffith, et al., "One-Year Effectiveness of the Atkins, Ornish, Weight Watchers, and Zone Diets in Decreasing Body Weight and Heart Disease Risk," presented at the American Heart Association Scientific Sessions, November 12, 2003, in Orlando, FL.

50 R. B. Ervin, J. D. Wright, C. Y. Wang, and J. Kennedy-Stephenson, "Dietary Intake of Fats and Fatty Acids for the United States Population: 1999–2000," *Advance Data* (November 8, 2004) 348: 1–6.

51 B. R. Hammond Jr., E. J. Johnson, R. M. Russell, N. I. Krinsky, K. J. Yeum, R. B. Edwards, and D. M. Snodderly, "Dietary Modification of Human Macular Pigment Density," *Investigative Ophthalmology & Visual Science* (August 1997) 38 (9): 1,795–801.

52 J. K. Campbell, K. Canene-Adams, B. L. Lindshield, T. W. Boileau, S. K. Clinton, and J. W. Erdman Jr., "Tomato Phytochemicals and Prostate Cancer Risk," *The Journal of Nutrition* (December 2004) 134 (12 Suppl): 3,486S–3,492S.

53 E. R. Miller III, R. Pastor-Barriuso, D. Dalal, R. A. Riemersma, L. J. Appel, E. Guallar, "Meta-Analysis: High-Dosage Vitamin E Supplementation May Increase All-Cause Mortality," *Annals of Internal Medicine* (January 4, 2005) 142 (1): 37–46. Note: The authors of the paper acknowledge several limitations to their analysis, the most important of which is that the studies that involved very high doses of vitamin E were often very small, and were conducted on patients with chronic illnesses.

54 Katherine Tallmadge, "Eat Less, Live Longer?," *The Washington Post* (May 19, 2004) F 01.

55 http://csde.washington.edu/downloads/01-04.pdf

56 J. A. Mattison, M. A. Lane, G. S. Roth, and D. K. Ingram, "Calorie Restriction in Rhesus Monkeys," *Experimental Gerontology* (January–February 2003) 38 (1–2): 35–46.

57 R. L. Walford, D. Mock, R. Verdery, and T. MacCallum, "Calorie Restriction in Biosphere 2: Alterations in Physiologic, Hematologic, Hormonal, and Biochemical Parameters in Humans Restricted for a 2-Year Period." *The Journals of Gerontology. Series A, Biological Sciences and Medical Sciences* (June 2002) 57 (6): B211–24.

58 W. R. Pendergrass, P. E. Penn, J. Li, and N. S. Wolf , "Age-Related Telomere Shortening i Lens Epithelium From Old Rats and Is Slowed by Caloric Restriction," *Experimental Eye Research* (August 2001) 73 (2): 221–8.

59 M. Barbieri, M. R. Rizzo, D. Manzella, R. Grella, E. Ragno, M. Carbonella, A. M. Abbatecola, and G. Paolisso, "Glucose Regulation and Oxidative Stress in Healthy Centenarians," *Experimental Gerontology* (January–February 2003) 38 (1–2): 137–43.

60 N. Libina, J. Berman, and C. Kenyon, "Tissue-Specific Activities of C. elegans DAF-16 in the Regulation of Life Span," *Cell* 115 (4) 489–502.

61 M. Tatar, "The Neuroendocrine Regulation of Drosophila Aging," *Experimental Gerontology* (November 2004) 39 (11–12): 1,745–50.

62 J. G. Wood, B. Rogina, S. Lavu, K. Howitz, S. L. Helfand, M. Tatar, D. Sinclair, "Sirtuin Activators Mimic Caloric Restriction and Delay Aging in Metazoans," *Nature* (August 5, 2004) 430 (7000): 686–9.

63 S. Jarolim, J. Millen, G. Heeren, P. Laun, D. S. Goldfarb, M. Breitenbach, "A Novel Assay for Replicative Lifespan in Saccharomyces cerevisiae," *FEMS Yeast Research* (November 2004) 5 (2): 169–77.

64 M. Kaeberlein, T. McDonagh, B. Heltweg, J. Hixon, E. A. Westman,

S. Caldwell, A. Napper, R. Curtis, P. S. Distefano, S. Fields, A. Bedalov, B. K. Kennedy, "Substrate specific activation of sirtuins by resveratrol," *The Journal of Biological Chemistry* (2005 Jan 31).

65 R. Gredilla, A. Sanz, M. Lopez-Torres, G. Barja, "Caloric Restriction Decreases Mitochondrial Free Radical Generation at Complex I and Lowers Oxidative Damage to Mitochondrial DNA in the Rat Heart," *The FASEB Journal: Official Publication of the Federation of American Societies for Experimental Biology* (July 2001) 15 (9): 1589–91.

66 S. X. Cao, J. M. Dhahbi, P. L. Mote, S. R. Spindler, "Genomic Profiling of Short- and Long-Term Caloric Restriction Effects in the Liver of Aging Mice," *Proceedings of the National Academy of Sciences of the United States of America* (September 11, 2001) 98 (19): 10630–5.

67 Ch. Barrows Jr., L. M. Roeder, "The Effect of Reduced Dietary Intake on Enzymatic Activities and Life Span of Rats," *Journal of Gerontology* (January 1965) 20: 69–71.

68 Sources include *The New England Journal of Medicine* (June 26, 2003); Dimitrios Trichopoulos, MD, PhD, professor of epidemiology; Vincent L. Gregory, professor of cancer prevention, Harvard School of Public Health, Boston; Alice H. Lichtenstein, DSc, senior scientist and director, Cardiovascular Nutrition Laboratory; Jean Mayer, USDA Human Nutrition Researcher Center on Aging, Tufts University, Boston; spokeswoman, American Heart Association.

69 *Consumer Reports,* September 2004.

70 Guohua Cao, Sarah L. Booth, James A. Sadowski, and Ronald A. Prior. "Increases in Human Plasma and Anti-Oxidant Capacity After Consumption of Controlled Diets High in Fruits and Vegetables." *The American Journal of Clinical Nutrition* (November 1998) 68 (5): 1081–7.

71 Ibid.

72 Eric T. Poehlman, Angelo Turturro, Noni Bodkin, William Cefalu, Steve Heymsfield, John Holloszy, and Joseph Kemnitz, "Caloric Restriction Mimetics, Physical Activity and Body Composition Changes," The Gerontological Society of America, 2001.

73 S. J. Colcombe, A. F. Kramer, E. McAuley, K. I. Erickson, and P. Scalf, "Neurocognitive Aging and Cardiovascular Fitness: Recent Findings and Future Directions," *Journal of Molecular Neuroscience: MN* (2004) 24 (1): 9–14. Review.

74 Mel Robin, *A Physiological Handbook for Teachers of Yogasana* (Tucson: Fenestra Books, 2002), 271.

75 Elissa S. Epel and Elizabeth H. Blackburn at the University of California–San Francisco, as reported online www.pnas.org/cgi/content/abstract/0407162101v1 in Proceedings of the National Academy of Sciences, November 2004.

76 S. Sandberg, S. Jarvenpaa, A. Penttinen, J. Y. Paton, D. C. McCann, "Asthma Exacerbations in Children Immediately Following Stressful Life Events: A Cox's Hierarchical Regression," *Thorax* (December 2004) 59 (12): 1046–51.

ACKNOWLEDGMENTS

THIS BOOK OWES its essence and its every word to the late Dr. Roy Lee Walford, friend to us both, father to Lisa, and mentor to Brian. Dr. Walford's work has given youth and life to thousands, and inspiration to us and to many others. We hope this book helps in some way to keep his spirit with us.

The authors also wish to acknowledge a debt to the untiring technical support of Ross R. Smith, who enabled us to collaborate despite only rarely being on the same continent. His wizardry with computers, wireless Internet connections, and Internet telephony proved invaluable. We are also grateful to the members of the CR Society who, through their pioneering spirit, pushed the envelope of CR and shared their experiences with the rest of us, thus enabling us and many others to fine-tune our health and longevity programs. In particular, we wish to recognize Warren Taylor, whose enthusiasm, ceaseless hard work, and limitless patience has not only benefited the CR Society, but also kept us going during an often trying writing process.

Iris Bass did an extraordinary job editing the manuscript, despite its arriving in disparate batches from all corners of the globe, and we thank our publisher, Matthew Lore of Marlowe &

Company/Avalon Publishing Group, for believing in this book through many reconceptions, revisions, and rewrites.

Brian would like to thank Florence Banks for her patient support many, many years ago when he first took up writing. Lisa would like to thank Shree B.K.S. Iyengar for his brilliant contributions to yoga, which helped her maintain her health and equilibrium through her father's passing.

INDEX

A

AA (arachidonic acid), 52, 53, 54
ADA (American Diabetes Association), 19–20, 29
adrenal hormones, lipids and, 51
adrenaline, effect of, 192
advanced glycation end-products (AGEs), 79
aerobic exercise, 182–84, 191, 194–95
aerobic fitness, 182
AGEs (advanced glycation end-products), 79
aging, 73–86
  calories and, 73–75
  cells and, 77–80, 181–82
  elderly on CR, 96
  free radical theory, 82–85
  insulin and, 81
  insulin sensitivity and, 28–29
  Longevity Diet and, 87–88, 96
  NIA research on, 19–20
  reproductive capability, 31, 71–72
  research on diet and, 3–5
  segmental, 6
  sexual activity and, 31
  system theories, 75–77
  traditional theories, 74–75
  understanding process of, 26–27
  wine vs., 82
"Aim for a Healthy Weight" (NIH), 19
albumin test, 94
alcohol, 82
alpha males, 69
alpha state of consciousness, 193, 205
American College of Sports Medicine, 182–84
American Diabetes Association (ADA), 19–20, 29
amino acids, 46–48, 79, 205
animals. See *under* research
anorexia nervosa, 42–44, 205
antagonistic pleiotropy theory of aging, 74–75
anthocyanins, 64
anti-aging medicine, 206
anti-aging properties of CR, 26–27
antioxidants, 63, 84–85, 111–12, 205
Anusara yoga, 190
arachidonic acid (AA), 52, 53, 54
arteriosclerosis, 191
arthritis, 32, 55
Athens School of Public Health, 109
Atkins diet, 50

INDEX

autoantibodies, 76, 206
avocados, 57, 114

B

bad cholesterol (LDL), 33, 209
balancing "cheating," 11
Baryshnikov, Mikhail, 191
biomarkers
  as motivation for CR, 16–17
  overview, 5–6, 206
  results measured with, 5
  weight loss and, 95–96
  WUSTL study findings, 33–34
Biosphere, data from, 24
blood pressure, 31–32, 33, 93, 174–76
blood sugar levels, 172
BMI (Body Mass Index), 9–10, 92, 206–7
body's essential needs. *See* calories; lipids/fats; proteins; vitamins and minerals
body temperature, CR and, 27, 39
body weight
  biomarkers and, 95–96
  disease prevention and, 70
  health correlation to, 4
  historical views of, 67–69
  losing, as CR side effect, 91, 174
  monitoring CR with, 92–94, 173–74, 176–78
  protein per pound of, 48–49
  rapid loss of, 178
  rational loss of, 176–77
  set point, 90–92, 212
  See also lipids/fats
bone-loading, 186–90
bones, exercise for healthy, 184–90
Boston School of Medicine, 191
brain agility, 12–13, 32, 51, 183
breakfast, value of, 106
buddy systems, 167–68
bulimia, 42, 207
Burkitt, Denis, 62

C

calcium, sources of, 117, 124, 147–50
CALERIE (Comprehensive Assessment of Long-Term Effects of Reducing Intake of Energy), 4
caloric allotment, 11, 207
calorie counting
  monitoring progress, 173–76, 178
  as reduction strategy, 94–95
  technique, 128–33
calorie reduction strategies, 90–96
calorie restriction. *See* entries beginning with CR
calories, 67–86
  aging process and, 73–75
  cellular theories of aging and, 77–80
  defining, 207
  empty, 41–44
  Internet information sources, 135, 215–18
  overview, 60–61
  reduction strategies, 90–96
  system theories of aging and, 75–77
  traditional view of overeating, 67–70
  U.S. government recommendations, 4
  Web sites about, 135
  See also calorie counting; *entries beginning with* CR
cancer
  deaths from, 23, 24
  from free radical damage, 84
  olive oil and, 109
  prevention of, 30–31, 59, 62
  telomerase in cancer cells, 78
  tumor growth and food consumption correlation, 26
canola oil, 109–10
Cao, Guohua "Howard," 111
carbohydrates

dietary fiber in, 60, 62–63, 118, 208
glycemic index, 7–8, 44, 79–80, 209
Internet information sources, 135, 215–18
overview, 60–61
properties of, 141–44
cardiovascular disease
deaths from, 23–24, 65
preventing, 57, 60
CBC (complete blood-cell count), 93
cells, aging and, 77–80, 181–82
cellular senescence theory of aging, 77–78
cellular theories of aging, 77–80
cerebrovascular disease, 23
cheese, properties of, 148–49
children, warning about CR and, 89
cholesterol
HDL, 33, 57, 209
LDL, 33, 209
as sterols, 51
total cholesterol, 33–34
chronic lower respiratory disease, 23
coffee, 15
cognitive function, 12–13, 32, 51, 183
collagen, 46
complete blood-cell count (CBC), 93
compound lipids, 51
Consumer Reports, 110
contract with self, sample, 159–60
control group, 25, 207–8
cortisol test, 94
CRAN diet, 8, 43–44. *See also* Longevity Diet
CR (calorie restriction)
anti-aging properties, 26–27
bone density loss, 186
food shortages and, 71–72, 74
glucose and, 79–80
history and, 25–26, 67–70
known benefits, 28–32, 73
maintenance and repair priority, 91, 174
in pill form, 81–82
preserving youthfulness with, 25, 71–72, 74
CR diet, 7–8. *See also* Longevity Diet
CREN diet, 14–15, 43. *See also* Longevity Diet
CRON diet, 8, 43. *See also* Longevity Diet
CRS Insider (newsletter), 216–17
CR Society
discussion forums, 18
overview, 208, 215–16
2001 Conference in Las Vegas, 101–2
cultural conditioning
food and, 17, 38–39
overeating as, 68–70, 71–72

D

daily caloric allotment, 11, 207
Daily Food Diary, 119–55
monitoring your progress, 168, 169
overview, 119–21, 134–35
sample pages, 122–23
successful user of, 170–73
table of food properties, 136–55
See also Nutrition Tracker
dairy products, properties of, 147–48, 149–50
deaths in the U.S., causes of, 23
Delaney, Brian M., 10–12, 36–37
DHEA-S test, 94
diabetes, 19–20, 29, 80, 170–73
dietary fats, 50–51, 56–57, 61
See also lipids/fats
dietary fiber, 60, 62–63, 118, 208
"Dietary Guidelines for Americans" (USDA and HSS), 4
Dietary Reference Intakes (DRI), 211
diet fads, 41, 50
Diet Simple (Tallmadge), 65

diseases
arteriosclerosis, 191
arthritis, 32, 55
cardiovascular, 23–24, 57, 60, 65
deaths from, 23
diabetes, 19–20, 29, 80, 170–73
high blood pressure, 174–76
ORAC foods vs., 111
osteoporosis, 61, 184–85, 210–11
overview, 23–24, 70, 100
susceptibility to, 6
See also cancer
disposable soma theory of aging, 74
DNA (deoxyribonucleic acid), 30, 77–78, 84, 85
doctors. *See* health-care professionals
DRI (Dietary Reference Intakes), 211
DWIDP (Dr. Walford's Interactive Diet Planner), 217

E

eating
fasting vs., 179
health vs. weight priority, 41–44, 91, 134, 174
hunger experience, 35–39, 106–7
See also emotional triggers; overeating
eating disorders, 42–44, 89
eggs, 49, 144
eicosanoids, 51, 53–56
eicosapentaenoic acid (EPA), 52, 53, 54
elderly on CR, 96. *See also* aging
electrons, free radicals and, 83
emotional triggers
on difficult days, 160
from food as punishment-reward, 38–39
recording in food diary, 119–20
volume of, 165–66
empty calories, 41–44
energy
from alcohol, 82
efficient use of, 75–76, 91
from glucose, 28–29, 33, 79
storage of, 68–69
See also carbohydrates; lipids/fats; proteins
energy density, 105, 113–15, 208
enriched foods, 125
enzymes, 61–62
EPA (eicosapentaenoic acid), 52, 53, 54
epidemiological evidence, 208
epidemiology, 208
essential amino acids, 47–48
essential fatty acids. *See* omega-3; omega-6
evolution, 71–72, 74–75
exercise, 181–95
aerobics, 182–84, 191, 194–95
benefits of CR and, 181–82
calories and, 187–88
permission from doctor, 66
physical stress from, 191–92
resistance training, 184–85, 186–87, 191, 194–95
weight-bearing, 184–86, 194–95
yoga, 188–90
explorer's trail, 168–73
extra-virgin olive oil, 109, 110

F

fast foods, properties of, 152–55
fasting technique, 179
fats. *See* lipids/fats
fat-soluble nutrients, 65
fatty acids
monounsaturated, 51–52, 210
overview, 51–53, 208
polyunsaturated, 51, 52–53, 56, 211
saturated, 51, 212

trans fatty acids, 56, 209, 212–13
See also omega-3; omega-6
feelings. *See* emotional triggers
fiber. *See* dietary fiber
fish and seafood, 50, 55, 117, 145–46
fish oil, 56
flaxseed oil, 110
food allergies, protein digestion and, 47
food diary. *See* Daily Food Diary
food reduction (FR), 42
foods
energy density of, 113–15
enriched, 125
fiber in, 60, 62–63, 118, 208
fish and seafood, 50, 55, 117, 145–46
glycemic index and, 7–8, 44, 79–80, 209
guidelines for non-CR diet, 65–66
human relationship with, 119–21
meal comparison, 107
priorities in choosing, 115–18
serving size, 59, 129–30, 166
table of food properties, 136–55
table of properties, 136–55
water content of, 113
Web sites about, 135
See also eating; fruits; vegetables
food shortages, genetic factors of, 71–72
free radicals, 82–85, 208
free radical theory of aging, 82–85
free testosterone test, 94
FR (food reduction), 42
frozen confections, properties of, 149–50
fruits
color guide to, 104
creative preparation ideas, 105
high-pectin, 62–63
ORAC ratings, 112
with soluble fiber, 62–63
table of properties, 137–39
functional age biomarkers, 6

G

genes
diseases and, 23
forced expression of, 27–28
in ob/ob mice, 91
oncogene expression, reducing, 30–31
overeating as factor of, 38–39, 70–71
resveratrol and, 81–82, 211–12
geriatrics, 209. *See also* aging
gerontology, 5, 209
GI (glycemic index), 7–8, 44, 79–80, 209
glucose, 28–29, 33, 79
glycated hemoglobin test, 94
glycemic index (GI), 7–8, 44, 79–80, 209
glycemic theory of aging, 79–80
glycerol, 52–53
goals, 161. *See also* priorities
good cholesterol (HDL), 33, 57, 209
grains and flours, 62–63, 139–41
Greenberg, James, 73
Greenland natives, 50, 55
green tea, 38
guppies, life-span of, 20

H

Harvard School of Public Health, 109
Hayflick, Leonard, 77
Hayflick Limit, 77–78
HDL (high density lipoprotein), 33, 57, 209
health. *See* priorities
Health and Human Services (HSS), 4

health-care professionals
  baseline data from, 16–17, 66
  basic tests given by, 93–94
  talking with, 16, 89–90
health marker calorie reduction strategy, 95–96
heart disease
  deaths from, 23–24, 65
  preventing, 57, 60
hemp oil, 110
high blood pressure, overcoming, 174–76
high-GI foods, 79, 209
high-low diet, 7. *See also* Longevity Diet
homeostasis, 76–77, 209
hormonal regulation, 76–77
HSS (Health and Human Services), 4
hunger, 35–39, 106–7
hydrogenated vegetable oils, 56
hydrogenation, 56, 209, 212–13
hypothalamus gland, 76–77

I

ice creams, properties of, 149–50
IGF-1 test, 94
immunological theory of aging, 76
insoluble fiber, 62–63
insulin
  aging and, 81
  glucose level and, 79–80
  overview, 28
  testing recommendation, 94
  WUSTL study results, 33
insulin sensitivity, 28–29, 80
Integral yoga, 190
Internet discussion forums, 18, 103, 216
Internet information sources, 135, 215–18
inversions (yogic exercises), 189
isoleucine, 47–48
Iyengar yoga, 190

J

Johns Hopkins School of Medicine, 59–60
junk food, eliminating, 44–45, 116
junk-food vegetarians, 47

K

Kenyon, Cynthia, 81
keratin, 46

L

label reading, 116
laxatives, fiber vs., 62
LDL (low density lipoprotein), 33, 209
legumes, 139
leucine, 47–48
leukotrienes, 53
life-extension, 22–25, 210
life-extensionists, 216
life-span, 21, 209
life-span studies
  efficacy of CR and, 73
  of mice, 20–21, 25, 26
  overview, 4, 20, 209–10
lifestyle with Longevity Diet, 103–11
linoleic acid, 53
lipids/fats
  dietary fats, 50–51, 56–57, 61
  digestion of, 115
  Internet information sources, 135, 215–18
  overview, 49–53, 210
  panel tests, 93
  quantity per day, 108–11
  saturated vs. unsaturated fats, 56–57
  triglycerides and, 52–53
  Web sites about, 135
  See also fatty acids; omega-3; omega-6
liver function panel tests, 93

Longevity Diet
  agenda for implementing, 102–3
  anorexia compared to, 42–44
  challenges to staying on, 38–39
  five key points, 99–102
  lifestyle on, 103–11
  overview, 7–8
  regimens of users, 8–16
  research-specific life extension, 22–25
  self-support, 157–64
  side effects, 39
  target weight, 92–96
Longevity Diet contract, 159–60
low-GI foods, 7, 209
lutein, 59
lycopene, 59, 64
lysine, 47–48

M

macronutrients. *See* calories; carbohydrates; lipids/fats; proteins
macular degeneration, 59
Masoro, Edward J., 28
Mattson, Mark P., 73
maximum life-span, 21, 210
Maximum Life Span (Walford), 31, 197
McKay, Clive, 26
meal comparison, 107
meat, properties of, 146, 147
mental function, 12–13, 32, 51, 183
metabolic panel tests, 93
methionine, 47–48
mice
  CR and exercise, 181–82
  life-span of, 20–21, 25, 26
  ob/ob set points, 91
  tumor growth in, 26
micronutrients, 57–61. *See also* vitamins and minerals
Middle Ages, 25
milk products, properties of, 147–48, 149–50
mimetic pill for CR, 81–82
minerals. *See* vitamins and minerals
mitochondrial DNA, 85
modified CR example, 10–12, 15–16
molecular biology, 26–27
monitoring your progress, 165–79
  calorie counters, 173–76, 178
  explorer's trail, 168–73
  warrior's code, 165–68
  weight watchers, 173–74, 176–78
monounsaturated fats, 57, 109–10
monounsaturated fatty acids (MUFAs), 51–52, 210
Montagu, Ashley, 100
Moorhead, Paul, 77
Moreschi, Carlo, 26
motivation, 157–64, 200. *See also* priorities; support groups
MUFAs (monounsaturated fatty acids), 51–52, 210

N

National Academy of Sciences (NAS), 190–91
National Cancer Institute (NCI), 19–20
National Geographic, 40–41
National Institute of Mental Health (NIMH), 191
National Institute on Aging (NIA), 19–20, 28–29
National Institutes of Health (NIH), 19
NCI (National Cancer Institute), 19–20
neural transmission time
  degradation of, 12–13
neuroendocrine theory of aging, 76–77
NIA (National Institute on Aging), 19–20, 28–29

NIH (National Institutes of Health), 19
NIMH (National Institute of Mental Health), 191
NutriBase Nutrition Software, 218
nutrient density, 113, 135
nutrition, 40–66
 dietary fiber and, 60, 62–63, 118, 208
 learning about, 160–61
 medical discoveries and, 43
 micronutrients, 57–62
 overview, 40–46, 61–62, 65–66
 phytochemicals and, 56, 63–65, 116, 211. *See also* carbohydrates; lipids/fats; proteins; vitamins and minerals
nutrition classes, 45
Nutrition Tracker, 124–33
 calories and, 128–31
 CR example, 132–33
 overview, 124–25
 sample pages, 126–27
nuts and seeds, 117, 144–45

O

obesity, 4, 40–41, 67–70, 91
ob/ob mice, 91
oils
 cooking with, 117
 fatty acids in fish vs., 50
 hydrogenated, 56
 olive oil, 57, 109–10
 omega-6 fatty acids in, 55
 table of properties, 150
 types of, 56, 109–10
oleic acid, 51–52, 210
olive oil, 57, 109–10
omega-3
 defining, 210
 overview, 53–56
 quantity per day, 109
 sources of, 110–11, 124
omega-6
 defining, 210
 overview, 53–56
 quantity per day, 109–11
 sources of, 110–11
oncogenes, reducing expression of, 30–31
online groups, 18, 103, 216
Optimal Living philosophy, 197–99
ORAC (Oxygen Radical Absorbance Capacity) assay, 111–12
osteoporosis, 61, 184–85, 210–11
overeating
 cultural conditioning and, 68–70, 71–72
 gene-based cravings, 38–39, 70–71
 obesity, 4, 40–41, 67–70, 91
 traditional view of, 4, 67–70
 See also eating
Oxygen Radical Absorbance Capacity (ORAC) assay, 111–12

P

pasta, properties of, 140–41
phenylalanine, 47–48
physical stress, 191
physicians. *See* health-care professionals
phytochemicals
 in eicosanoids, 56
 overview, 63–65, 211
 servings per day, 116
phytonutrients. *See* phytochemicals
pleiotropy, 74–75
PNAS (Proceedings of the National Academy of Sciences), 190–91
polyunsaturated fatty acids (PUFAs), 51, 52–53, 56, 211. *See also* omega-3; omega-6
Pomerleau, Dean, 12–13, 106, 199–201
portion sizes, 59, 129–30, 166
poultry, properties of, 146–47

predictive biomarkers, 6
pregnancy, warning about CR and, 89
primate studies, 28–29
priorities
  in food choices, 115–18
  goals as, 161
  health, 41–44, 91, 134, 174
  intention as, 200–201
  maintenance and repair, 91, 174
  overcoming inner wimp, 165–68
  self-support, 157–64
  See also monitoring your progress
probability value in WUSTL study, 33–34
Proceedings of the National Academy of Sciences (PNAS), 190–91
progress. *See* monitoring your progress
prospective studies, 211
prostaglandins, 53
proteins
  damage from excessive, 61
  defining, 211
  Internet information sources, 135, 215–18
  overview, 46–49
  in plants, 117
  quantity per day, 108
  table of properties, 144–47
protozoa, life-span of, 20
psychological changes, 199–201
psychological preparation, 161–64
psychological stress, 190–91
PUFAs (polyunsaturated fatty acids), 51, 52–53, 56, 211. *See also* omega-3; omega-6

R

rate of living theory of aging, 75–76
ratios in diet
  omega-6 to omega 3, 54–55
  vegetable oils to fatty acids, 50
rats, CR studies with, 20, 25
RDA (Recommended Daily Allowance), 59–60, 211
Recommended Daily Allowance (RDA), 59–60, 211
relaxation, value of, 190–93
the relaxation response, 193–94
reproductive capability, aging and, 31
research
  biomarkers and, 6
  certainty in, 87–88
  control group, 25, 207–8
  discovery of CR, 26
  Hayflick Limit, 77–78
  on humans, 24, 32–34
  on insulin sensitivity, 28–29
  methods, 27–28
  overview, 3–5, 19–22, 73
  on primates, 28–29
  on rats, 20, 25
  See also mice
research studies
  in Biosphere, 24
  cardiovascular disease, 23–24, 65
  diseases, at WUSTL, 32–34, 65
  exercise, 181–82
  fitness and cognitive function, 183
  mimetic pill for CR, 81–82
  olive oil and breast cancer, 109
  stress, 191
  vitamin E, 59–60, 225*n*53
  See also life-span studies
resistance training, 184–85, 186–87, 191, 194–95
resting metabolic rate (RMR), 187–88
resveratrol, 81–82, 211–12
retrospective study, 212
rigid CR example, 12–13
RMR (resting metabolic rate), 187–88
rT3 test, 94

S

salad dressings, properties of, 151
Sandstrom, Kim, 101
saturated fats vs. unsaturated fats, 56–57
saturated fatty acids (SFAs), 51, 212
Schaefer, Ernst, 41
seafood. *See* fish and seafood
seaweed, 63, 144
seeds and nuts, 144–45
segmental aging, 6, 212
selenium, 58
self-support, 157–64, 200
serving size, 59, 129–30, 166
set point, 90–92, 212
sex hormones, lipids and, 51
sexual activity, aging and, 31
SFAs (saturated fatty acids), 51, 212
side effects of Longevity Diet, 39
Sinclair, David, 82
Sivananda yoga, 190
Skelton, Francesca, 201–3
skinniness, severe, 39
Smith, April, 106, 168, 169
societal conditioning
  food and, 17, 38–39
  overeating as, 68–70, 71–72
software, 217, 218
soluble fiber, 62–63
sorbets, properties of, 149–50
soups, properties of, 152
soy milk products, 148
spiders, life-span of, 20
squalene, 109
standard metabolic panel tests, 93
starches, 60–61
stearic acid, 51, 52
steroids, 51
sterols, 51
stress, 168, 190–93
Stress and the Developing Brain (National Institute of Mental Health), 191
success tips, 159–60, 203. *See also* monitoring your progress; priorities
sugar, refined, 118
Sullivan, Ed, 14–15
supplements. *See* vitamins and minerals
support groups
  beginning CR with, 17
  buddy systems, 167–68
  life changes and, 215–16
  self-support, 161–64, 200
  value of, 18
survival curve, 21–22, 25
sweets, 125
system theories of aging, 75–77

T

T3 test, 94
Take Control (margarine-like spread), 14
Tallmadge, Katherine, 65
Tatar, Marc, 81
telomerase, 78
telomeres, 77–78
TG (triglycerides), 33, 52–53
thoughts, effect of, 192
threonine, 47–48
total cholesterol (Tchol), 33–34
trace minerals, 58
traditional theories of aging, 74–75
trans fatty acids, 56, 209, 212–13
trial period recommendation, 159–60
triglycerides (TG), 33, 52–53
tryptophan, 47–48
tumor growth, food consumption and, 26
2001 CR Society Conference (Las Vegas), 101–2
type 2 diabetes, 80

U

University of Illinois at Urbana–Champaign, 183

unsaturated fats, 56–57
urinary calcium excretion, 61
USDA (U.S. Department of Agriculture), 4, 111–12

V

valine, 47–48
vegetable oils. *See* oils
vegetables
  color guide to, 104
  cooking guide, 64–65
  creative preparation ideas, 105
  fiber in, 58, 62–63
  low energy density of, 111–12
  meal comparison, 107
  nutrients in, 58–59, 64–65
  ORAC ratings, 112
  table of properties, 136–37
  value of, 169
vegetarians, 47, 69
Victorian era, 69
Viniyoga, 190
virgin olive oil, 109
vitamins and minerals
  calcium, 117, 124, 147–50
  Internet information sources, 135, 215–18
  overview, 57–61, 62, 68, 210, 213
  in proteins, 47–48
  value of, 58, 84–85
  vitamin A, 59
  vitamin E, 60, 225*n*53
Voss, Peter, 169, 176–78, 197–99

W

Walford, Lisa, 9–10, 37, 179
Walford, Roy L., 10–12, 76, 100, 197
Walford diet, 7. *See also* Longevity Diet
walnut oil, 110
warrior's code, 165–68
Washington University in St. Louis (WUSTL), 32–34, 65
water content of foods, 113
water fleas, life-span of, 20
wear and tear theory of aging, 78
Web sites with nutrition information, 135, 215–18
weight. *See* body weight
weight-bearing exercises, 184–86, 194–95
weight watchers, 92–94, 173–74, 176–78
Weindruch, Richard, 73
Western diet, fat in, 50
whole grains, 111–12, 117, 139–40
wine and aging, 82
Wistar Institute (Philadelphia), 77–78

Y

yoga, 188–90
youth span, 25, 213